THE GREATEST STORY EVER...

RETOLD

Leah Rodriquez DeSalles

ISBN: 978-0-578-85435-9

DEDICATION

This book is dedicated to all those who have yet to receive true redemption in hopes that liberty may come through reading it.

CONTENTS

ACKNOWLEDGMENTS

To my beloved Husband, Rudy. I know everyone always says, "I couldn't do this without you!" But truly– there is no way on God's green earth that I could have ever done this without you paving the way for me to have the time and ability. I cannot express my love for you and my gratitude for God's provision of you, my hero. You are the one. This is it.

Thanks to my parents– all of you! Selma, Dolpie, Bill, Lynda, Ed, Linda, Mama Mary! I love you all. Each of you has contributed to my world in ways for which I am beyond appreciative. But Mom– I praise God for the foundation of faith you provided and the seeds you planted. Thank you.

To my family and brothers (Bill, Craig, Doug) – here's your line, hehe. Thanks for believing in me and not always believing in me. It made me who I am.

To my beloved soul mate, Beckie. Rebecca Wells McDonald– you know. Thank you for your intentional help and support in content. Let's do it again. And again, and again… I love you beyond.

To Dan Wood– Thank you for believing long before I did and encouraging me so well since the second grade!

Ultimately, thank you to Emmanuel, whom I know in person. My life is forever changed by the acceptance and telling of your life.

CHAPTER 1:

YOU DON'T UNDERSTAND

The nurse came to the lobby door and looked down at her chart, "Elizabeth?" Liz looked over at her husband with a nervous, 'here we go.' They had made this visit numerous times. The staff each smiled as they walked by, having seen them so regularly for months now. Everyone was kind, but behind their greeting was an air of sympathy. That was the worst part. Zachariah squeezed Elizabeth's hand tightly as they walked the familiar path to the exam room.

What a ride this had been. Working at the adoption agency had given Liz a complete education regarding infertility. She didn't know when she first got the job that God had placed her there for more than one reason. At the first educational seminar for new clients, the testimonies she heard were so close to her own. Miscarriages, fear, and revelation of a larger problem. Getting pregnant seemed so easy for everyone else. How many times had she seen women on drugs with no desire to have a child get pregnant if someone simply looked at them sideways? How many stories had she heard of abortions and teenagers abandoning babies? Yet here they were. A solid couple, for the very most part, praying, hoping, trusting, and trying. Oh, the trying. Trying not to let lovemaking become a task on a clock. Trying not to walk in fear but trust that all would work itself out. Trying not to be offended when yet another person encouraged them to 'just relax! Have a glass of wine and put your feet up on the wall.' Trying not to let the feeling of sinking lower and lower show every time she walked into the church nursery or when another friend announced their 'good news.'

In the beginning, it was easier. There was finally an answer to all they had been going through. She wasn't crazy! There was a path they could take and options they could try. But as time went by, seeing things like little families at a Fourth of July parade all in matching shirts was like a dagger. Zach had been outstanding. He was so dedicated to her and to the heritage their fathers had given them. Both had come from families with fathers who were priests and pastors. They both believed all things truly do work together for the good of those who love God and are called according to His purpose. Hadn't they dedicated their whole lives to Him? Hadn't they walked in the utmost obedience down to every tenth tithed? How, then, could He let this happen to them? How could He see their dedication and hear their prayers only to allow them to be here again in this cold examining room with yet another round of anxiousness regarding a pregnancy? Surely, this time would be different. Surely, the doctor would tell them that this latest treatment worked, and in nine months, they would be the proud parents of their long-awaited bundle of joy.

"Elizabeth, Zachariah… hello." The doctor entered and greeted the wary couple. "How are you guys doing? Feeling okay?" Wheeling a stool over, he sat directly across from them. Dr. Lemon was kind enough and didn't waste too much time with the small talk. "So, here we are," he started, "as you know, we had determined in the past that should this last round not take, we would move forward into other options…" The words were clear, but Elizabeth started to fade. His tone was all too familiar, and the matter-of-fact demeanor with which he delivered the news left her convinced of only one thing, and it was not that this was going to work together for their good. Dr. Lemon's mouth was moving, but everything went into silence. Zach was there, steady as ever, and shaking his head. He seemed to understand without issue. He said something positive to her, but she was slipping into a state of shock. "The numbers weren't good and didn't show a rising hormone level…" she was in and out, head reeling, remembering every promise and the positive words spoken by those who were supporting them.

The next thing Liz knew, Dr. Lemon was patting her on the shoulder. Zach was shaking his hand and thanking him for all of his efforts on their behalf. 'Anne. ANNE,' she thought. Anne was one of Liz's closest friends. They had always been more like sisters than distant cousins. Anne was waiting for them in the lobby of the doctor's office as a loving show of support. She had to tell Anne, who herself was several months pregnant with her first child, Miryam. Standing up and rushing out, Liz made a beeline for Anne. Holding it together until the moment she saw her, Liz fell into her girlfriend's chest.

"Oh, Anne… *Anne,"* she sobbed. "It didn't work. It didn't work! I'll never have a Miryam of my own." Crying, she laid her hand on Anne's belly and gave in to the betrayal that she would never be a mother.

~~~

16 Years Later

It was a morning like any other, as Zach was preparing for work. Running a little late, he was not like his wife's relative Joaquin, who would never dream of being even a minute late for his responsibilities at church. Zachariah was a multigenerational pastor. His father, his father's father, and his father's fathers before them were all pastors or priests. You'd think that one of them by now would have chosen a different profession, but somehow all things always led back to this one steady course, as for each of them and their households, they served the Creator. Coming from a line of men who had chosen to serve in this way, Zach had many examples of who he did and did not want to emanate. The spirit of religion had overtaken so many of them with their rules and regulations that the relationship he felt with the Creator seemed neglected when he followed them too rigidly. This is how he often thought about Joaquin, Anne's husband. As devoted as Joaquin was–as driven and intentional to do the right thing– something seemed lost about him. Joaquin had all the right objectives but remained bound by unseen confinement. Zach had seen it too many times before and wished he could help his cousin-in-law find freedom. 'How easily people of religion find themselves restrained if they aren't careful,' he thought.

Zach, on the other hand, was as genuine and down-to-earth as a pastor could be. Educated at all the right seminaries and having fulfilled all of the ethical requirements, he held his appointment with a bit more ease. Maybe it came from the heritage of examples, or perhaps it merely stemmed from an inner belief that the Creator wasn't waiting to pounce on every accidental occurrence or choice. That seemed to be a very earthly father's perspective. The Creator had always seemed so close to Zach. He didn't have to search for Him; He was there in every sunrise or crashing of a wave. Zach didn't have to chase after the question of Him; he simply had to be still and know that He was there. Exercising faith hadn't always been easy; it was just never
~~~

questioned. He unpretentiously had faith. In all things, he chose to know that the designer of every star, every energy source, every astounding fact that science could prove, all originated from the same place as his heartbeat– the Creator.

Grabbing his coffee, phone, and keys, he kissed Liz and rushed for the car. They had settled into a quiet routine, just the two of them. In the beginning, they had thought about having pets, but it seemed like a replacement for the children they couldn't have. Then they enjoyed the ability to get away whenever they wanted; at least that's what they told themselves. Into the office and firing up his computer, he started on his daily tasks. "Drat!" Remembering it was his turn to lead the morning devotional, Zachariah rushed down the hall to find the staff all gathered and ready to go. "Sorry, all," he offered, "No excuses, just one of those days." Taking his place at the head of the table, Zach sat and closed his eyes. Pausing to receive a direction for the morning, he sighed, and something very abnormal happened. He felt a swoon in his head. It was so strong that he opened his eyes to see if anyone else had felt it. No one seemed to be reacting. It almost seemed as if they were experiencing an earthquake. He closed his eyes again. The swoon came stronger. So much more robust that he grabbed the arm of his chair, feeling like he would fall over if he didn't. He opened his eyes, positive that the others would have experienced that one, but instead of seeing his coworkers, he saw a great being of light standing next to what appeared to be an altar with smoke rising from it. 'What the–' Zach became anxious, and fear fell upon him.

Straining to see anything past the light, he searched for his coworkers, which were faint and vague. It was as if they weren't real, and the being of light was the only absolute thing.

"Don't be afraid, Zachariah," the messenger said. "Your prayer has been heard. Your wife Elizabeth will bear you a son, and you shall call his name John."

'John?! Prayer?!' his mind raced. It had been years since Zach had prayed for a son. Someone to carry on the heritage handed down in his family from generation to generation. 'I haven't prayed any prayers,' he thought. Then a revelation came upon him that was profound and complete, 'it didn't matter how many years it had been; he had been heard. The *Creator* had heard him.' With thoughts swirling and heart-pounding, Zach tuned back into the being's words.

"You will have joy and gladness, and many will rejoice at his birth, for he will be great before the Creator. He must not dull himself with common substances but will be filled with the Essence of the Creator, even from his mother's womb."

Zach wished he could write all of this down or click Voice Memo on his phone. How would he ever explain what was happening? The Essence of the Creator? What was the Ess– suddenly, the questions in his mind were all still. He had a knowing that he couldn't deny. The Creator and The Essence were one. They operated out of the same expanse. How did he know that? It was so clear. Why was it so clear? It seemed to be so simple. Why didn't he know of this *essence* spirit before? Why didn't he know that was what he had always felt and been confident in? Had he been asleep?! The messenger continued.

"–he will operate in a mighty spirit, turning the hearts of many fathers back toward their children and the disobedient to wisdom. He will make the people ready for what's coming next."

'What's coming next?' Zach wondered, 'What *is* coming next?!' This was all too much. With a shaking of his head and the ability to finally speak, Zach addressed the messenger, "Look… I mean, thanks, thank…*you*…but– how is this even possible? It's all so– I am not a spring chicken, and Liz is– well, hardly at the age to be giving birth. I'm just– how is this– *why* is this– and why *now*??" Zach became overwhelmed with emotion. "We've finally become settled. It took so long, and it's been so hard. This can't be real. This cannot be happening."

"Settle down, Zachariah," the messenger replied. "I stand in the presence of Supremacy, and I make known to you this good news." All at once, Zach felt unappreciative and irrational. "These things *will* take place, and because you didn't believe my words, you will be silent and unable to speak until the day that they occur." Zachariah rose to plea against the decree.

"That's not right…please, I…I didn't mean to– I was just saying that…" but he wasn't *saying* anything at all. No sound came from his mouth as he tried to defend himself. Grabbing his throat, he looked up, and there, with perfect clarity in the absence of the excessive light, were his coworkers waiting for him to speak. For them, it had been but a few moments. Zach spun around, but the messenger was nowhere. His peers were looking to him in expectation for the morning delivery of devotion. Standing there with his hands on his throat, Zach tried to speak, "eeeeeh," was the only exhale he could manage. Shaking his head, he tried again, "Eeeehhhh." 'This isn't happening,' he thought. This whole thing can *not* be happening.'

The staff sat patiently. Some were thinking Zach may have shifted into a bit of a skit to illustrate a point he would make. Others chuckled as he seemed to be entirely off his game. One or two had squinted eyes and the look of discernment as they started to tune into something larger at play. Finally, Zach flopped down in his chair with a face of despair and defeat. How could he ever explain what just happened? Ida, a woman with particular insight, stood and laid her hand on his shoulder.

"Zach," she had such peace about her. "Zach, are you all right?" Relieved that someone was seeing him for the issue he was having, Zach shook his head, 'no.' He felt that he was about to cry, and if he had, Ida would have been the perfect shoulder to bear it. Turning to the table, Ida simply said, "Perhaps Zach is experiencing 'one of those days' that requires returning home to sort some things out." She looked to their boss and raised her eyebrows as if to ask permission on his behalf. Ida was well respected. So, the elder consented with a nod, and off they went. Escorting Zach back to his office to grab his things, Ida looked over to their coworker Parmeet and nodded her head for him to 'come with us.' Parmeet was already there.

Once in his office, Zach altogether lost it. Falling to the ground on his knees, he started weeping. Parmeet grabbed the tissues and knelt beside him. Neither Ida nor Parmeet spoke for several minutes; they quietly prayed and supported their friend. Eventually, Zach sat up and leaned back against his desk. Breathing heavily, he shrugged and put his face in his hands. He had no idea how or where to begin. How could he possibly explain and without words? Parmeet looked to Ida. Ida smiled a calm, knowing grin.

"You've had a vision, haven't you?" Parmeet asked. Zach shot him a wide-eyed look and nodded a passionate 'yes.' "Can you tell us about it?" Zach made another attempt to speak, and with a look of anguish, shook his head, 'no.' He pointed to his throat and waved his hand as if to say, 'I can't speak.'

"Wow." Ida chimed in. "Well, it's okay, Zach. It's going to be okay." Handing him a pad of paper and pen, she encouraged him to rest a bit. "Would you like me to get you some tea? Do you think you'll be able to drive home, or would you like us to drive you?" Zachariah thought of Liz. Tearing up a bit, he bucked up. 'No,' shaking his head adamantly. He could make it home on his own. He needed to get home and try to explain to Liz what had happened. With a sudden sense of mission, he stood. He wasn't sure that she would believe him or even if any of what the messenger had said would come to pass. He wasn't sure of much. All he knew is that he needed to get home and try to wrap his head around how he was going to move forward if his voice didn't return soon. Standing, he hugged Parmeet and Ida thoroughly. Zach didn't know much sign language, but he did know the sign for, 'Thank you.' Placing the four fingers of his dominant hand flat against his chin, he moved it out and down in each of their directions. With love, they blessed him.

Having received a call from Ida, Liz was home by the time Zach arrived. Rushing out to his car as he pulled in, she greeted him with concern.

"Zach, honey… what is it? Are you okay? Should you have driven?"

Zach was already exhausted. 'Yeah, yeah,' he nodded as if to say, 'it's fine.' Taking Liz by both arms, he looked her directly in the eyes. "Honey," he tried to speak, "eeeeeeeeh." Elizabeth's eyes widened. Ida said he hadn't spoken, but she thought perhaps he might have calmed enough to express himself by the time he got home.

"Ida said you had some kind of experience. Are you in pain? Do we need to go to the hospital?"

'No, no.' Zach was resisting.

"Don't be stubborn, Zachariah. Maybe something is wrong. What if you've had a stroke?" Zach froze and motioned back to the car as if to say, 'hello… I just drove home.'

"Fine. For now. Let's get you inside."

They were particularly good at taking care of each other. Having been alone and the sole focus of the other's affection for so many years, they were quite adept at caring for the other without many words spoken anyway.

Tucking him in and getting some hot tea for his throat, Liz sat down on the edge of the bed. Zach held his hand up like a pad and imitated writing. Liz handed him a small pad of paper and a pen.

"I need to sleep," he scribbled. "I'm okay. I will try and tell you everything, but right now, I have to sleep." Of all times for this to be happening. Liz hadn't been feeling quite up to par herself, but now none of that mattered. Full focus was on her beloved, her life.

"Okay, okay," she complied. "I love you, Zach. I'm going to be very nearby, so just ding the pen on the side of your mug if you need me, okay?" Rolling over, Zach was asleep before her sentence was complete.

Zach slept the rest of the day and well into the night. Liz was concerned and searching all sorts of information on how long to let someone sleep after a trauma. Did he have a concussion? How would he have gotten it? Did he have a stroke? Was it a physical or emotional episode? When Zach finally woke in the morning, Liz was already sitting up beside him in bed.

"Hi," she said, "How are you feeling?" Clearing his throat and confident it had all been a bad dream, Zach answered.

"Eeeeech." Sitting up, he cleared his throat again. Looking at his wife with a calming, 'it's okay,' he attempted once more, "eeeeech."

"That's it." Liz shot out of bed and started dialing the phone. "We're going to the doctor, Zach. Don't argue with me. You've had plenty of rest, and if something is wrong, I don't want to waste time. Get dressed."

Knowing she was right, Zach got up and started to dress. He didn't feel bad. In reality, he felt pretty good. That sleep had done him justice. Now, he was just concerned about his inability to speak. He hadn't even been able to tell Liz what had happened yet. Poor Liz. He hated putting her through this. Strangely enough, he was slowly coming to a real sense of peace after sleeping. He had a knowing he was going to be okay. He even knew that what he had experienced was real. Now, he just had to find a way to type it all up and share it with Liz. What would she think? How would she feel? First things first, they had to get to the doctor so that she could realize it all too.

When the doctor's office heard that Zach had had an episode, they got him in relatively swiftly. All of his vitals were good, and he had a real sense of calm about him. He was curious what the doctor would say about the condition of his vocal cords. But his main concern now wasn't for himself but Liz when he tried to explain the messenger. Liz, on the other hand, was worried sick. Her stomach was turning as a result of this whole thing. When the doctor finally came in, it was Liz who had to try to explain because Zach, of course, could not. As she spoke, she started to sweat a bit. Reaching for the tissue, she dabbed her forehead. Shaking it off, she tried to explain that Zach had been at work the previous day and had some sort of an episode that left him speechless. She said how he had driven home okay but hadn't spoken a word since, and suddenly, the sick with worry feeling in Liz's stomach turned to full-blown nausea. She paused, trying to reason with her body and that, 'uh-oh. I think I'm going to be sick,' moment. Without more than a moment's notice, she jumped up and lunged for the garbage can.

Vomiting all that she had not eaten in the last several hours, Liz hugged the can. Head pounding, she was grateful that this had happened in front of a doctor and not in public.

"Wow," she gasped. "I'm so sorry; I think I just need to calm down a minute." The doctor stood and helped her back to her seat. "I think this has all just been really traumatic, and I'm really…just…" The doctor took his light and looked into Liz's eyes. He took her temperature and checked her complexion.

"How have *you* been feeling lately, Elizabeth?"

"What? Oh, um– a little weary, actually, but I'm okay. Just tired, like I can't really catch up."

"Mm-hmm. Any tenderness in your breasts?"

"What?! No, I'm fine, just a little…" a light bulb went off in her mind regarding the direction of the doctor's questioning. She felt her breasts, and indeed, they were quite tender. She looked at Zach then back to the doctor. "Oh, no," she started, "you don't understand. Thank you for thinking– but no. First of all, I'm way too old for that, and second, well, I'm infertile."

"Mm-hmm," the doctor continued. Pulling something out of a drawer and handing it to Liz, he said, "Why don't you go ahead and pee on this stick for me?" Liz started laughing nervously. "On the house."

A wave of frustration, fear, and then anger flooded her. How could he ask this of her? He didn't understand everything they had been through. How could he be so nonchalant with even the slightest chance of hope? Suddenly, Liz became defensive.

"You don't seem to be hearing me. I'm infertile," she said, making direct eye contact. "This is… well, it's just… nonsense. So, thanks, but no thanks. We're here for Zach." The doctor looked at Liz and cocked his head sideways.

"You know, Elizabeth, I know it's hard to believe, but there are perimenopausal pregnancies sometimes. Granted, it's quite uncommon but not impossible. I'll tell you what. You can take this stick home and just use it later should you feel like it. Okay? No pressure. On the house." Why did he keep saying that?! Now, she was just irritated with him.

"Oh, give me that thing," she said. "You want to know that I'm not pregnant? Fine, I'll just go show you right now." Liz left the room, and the doctor proceeded to examine and attempt communication with Zach. She didn't wait for a second line to not appear on the stick. Returning immediately, she handed the doctor the stick. Sitting down, she looked to Zach with disgust and was thinking, 'see if we ever come to this guy again.'

"Well, well, well…" the doctor said. "Congratulations." Shaking Zach's hand, the doctor smiled started gathering brochures.

"Excuse me?" Elizabeth quipped. It wasn't funny.

"Congratulations," he responded. "Now, look… there will need to be some precautions taken, and you want to be sure to make an appointment for yourself sooner rather than later. Late age pregnancies may require some additional care, so don't put off having your bloodwork done and getting into a recommended regime. In the meantime, I will prescribe some prenatal vitamins to get you started. This is very exciting." Elizabeth was shaking her head. How could he do this? How could he be so cruel?

"You're not funny," she whispered. Zach knew every word was true. He reached over and put his hand on his wife's forearm. The doctor handed her the positive pregnancy test. "No," she uttered. Looking down at the test and then to Zach with pain and tear-filled eyes, she noticed the look on his face. He was calm. He wasn't shaken at all. As a matter of fact, he was smiling at her– smiling at her and rubbing her forearm. He looked like he knew something she didn't. He looked like he had known before. "No…," she said again and looked back at the two lines on the stick. Zach nodded, 'yes.' "No," she said firmly with more volume. Zach looked at her and got face to face, 'Yes,' he nodded. "Yes?" She whispered. "No… no, I won't get my hopes up." Zach stood and pulled her up into his arms. As he hugged her and rubbed her back, Elizabeth broke. "Do you really think?" she dared.

"Well, *I* really think," the doctor chimed in. "And I kind of have a degree in this sort of thing, so… you might want to believe me when I say these tests are rarely faulty." They shared a chuckle for the first time. Elizabeth was thinking, 'if this is true… we are never going to another doctor ever again.'

CHAPTER 2:

IN THE BEGINNING

Joaquin slammed the phone down with the giddy excitement of a teenage girl, "I got it! I got it!" Yelling at the top of his lungs and running from his den, he searched for the one person who might care as much as he did. "Anne!" he continued, "Aaaannne!!! I got it!! Where are you, for the love of Michael?!"

Anne was dropping laundry as she walked. "What? What are you yelling about?"

"I got it!" Joaquin stared her straight in the eyes, eyebrows raised, waiting for the news to strike her understanding.

"You *got* it?" With her head slightly shaking, Anne was more focused on the load in her arms than Joaquin's news.

"I- GOT- IT!" he repeated.

"You- got- it." She mimicked with less enthusiasm. Revelation swept over her, and she met his raised eyebrows, "You got it?!"

"IIIIIII GOOOOT IT!! I GOT IT!"

"AHHHHHH!" Anne shrieked, "You got it!!!" Throwing the laundry into the air, the two embraced and danced around in circles on the clean scattered pieces. They laughed and released noises of exaltation.

Miryam came out of her bedroom to see her parents dancing around like children just told they were going to Disneyland. "What's going on?!" she asked. Through laughter and catching of breath, Anne shared the news.

"Your father has just been given the Office of Overseer at the church!"

"I thought those meetings and interviews would never end," Joaquin sighed. "Dinners with the Elders and lunches full of 'what would you do if' scenarios. But it's all paid off! We got it, oh, honey. We got it."

"YOU got it," Anne replied. Always the graceful supporter, Anne knew how much this position meant to her husband. He had watched every P and Q for as long as she had known him. A devout and upright follower of the church, Joaquin lived as best he could, always above reproach. Joaquin was focused, sober-minded, intentional in all things, and respectable. He had given long hours to the church day and night. Anne knew that she had to use all the natural grace she was given and then some to be the loving, submissive, dignified, and never slandering wife that an overseer was required to have. Heaven forbid she be the reason Joaquin's long-time dream did not come true. They must keep themselves blameless and well thought of, even by outsiders. "What's next?" she asked, "What happens now?"

"Now?" Joaquin chuckled. "Now, we pick the laundry up off the floor before anyone sees it." They both laughed. "What if someone comes by to congratulate us?" Miryam turned to walk away when her sister Salome came bounding up the stairs.

"What the what?" knowing her mother would never trample a pile of clean laundry on the floor, Sally asked, "What's going on?" Shaking her head, Miryam answered.

"He got it."

Roles seemed somewhat reversed where Miryam's parents were concerned, even though she was just 16. She would never dishonor them by challenging their devotion to the church. She admired it- to a point. But a relationship with a higher power was more natural for her. She didn't strive to enter into a place where she knew she was loved. She didn't feel the need to please others by proving her every action. Granted, Miryam's every action was upright intrinsically, but she didn't think she would ever endure the scrutiny of allowing others to impose such stringent demands on her. After all, the Office of Overseer required that the official, at all times, be self-controlled, hospitable, able to teach, not be a drunkard, violent or quarrelsome and not be a lover of money. For Miryam, it was common sense to be these things. She didn't like anyone making a law of it.

Dinner to celebrate was the next logical step. Holding his head just a little higher than usual, Joaquin led his family into a restaurant that was pricier than he would typically allow. Miryam couldn't help but chuckle to herself, seeing his pride. Anne was beaming with the knowledge that her husband would now be welcomed into circles considered elevated by church society. They had built their lives around the teachings of the Ancient Writings and were finally seeing the fruit.

The menu offered a spectacle of delights and every choice a temptation. Decisions made and belly's full; they were contemplating dessert when a hand landed square on Joaquin's shoulder.

"Joaquin! Anne, hello." Standing above them with his towering presence was one of the Elders from the church.

"Darrold! Hello! What a pleasure to see you here."

"Especially tonight, eh Joaquin?" Darrold said, smirking. "Congratulations, old boy. It couldn't have happened to a more devout member." Joaquin lit up like a Christmas tree but lowered his head in presented humility.

"Thank you, thank you so much, Darrold."

"Miryam, isn't it? Are you proud of your dad?"

"Proud?" Miryam asked.

"Yes! Pleased with the way all of his hard work and endeavor has been rewarded?"

"Rewarded?" Miryam chuckled. Joaquin squinted his eyes and wondered what his daughter was getting at. Undoubtedly, at this moment, she would know to exercise all the years of manners that she had been taught. Especially tonight, especially now, in front of a Senior Elder.

"Miryam," he said firmly.

"Of course, I am, Elder Darrold," Miryam answered. "I've admired my father's drive to be pleasing to those he thinks matter."

"Miryam–" Joaquin warned.

"What I mean is, I'm glad all of his devotion has been recognized by those he considers so dear."

"Yes, well…" Elder Darrold hesitated, "You all enjoy your evening. There is much to be grateful for." Darrold shook Joaquin's hand and nodded to Anne. He looked at Miryam and furrowed his brow just enough to show question. "Miryam, Salome," he said in a good-bye tone.

"Miryam!" Joaquin started, "What was that?!"

"Miryam, you really shouldn't have." Anne chimed in.

"What?" Miryam defended.

"What were you thinking? Tonight, of all nights?" Joaquin's concern was peaked. "You know that Elder Darrold is a senior member of the council; why would you not be completely respectful?"

"I wasn't disrespectful, Dad. I was just acknowledging your devotion." In truth, she hadn't been disrespectful. She modestly considered the whole song and dance thing a bit much. They say this, and you say that; everyone shakes hands and so on.

"Miryam," Joaquin scolded, "If they think I don't have control over my own child and that I can't manage my own household, they may think I can't manage the church. Now, fall in line." That was always what he said when he wanted Miryam to tuck it in. She was such a good kid that he really couldn't punish her for much. So, when he was displeased, he told her to *fall in line*. Joaquin looked at Anne with concern. Anne looked at Miryam and shook her head.

"I'm sorry, Dad. If you want me to call Elder Darrold tomorrow and apologize, I will."

"No. Don't make anything worse."

~~~

Miryam sat in a small circle of friends, laughing and talking about all the things girls do: boys, clothes, and a choice smelling lip-gloss. The light from the bonfire was causing her eyes to sparkle, and Joey was noticing. As he glanced around at the activity, his eyes kept finding their way back to Miryam. How obvious it was to him that she was truly a good person. Now that he thought about it, Miryam never seemed to be false. Everything about her seemed to exude goodness. She was a straightforward type of person but not out of assertion. Miryam simply was straightforward. At that moment, thinking about how easy it always was to talk to her, to know that she would be genuine, and remembering how awkward experiences had been with other girls, Joey had a warmth come over his entire being; a knowing.

"I'm going to marry that girl someday," he said softly.

"What?" Jackson halted. He noticed Joey lost in thought, staring at the girls. "Dude," he waved his hand in front of Joey's face, "Dude… what did you say?" Joey stirred, not having realized his words were aloud.

"Hmmm? What, man?"

"Helloooo…earth to Joey… come in, Joey." Joey nodded his head in acknowledgment.

"What?"

Jackson started shaking his head and chuckled at his friend, placing his
~~~

hand on his shoulder. "Yer' killin' me, Joe. Are you seriously thinking about marriage right now?"

"Marriage?" Joey snapped out of it. "What are you talking about?"

"DUDE." Jackson retorted, "What are *you* talking about?" Joey had a slight realization that he *had* been thinking about marriage and, indeed, he may have muttered it out loud. He had to save face, and he had to do it now, but before he could, Jackson came in close, putting his face side by side with Joey's and began talking in his ear. "Look around, my man, before you lay an assortment of ladies. The night is young, and you, my brother, are free to be."

But Joey wasn't free to be. Home periodically to visit, he lived a couple of hours away, attending school to be a contractor. Netzer was home, but living in Breadville had taught him to be a man. He had become a focused, well-rounded young man, but truth be told, Joey had always been a bit awkward with girls. He hadn't even ever had a very serious girlfriend. Girls liked him from time to time, but nothing ever really took. Everyone wondered why this was in that Joey was a perfectly good guy. He was generous, considerate, and had a definite way about him. He was funny, hard-working, and not at all ugly. But for whatever reason, he made it to 24 without a single legitimate commitment. Looking at Miryam, he had a feeling he knew why.

Miryam, on the other hand, had not been dreaming of marriage. She was a mature 16 but was much more concerned with school, family, and making time for friends. She was a tender and considerate creature who always addressed anything that came her way head-on. Tonight, she noticed Joey watching her. She had that feeling in her knower that something was in the air. It wasn't creepy, but it was intense. The strangest part was that when she held his gaze for a moment, she wasn't even sure he noticed. His eyes were on her, but his thoughts were somewhere else. What was he thinking, she wondered? Miryam liked Joey. Their fathers worked together, so Miryam had seen him at company picnics and events from time to time. Even though they were years apart, Joey had always been kind to her. A couple of times, it seemed he had even gone out of his way to be courteous to her. Funny, she had never noticed how attractive Joey was until tonight. Something about the way he was looking at her with the firelight between them. How old was Joey, again? Too old for her parents to approve, that's for sure. He would never be interested in someone her age anyway. Still, he was such a nice guy and so considerate.

It was starting to get late, and Miryam thought she should get home. Her curfew was 11 pm, and it had to be getting close. Some of the crowd had been drinking, and the alcohol's effects were starting to exhibit themselves. As Miryam stood to dust off the sand and give good-bye hugs to her friends, she noticed Joey once more. Standing near the water ice chest, he seemed to be tiring of the scene as well. His friend Jackson, on the other hand, was dancing about and flirting with the ladies. She chuckled at him a bit and looked back to Joey, who noticed her laugh. He shrugged his shoulders in a, 'what are you going to do?' kind of way and then smiled at her. As she started to head off the beach, Joey met her stride.

"Hey, Miryam. Leaving?"

"Yeah," she answered, "Time to get home."

"Walk you to your car?" he offered. It was safe enough on this stretch of beach, but Joey was a gentleman and wanted the opportunity to say hello.

"Sure," Miryam replied, but right then, they heard harsh words rising. Turning to see who was talking, things escalated quickly. Two intoxicated guys were pushing each other a bit. Chests were out, and arms were flailing. Others were starting to step in and try to speak sense to them. With a bit of embarrassment, Joey looked at Miryam and simply said, "Alcohol. In the end, it bites like a snake and poisons like a viper." Before she could nod in agreement, the voices began yelling. One of the guys pulled a gun out and was pointing it at the first young man.

"You think you're so smooth!" he was screaming. "You think you're better than me? You think you deserve anything more than me?" Miryam had not met this guy, but she did see him drinking rapidly and questioned his stability. He seemed brooding and touchy. She had noticed him talking to a girl and wondered if perhaps this other guy tried to step in or something. Whatever it was, things were getting out of control. Joey took Miryam's arm above the elbow.

"Why don't we get out of here?" He started ushering her up the sandy hill when shots rang out, echoing in every direction. Joey and Miryam both dropped to the ground. Screams started piercing the air. Keeping her head down but wanting to look back, Miryam shrieked.

"What's happening? What is happening?!"

Joey did look back and saw the disturbed individual pointing the gun haphazardly. He was ranting about what seemed to be years of mistreatment and spewing anger. The civic climate in Netzer was becoming more and more oppressed, and everyone felt it. Back-to-back, gunshots fired directly into the crowd. People started dropping, and the sound of begging ensued. Joey saw Jackson try and rush the shooter but took a shot straight to the chest. Scrambling for her bag to get her phone, Miryam wanted to call 9-1-1. Joey started pushing her along the ground in an army-style crawl.

"Go, go, go," he was ordering. His only and total instinct was to see Miryam safe.

"My friends… My FRIENDS!!" Miryam cried.

"Miry, just go, sweetie, we have to go…. GO!"

After dropping to his knees and awakening to the calamity he had caused, the shooter turned the gun on himself. He knew there would be no escaping the political grip of the Region of Circuit. With one quick shot to the head, he fell over lifeless.

Joey and Miryam reached the top of the dune after what seemed like an eternity. Miryam turned and looked down at the figures on the beach. Sirens could barely be heard in the distance as someone had been able to reach their phone first thing.

"Are you alright?" Joey asked. Miryam nodded positively but couldn't quite make the words out. Dropping to the ground, she put her face in her hands and started to sob. Joey covered her entire being in an embrace. He didn't speak comfort or try to put words to the moment at all; he simply held her. Encompassing her whole person, the two of them lingered there in what felt like an out-of-body experience. Was this really happening?

"You'd better call your folks. It looks like we might be here a while."

~~~

Weeks passed since the tragedy at the beach. The whole Region of Circuit had been glued to the news. Why did they feed on tragedy so? Governor Tetrarch, a weak, self-centered man, had taken every opportunity to address the issue publicly. Joaquin and Anne were immensely grateful to Joey for having been so attentive to Miryam. Even though he usually lived at a distance for school, Joey had been staying with his parents on break. There was much trauma to work through. Miryam's friends from the scene made it out without any physical harm, but Jackson hadn't been so fortunate. A bit of a goofball, Jackson had shown courage in the last moments of his life. He made it close to the shooter but wasn't fast enough. His memorial portrayed him as a hero. Joey was still processing his absence, but he and Miryam had
~~~

become authentic friends. He was welcomed for dinner and unforeseen discussions in their living room that turned into hours of processing together. Anne and Joaquin grew to love and admire Joey for the honorable young man he was. They even allowed him to take Miryam to dinner a couple of times. She felt safe with him, and because they had shared a foxhole experience, there was a natural camaraderie that developed between them.

Joey was pacing himself. He knew that it would be a couple of years before he could formally ask Miryam out on a date. He had been earning the family's trust and didn't want to seem like the creepy older guy taking advantage of the situation. For now, he found honor in having Miryam's friendship and trust. 'She sincerely is something special, though,' he thought. The way she could be so articulate and expressed herself. It wasn't like she was any younger at all. They could talk about any subject and voice any differing opinions without offense. Joey particularly liked the way Miryam looked. She was beautiful but not in an ornate way. If she wore make-up, it was always so slight that she seemed to be natural. He had seen her use lip-gloss, but he tried not to focus on her lips; it would only lead to wanting to kiss them, and he knew that day was far off, if ever. He loved the way her hazel eyes lit up when she laughed and how sharp her wit could be. Miryam seemed to have discernment about her and wasn't afraid to ask the tough questions or have tough conversations. And as difficult as things had been since the shooting, Miryam handled herself with an absolute resilience. It was as if she would be able to handle anything this world threw at her. She was solid and capable.

Miryam was pacing herself. She knew that Joey was too old for her and would never think of her in a romantic way. He must have seen her as someone to take care of and watch out for. Nothing more. He had known her since she was a young girl and must have seen her merely as Joaquin's daughter. 'He sincerely is something special, though,' she thought. He listened to her as if every word was worth hearing. He was so strong and commanding during the tragedy, a natural leader. He was responsible and quirky. He had reddish-brown eyes and could obviously grow a great beard if he ever wanted to. Why wasn't he already snatched up? He was a little on the thin side, but she didn't mind. When Joey talked about the future and steps he wanted to take to become a contractor, Miryam believed he could do it. She loved DIY projects and pictured herself working alongside him to create a home where they could both be proud. Miryam knew she was crazy. She was wise enough to know that most girls her age probably developed crushes on guys who had rescued them in some way and that dreaming of marriage and a home was ridiculous. Besides, it would be another two years before she would even be able to date someone older, and by then, she was sure, a catch like Joey would have long since been taken. So, she decided to enjoy his friendship entirely while she could.

One evening, Miryam was reflecting on the night of the shooting. She always thought of it in the light of what happened. This evening Miryam was thinking about everything that led up to the actual event. The conversations she had with her friends and how perfect the weather had been. Then she flashed on Joey's face. She remembered him looking at her from a distance and Jackson's hand on his shoulder, saying something in his ear. She wondered what it was he had said. She remembered meeting Joey's eyes and him seeming far away. There was a quickening in her spirit, an energy that flowed through her making her feel suddenly awake. What had Joey been thinking? Would he remember anything before the event? She wanted to ask him. Trotting downstairs in a lighthearted fashion, Miryam asked Anne what was for dinner.

"Oh, sweetie," Anne confessed, "it's been a crazy day. It's going to be a 'fend for yourself' night." Miryam tried to act disappointed. If her mother hadn't made an effort toward dinner, then she probably wouldn't mind if Miryam ate out.

"Mom," Miryam led, "if there's no dinner, do you mind if I text Joey? Maybe he'd like to get a burger or something."

"Miryam, try not to take advantage of that boy. He's been very kind to you, but we don't want to exhaust his courtesy. Besides, you need to guard your heart. I've seen the way you look at him, and it's not realistic thinking."

"Moooom…"

"Seriously, what is your motivation in wanting to see him tonight?"

"Mom! I just wanted to get a burger, sheesh."

"A burger?"

"Yes! It's not like that. He just– gets me. We talk a lot. About a lot of things. I thought you liked Joey?"

"We love Joey. But I want you to keep things in perspective."

"So, I can't text him."

"Miryam, just keep things in perspective."

"Okay! I will," she conceded. "So… can I go for a burger?"

Anne sighed. "If he's up for it, but don't push. He might be in the middle of something." Miryam walked away at a pace she hoped didn't look like she was rushing to text, but she was.

Joey was in the middle of something, but he didn't mind putting it off for a burger with his friend. Making sure to greet Joaquin and Anne when he picked Miryam up, off they went to grab a bite. They went to a local diner and chose a booth next to the window.

"I always like to look out if I can," Miryam said.

"Same," Joey answered. "Miryam, does anyone ever call you Miry?"

"I have a relative who does," Miryam chuckled, "but no one else ever does. Why?"

"I just think of it sometimes. It's like it almost comes out of my mouth, and I stop myself."

"You called me Miry at the shooting."

"I did?"

"Yeah, as you were pushing me up the dune."

"Wow, I don't remember that."

"You can call me Miry. If you really want to." They both smiled at each other and turned away from a gaze that hooked a bit too hard. Miryam shot straight to her real reason for texting. "I saw you." Joey looked back at his friend. She had a look on her face that he hadn't seen before. "That night," she continued, "I saw you."

"You saw me? You saw me what?" Miryam nodded. "You saw me what?"

"I saw you looking at me." Joey's heart skipped a beat. He may have even felt himself break into a bit of a sweat.

"Oh, yeah?" Trying to play it cool, he went along, "Hmm. Okay."

"Joey," Miryam pressed. "I saw you looking at me, and I saw Jackson say something in your ear. Do you remember that?"

"Ah, Jackson…" Joey knew *exactly* what Jackson had said. He had caught him dreaming of marriage and encouraged him to engage some other ladies that night. He chuckled, remembering his lost friend. "I remember."

"You had a look on your face. I looked at you, but it wasn't as if you saw me. I mean, you saw me, but you didn't see me see you." Miryam wavered, feeling like she wasn't making sense. "Ugh. Do you know what I'm talking about?" Joey did know what she was talking about, but he wasn't about to tell her any of it.

"What made you think of that?" he asked.

"Answer the question."

"You answer the question!" They both laughed.

"Joey… answer the question," Miryam pried.

"Miryam…no. It's none of your business." He smirked at her and shook his head.

"I saw you, Joey." Her tone turned serious. "I saw you looking right through me. Nobody's ever looked at me like that before."

"Miry," Joey had to choose his words very carefully. He valued this young woman and didn't want to be inappropriate in any way. "Miry, I am so grateful that we have developed this relationship. I mean friendship. This friendship." Joey sighed. Even now, he wanted to protect her from anything that might make her feel unsafe, including himself. "The truth is that I can *not* tell you what I was thinking that night."

"You don't remember?" Miryam interrupted.

"I remember; it's just not for you. Not now." Miryam saw the look of authority in Joey's eyes. He knew what he was saying was correct, and he wasn't going to come off of it. She loved the way he gently refused her without being offensive. He was ever aware of her feelings. Would anyone else ever be that considerate?

"Will you tell me someday?" she asked.

"You don't quit, do you?" They both laughed. "Man, where is this waitress already?!"

"Joey…" Miryam looked at him. Half-girl and a half-woman, she had a look that was hard to deny. "Will you tell me someday?"

"Someday," he relinquished. "If we're still friends, and it still matters." Miryam squirmed in her seat with joy. 'It will matter,' she thought to herself. 'It will matter.'

CHAPTER 3:

VISITATIONS

Liz had been hiding out at home for five months. Not wanting to walk in fear but making sure she wasn't required to do any excessive physical labor or engage in any substantial stress from a day-to-day job, she and Zach agreed that she would not work outside the home but focus on a healthy pregnancy. The Creator had dealt generously with them and taken away any reproach of their former grief; they lived a season of joy and anticipation. Liz would have found Zach's experience with the messenger harder to believe had she not shown up pregnant immediately afterward. It took their allegiance to the Creator to a new level. Not only were they thrilled with the opportunity to be parents, but the messenger said that this child would be a person of great significance and purpose. They were to call him John, which they loved because it meant, *the Creator has been gracious and shown favor.* Wasn't that the truth?!

In the sixth month of Liz's pregnancy, the messenger that visited Zach made another appearance. This time, Miryam was sound asleep when a bright light filled her room. Thinking that something was happening outside, she woke to find the light inside the house and not out. Instead of alarm, Miryam felt great peace. Turning herself to exit the bed, she realized she was not alone in the room. Suddenly, her peace level dropped as she gasped at the enormous figure of light in her room. His head reached to the ceiling, and his shoulders were broader than any man she had ever seen.

"Hello, Miryam," he said in a calming voice. "You are favored and more blessed than other women." Miryam thought she must be dreaming. She shook her head and slapped her face.

'Wake up,' she thought. 'What kind of a greeting would that be to me?' Upon not waking up, she contemplated again. 'Wait– if I'm dreaming– this might get good. Let's see where this goes.'

The messenger chuckled and spoke again, "Don't be afraid, Miryam. You're not dreaming, and you really have found great favor with the Creator." Miryam pinched herself and looked outside. The light was only in her room. She could see that the shadows outside were the same as always at this hour. With a sudden consciousness of her reality, Miryam turned her whole body towards the messenger and stood up. She was aware that she should probably be dropping to the floor but instead felt the fullness of her being standing wholly upright.

"Miryam, you've been chosen to carry an exceptional child. You will call him Emmanuel. He will be great and called the Son of the Highest Deity. His purpose will fulfill all of the strivings of the world, and his sphere of influence will know no end."

Miryam felt her stature slack a bit. She heard every word but contemplated for another moment whether she was indeed dreaming. Did he mean now? Or years from now? Certainly, he couldn't mean now. She was too young and hadn't ever slept with a guy. Patiently the messenger stood as if he could read every thought process Miryam was having.

"How can this be?" she asked. "I've never slept with anyone and–"

The messenger intervened, "An efficient source of power, a life-giving spirit of the Creator's Essence, will come upon you. This endowment will overshadow you, bringing a physical representation of the Creator to earth." Even though it didn't make sense to her, it made perfect sense to her. "In addition," the messenger continued, "your cousin Elizabeth has also conceived a son. Even now, she is six months pregnant. With the Creator, nothing is impossible."

At this point, Miryam did lower herself slowly to the floor. Knowing the impact this would have on Liz, and how deeply she had longed for a child, Miryam pondered all of these things in her heart.

Were these things connected? Why would Liz be given a child now? She had to see her. Had the messenger visited her too? Looking back up toward his radiant presence, Miryam felt a sense of purpose. It was more than that. It was as if everything that had ever been wrong in her was wiped clean.

There was no anger, no frustration. There was no generational guck clouding up any thought that passed through. Miryam knew that she had been made whole in a way that would allow her to carry this perfect creation within her womb. She was entirely cleansed in her soul. Her perspective was sharp and crystal clear. She had an understanding. Somehow, she felt healthier without any physical pain. Again, the messenger patiently stood as if watching her whole thought process transpire.

"All right then," she affirmed, "Let it be just exactly as you have said. I am the Creator's willing servant." In that instant, the messenger vanished.

Miryam crawled back into her bed and sat with her knees against her chest, wide awake. The world outside hadn't even started rousing yet, but she was as conscious as a person could be. Revisiting all of the words the messenger had given her, she felt an anxiousness. There was so much to do; who could she tell? What would they say when they learned she was pregnant? She would have to tell everyone eventually, but who would she go to first? Her mother? Liz? Liz, of course. As quickly as the messenger had come and gone, Miryam felt an unusual peace come over her. Even though she didn't know how she would explain all that had happened, she felt a liquid warmth pour over her body. She became so relaxed that she let her knees down and leaned back against her pillow. She snuggled down and breathed a deep sigh. Suddenly, the liquid warmth became hot over her mid-section. Miryam became so hot that she felt like she might melt, but the strangest part was that there was absolutely no discomfort. She was not sweating, nor did she want it to stop. In fact, Miryam felt so much ease and comfort she found herself wishing it would never stop, and she could linger in this presence forever. She believed she could let everything go and leave behind any hope of any future for the continued fullness of this moment.

~~~

First things first, Miryam had to see Liz. Convincing Anne to allow her to borrow the car, Miryam did her best not to speed the whole way there. She didn't call or text in advance, but she knew Liz had been working from home online for the adoption agency. When Liz opened the door, Miryam greeted her with a huge hug. Immediately, Liz gasped as a filling of power, the energy of the Creator's Essence, came upon her.

"Oh, Miryam," she breathed. Liz's baby leaped inside her with such vigor that she felt the sudden urge to sit down. "Whoa."

Once it passed, she looked at Miryam with wide eyes, raised eyebrows,
~~~

and an expression of surprise and joy. "Oh my gosh– Oh, Miryam." Liz had a sense that Miryam was somehow significantly involved in the miracles that were taking place. Miryam reached out and embraced Liz's belly with her hands, smiling from ear to ear. She could tell by the look on Miryam's face that she was well aware of the pregnancy, even though they had not yet begun telling family. "Come in, come in here right now!" Liz exclaimed. Rushing towards the couch with Miryam's hand in her own, she burst out, "What is going on here? Have you had a visitation too? The moment I heard the sound of your voice, my baby about busted my gut kicking around!" Both women laughed and embraced again. "Oh, Miry… how did you know I was pregnant?" Miryam was about to burst with the satisfaction that someone else was in the midst of the extraordinary things she was experiencing.

"Liz, last night, this huge guy showed up in my room…" Liz's face dropped. "Not a huge guy," Miryam corrected, "I mean, he was huge, and he was a guy, but… he wasn't a guy…"

Liz interrupted her dear young cousin, "A messenger."

"Yes!" Miryam exclaimed, "Yes… a messenger. Oh, my gosh! It was so scary, but not. It was–"

"Divine." Liz completed.

"Yes," Miryam calmed, "yes, divine. But Liz, you're never going to believe what he told me. And what happened afterward. My parents are going to flip."

"Miryam, blessed are you among women, right? You've found such favor with the Creator– and you're pregnant."

Miryam leaned back against the couch in shock. "Yes! How did you know that?! Did the warmth come over you too? Oh, my gosh– did you not ever want it to stop?"

"No… the warmth? No, I just went to the doctor, and he figured it out. It was crazy. But Zach knew. The messenger actually visited Zach! At work!"

Both women started laughing. Zach came around the corner and was a bit stunned at the scene. Liz had kept somewhat isolated in the last six months, wanting to make sure all was well before telling family. Zach was surprised to see the two ladies sitting so close and sharing so openly. He noticed that Miryam looked older, somehow, and thought she looked as though she had come into her womanhood overnight. Without saying a word, he greeted her with a side-hug. Liz explained how Zach had become mute since the news from the messenger. "It's been so nice," she teased. "Actually, it's been really hard. There's so much we want to talk about, but communication has become a whole other ball game. I think we've become closer, though. It's like, we don't take words for granted, and a look can say so much." Zach nodded in agreement. Turning and looking into his eyes, she agreed with them, "Love you too, honey."

The ladies chatted all morning and well into the afternoon. Finally, Anne called, wanting her daughter and her car back. This was only the first of many personal visits the two would have over the next few months until Liz gave birth. But the firestorm had just begun.

~~~

Miryam had not yet told her parents about the messenger or being pregnant. She knew it was all true by a few different things. First, her breasts were tender beyond any typical monthly issue. Second, she hadn't had a period, and there was this constant issue with smell. She would have to tell them soon, as she could not keep sleeping so late and taking naps all the time without them starting to think something was seriously wrong. Liz and Zach's baby announcements finally hit the mail, and everyone was in a bit of shock. How could she come behind that with her shocking news?

Miryam started formulating a plan to sit down with her parents. Perhaps she would ask Liz to come and be with her for backup. After all, her own miraculous story would add validation to Miryam's. Miracles or no miracles, Miryam knew her parents were going to have a difficult time. Joaquin was so content in his new position at the church, and Anne would be so ashamed of her daughter being found in any compromising condition. Girls Miryam's age got pregnant all the time, but that didn't mean it was the most ideal or upright situation. No one ever likes to hear that a teenager is pregnant, and even though Miryam was not a typical teenager as far as maturity went, she was a teenager nonetheless.

School had become more difficult as well. Normally, Miryam was an attentive student with good grades. Since the change in her body, she had difficulty focusing and was preoccupied with how to move forward. One of her favorite teachers even called home with concern for her wellbeing these days. Miryam had a hard time relating to the girls her age and wondered how many teenage mothers went through this. Even though her circumstance was much different, she still felt the stress of how others would view her and how she could possibly support a baby. Undoubtedly, the Creator who had
~~~

deemed her suitable for such an assignment would provide and not leave her alone in this major undertaking. She just couldn't see how. After all, it wasn't Joaquin and Anne's assignment; it was hers and hers alone.

It was definitely time to have the talk. Miryam practiced with Liz and invited her over for the main event. Joaquin and Anne agreed to sit down for Miryam's disclosure. They thought it would be that she wanted to buy her own car or attend the mission trip with the church youth group and needed money. Little could they have imagined. After dinner, they all took their places in the living room. Miryam sat directly across from her parents with Liz by her side. Joaquin and Anne were almost beaming with pride. Their little girl was growing up, and now she would work towards a car or take a trip with other productive youth wanting to make a difference in a hurting world. Either way, she was maturing and headed toward independence. Miryam was hoping that the same energy of the Creator's Essence would show up as it had with Liz and that miraculously her parents would embrace her and be proud. Liz wanted so badly to speak for her loved one but knew it had to originate with Miry. Miryam looked at her parents nervously.

"Well, this is a bit difficult," she began. "I want to thank you, actually, for raising me with such a profound understanding that there is a Creator and that He, or even they… are truly involved in our lives." Anne and Joaquin were still beaming. What a treasure their daughter was to have the mindset of honor to thank them for initiating her relationship with the architect of life. With a full sense of self-satisfaction, they turned to each other, relishing the moment. They weren't sure what she meant by 'they,' but they weren't about to ruin the moment to find out. They were too eager to hear her good news and plan.

"Mom…Dad… My soul magnifies the Creator." A lofty start from their daughter on the brink of womanhood.

"Yes, yes," they agreed. "Ours does too."

"Yes, of course, it does." They smiled. Miryam could see her parents being *themselves* and turned to Liz. Liz smiled a warm knowing smile and encouraged her to proceed with a nod.

"My spirit rejoices in the Creator Who saves me. He has looked at the humble state of my life, and every generation from here on out will call me blessed– because, in His mightiness, He has done truly great things for me, and, well– I praise Him." Joaquin cocked his head and looked to Anne. He wanted to see if she was following Miryam's point or if he was the only one who felt lost. Anne raised her eyebrows with a look and shook her head like she had no idea. "Guys," Miryam cut to the chase, "I'm pregnant."

There was a long pause before Anne burst out with a laugh. "Oh, honey," she chortled, "Miryam," she came to a light rebuke, "how could you do that to your parents?" Laughing, she continued, "Joaquin…it's a joke. She's joking. That's not the real thing–" Joaquin acted like he was understanding but still felt a bit lost.

"No, Mom… guys. That *is* the real thing. I'm pregnant. Seriously. *That's* the thing. But it's going to be okay." Anne looked to Liz; Liz nodded. Anne looked to Miryam; Miryam raised her shoulders and smiled a fake smile.

"You're not really pregnant," Anne contested.

"Pregnant?!" Joaquin stood up. In an instant, his whole career flashed before his eyes, as did the face of every elder that would look down on him. This could not be happening to him. "Oh!" he exclaimed, "It's a joke!" a delayed revelation seemed to be his only hope. "It's a *joooooke.* Oh, wow. Not cool, Miryam. Not cool. Whew." He sat back down.

"It's not a joke," Anne said solemnly.

"No, honey, it's a joke… a dumb joke, but it's a joke," he protested.

"Dad, it's not a joke," Miryam established. "I am pregnant. But it's the most incredible thing; wait 'til you hear…"

"Oh, God!" Anne interrupted, "It's that boy! It's that older boy! My God! How could we have let him near you! How could he betray our trust like this?!"

"What? No– Mom– it wasn't Joey. Please, just calm down."

"Calm down? Seriously, Miryam? You step out of everything we have ever taught you and ruin all of our lives in a moment and seriously expect us to calm down? What were you thinking? How could you let this happen?" Anne admonished.

"Did he force you?" Joaquin was standing again, "Miryam, if he forced you, then nothing is your fault, and we can go to the elders with this. We will go straight to his father and let him know what kind of a son he has raised."

"Stop!" Miryam yelled.

"Okay, okay," Liz chimed in, "Listen. Everyone calm down. Joaquin, have a seat. Look, something is happening in this family. Maybe it's years of serving Him, maybe it's strictly unearned, unmerited favor, but *something* is happening in this family. The Creator has chosen to bless us with visitations and babies."

"Look, Liz… my kid is pregnant, okay? She's 16, and she's pregnant. She's not some forty-something-year-old woman past her prime. She's a kid, and this ruins everything."

"Anne, you're not listening. Both of you get out of your heads for a minute and listen to what we are telling you. These pregnancies are miracles. Both Zach and Miry had visitations by a messenger that resulted in us being pregnant. A divine messenger, Anne. Your daughter is not a strumpet. This was not done by flesh or the will of a man but by the Creator. He has a great plan to reconcile the world to Himself."

"Alright," Anne said in a huff, "I don't know which of you is worse. My daughter, who has the nerve to bring us this news, or the closest thing I have to a sister in this world. What the hell is going on here?" Joaquin shot a look at Anne, appalled that she would resort to such language. "Oh, really, Joaquin? That is what you're going to get upset about?" Miryam knew things were bad when her mother lost her ever graceful demeanor.

Starting from the beginning, Liz told the story of Zach and the messenger's visit to him. Then Miryam, with intimate detail, shared the story of her visitation. She explained the way it felt and the complete peace that she experienced. She apologized for not telling them sooner but expressed that she had to get her wits about her and how helpful Liz had been. Even though they accepted each of the ladies' experiences, it took every ounce of their being and then some to apply what faith they had to consider the Creator they believed in would do something like this. Whatever the case, they were all in it now. A tug of war in emotions consumed the next days. Anne and Joaquin fluctuated between support for their daughter and being disconcerted. They knew that the Creator had done miracles in the past; the Ancient Writings said so, but He was not in the business of doing grand things like that today. Today, they were just supposed to believe that He was there, give Him the honor due to Him, and try to live a life pleasing to Him and others. Right? How could He allow a 16-year-old girl to make such a sacrifice? And what about them? They had spent their entire adult and married life following all of the rules. Why would a loving Creator allow them to go through this humiliation? Couldn't He have chosen someone else? And someone older?! It seemed to them that an all-knowing God should know better.

CHAPTER 4:

STAND BESIDE HER

Miryam hadn't spoken to Joey in a couple of months. He texted her a couple of times, but she always responded vaguely. Joey was saddened but assumed she was ready to move on from a traumatic time in her life, and he was associated with it. He tried to convince himself that it wasn't healthy to adore her the way he did. He sometimes caught himself in that faraway place that allowed him to dream of perhaps running into her someday years later and sweeping her off her feet. Miryam, on the other hand, would not allow herself to think of Joey at all. She was far too attached to him for something that had never even been established. Whenever he came into her mind, she would take the thought captive and dismiss it. She had become too dependent on him, anyway. Now more than ever, Miryam believed she needed to become self-sufficient. She needed to prepare for being a mother and find some way to earn an income. She was looking at jobs online that would allow her to make a decent wage, but her age and lack of education for the position always seemed to be factors. They all agreed that she would finish school, but perhaps from home online. Things were becoming intense, and she wasn't even showing yet. Only a couple of her friends knew; it was a hard story to believe. Even the most devoted friends questioned her sanity a bit. They wondered if someone took advantage of her somewhere or if she let herself go and regretted it. Either way, claiming to be a virgin and suddenly turning up pregnant were hard pills to swallow.

The family was suffering as a whole. Joaquin was removed from the prestigious Office of the Overseer at church. Citing it as 'just not the right time for his family,' they encouraged him to step down and lay low. Anne was all but shunned from the ladies' group. The concept of an actual miracle taking place was far more than the distinguished wives of esteemed board members could allow. The family was even considering moving to a new town and quietly starting over. How could they ever get past all the whispers and judgment? Joaquin barely believed his daughter himself; how could he ask his peers to embrace her? Anne struggled to believe, but she did conclude that Miryam was convinced of what she was saying. Perhaps someone had slipped her one of those date rape drugs and forced themselves on her. Maybe she had no remembrance of it. They simply could not wrap their heads around how the Creator could do this to them. Everything they had done for him. All their service and sacrifice– shattered. Still, what could they do? Miryam was their daughter. Were they supposed to put her out in the street for something that so many other young girls had done? It was commonplace in society, just not in the religious sphere they walked in.

Anne threw herself into planning a baby shower for Liz. Hers was a pregnancy they could rejoice in. That seemed like a miracle they could get behind, even though she and Joaquin had discussed feeling a bit sorry for the child. Liz and Zach would be such older parents. They would undoubtedly face strangers thinking that they were the grandparents and not the parents. What would people think? Why would the Creator choose *now* to bless them? Anne didn't honestly think Liz would be able to carry the baby to term. Conceivably that is why she waited so long to tell everyone. Maybe Liz had a hard time believing too and wanted to give it time. Anne was facing a lot of thoughts and convictions with struggle. It may be that she and Joaquin, in their search for an upright life, had entered an arrogance that led them to this inevitable humbling. They never dreamed that Miryam would put them in this kind of a position, or greater yet, that the Creator would. Ultimately, they were lost. They had no idea how to come back from this or how things would ever be okay again. What were they going to do? What were their options? Was this baby really for Miryam to raise? For years, they had heard Liz praise the women who placed their babies for adoption with couples who couldn't have children; such a brave thing to do. Perhaps Miryam could do that. Maybe this baby was supposed to be a miracle to an infertile couple? If she did, they could resume their lives. Anne was overwhelmed with the lack of direction for their future. She flopped down on the couch and put her head in her hands.

"Seriously, what are we supposed to do?"

~~~

Word spread through the church where Joaquin had stepped down. Veiled in confidential prayer requests, the talk of Miryam's pregnancy spread like wildfire. Eventually, it spread to Joaquin's job as well and landed in the ears of Joey's father, Jacob. Knowing that Joey and Miryam had been somewhat close for a bit, he vaguely wondered if his son might have anything to do with her condition. Jacob slipped into his office and called his son. Joey's ears were burning upon hearing the news. His father asked if he was involved. Joey's heart sank, and he hung up as soon as he could get a denial out of his mouth.

'This is why,' he thought. 'This is why she won't talk to me. What could have happened?! Miryam was *not* the kind of girl who would allow anyone to…' Joey became sick to his stomach. He wanted to call her. He didn't want to call her. He wanted to let her know his mind on the subject; he wanted to never speak to her again. After surviving a trauma of some sort, Joey had read how people would act out in ways they wouldn't typically. Perhaps she had met someone. Perhaps she had let go in some hazardous way that had taken her further than she would typically agree to go. It just didn't add up. Miryam was so strong, at least he'd thought she was. Knowing that this sealed the deal on his ever being with her, Joey cried himself to sleep and had a dream.

He was on an airplane. He was panicked because he believed he had boarded a plane for a different destination. He wanted to get off, but they were already thirty-eight thousand feet in the air. A flight attendant came over to him and encouraged him to relax. She said the Captain was in full control and would be able to land the plane without issue. She gave him a drink of water and told him that the copilot would be with him shortly. Joey drank the water. The next thing he knew, he was sitting in a wide-open field of green. The copilot was walking directly towards him. Joey felt a sense of reverence. He was so intimidated; he wanted to run but also wanted to stay and hear what the copilot was going to say. He knew it was a great honor to be visited in this way. He didn't understand why he had been chosen.

"Hello, Joseph," the copilot greeted him. His voice was deep and calm. He smiled at Joey, and everything seemed to melt away; all pain and sadness were dismissed. "Enjoying the flight?" Joey looked around at the soft green
~~~

grass.

"It's so beautiful. I wanted to go somewhere else, but I see now how this was the right choice."

"Joseph, I want to talk to you about Miryam." Joey lowered his head and wanted to cry. The pain he felt was so profound, much deeper than it had been before. "There's no need for that now," the copilot corrected. With just his word, the pain lifted, "Don't be afraid to take Miryam as your wife."

"My wife?" Joey was confused, "No, no, I can't. See, she has– Well, she was– but now she's…"

"Joseph– Miryam is innocent. She has been chosen, as have you. For that which is conceived in her is from the Essence of the Creator. She will bear a son, and you will call him Emmanuel, for He will rescue all people from the consequence of their wrongdoing."

"The Essence of–? But how is that possible?"

"The Captain is getting ready to land the plane."

"But it's too much. For Miryam, I mean– it's so much to ask of her…"

"Then you'd better stand beside her. She will need your leadership, Joseph."

With that, the copilot pinned a pair of golden airline wings on his lapel. A loud whirring came and grew in volume. Joey looked up and saw the plane in a direct nosedive headed straight for him. He gasped, but instead of running, he reached out and, with superhuman strength, caught the aircraft by its nose. He lowered it gently to the ground. Suddenly, he was wearing the Captain's hat. He looked over at the copilot. With a sharp whip of his hand to his forehead, the copilot saluted him. Joey knew what he had to do.

~~~

Anne heard the house phone ringing. She almost didn't answer it. She had nothing to say to anyone, and nobody called on the landline anymore. After several rings, she picked up, "Hello?"

"Hello… Anne. Oh, I'm so glad you answered. I almost hung up. This is Joey. I'm sorry for calling you at home, but I haven't been able to get ahold of Miryam, and I need to speak to her. I mean– I *really* need to speak to her. Is she home?"

"Oh, Joey, hello. Um…" Anne knew that Miryam insisted Joey was not the father. This, for some reason, they did believe. "Joey, it's so good to hear your voice. Miryam, um…" Miryam had not told Joey or spoken to him. Anne was not about to drop the bomb. "You know, I think she's
~~~

upstairs; let me check– I haven't spoken to her much today."

"Wait…" Joey stopped her, "If it isn't terribly rude, I'd actually prefer to come over and see her. I just wanted to know she was there and attain your permission."

"My permission? Oooh. Um, that's a tough one. I mean, of course, you have my permission, Joey, you are welcome here anytime, I'm just not sure it's a good time for–"

"Wonderful, thank you so much, Anne. Is Joaquin there, too? I was hoping to speak to the whole family." In all her graciousness, Anne had never been good at turning anyone away when they sincerely asked for something.

"I'll tell you what," she offered, "why don't you just come for dinner. We'll be sitting down in about two hours."

"Yes! Yes, thank you so much. I look forward to seeing all of you. Until then." Hanging up, Anne hoped she hadn't just made a big mistake.

Miryam came down about 10 minutes before their standard dinner time. She thought she would set the table for her mother and knew that Sally wouldn't volunteer. Anything she could do to stay on her parents' good side these days was beneficial. Anne had not mentioned Joey to Miryam. The family was in survival mode, and Anne didn't feel the strength to argue with her about it. After all, Joey had become friends with all of them during the last crisis, and Anne could invite him if she wanted; at least that is what she told herself. Joaquin came in and kissed his wife on the forehead. Sally came wandering down the stairs and announced how good everything smelled. Miryam longed for a kiss on the forehead from her father. Even though she knew the Creator called her, the situation caused a degree of shame culturally, which ended up sitting between her and every person with whom she came into contact. She wondered if that would ever end.

The doorbell rang, and everyone looked at each other. Anne started bringing food to the table and instructed Sally, "Well, don't just stand there; answer the door." Sally bound to the door and swung it wide open. There stood Joey holding a bouquet of flowers. He was wearing an old, slightly too large, dress coat with a tie. Sally's eyebrows went up, and her jaw dropped. She would have laughed out loud, but the look on Joey's face was too sincere.

"Ummm," she started, "I think you might have the wrong house."

"Hey, Sal," Joey chuckled nervously, "your mom invited me."

Sally nodded, thinking to herself, 'Oh, this is going to be good.' "Come on in," she obliged.

Walking into the dining room, Sally stepped to the side as quickly as possible to give the family a full presentation. By this point, she couldn't help but chuckle just a bit. Everyone's eyebrows went up this time, but upon seeing Joey, Miryam gasped. What was he doing here? And why was he dressed like that? What could he possibly be thinking?

Joaquin took the lead, "Joey… long time no see."

"Yes, I know; I'm sorry about that."

"What brings you by this evening? You're obviously headed someplace special." Joey looked to Anne, whose face said, 'I'm sorry,' and 'I'll fix it,' all in one moment.

"I invited him," she said.

"You what?" Miryam asked defensively.

"I invited him," Anne's tone had shifted to the guarding mother, "now everyone quit acting so weird. We haven't seen Joey in a while, and I think he looks very nice. Would you like me to get a vase for your flowers?"

Sally was chuckling again. Miryam sighed heavily. She couldn't believe her mother wouldn't tell her he was coming or give her the opportunity to sneak out of it somehow. Miryam wondered how she could be around him. How could she not spill over and weep into his chest? How could she pretend that she was anything but upset to see him? She would not be able to control her emotions with him in the room. All-day, every day Miryam did her best to keep her head up and trust the Creator to help her through. But how could she be expected to look Joey in the eye on top of it all? It was too much.

"If you don't mind, Anne, no. I mean, thank you, but– I was hoping there was something I could do first." The whole family got quiet; even Sally couldn't muster anything but reverence for the weight that had just come into the room. Joaquin ushered everyone into the living room. He was hungry and wanted to get whatever this thing was over with swiftly. Miryam had not even said hello. Everyone sat down; everyone except Joey. His heart was pounding. Either he was about to make a complete fool of himself or be greeted with hugs of acceptance. There was no way he could know if Miryam even felt the same way he did, but he had to try. He closed his eyes and envisioned himself in the Captain's hat and wings pinned to his chest. He looked at Miryam and waited for her eyes to meet his. It took several seconds, and the wait seemed eternal. When she finally looked at him, she cracked. Silent tears started flowing down her cheeks. Joey addressed her as if no one else was in the room.

"Miryam," he started. His voice was soft and tender, every bit the man she had adored so completely. She didn't look back at him too quickly. She looked at her parents and felt the familiar shame between them. "Miryam, my dad told me what was going on with you. I wish you would have known you could tell me yourself. But I understand why you didn't." Miryam's tears became harder to restrain. She found herself holding her breath and taking quick gasps here and there as silently as possible. "I want you to know; you are one of the most special people I have ever met. I know we went through something awful together and that it gave us common ground to connect on, but it was more than that for me. I know it's awful, and I would never wish what happened upon any of those people, upon Jackson, but that situation gave me an in to your life that I wanted very much. I've always admired you, Miryam. I've hoped that someday, maybe years from now, you would even consider me…" Miryam jerked her head around and finally made direct eye contact without wavering. Was he really saying what she thought he was saying? "Well, consider me as someone you might like to date." Joey looked over to Joaquin and repeated, "Years from now." Joaquin softened and offered the boy a slow blink and close-lipped smile followed by a nod. "But– and this is going to sound crazy, I know… but I was given a revelation." The room shifted from an awkward strain to a warm charge of the Creator's Essence. "I know that this whole thing wasn't of your doing. I know that you have conceived in some miraculous way and that you aren't guilty of any shame. But I also know the world won't understand that." As Miryam looked at Joey, she realized it made perfect sense that he would be the one person who didn't look at her with that burden in the midst.

"Oh, Joey," she whispered. She had missed him so.

"I know you're walking through something complicated and life-changing. Shoot, world-changing! So, with the permission of your parents, which, legally, we would require," Joey got down on one knee in front of Miryam and placed the flowers at her feet. From his pocket, he pulled a very humble but very respectable diamond engagement ring, "Miryam, if you'll have me, I'd be so honored to love you and walk with you through everything that you are called to." Joey started to choke up and had a hard time finishing his offer. "Miryam, will you marry me?"

Every ounce of Miryam's being shot up out of her chair, throwing herself around Joey's neck. Standing up, they cried and hugged and felt the void of the last weeks gone. Anne put her hand on Joaquin's. He was fighting a flow of tears of his own; this could solve everything. Yes, they were young, but if Joey would assume responsibility for this situation and take Miryam as his own, they could carve out a respectable life somewhere in upright standing.

Miryam came away from Joey's neck long enough to look at her father, "Daddy?" she asked, "Can I please?" Joaquin stood up, and Anne swiftly joined him.

"With all of my sanction and blessing, honey." Miryam threw her head back with a full-blown laugh and simultaneous sob of relief.

"Yes!" she shouted, "Yes, Joey! Yes– I will marry you!" Joey had never kissed his soon-to-be bride, but with a gentle and heartfelt impression, he committed, 'til death do we part.'

CHAPTER 5:

BIRTHS AND BABIES

The day had come for Liz's baby shower. After three months of planning, Anne hosted a long-awaited event with the theme, *Dreams Come True.* The men were all out back with cigars while the ladies enjoyed hors d'oeuvres, sweet treats, and presents. Many friends were there to rejoice with the couple, but few knew the details of how this pregnancy had come about. They knew it was a dream come true, and they knew Zach had suffered an episode of some sort. It was an ironic joke that he was 'speechless upon finding out and hadn't found his tongue ever since.' They played games, opened onesies, and gave every conceivable offering to the mommy and baby-to-be. Miryam was thrilled for her cousin. She knew her baby wouldn't have the same sort of reception, but with each week, she felt more and more love for the life growing inside her and wasn't bothered if they barely had a thing. All she wanted was this baby and her newlywed husband, Joey. Looking down at the gold rings on her finger filled her with satisfaction enough.

Miryam and Joey had a small civil ceremony at the county courthouse. Only their parents and siblings were present. These days it seemed that family was the only thing that truly mattered. Anything anyone else had to say on the topic of marriage and pregnancy was wholly disregarded. Although Miryam was young, she had taken to the idea of being a wife quite nicely. Joey committed to not knowing her sexually until after the baby was born. It didn't seem right for her first experience to be under the pressure of everything else she was dealing with, and contrary to popular belief, he didn't mind the wait. Actually, he was nervous at the thought. Quite willing but nervous. He figured he had waited this long for the love of his life, what was a few months more, while they prepared for their anointed bundle of joy to arrive. They were content to get to know each other further and prepare for officially starting their lives together. It had all happened so fast, and even if Miryam was the strongest person he'd ever met, she needed time to process and prepare. They hadn't started living together just yet. Joey lived in Breadville, after all. He was a student living in a dorm with another guy. It would never suit Miryam and a new baby. He had been keeping his eyes open for something more adequate and completing his degree but hadn't seen anything he could afford. Joaquin generously offered to help get them into a place, and soon he would be able to step out into the dream of his own construction business. He dreamed of a Father and Son Carpentry business.

"What are you going to name the baby, Liz?" one friend asked.

"Yes, yes…" the others were eager to hear. "Is it a boy or a girl?"

"It's a boy," Elizabeth answered. "And we're going to name him John." Oohs and awes came from the room until one cantankerous friend piped up.

"John? Doesn't this world have enough John's in it? Why don't you name him Zach Jr. after his father?" With laughter and hushed tones, some agreed. Elizabeth started to answer, but just then, the men came in to refresh their drinks and use the facilities. Again, the testy gal piped up.

"Zach! Wouldn't you rather have a Junior? What's with this John business?" Reaching for the little pocket pad of paper he had become accustomed to carrying, he started to write.

'His name is John.' As he wrote, he began saying the words out loud simultaneously. Liz stood and went to him, hearing him speak for the first time in months. Her face lit up, and she put her hand on his arm.

"What?" Zach asked her. Taking a second click to realize he had just spoken out loud, he looked at his wife and gasped. With a burst of laughter, he swung her around. "Yes!" he blurted out. His voice softened, and tears came to his eyes. Forehead to forehead with his wife, he said softly, "His name is John."

Turning to the group, Zach began to share openly, "What a crazy time this has been." The company was hushed in awe of his ability to speak after so long. "The miracle of Liz's pregnancy and my loss of speech. It's been a difficult and humbling season. We didn't know what to think! This is crazy."

He put his hand to his throat. "We've learned so much about everything we take for granted and how treasured communication is, with or without words." Gravity came into the room. A stillness that caused each person to feel the significance of what Zach was sharing. "We haven't had the words to tell you– well, I literally haven't had the words– but we haven't known how to tell you of everything that comes along with this baby. Obviously, it's a miracle. But it's more than that. There is a destiny on him; on John." Eyes were exchanging looks of interest, and hearts were beginning to shift. Zach laid his hand on his wife's stomach. "You, child, will be a forecaster. You will speak on behalf of the Creator and go before the One Who will fulfill all the strivings of the world, bringing peace. You will prepare a way for Him– somehow, you will. You will bring a message of knowledge, leading people to the restoration of their lives from all our pain and missing the mark. Because of the tender mercy of the Creator, you will be a part of bringing light to those who sit in darkness and the shadow of death, guiding our feet into the way of peace."

No one spoke a word. Liz was crying. The Essence of the Creator was heavy upon all who heard. Finally, Zach looked up at the people and breathed deep. "Wow," he said. "Alrighty then." After an appropriate pause, he asked, "Refreshments?" Some chuckled, and some sat in contemplation for a moment or two more. Some did get up for refreshments. Liz hugged her husband and felt a sudden warmth running down her legs.

~~~

The military statesman, General Cesar August, was making changes. His most recent appointment caused him to want any and all information at his disposal. He determined an updated census needed to take place for an accurate count and registration of all citizens. General August's census dictated that one must register in their town of residence. Joey considered Breadville his home away from home. His family and all Miryam's family were in Netzer, but it was the family's history and beginnings in Breadville that had led him to go to school there in the first place. He looked forward to the days when he could finally bring Miryam and show her all his favorite spots. They were still trying to finalize when the transition would take place, but he was sure he wanted to bring her there for the registration and census. She was his wife now, and there should be nothing odd about them traveling and staying together. Except that it was foreign, and he was a bit apprehensive. Joey was short the cash that would enable him to get a hotel
~~~

room in advance. He knew Joaquin would be willing to help, but he didn't want to ask for more than the offer of getting into a place when they were ready. His own parents thought he was crazy for marrying such a young girl and one who was in trouble at that! Needless to say, he was not going to ask them for a thing. Joey had been saving for a new car but dipped into that savings for Miryam's ring and the special first night they had shared at a local Bed and Breakfast as man and wife. He would continue to drive his trusty old Volkswagen bus a bit longer. It wouldn't do for long, though. Thankfully, Miryam's parents had mentioned getting her a car as a wedding present. But she would need other comforts, and the baby would need *everything.* Joey felt the stress of all that he had stepped into. He wished Jackson was available to talk.

~~~

Baby Johnny had grown to a fat and happy six months old. He was strong in spirit and full of things to say. Always babbling and pulling himself up, they joked he was born with the ability to stand and proclaim some important news. Liz and Zach thought he was advanced for his age but were a bit prejudiced and had no real reference. Miryam went to visit as often as she could and was learning alongside Liz how to care for a baby. The two would laugh at little boy pee going everywhere and poop up the back. It was the best kind of awful either of them could imagine. Miryam was comforted by Liz and grateful that their boys would be related. They had long conversations about marriage and the miraculous things in store for their families, even if they didn't have a clue what that might mean. Miryam was able to talk more easily with Liz and ask her questions about intimate things. She wanted to be a good wife and mother. She wanted to protect her son and make sure that he would always be taken care of. She wanted him to have everything he would ever need.

Miryam's belly had grown, and with it whispers from the neighbors and church members. She could not wait until Joey found a place and took her away from it all. She longed for the new enterprise of Breadville. Miryam was checking places online and looked forward to the next weekend with Joey when she could run them by him. Anne told her she was nesting, but whatever it was, Miryam could not stop thinking about it. Since her 24th week of pregnancy, she experienced more tightness and a hardening of her stomach. Now and then, she even experienced some mild contractions that the doctor said were normal from here on out as her body prepared for
~~~

delivery. Delivery. Miryam did not look forward to that part of this 'miracle.'

In the months at home, Miryam easily accomplished her studies and passed exams to complete her education. She graduated early and was only vaguely disappointed she wouldn't experience the standard cap and gown routine. These days she had grown physically uncomfortable and was not as full of energy to shop with Anne to gather all the things they needed for the baby. She didn't usually like to venture outside of the house but was looking forward to the weekend when she and Joey would get out of town to Breadville to register for the census. Many people registered by mail, but Joey wanted to handle it in person; he was the same when it came to voting. For Miryam, any excuse to get away with Joey and escape prying eyes was good enough.

Finally, the weekend came. Miryam had begun packing a week in advance from excitement. She and Joey were still learning much about each other. The freedom of already being married eliminated any petty precursors to commitment. Because they were already devoted, all that they discussed or learned was with the foundation and safety of their pledge, not only to each other but to this baby. It provided uncommon solidarity. Joey gathered his bride and loaded her belongings into the van. He apologized once more that he didn't yet own a more appropriate vehicle for the trip.

"Maybe I'll end up getting some sort of mini-van," he teased.

After all, they hoped there would be more children in the future, but not for quite some time. They started their trip around 2 PM, hoping to miss most of the commuter traffic that happens after 4 PM. Joey asked if she wanted to stop and eat somewhere, but Miryam had been feeling a bit nauseous all day. He figured that by getting into town around 4 PM, they would have plenty of time to eat and find a place to stay. Miryam didn't look forward to eating. Even if they were married, she didn't look forward to sharing physical issues just yet, and it seemed that everything she ate lately went right through her, and when she needed to go– she needed to go!

The drive went well. They laughed a lot and made good time. They made jokes about Miryam being the size of a house. She figured if she made fun of it, maybe Joey wouldn't see her as unattractive as she felt. He seemed to be okay with it, but she knew he was so kind that he would never say anything that might feel like an insult. Miryam was thrilled to be in Breadville with her husband finally. She wanted to see everything. Even though she knew it would be a quick in and out weekend trip with the business of the registration to handle, she was determined to work some fun in as well. Once Miryam got it into her mind to do something, she usually did it. Not even being the size of a house was going to stop her. The first stop had to be for a restroom, and Joey suggested again that they eat. Miryam was only able to get down some broccoli cheese soup and crackers. Refusing to give in to her discomfort, Miryam didn't mention the severity to Joey. She looked forward to checking in somewhere and resting for a bit before doing a bit of sightseeing that night. Joey suggested his favorite place to get frozen yogurt, so they decided to go there.

After dinner, Joey headed to the motel he had in mind to stay. Traffic was greater than he had anticipated, as many people had come into town for the registration. Leaving Miry in the car, he ran in to get a room.

"A room?" the attendant chuckled. "Tonight? Sir, I'm sorry, but we've been booked for this weekend for weeks. Everyone is here for the registration."

"Yes, but… Okay, well. I'll just try someplace else, thanks."

"Good luck, man."

Back out to the car, Joey explained they were full and knew of someplace else that would be just fine. As they headed over, the traffic grew thicker and thicker. People were also out walking everywhere. Joey had never seen Breadville so packed. "This is crazy!" he commented. "It's not normally like this. I don't know why I didn't think about people coming in this way." Miryam was somewhat unresponsive. She listened politely but was having a hard time not focusing on her discomfort. She didn't want to complain, so she just made little comments here and there to let him know she was paying attention. Reaching the second location, Joey couldn't find a place to park.

"I don't have a very good feeling about this," Miryam said after the third trip around the block. Joey apologized and finally double-parked just to run in. He was starting to realize that he needed to get Miryam into a room as soon as he could. The clerk informed Joey that there no vacancies. He asked if the clerk knew of any place that still had vacancies. The clerk suggested one of the higher-end hotels. Joey's heart sank. It was true; he had tried two of the lower-priced motels in hopes of not blowing his whole wad on just the room. He should have booked weeks ago. Why had he let money be the factor in not making sure they had a secure location to stay? In the future, as a father, he couldn't be so careless. He would need to become more safe than sorry.

Apologizing to Miryam again, Joey headed to a high-end hotel just a couple of miles away. Even though it was close, it took nearly an hour to get there. Traffic had become horrific, and if Miryam hadn't been pregnant, Joey determined it would have been faster just to park and walk. Joey pulled into the front entrance and spoke briefly to the valet. Before parking, he wanted to get their room and things. The lobby was a madhouse. When Joey finally reached the concierge, he was informed the hotel was full, as were all the hotels in the area. They would have to go out of town to find a room available. "Out of town?!" Joey was vanquished, "We just got into town! Are you sure there aren't any rooms anywhere? Anything?" The concierge just shook his head, 'no' for the millionth time that evening. Joey was at a loss. What was he going to tell Miryam? Did they need to head back towards Netzer? *Why* didn't he just register by mail?! He couldn't take Miryam to the dorm. Men and women's dorms were separated, and his roommate was not the kind of guy who would be cool with sneaking her in. Joey was desperate. In the car was his beloved wife, uncomfortable and unprovided for. He wanted to cry or punch someone in the face, but neither would get him any further toward what he needed. He dreaded the thought of Joaquin and Anne learning that their weekend away had turned into such a failure, and they hadn't even been there one day!

Heading back out to the car, Joey noticed a look on Miryam's face. She didn't see him watching her or approaching; she was too engrossed in her own experience. She looked in pain. His heart stopped. Was she suffering and hadn't even mentioned it? Was he so selfish that he hadn't tuned in to her true state? Now he really wanted to cry– or punch someone. Tapping on the window, he motioned to roll it down.

"Miryam, honey… are you okay?"

"Yeah, yeah… I'm just…"

"Miry…" his voice was the tender sound that cut directly to the truth. There was no more being polite.

"Joey, I don't feel so well. I hurt all over and really have to go to the bathroom again."

Slipping the valet a few dollars to let the car sit, Joey ushered Miryam into the lobby and to the restroom. As he waited, he felt like a complete failure. They would have to head back out of town. He had to get her a room, even if it meant a longer drive into Breadville for registration the next day. Joey hated that Miryam would have to wait for the length of another drive before being able to rest properly. Miryam felt feverish. When she went to the restroom, there was more mucus than usual, and she was having some of those false contractions the doctor mentioned. Worst of all, she was nauseous and hungry all at the same time. Why hadn't she tried to eat more than soup? Joey grabbed a ginger ale from the soda machine, and they headed back out to the car.

"So, I have some bad news," he told her, "it looks like there are no rooms in town. Anywhere." Miryam's face dropped. She couldn't pretend she wasn't hurting. She took a couple of deep breaths and nodded her head that she understood. "We're going to have to head back out of town, and with the traffic being so bad, it's going to take longer than normal. Can you make it another couple of hours?" Miryam was trying to be a good sport but really just wanted to cry and lay down. She wished her mother was there. Seeing the look on her face, Joey asked, "Miryam, are you okay? Do you think we should go to the hospital?"

"Oh, no," she answered, 'surely it isn't that bad,' she thought. She just needed to get to a place of rest. "How long do you think it might take?"

"When we get to the car, you can use my phone to search for rooms in the next town, if you feel up to it? Do you think you can? Otherwise, I can do it– I just wanted to start driving right away."

"Yeah, yeah. I can try." Miryam whimpered a bit on the way to the car. Joey apologized multiple times for letting her down. She wasn't upset with him. She knew it hadn't occurred to him that Breadville would be this congested, and she was confident she could make it to the next stop if she could just lay back in the car.

Joey made a makeshift bed in the back seat of the van. All of a sudden, he hated this van for not being the real comfort Miryam needed. Still, he was grateful that their bags were in the back, and she could lay down while they drove. Asking her again if she thought the hospital might be necessary, Miryam declined, just wanting to get to where they needed to go. Trusting her judgment, Joey hopped into the van and put the peddle to the medal. Traffic had become a standstill. Even though they were headed in the opposite direction out of town, roads were congested and overflowing. Inching along, Joey tried to talk about things to keep Miryam's mind off the discomfort. Finally, Miryam confessed, "Honey, I think it's better if we just don't talk." The hour got later and later until eventually, they were both past the point of being cordial. Joey started wondering if it wouldn't be acceptable just to pull over and make a full bed out of the back of the van. He could try to make Miryam as comfortable as possible, and– Joey's thoughts were interrupted by a shriek coming from Miryam.

"What the– are you okay?! Miry, what's wrong?!"

"Not good, not good…" Miryam responded. She was trying to breathe and was grabbing her stomach. When a break in the pain finally came, she gasped as if she had never breathed before. Hearing Miryam take long, deep breaths of relief frightened Joey.

"Talk to me," he insisted.

"Joey, I think we should have gone to the hospital. I didn't know."

"You didn't know what?"

"I didn't think this might be it."

"Might be it?" he questioned, "You mean, might be IT? Like– IT?"

"Yes."

"Like, *labor*. You think you're going into labor right now?"

"I don't think I'm *going* into labor… I think I'm *in* labor."

"Right now?"

"YES… right now. Oooouch!" Another wave struck as she gasped and held her breath.

"Breathe! Breathe! Are you sure?"

"Joseph, for the love of Michael, what else could it be?" she admonished. Joey had never heard her call him by his full name, nor did he think he ever wanted to again.

"Okay, hospital… hospital… I neeeed a hospital." Of all times to not be able to reach his phone. "Are you able to reach your phone? Get Siri to tell us where the closest hospital is."

"Aaargh. Are you kidding me?" The pain was reaching its peak, and the contractions were hardly letting up. "Joey, I can't. I can't," she was letting go and crying now. "It hurts. It really hurts. I want my mom!! Dadgummit– this sucks!"

"Okay, that's it." Joey was trying to find a place to pull over. He had to search for a hospital. Miryam was crying and trying to breathe. "I think it's coming," she said.

"No, no, no… I'm finding a hospital."

"Joey, seriously. It feels like it's coming."

"Are you serious, Miryam? That cannot happen! Hold it in; we are not prepared for that. I'm going to find–"

"HOLD IT IN? Are you crazy?! Joseph, get back here right now." There it was again. His name in that threatening manner. Miryam was taking control, "I'm serious pull this crap-mobile over and get back here right now." Joey flashed on the image of them on the dune. The same feeling of absolute concern for Miryam's safety shot through him. He flashed on the copilot saluting him. He flashed on the Captain's hat and wings. He pulled over. Not on a side road, not far out of the way of traffic; he just pulled over. He didn't even turn the car off. He just jumped out and threw open the side door. Miryam was panting and pulling off clothes.

"Okay, Okay, here's what we're going to do," he instructed.

"We're going to have a baby!" Miryam cut to the chase.

"Yes, honey. Yes, my darling, we *are* going to have a baby."

Joey was scrambling for the bottled water he had in the back. He had his old fleece blanket that never left the car. Everything felt far from clean, and he was sure it was anger pushing him through each step as much as compassion. Joey washed his hands with half a bottle of water and prepared the blanket under Miryam's bottom. The last thing he wanted was to drop their brand-new baby onto the gravel at the side of the road. He wasn't thinking about her body parts or any embarrassment. All of that was utterly aside. Miryam was in pain, and this baby was coming.

"I'm so sorry," he offered, "I'm so sorry I didn't take better care of you. I'm so sorry you're in pain– You're doing great, Miry; you are doing so well. You've got this. You've got it– that's it."

Miryam was crying and screaming occasionally. Joey was crying and encouraging her to let it out. Inch by inch and push after push, they did, in fact, have a baby. Right at the side of the road on the interstate, with cars zooming by. Just the two of them amidst the mess. Joey took his jacket off and wrapped the baby in it. He thought it would be cleaner than the fleece blanket at this point and didn't want it to be too cold. Laying him on Miryam's chest, she laughed, and she cried.

"Well, we will certainly never forget this," she said. Joey squatted in the floorboard next to the seat and held her head.

"I love you," he said. "That was insane… and I love you."

"I love you, Husband," she said, "Now, about that hospital…"

CHAPTER 6:

THE SEERS

Sibyl sat straight up in her bed. Her breathing quickened, and the scene in her mind was perfectly clear. The same dream about a new king coming. A righteous king who would bring equality and justice for all people. Sibyl always saw herself among his subjects and felt the deepest love and loyalty to him. The peace in his kingdom often left her saddened when she awoke. She would much prefer to stay in his presence than avoid the ache upon waking in the absence of it. In reality, Sibyl and her brother Quest were not subjects of any king in any kingdom. They stood entirely on their own, both in life and society. Born with the ability to see outside of natural or scientific knowledge, Sibyl was super sensitive to influences and forces of a nonphysical and supernatural nature. At 28, she had spent the better part of her adult life isolated. No man had ever been altogether able to handle her gifts, and women often found themselves intimidated by the constant influence of another realm. Her only authentic and best friend was Quest. At 32, Quest was strapping and completely self-assured. He had lived his whole life with not only Sibyl's gifts but his own. Quest graduated summa cum laude with his doctorate degrees in Psychology and Astronomy. The ladies loved Quest. He was like a real-life Persian version of Indiana Jones, always searching the stars and planets for a worthy find. He could teach anywhere he wanted but preferred the freedom that grants provided for research and travel.

Stumbling out to the kitchen, Sibyl made her first pot of strong coffee. She tied up her long black hair and sat in her cozy chair, staring out the window. Quest soon rolled out to the pleasant aroma. Seeing Sibyl in her own world was normal, but she had a particular faraway look in her eye on certain mornings.

"The King?" he questioned. Sibyl didn't look toward him but slowly nodded her head affirmatively. Her eyes filled with tears. "Sib," Quest consoled, "you are loved."

"I know that. But– it's different. You–"

"'–you don't understand,' I know. But it bothers me to see you like this. You've really got to snap out of it." Sibyl looked sharply at her brother.

"Snap out of it? You of all people, Quest."

Some years earlier, the siblings lost their parents in a dreadful car accident and were left with a substantial inheritance. Free to study and live in whatever manner they chose, they remained humbled by the whole experience and clung to one another.

"I know… I know you feel things on a different level, but when you fixate on something that's not real, it concerns me that you might hurt yourself or something."

"It *is* real. That's the thing. It is so… *real.* Maybe I lived in another time; maybe he was my father. Maybe there really is a new kingdom coming. I just can't put my finger on it, but it's too consistent to be nothing. And, you know I'm not going to hurt myself, Quest. I could never do that to you. And it wouldn't matter. Energy continues, so I might as well work on myself here because I would only transfer it into another realm. Unless… unless this kingdom is a glimpse of a place where all of it is finally resolved– and we really can live in the peace and love of… this King."

Quest kissed his sister on the top of the head and started toward the shower. As he did, he passed his computer, which continuously ran a star program and scanned the known universe for irregularities. There was a blinking indicator signifying a change. Pausing to click on it and investigate, Quest couldn't believe his eyes. There, in a spot where nothing had previously existed, was what appeared to be a supernova. "Holy cannoli…" he whispered. Sitting down, he pulled all the data that the program had been gathering to investigate further. Certainly, NASA was already onto this. He went to their website and into their public files. There was no indication that they were aware of the activity. If they hadn't made it available, they either wanted to keep it hush-hush or felt there was something not worth alarming the public over. Ten hours passed like ten minutes. Figures and sightings, anything he could pull up and read. Quest pulled out his high-powered telescope and equipment to set up in the backyard. Tonight, he was going to catch sight of this star himself without fail. Sibyl tried to feed him a few times during the day to no avail. When Quest was on the trail of something big, he would forget to breathe if it wasn't automatic. Living like a little old couple, they knew when to press in and when to leave the other alone.

That evening, they both sat outside, waiting for the sky to grow dark enough. Quest was like a little kid and could barely contain himself. The strangest part was that the numbers showing the supernova's explosion weren't growing or depleting. Granted, he had only been watching it for ten hours, but the program numbers showed absolute consistency. Almost like a picture had been taken, not like it was a currently active nova. With ordinary novas, it would take less than a quarter of a second for its core to collapse. It would take just a few hours for the shockwave to reach the surface of the star, a few months to intensify, and then a few years to dissolve and disappear. It absolutely seemed to be in the intensify stage by the brightness indicated, but that would show increasing numbers, not constant. Sibyl made popcorn and sat outside, wrapped like an Eskimo. Quest was in a t-shirt and jeans. Finally, the stars began to show, and the beauty of the universe settled in for the night. Breathing it in like an old friend, Sibyl let her head fall back onto her shoulders. With her knees tucked up into her chest, she smelled the night air as Quest ran about adjusting instruments and checking equipment. He was in his element.

After quite some time, Quest found the star. "Woooo-Hooo! Would you look at that?" Sibyl didn't move. This wasn't yet the real offer to check it out for herself. He would not be relinquishing the site on his telescope anytime soon. "Oh, it's beautiful. It's so big and bright! Sib, this is incredible." Taking pictures and scribbling down settings, Quest was a kid in a candy store. After quite some time, Sibyl decided to grab a glance for herself as Quest paused for one of his writing breathers. "Be careful," he said, "don't touch anything."

Sibyl rolled her eyes. She had heard the same warning for years on end. With a sigh, she stepped up and leaned into the scope. There, in all its glory, was the star. As she stared, a warmth overcame her. Initially, she thought about removing her jacket but then realized it wasn't a natural warmth. Tuning into it a bit, she looked deeper into the star. Sibyl was overcome with a familiar wave. She jerked back from the telescope and stood erect. Could it be? She looked again with the hope of a thousand lifetimes. Holding her breath, she peered into the vision. Without hesitation, she gave herself over to the force. It was. Love flooded her waking soul. First, it was the ache she had awoken with that morning but then swept into the most engaging and fulfilling love– the assurance of peace and provision.

"The King," she whispered. She could not look away.

Quest stepped back to the scope and shooed her away from his position, but Sibyl didn't move. "Sib, move," he said. Sibyl did not move. "Sibyl… move," he repeated. Pulling back from the scope, she looked at her brother in the eyes. Noticing her tears, he smiled. "Amazing, isn't it?"

"It's the King," she answered.

"What?" Thinking she wanted to name it herself, Quest didn't register her meaning.

"The King. The King, Quest. It's him. He's here."

~~~

Sibyl was determined to go. She began packing her things immediately, not knowing how long she might be gone. Quest was trying to speak reason to her, "C'mon, sis. Give it some time. I know you are catching something in the spirit, but wisdom would say to slow down. Let's make a plan; let's gather some more information before you start running off into the night after a star."

"I'm not running off after a star, Quest. I'm going to the King."

"Do you know how crazy you sound? This is exactly the kind of thing that keeps people arm's length from you."

"I don't care. I don't care what people think. This thing has been pursuing me for months. Night after night, the same dream. He was speaking to me– he was letting me know he was coming, and I am going to find him."

"What do you think you're going to find when you get there? A nobleman in a crown with a broad chest decreeing salvation for all who come to him? Get real. And do you know how long it will take you to get to where the star is actually hovering directly above? Sibyl– are you listening to me?"

"Yes, Quest. I'm always listening to you. Now, you listen to me for once. I am going on this trip. I am leaving as soon as I am able. I'm going to go to wherever this thing is and find whatever it is I'm supposed to find. I'm trusting that you will support me in that and know that this is bigger than either of us. Don't fear the process. I'm not going to linger here. I've
~~~

lingered for too many years in my fear. Afraid of what people will think of me if I say *half* of what comes into my head out loud. I see things. I know things, but no one really wants enlightenment. They say they do, but when it comes at them and stares them right in the face, they cower. Or they don't want to give up all that they have embraced, even to try a different way. Whatever. To each his own. But I have been given a glimpse of something more, and nothing, not even you, my beloved brother, is going to keep me from it. Do you hear me? I am going. Please. Please, Quest. I am going."

By this time, Sibyl was crying with the passionate cry of a lover long lost or a mother losing her child. Her understanding was from the gut, and Quest knew better than to argue with Sibyl's gut. When she knew something in her knower, one was wise to get on board or get out of the way.

"All right. All right," he complied. "I hear you, alright? I hear you. Just give me a couple of days, will you do that? Let me gather some directional data and a general starting point. I'll make some phone calls and start to see how much anyone else knows about this thing. Maybe we can know exactly where we are aimed before starting, okay? Will you do that?"

"Where *we* are aimed?" Sibyl questioned. Quest took a deep breath and nodded his head.

"Yes, Sibyl," he chuckled. "You don't think I'm going to let you go alone, do you?" Running into his chest, Sibyl hugged her brother. His was the most faithful love she had known. When it came to investigation and research, there was no better team.

"You'd better get started," she warned, "when I get the 'it's time to go,' I'm not waiting for your lazy ass."

"What?!" The hug turned into a wrestle with Quest giving her noogies.

"Stop! I'm not kidding!" She pulled away. "Quit wasting time!" She threw a pillow at him from the couch and went to find boxes for groceries. "I'm packing. You'd better do your part." With a sigh, Quest dug into his part.

~~~

Governor Mashaka Mondo's office in the Region of Peace was contacted by a brother and sister astronomy team who were seeking any information regarding a star they had found. It wasn't often that the Governor's office would make themselves available to such an outrageous pair. Still, the politician's marketing team had encouraged the meeting and even suggested he allow a reporter to be present or, at the very least, someone to take pictures
~~~

for his social media pages. It would make him look like a Governor who cared about the individual and things happening in the astrological field. It would be spun just right so he wouldn't be considered a crackpot but show that he thinks outside the box. The meeting was set, and after days of travel, Quest and Sibyl were eager to talk to someone higher up who may be able to offer further information regarding the star and any events surrounding it. Sibyl's dreams had only intensified since going on the road, and she was gathering that there was a distinct shift in leadership taking place in the region. With only a 30-minute window given in the Governor's schedule, they would have to be clear and concise.

After the pictures were taken, which made Sibyl beyond uncomfortable, they had about 20-minutes to explain to the Governor that they were in search of a new leader on the rise who would bring radical change to the region. His arrival coincided with this supernova, so the brother and sister were in pursuit of any and all information regarding either entity. All the Governor could hear was that there was an upcoming leader of substance who would most certainly take his place. Ever mindful of how everything worked together toward the next election, Governor Mondo quickly formulated a plan in his head to gather his own information on this leader.

"Well, by golly, I'm sorry I don't have more to offer you, kids, on the matter," he danced, "But let me tell you what I'm going to do– I'm going to put my best people on this, uh, star thing, and I will also gather information on this leader… what did you say his name was again?"

"We don't actually have a name, Sir. We were hoping perhaps you knew who the upcoming leaders in this region may be and how we could reach them for–"

"Well, yes… I mean, yes, of course. We know most things, but your description left a bit to be desired. Still, I will get my people on it, and we will get ahold of you when we gather anything of substance. Also, please, keep us informed if you locate the gentleman before we do. We would be most honored to pay our respects and follow his career into whatever field he chooses to pursue." With handshakes and agreements made, Quest and Sibyl were ushered out.

"What just happened?" Sibyl asked.

"I have no idea. Nothing beneficial, that's for sure. I think we just agreed to give him *our* information as *we* found it."

"Good grief. What a waste of time." Sibyl had a quick vision of a rope swinging from a tree. The noose had blood on it, and with it came a flood of suffering. Heavy, wicked torment. "Whoo." She shook her head, trying to rid herself of the image. Quest said nothing but waited for any word. "That man does not have good intentions," she said.

Inside the Governor's office, Mondo was already making private phone calls. A sinister man at heart, he was not about to let any up-and-comer move into the office he had worked so hard to build. Mondo assigned a private investigator to find information on any bright and industrious people seeking to run for office in the next term. With any luck, he would be able to squash that option and maintain his position. He had hopes that the brother and sister would follow through and send him word when they found the man they had come so far to honor. If their allegiance had brought them from such a distance, what would people from his own region be willing to do? He placed a tail on the brother and sister duo in case they reached their destination before his private investigator could. Not your typical investigator, Mondo's man had an order to put an end to this 'shining star's' life should he show the potential of being the hope of the future.

Quest and Sibyl headed back out onto the road. Quest's data and the ability to physically aim toward the star at night meant most of their travel was from dusk to dawn. They had long conversations about what they would say to the man when they found him. They wondered what their parents would think of yet another crazy adventure and hoped that in some way, this leader really would bring an end to all the striving in the region. Sibyl knew it was greater than a region. In her dreams, when she stood among the crowd of subjects, there were people from every nation and tongue– old, young, lowly, and elevated. No one was exempt from the love of this man. She felt the depth of his love for her personally. But when she looked at those around her, she could tell by the expression on their faces and by her sense that they were feeling the same way. Every one of them held his full heart and pleasure in some way. The noose in her most recent vision bothered her immensely. There was an element of suffering attached to it that was unjust. If someone were going to hang a man, there would be no reason for there to be blood on the noose. Blood indicated a beating or physical wounding of some sort before the hanging. There was a lack of integrity in it. The King. The noose. The King. The noose. Sibyl refused to connect the two. He was their great hope and the epitome of love. This noose had to be for someone else. She wouldn't think of it any other way.

CHAPTER 7:

ORCHESTRATION

A Breadville division road crew was only about an hour into their night shift. Working on the outskirts of town kept the horrific census traffic away from their project. They were grateful not to be dealing with idiot drivers in town for the registration. Suddenly, a great light shined all around them. Initially thinking it was a large vehicle approaching, men ceased their work and covered their eyes. "Damn monster trucks," one of them complained of the blinding light. But the light did not pass by; it shined brighter and brighter. Squinting through their hands, they saw a figure. Standing before them was a man larger than any of them had ever seen. Instinctively, a few of them ran off in fear; others froze in their tracks. Some dropped to their knees. The figure spoke with a thundering voice.

"Don't be afraid. I'm here to tell you of something incredible that will benefit everyone."

The men were still and silent.

"Tonight, in Breadville, a baby has been born who will become a liberator for all people. He will carry an anointing of deliverance. As evidence, you will find him at the side of the Interstate in a Volkswagen, wrapped in his mother's arms and a jacket."

This was too farfetched. This messenger looked like a construction worker himself. He had a white tank top on, and his arms seemed to have swung a million roughneck sledgehammers. Upon further inspection, they believed they saw wings, but they weren't solid. They seemed to blend in with the light. They were translucent and well worn. This guy was no slack. He had seen his share of worksites and done his part. As the men were processing all they saw, there suddenly appeared before them a multitude of supernatural workers. They were chanting some sort of hard work labor song in a rhythm. It was as if some great work was being done in another realm, and they were catching a glimpse of it. They could feel the pound and pulse of each syllable and were overcome with the magnitude of the message. They couldn't help but sway to the power of the verse.

"Triumph to the Creator most elevated!" the messengers sang, "Coexistence on earth and unity among men."

The light began to lessen, and the thump of the rhythm started to fade. The celestial workers were gradually gone, and the remaining work crew stood staring into the expanse they had occupied. After a few deep breaths, they began to look around at each other. Some began to cry without shame, so overwhelmed by what they just experienced. Some dropped down in silence, unable to speak. Finally, one of the men broke the silence.

"I don't know about you guys, but I'm going to the Interstate. I've got to see this for myself."

"Wait for me," another joined, "It's a Volkswagen, right?"

"I wouldn't miss this for the world," another agreed. With haste, the men gathered their wits and headed out.

At the side of the Interstate, Joey tended to Miryam the best he knew how. He gave her water and wiped her down. He wrapped her in the fleece and tucked her in for the trip to the hospital. They were both eager to know that the baby was okay. Just as he pulled his phone out to search for the closest facility, blue and red lights came up behind the van. Instead of fear, a wave of relief came over Joey. An officer stepped up to the side of the vehicle.

"Sir, step away from the vehicle. What is the situation here; are you having car trouble?"

"Officer, thank you so much," Joey answered, "My wife has just had our baby– it was crazy. We need a hospital. Can you please help us?"

The officer stepped closer, looked inside the open van, and saw an exhausted Miryam, weak and tightly holding her newborn son.

"Holy cow!" he exclaimed and took up the hand mic on his shoulder. "Officer 4632, I have a code two at Interstate marker seven. Will be escorting an older model Volkswagen bus to Rosa Parks Hospital. I repeat; Officer 4632 encountering a code two at Interstate marker seven. Escorting older model Volkswagen bus to Rosa Parks Hospital. Requesting immediate assistance upon arrival for a newborn infant and mother. Immediate assistance upon arrival."

"Roger, 4632. Immediate assistance, Rosa Parks Hospital."

"Ma'am, are you secure and able to travel?" Miryam nodded her head with the most gratitude she could muster. "Son, you're going to need to follow me on the edge of this road until we can make a break in this traffic. How fast is this vehicle able to go?"

"Oh, I'll be right behind you," Joey swore.

"All right, let's do it."

Just then, a truck of road crew workers stopped and ran towards the van. "Is everything okay here? Is this the baby? Can we help? Is there anything we can do?" The officer assured them all was under control and let them know they were headed to Rosa Parks. Joey was confounded as he stepped up into the van. Who were these guys, and how did they know about the baby? How had they known to come for help?

Once at the hospital, a troop of doctors and nurses rushed out to meet them at the emergency entrance. The officer had successfully led them directly to the hospital in what felt like record time. The road workers, for some reason, had followed. Once they were all inside and directed to their respective waiting areas, Miryam was able to relinquish the baby for proper care. She and Joey laughed and cried. Miryam was given something for her pain. They swiftly ushered her in for attention and any stitching up she may need. Noticing her age, they were concerned and asked after her parents. Joey agreed they should be called but assured them that he was, in fact, her husband. The hospital workers gave him less than kind glances and stood in a bit of judgment during the length of their stay. Joey wanted to thank the officer, so he headed back out to the entrance to find him. Instead, he was greeted by the crew of road workers, all eager to speak to him. One guy even had his phone out and took a picture of Joey as if he was some sort of celebrity.

"What– what's going on here?" Joey asked, "What do you guys want?"

As the group's momentary leader explained all the incredible things they had seen and heard, Joey had to sit down. Wandering nurses and hospital workers started to gather to listen to the news of the young couple. The workers explained the supernatural visitation they experienced and wondered if they might see the baby.

Joey knew that this pregnancy was a miracle. He knew that the Creator had chosen them, for some reason, and he knew that this baby would make a difference in the world. But he couldn't wrap his head around how this grand plan could include the baby being born at the side of the Interstate with no proper place available to them. How absolute strangers in the middle of the night would be visited to make known his arrival and how random passers-by would become so engrossed in the story that they would all start to hope for something great to come of it. Electricity seemed to be in the air. Joey was numb. He thanked the men and headed back to Miryam. Just then, a reporter came in hoping for information about the couple who had a baby at the side of the Interstate. Joey didn't know the level at which they were supposed to divulge information just yet, and Miryam's parents hadn't even arrived. He directed the reporter to the workmen. They certainly had plenty to say. Again, Joey headed back to find Miryam. He told her of everything that was happening, and she pondered all of it in her heart. They were in awe that this baby was already making such an impact; so many people were already caring.

With the morning came Anne and Joaquin. Overwhelmed with love for their new grandbaby and gratitude once again for Joey taking care of Miryam, they weren't even disappointed in his failure to secure a room in advance. They were just grateful that all had turned out well and that each person involved had seemed positioned in the right place at just the right time. In came the nurse to gather birth certificate information. Father's name: Joseph Paladin. Mother's Name: Miryam Paladin. Child's name: the room fell still as Joey and Miryam looked at each other, smiling. Miryam answered, "Emmanuel Paladin." Emmanuel reached up and touched his mother's face. His eyes were small and dark. His face was swollen from the stress of birth. He was silent. His little breath rose from his perfect lips. Miryam smiled at him with tears of joy filling her eyes. "Hello, little man," she welcomed. "What a beginning this has been, huh?" Joey came over and held them both.

"Emmanuel Paladin," he pronounced. "The Creator sure knew what He was doing with you." As momentous as the occasion was, they both knew this was just the beginning of the new world this child would bring. They were willing.

~~~

Joey did not want to leave Miryam and little Manny, but he still had to register for the census. Anne and Joaquin offered to give them a ride back to Netzer, but Joey asked them to secure an infant seat instead. He would gather them once he had completed the registration and take his family back
~~~

to Anne and Joaquin's later that day. He hated the thought of separating from them now. It wasn't right. First, he hadn't gotten a room in advance, and now, he hadn't secured a place for them to live yet. Frustration rose in Joey. He felt that he wasn't off to a good start with all that had been entrusted to him. He said his good-byes and headed out to the registration. Before he could pull out of the parking lot, his phone started ringing. Normally, he would not answer, but for some reason, he paused to answer it. It was Jackson's father; Joey's heart sank a bit. His best friend wasn't here to enjoy the major events that were taking place right and left. Even though Jackson was opposed to the thought of marriage at the time, Joey was confident that he would be completely supportive of all that was coming together now. It was all too profound to ignore.

"Hello, Son…" Jack greeted.

"Jack, hey… how are you doing, Sir?"

"Joey, how many times do I have to tell you? You don't need to call me Sir."

"I know, I'm sorry… I just how are you?"

"Well, we're doing all right, son. How are you? Lots going on, I see."

"So much, Jack. You have no idea."

"Actually, I do," Jack indicated. "We saw your story in the paper this morning. We could hardly believe it was you! We hope your new bride and son are faring well." Joey was confused and put the car back into the park position.

"You saw our story in the paper?" Joey asked.

"Yes… quite jarring, 'Young Couple has Baby on Interstate.' I guess the Registration traffic had you locked in, eh?" Joey's mind was spinning. This whole thing just got crazier and crazier.

"Wow, that's insane… yes. It was… very uncomfortable!" Both men laughed.

"Look, Joe– This is going to sound strange, but there is a reason for my call. Beyond the congratulations, I mean. I hope you will hear me out."

"Of course, of course…"

"Jackson's mother and I had gone to a bit of a length to secure an apartment for him as a surprise after he graduated from college this next month. It was selfish now that we think about it. It's here in Netzer; we just kind of wanted to help and keep him close. We've been debating and taking our time with what to do with it. Grief kept us from making any sudden moves in getting rid of it. Well, now– I mean– it seems that you might be needing a place of your own. I assume you already have one; I mean, it's not like you didn't know you were having a baby…" Joey's heart leaped in his chest. "But we thought, especially after reading the paper this morning– we wondered if you might be interested in the place for your little family." Joey could not believe his ears; the timing continued to be perfect. Is this how things would always come from now on? Perfectly aligned and on time, though not always easy. "It's in a great neighborhood close to the shops and things. It's just a little two-bedroom, one bathroom. And it's not–"

"Jack…" Joey interrupted, "Dude. Oh, Jack. You have no idea how interested I am. When can we move in?" He didn't care about the price; he didn't care what it would take; he knew if the Creator had orchestrated all the preceding events, this one was going to be the right fit, too. The two men laughed, and each expressed gratitude. "Is today too soon?" Joey asked.

"Not at all!" Jack replied, "It's fully furnished, so it's ready when you are. I'm sure Miryam will want to make changes, but it will certainly be enough for right now. We can go over and wipe things down for you. Is there anything you want us to grab for the baby just to get you started? We'd be happy to run that over as well."

"Jack," Joey inquired, "why are you doing all of this? I mean, it's beyond kind, you know?"

"Joey," Jack's voice softened. "Jackson loved you like a brother. Seeing the two of you always did my heart good. I was so glad he wasn't mixed up with some hooligan, you know. That kid was a nut, and it could have easily been the case." They chuckled again in memory. "I just figure– and please know, it's not a condition of the place, but– you're the closest thing I have to a son now. If I can help you, especially at the time that is so trying for every new father, then I am honored to do it." Joey put his face in his hand and started crying. What an emotional 19 hours it had been. With his own parents being less than supportive, an offer of paternal reinforcement could not have come at a better time.

"I am deeply grateful," Joey whispered.

"Great. Well, let me give you the address, and we can run over and get this show on the road for you." Joey felt a weight lifted.

The registration office was packed, but he was prepared for that. With such a lengthy wait, he was able to call and tell Miryam everything about their new place and all that was being provided. Miryam was ecstatic to be coming into their own and not be dependent on their parents. She had been looking forward to life in Breadville but found herself content with a place in Netzer. She stood in awe of how things were coming together. This location would put her close enough to her mother while she needed help with the baby but should give them sufficient space that no one would be just stopping by unannounced. They googled and found nearby schools and parks. Jack was right; there were plenty of shops and markets nearby. Eventually, Joey made it to the front of the line and was able to turn in his registration paperwork. The clerk confirmed the information with him and took their new address for the system. With the report that Joey just had a son the night before, the clerk congratulated him. Grinning from ear to ear, Joey registered three; himself, his wife, and his son. *His son.* Oh, how things had changed in such a swift period. And oh, how they would continue to do so.

Returning to the hospital, Joey gathered Miryam and baby Manny. Joaquin and Anne bought and loaded a new baby seat into the backseat of the Volkswagen. They hated seeing the baby go home in this heap and revisited the idea of getting Miryam a car. Still, they knew that every young family had hurdles to overcome, and Joey and Miryam were no different. As the new family was released, they passed the little hospital chapel. Joey paused in front of the door and looked down at Miryam in the required wheelchair. Miryam noticed the plaque and the look on her husband's face. She simply nodded, 'yes.'

The chapel was small. There was a wall of little candles lit toward the front. It was quiet and still. There were only a few people inside, a man and two women, all seated separately. Joey slid Miryam's chair up toward the front. He felt the need to kneel. They were quiet and seeking to revere the powerful force that had visited them and brought them into their new season. Even baby Manny was still, without a coo or cry. Suddenly, the energy of the Creator's Essence fell upon the room. It was a peace that made them want to linger there. Baby Manny put his arms straight out from underneath his wrap. It was as if he was asking to be held by the tangible presence. His perfect little fingers stretched out toward the ceiling.

A man approached Miryam and knelt beside her. She looked at him. His eyes were soft. He had a long white beard, and he wore a yarmulke. He seemed to be 90 years old but had grace and fluidity about him. He bowed his head to Miryam and wanted to see the baby. The man touched his chest and whispered.

"My name is Simeon." Miryam smiled and pulled the wrap back to expose baby Manny's round belly in a perfectly white onesie. Simeon grasped one of the baby's outstretched hands. His eyes filled with tears. A warm wind passed through the chapel. Joey startled and turned to check on Miry and Manny. Simeon held the baby's hand as the wind whirled about, causing the flames of each candle to swirl but not blow out. "The Creator made me a promise," he sighed. "I have long waited for the consolation of the world. His Essence assured me I would not see death before the salvation of all trouble had come into the world." Miryam had a knowing in her heart that Simeon had been on this path long before she was. Joey came and sat beside her. She extended the baby, offering Simeon the gift of holding him. Simeon's face lit up as he accepted the generous donation. "Gracious Creator… now you will let me depart in peace. Here is all that Your Essence has assured me of– the arrival of Your light, word, and energy for the revelation of all people. Oh, make yourself known, Maker. Magnify Yourself through this bundle and blessing." Miryam and Joey marveled at the old man. He blessed them and told Miryam, "This child is appointed for the fall and rising of many. He will be distinguished from others and opposed. Even you, sweet one, will experience a piercing through your own heart and soul. But, by such, the thoughts and intentions of many will be revealed." Everything this man said resonated in Miryam as truth, though she didn't understand it all.

Then, one of the women approached. She, too, was advanced in years. As Simeon passed the baby back to his mother, the woman started praising the Creator out loud. It would have been creepy if she wasn't so sincere, and the Essence wasn't so strong. This woman spent years coming to the chapel. She had spoken over many souls in their hours of distress. Married as a very young woman, she was united only seven years before becoming a widow and lived until her current 84-years-old without knowing any other man. Without a habit or any other formal invocation, she was one who had devoted her life to a connection with the Creator and helping others with predictive knowing. Miryam and Joey knew this visit to the chapel was not happenstance. With hugs and genuine exchange, Joey, Miryam, and Emmanuel left the hospital with the fullness of their positions upon them.

CHAPTER 8:

GOLD, FRANKINCENSE, AND MYRRH

Sibyl and Quest had been on the road for six months. They followed the star as far East as they could until they ended up in the town of Netzer. They were led as much by the star as they were by Sibyl's dreams and visions. Quest loved a good road trip, but this one had become a bit long. He knew Sibyl wasn't going to give up until she met the man who would bring so much change. They traveled the entire lower region. They passed through Breadville in the Region of Peace, over Watch Mountain, and into the Northern Region of Circuit. Netzer, meaning the branch or shoot, was a city in the Region of Circuit. There was a beach about 40 minutes from Netzer, and Quest hoped, at least, that their next stop could be there. It was early morning, and they, per usual, traveled by night. The star seemed to be directly above them now. Quest's numbers showed it had transitioned from its initial burst of light phase into its proper Supernova phase, meaning the remains of the former star would soon spread over light-years of space, leaving a faint but beautiful glow behind.

They bought a camper to hitch to their car somewhere in the third month. Tired of hotels and missing home, they desired their own beds and space. As always, Sibyl diffused some essential oil for revelation and hit the sack. This morning she had particular anxiety that would not seem to rest. Quest noticed and questioned, "Are you going to be able to sleep? Or are we going to go get some pancakes?" Sibyl did not respond but took a few deep breathes to feel the atmosphere. She tried to focus on the King. She tried to feel his presence. Slowly, a warmth entered the camper. Sibyl laid as still as possible. Clearing her mind's eye, she waited for any direction. The peace of the King came upon her. She identified that this Essence was of the King, but not the King himself. It was equal to the King. How could that be? Trying not to reason, Sibyl allowed the flow to assert itself. Clearly, she saw a white building and staircase. Following the stairs up, she came to an entry. The number 111 was on the front of the door. She opened it and saw a man and a woman cradling a baby with joy. This man did not look like the King. What was she seeing? Is this where they were supposed to go, or something else? Sibyl asked the Essence for a specific location.

"Elevation," she heard. Opening her eyes, she lingered in the peace of the Essence.

"Ummm, Sib? Are you asleep? Okay– no pancakes." Quest rolled over. Sibyl shot up and out into the driver's seat. "Okay! Pancakes it is!" he quipped. Sibyl started the engine and grabbed her phone. Quest followed and offered, "I can find the closest place."

"We're not going for pancakes," she answered.

"What… you'd rather have huevos rancheros? Doesn't IHOP have both?"

"We aren't going for food," Sibyl remarked.

"What is this? Did you see something? What is it?"

"Elevation. That's all I heard, 'Elevation.' But I also saw a number on a door. An apartment, I think."

"An apartment? What kind of king lives in an apartment?" he said with a smirk. Sibyl shot him a look and searched for Elevation Road.

"Results: Mount Evans Scenic Byway, Road Elevation Profile, Circuit Region's Highest Roads, Ten Highest Elevation Roads in the World…" Ugh, this wasn't it. She typed in, "Elevation Road near me." Quicker than she could get the results, Sibyl felt a hand on her shoulder. She knew it wasn't Quest; she could see him sitting in the passenger seat out of the corner of her eye. Sibyl had experienced many kinds of obscurities, but this came with a calm sense that equated the King.

"Follow me," she heard in her spirit. Pulling out of their spot, she decided just to drive.

"Where are we going," Quest asked, "Did you find it?"

"Quest, I don't know what I'm doing. You're just going to have to trust me."

Quest squinted his eyes and cocked his head. That statement made no sense. Suddenly, Sibyl felt a presence on her lap. She felt hands over her hands on the steering wheel. She knew that she was driving, but she wasn't the one leading. As she went, she knew each turn before it came. She sensed every indication, every light. She was tuned into a higher power that was literally directing her every move. Anticipation grew within her as she knew they were about to receive some sort of breakthrough. She agreed with Quest; she couldn't imagine this King being in an apartment. But she was sure it was a significant step in the right direction. These people must know something. They must have some information regarding the King's whereabouts.

They pulled into a left-hand turning lane and waited for traffic to pass. Sibyl looked to the left and saw a set of white apartment buildings. Her eyes searched for the name of the apartments, "Elevation Apartments." Sibyl let out a sigh, squeal, and chuckle all at the same time. Turning into the apartments, Quest asked, "So this is it?"

"This is it." She answered. Feeling the presence lift, Sibyl didn't know where to park. The camper wasn't a typical parking spot job, and she knew she needed to find #111. After finding a spot outside a rear entrance on the sideroad, she parked and was ready to bolt.

"Hey, hey, hey…" Quest slowed her. "Does one meet a king in her pajamas?"

"Oops." She blushed. They both changed and headed out to find the apartment. Even though Quest was eager for this next step in their journey, he secretly wished the whole visitation could have come *after* the pancakes.

Upon entering the courtyard, Sibyl saw the staircase from her vision. Heading straight for it, Quest followed. They were by no means trashy apartments, but they were far from a gated, upscale set of luxury apartments. Rounding the walkway to each door, she counted out loud as they passed, "109, 110… here it is. 111." Looking to Quest, she breathed deep and gave him a side hug. She was nervous and excited all at once. Being a weekend, Sibyl hoped that someone–anyone– would be home.

~~~

Manny had grown to a fat and happy six months old. Already sitting up and scooting around the floor, he was the pride of his parents. With Manny sleeping through the night, Miryam and Joey had settled into a comfortable routine. Mostly gone were the glares and questioning eyes of disapproving former neighbors. They carved out a little life that sometimes seemed too
~~~

good to be true. Joey completed his degree and was working toward starting his own construction business. They teased that someday it would be *Paladin and Son Carpentry and Construction.* Joey bought Manny a little plastic tool kit and was already teaching him always to put the tools back in their pockets so you could find them the next time. Somehow, Manny did it correctly every time, even at six months old. They knew he was special, but they didn't think he would be *that* special.

Sundays were their favorite day as Joey wasn't out working, and they could all be home together. Miryam had just finished cleaning up breakfast and was preparing to settle onto the couch with her boys when there was a knock at the door. They didn't get many visitors, and Miryam didn't usually answer the door when she was home alone with Manny. They hadn't had a call that anyone was coming, so Joey stood to answer the door. He checked the peephole and saw a man and woman standing on the other side. Thinking they may be from some religious sect, he simply called out, "We aren't interested; thank you." The knock at the door came again, along with a voice.

"Sir, we aren't selling anything. We are just hoping to speak to you and your wife." Joey looked over at Miryam, and they both shrugged. How did they know he had a wife? They must have some specific business– but on a Sunday? Joey slowly opened the door and stood between the opening and the view of his family.

"What is this regarding?" he asked.

"Sir," Sibyl started, "I don't even know where to begin. My name is Sibyl, and this is my brother Quest."

"Hello," Quest waved in a goofy ice breaker kind of way. Joey half smiled and nodded, 'hello.'

"Sir, we have traveled for the last six months trying to find information regarding– well, how do I say this without sounding like a nut job?" Joey firmed his stance and held the door tight. "Maybe you have noticed the supernova that has been hovering for the last several months? My brother is an astronomer, and I have– well, I flow in a supernatural ability and am very susceptible to major occurrences in the natural and spiritual realm. Sir, have you experienced, or do you know of any major occurrences that have brought a shift in the last six months? Perhaps having to do with a man of great power; a leader who is going to change– well– the world?" Joey's shoulders dropped a bit from his stance. He turned around and looked at Miry, holding Manny. She sighed deeply. Manny's straight arms flapped up and down in front of him with excitement. He cooed and seemed happy to hear them.

"A man of great power, you say."

"Yes, Sir… do you know him?" Joey made direct eye contact with Sibyl and greeted her warmly for the first time.

"I absolutely do," he answered. Joey opened the door wider and allowed the two to see Miryam seated on the couch with Manny on her lap. Miryam took Manny's little hand and waved to the couple at the door.

It took Sibyl a few clicks to catch on. First, she smiled at the cute baby and chuckled at his mothers' wave. Then she felt the warmth of the King and the Essence of his presence wave through her. The smile on her face dropped as she came into the consideration– the possibility that *this* might be the King. Next was denial. Surely, she hadn't been dreaming of a father figure king who would come to change the world only to find a baby. How would he do all that needed to be done? How many years away would it be before he could– Finally, it was as clear as any revelation she had ever known. The King had come as a baby. He had his whole life to grow and become the man she had seen in her visions. How had she not caught on to the fact that he was not going to be fully grown? She turned and took Quest's hand. With tears in her eyes, she chuckled as if she was telling an inside joke.

"That's him," she said. Quest raised his eyebrows and met her joy.

"That's who?" he asked.

"The King," Sibyl whispered. Quest's eyes met hers with a laughter that was moments away from exploding.

"No…" he said.

"Yes…" she wrinkled her nose. Both laughed, and Joey waited. Turning back toward him, Sibyl apologized. "I'm sorry. I expected someone… older." Joey joined the laughter and invited them in. Miryam had a feeling this would be the first of many unexpected visits by divine appointment. They would just have to become accustomed to it.

Sibyl walked in with her eyes directly on the baby. She met his eyes, and he held hers. As she approached him, he never looked away. She kneeled before him and began to reach out for his hand. Stopping, she looked up to Miryam, who nodded approvingly. Sibyl's eyes filled with tears as she reached out and took Manny's hand.

"There you are," she said. "I've been waiting for you. We've been searching for a long time. Yes, we have. Yes, we have." Quest came up behind her and laid his hand on her shoulder.

"Thank you for letting us into your home. My sister has been… aware of his coming for some time." Sibyl continued speaking to the baby. "She loves him very much."

Miryam motioned to the couch beside her and encouraged Sibyl to sit. Passing the baby over to her, she said, "This is Manny. Emmanuel." Miryam was relieved that someone would seem to understand the magnitude of Manny's birth and eventual call. "So, you've known of him for a while?" Miryam asked.

"It feels like forever. Oh! The gift! Quest, will you run and get the gift?!" Quest agreed and shot out the door to grab a gift that his sister had put together months in advance. Joey offered her some refreshments, and Sibyl accepted. When Quest returned, Sibyl handed the baby back to his mother.

"So, if I may," she began, "this gift has significance on many levels." Miryam felt the weight in her words and began to tear a bit. She nodded in encouragement for Sibyl to continue. "We lost our parents some years ago, but they had become quite successful with an essential oil company." Sibyl pulled out a gold box. "Perhaps you've heard of Healing Balm Oils."

"Oh, my gosh… yes," Miryam responded.

"Well, that's us," she shrugged like it was no big deal. "I've brought the Kin– I've brought Manny some oils as an offering. The gold box is a symbol; gold is what one would offer a king. Inside, I've given him some oils to help establish his strength and bring durability to his vitality. Do you know much about oils?" Miryam shook her head negatively and lowered her eyes with a bit of embarrassment. "That's okay, no big deal. Lots of people don't. But here, I've given you guys some Frankincense. Frankincense has a wonderful woody, spicy smell. It can be inhaled, absorbed through the skin, diffused, or even steeped into some tea. Frankincense is a bit of a wonder drug," she chuckled. "It has healing properties that help improve a ton of things: arthritis, digestion, it helps reduce asthma, and can even contribute to better oral health. It may also help fight certain types of cancer. Um, let's see– it has anti-inflammatory effects that traditional medicine has used to treat bronchitis and asthma for centuries. Oh, and it helps to just put a couple of drops on the soft spot in the roof of your mouth if you ever get severe headaches. Frankincense symbolizes a priestly role. So, there's that."

"Thank you," Miryam accepted.

"And Myrrh. This will be beneficial. You can combine this with Frankincense or use it alone. Myrrh can directly kill bacteria. It has antimicrobial properties, so traditionally, Myrrh has been used to help with oral infections, inflammation, stomach parasites, and stuff like that. If you use it topically, it can fight infections. Look out, boo-boos! It counters skin fungi like ringworm or athlete's foot. I know, more information than you wanted– but it should never be ingested. So, no swallowing, but if you want to put it in the diffuser, that would be perfect. Again, I thought I was coming to someone much older, so you may want to keep it a bit of distance from Manny, but it should be fine in the same room. The thing about Myrrh is, it's one of those oils that are very concentrated, so you only want a few drops at a time. If you're going to put it on topically, you may want to mix it with another oil for better absorption, so I've included some fractionated coconut oil."

"Oh, wow, this is so generous. You gave us such large quantities. Thank you so much." Joey appreciated.

"Oh, we're honored to do it. Truly. You know, back in the day, places of worship would burn Myrrh and Frankincense together to purify the air and prevent the spreading of contagious diseases."

"Okay, okay," Quest chimed in. "Not everyone is as passionate about oils as our family. Nice lesson, though." They all laughed. Miryam and Joey were deeply touched.

"Thank you," Miryam said. "This shows your heart and honor for Manny. We receive it with gratitude. I'm going to put it all to good use! And this box is so lovely."

"Thank you," Sibyl paused. "It belonged to my father. It was one of his most treasured possessions. He received it as a gift to honor him for always managing his team and employees with dignity and friendship. I'm sure that Manny will do the same."

Sibyl again was honored to hold Manny. She stepped out on the balcony and rocked him in the sunlight. Sitting down on a patio chair, she turned him toward herself. "Hello, Your Majesty," she said. Manny spit up a bit, and she wiped it away with her sleeve. It didn't disgust her at all. There was such a sense of reverence for this miracle baby before her. Sybil could see him flowing as an adult. She could see him surrounded by crowds of people who loved him but also by those who only wanted what he could give them. Wasn't that always true of people? She could see miracles and healing. Manny sat silently, looking up into her eyes. He smiled as if he knew exactly who she was and why she had come. Then, he babbled as if trying to tell her all sorts of things. It was the strangest dichotomy between him being a baby and having eyes that looked straight through her soul as if he knew everything about her. He was defenseless but had messengers and spirits of boundless power moving on his behalf. She knew because they had led her to him. "Thank you," she said, touching his round cheek. "Thank you… in advance." Manny let out a few gurgles.

After spending a couple of hours together, Quest suggested they not take advantage of the Paladin's generosity. Sibyl agreed but found it difficult to say goodbye. She had waited so long to find him and didn't know if she would ever see him again. "Of course, you will," Miryam offered. "We can exchange information. Feel free to give us a call anytime. We would be more than happy to give you updates on our little prince." Sibyl gave them each a huge hug; the men shook hands and patted each other on the back.

"Let us know when you run low on oil, too, because we will be happy to send refills anytime. Let me know if you see anything else you're interested in, too– there's always oil that's good for–" Quest interrupted her.

"Okay, let's not start that again. But seriously, just let us know." Heading out the door, Sibyl turned back and met Miryam's eyes.

"Oh, and… he's a King."

The brother and sister headed down the stairs and through the courtyard in silence. What an experience. They had searched for so long; it would feel strange to head back home. Sibyl couldn't help but cry. Even though it was wonderful, she was sad. Sad she couldn't stay with him in a kingdom where peace and justice prevailed. The ache remained. She hadn't realized it would be a process. Of course, it would be a process. That made perfect sense. But she hadn't thought about it in those terms. She hadn't realized the King would be a baby, either! Still, the peace of his presence was indescribable. She hoped it would stay and that she would be able to experience the Essence that had escorted them again.

Getting into the car, Sibyl flashed on Governor Mondo. Knowing that they would not be sharing any information with him, they decided to head home a different way than they had come.

"Okay!" Quest concluded, "Now… pancakes."

CHAPTER 9:

PERFECT TIMING

Months had passed since Governor Mondo had the brother and sister duo visit him with news of a great leader coming to take his place. In his ruthlessness for power, Mondo had a couple of serious contenders eliminated by the most brutal means. Without knowing that the new leader was merely a child, Mondo had seen fit to clear any path of his removal from office. He was obsessed with the thought of someone growing to influence beyond his own and was willing to go to any means to stop it. Mondo's investigator had followed the trail of the brother and sister duo to an apartment complex. He knew they visited a small family there, but no one of political stature would catch themselves dead living in such a place. He planned to visit the family and strong-arm them for any knowledge they had regarding his pursuit. Perhaps one of them was related to the ensuing leader. It was fortunate they had a baby. Babies were always the perfect influence when pressing someone for information: babies, mothers, or loved ones.

Miryam was not in the habit of answering the door when Joey wasn't home. Of course, she would sometimes, but they were cautious. There was an increased number of murders in the city, and Joseph always warned his wife against strangers. This day, Miryam wasn't thinking about any of that. She had grown accustomed to being home with Manny without issue. He was a pleasant baby, and she loved watching him grow. He seemed to be an old soul who understood as she spoke to him. His eyes were attentive and wise. He watched his mother with such love. Miryam often wondered how her child was different from other babies his age. Did he know who he was?

Was he smarter than her? Or would he grow up learning everything on a regular timetable? All she knew was that he was wonderful and created for a purpose. But the details were as lost to her as to any other new mother. She was learning one day at a time and praying to do everything well.

The investigator knocked firmly on the door. Miryam bounced up from the floor with Manny and thought nothing of answering the door. As she was in mid-flow, she realized what she had done. Opening the door to find a man in a suit, she looked around behind him, hoping two things: first, that one of her known neighbors would be out and about, and second, that he was merely a salesman or someone she could dismiss quickly. Neither of these things was true.

"Hello, Miss," the investigator charmed. "How are you this fine day?" Miryam had an uneasy feeling right off. She knew Joey would be disappointed she had been so careless, and she didn't like the feel of this greeting. He wanted something.

"It's Mrs.," she replied. "How can I help you?"

"Well, that's a great question! I appreciate people that are willing to help me." The investigator stepped inside the apartment and headed straight for Manny.

"Excuse me–" Miryam objected. "I did not invite you in."

"Oh, now… calm down, Missy. There's no reason to get upset. Is your husband home?" The investigator looked around, casing the apartment. Miryam's heart leaped in her chest. "What a cute baby. Hello, laddie." The man squatted down and was reaching toward the baby. Miryam rushed and swooped him up.

"Who are you? What are you doing here?"

"Now, now, Missy. There's no need to get upset. What happened to you wanting to help me? I could use something to drink. I don't suppose your husband is here to get it for me." He smirked and looked Miryam in the eye as if to say, 'I'm in charge here, and you know it.' Miryam felt a wave of panic. She looked at the open door. She could just leave. She could just take Manny and walk right out. "Don't even think about it," the investigator said. He walked over and closed the door. Miryam thought about the murders. She thought about those horrid investigative shows that always show right where the victim went wrong. She thought about Joey, and she wondered what this creep was after.

"What do you want?" She asked.

"Oh, just a little information. That's not so bad, is it?" Miryam didn't speak. Manny was beginning to fuss. He could feel her discomfort. "You had a young couple visit you within the last couple of months," he was sauntering around the apartment, looking around every corner. "A brother and sister. They were seen here." The investigator wiped his finger along a piece of furniture and checked his finger for dust. "Tsk, tsk." Turning back to Miryam, he came to a standstill and spoke directly. "They were looking for someone that I am looking for." Miryam's heart dropped. "Apparently, they found him, but I am still, well... *looking*." Miryam became visibly nervous. He was here for Manny! She gripped the baby tighter and couldn't think of how to escape. The investigator noticed her grip tightening and body becoming tenser. Walking over to her, he lifted the baby out of her arms. Miryam didn't let go but pulled back.

"Don't. Don't you dare!" she threatened. Without regard, the investigator pulled the baby out of her arms. Not wanting him to be hurt, Miryam gave into the pull. She was instantly sick about it. "What do you think you're doing?" she yelled. "Give me my baby right now." Manny started to cry.

"Shhh, shhh... there, there." The investigator simply looked at Miryam with a wicked grin. "Now, Missy. You're going to need to calm downright quick. You're upsetting the baby. What kind of mother would do such a thing?" Miryam was officially freaking out inside.

"I'm going to call the police," she threatened.

"Oh, no. That wouldn't be wise. Besides, you couldn't be fast enough; if you know what I mean."

"What did you say you wanted?"

"Information. That's all. Information. Who were the siblings coming to see that day? What brought them here to you? I ask because I need to speak to the person they were seeking. I need to have a little conversation with him about his future." Looking at the baby and bouncing him up and down, he added, "Don't I? Yes, I do. Don't I?" Miryam felt that she might vomit. However, the investigator didn't seem to know that he was holding the person he was looking for. Perhaps she could lie. She had never been much of a liar, but for her son, she would be willing to do anything. Lying was nothing.

"What do you want to know?" she asked.

"Well, now that's better. Who is he? Where can I find him? What do you lot have to do with him? And don't play games with me, Missy. You wouldn't like to see me when I think someone is playing a game with me. Never much liked games." Miryam's eyes were searching for what she could use as a weapon. How could she take him? How could she get Manny before he was hurt? The investigator tisked again, "Now see… I can see in your eyes exactly what you're thinking. The difference between you and me is that I've been here a dozen times, and you have never been in this position before. If you're not very careful, you will find yourself in no position at all, and then who will take care of this precious baby?"

"Please, do it," Miryam responded. She flopped down to the floor and put her head into her hands.

"What?" the investigator questioned.

"Pleaaaase, do it," she repeated. "I'm so tired. I'm too young to be a mother and be in the middle of a political coup." The investigator froze.

"A coup, you say."

"Yes… this baby is the son of a so-called great man. He plans on running for office but knowing that he had a baby with a teenager would ruin his career. So, please, if you would just put us out of our misery, that would be a relief. At least we would go together. Only please be quick. Don't make us suffer. It's not our fault, and we have suffered enough." The investigator's wheels were spinning. Miryam ran and grabbed his arm. Looking up into his eyes, she begged him, "Please… please do it. Do it before my husband gets home. He only married me to save shame for this man."

"You're crazy," the investigator snipped, handing the baby back to Miryam. "Leaving you alive would ensure he doesn't get far in his conquest for office."

"No, please!" Miryam pleaded. She began to allow herself to look extremely unstable. Her eyes widened, and she started rocking back and forth. Manny looked at her and smiled with a coo. "Please! This would solve everything! He would leave us alone, and I wouldn't have to go through with this horrible existence!" The investigator headed for the door, and Miryam was following him out, pleading the whole way for him to help her. "Don't go!" she begged, "Wait!" The investigator was out the door. Miryam let out loud fake sobs of distress. She closed the door, bolted it, and leaned up against it holding Manny. Sliding to the floor, she began to cry for real.

What just happened? That man was coming to kill Manny. Would there be more? Would they always be on the run for their lives? What would Joey say? Oooooh, no. What would Joey say? Maybe she wouldn't have to tell him. How could she not tell him? Did she have it in her to deceive him in that way? What if she didn't tell him and the man came back? She would have to tell him. He was going to be so mad at her for not checking the peephole and answering the door. How many times had he told her to be careful? What was she thinking? That was far too careless. Gratefully, Manny was okay. Looking at Manny, he was starting to get sleepy. Completely unphased, he began to drift off in his mother's arms. Miryam, on the other hand, was exhausted but wide awake.

~~~

Telling Joey had not gone well, but eventually, they settled down and were able to go to bed. He was impressed with how quickly Miryam had contrived the story to save them. Joey was thinking of ways to safeguard the apartment, complete with bars on the windows, a panic button, and an alarm system. This could not happen again. He wished he could afford someplace more secure. This job was going to be more challenging than either of them could have imagined.

That night, Joey had a dream. He was sitting in a small boat on the lake at his grandfather's cabin. He hadn't been there since he was a boy. Skipping rocks, he heard a voice behind him.

"Hello, Joseph."

Turning, he saw a man wearing blue slacks and a white button-down shirt. He was barefooted and standing at the end of the dock. Joey knew him somehow and rushed to reach him. When he did, they were instantly standing inside the cabin near the fireplace.

"It's been so long," Joey said.

"It hasn't been that long," the man said.

Looking around, Joey remembered every detail of the cabin; how it smelled, where the gas key for the fireplace was kept, how it snowed in the winter, allowing them to sled down to the frozen lake. The old pine walls and the same red area rug that had been there for generations. Joey's grandfather had been a fighter pilot in the Vietnam war. There were candid shots of him with a cigarette hanging out of his mouth, posing with his platoon, and then as an older man holding Joey as a baby.

"You like it here," the man observed.

"I used to," Joey replied.

"It's time for you to return to this place."
~~~

"That would be nice," Joey answered. "But I can't really afford a vacation. I'm working random jobs until I get my business going. I'm married now; I have a son."

"You are in danger, Joseph. Emmanuel is being hunted, and this investigative man seeks to destroy him. Bring your wife and son here until I bring you a word that it's safe to return."

"How do I know you?" Joey asked. The man smiled and pointed to a picture of Joey and the copilot standing with their arms around each other's shoulders, smiling broadly. "I love that guy." All at once, he noticed that this man *was* that guy, he went to hug him. "How've you been?!" Joey asked as if he had just seen him for the first time.

"It's time to prepare for the flight," the copilot answered.

"But I don't have a plane."

"Trade in your old one."

"Oh, yeah… I can trade in the old one. Where did I put that thing?" Joey turned to shake the copilot's hand, but he was gone. He heard a hum and looked out the front door to see a plane where the lake should have been. It was running and ready to take off.

"Don't waste time," Joey heard. "It's time to go."

~~~

The next morning Joey awoke with an urgency to turn in his old VW bus and get a new car. Enough was enough. He needed a truck for work anyway. Without haste, he told Miryam to start packing and started checking out used trucks online. Going with a certified used vehicle, Joey made a record fast purchase and loaded up his little family.

"Where are we going," Miryam asked. "Is this about yesterday? I'm sorry, Joey. What about work?" Joey was in protection mode. His instinct to save the life of his loved ones was in full gear. Locking up the apartment, he assured Miryam that he could get work as an overqualified handyman anywhere. The lower the profile, the better. After driving through the better part of the night, Joey pulled into his grandfather's old cabin in Double Straights. There were no lights on, save the solar lights lining the path to the front steps. Joey was grateful it was not the season for snow.

"Give me a minute," he told Miryam. "I'm going to get inside and turn some lights on." Heading to where a key was hidden for eons, Joey entered the cabin. The familiar smell greeted him. He hoped there were no critters that had decided to take up residence since the last human visitor. Finding
~~~

the light switch as if he had done it yesterday, Joey turned on the lights and looked around. Ensuring that the coast was clear of anything that might alarm Miryam, he headed back out to gather her, the baby, and their bags.

"How long are we going to be here?" Miryam asked.

"Until I receive word that Manny is safe." Joey had told Miryam about the dream and messenger telling him to flee. Miryam was grateful for a defender who listened when heeded.

"Well," she teased, "If I knew sooner you would trade in your bus for a nice truck because of a dream, I would have told you I had a dream months ago."

"No, this is perfect timing," Joey reasoned, "No one knows us by this vehicle. No one can make any connection to us."

"Except that, we came to your family cabin," Miryam chided.

"No," Joey laughed out loud, "I assure you; no one will make a connection there either. I haven't been to Double Straights in *years*."

The next months were good ones. Joey introduced himself to neighbors and had steady work as a handyman for the closest village. Miryam did her best to clean up the cabin. Joey did all the shopping, so most people didn't even know that she and Manny were there. It was a peaceful time on the lake with unforgettable memories made. They celebrated their first anniversary and took pictures amidst the trees to celebrate. Miryam dreamed of having them printed and framed when they returned to their apartment in Netzer, if they ever would. She found herself missing the city but thoroughly enjoyed the life they were experiencing at the cabin. Manny was growing like a weed. He was strong and filled with wisdom for his age. It was apparent the favor of the Creator was upon him.

One evening after dinner, Joey started a fire in the fireplace. Manny was down for the night, and Miryam was cleaning up the kitchen. It was the glorious time of year at the cabin when the days were warm enough to swim in the lake, but the evenings were cool enough for a fire and marshmallows. Joey stood leaning on the mantle, letting his mind wander. He watched his wife clean up. He thought of the dream that had led him to return here. He glanced up to the spot where the picture of him and the copilot had been. It seemed empty without an actual frame there. He reminisced on their days of late and the new memories they were making in this place. He looked at the fire and remembered the fire on the beach the night of the shooting. It seemed so long ago now. He remembered the way Miryam looked with the light in her eyes and wishing he could be close to her. He remembered Jackson and chuckled out loud. He remembered months later being in the diner with Miryam probing him to learn what he had been thinking that night on the beach. Coming up behind him, Miryam slid her arms under his and around his torso. "Earth to Joey… come in, Joey." Joey laughed out loud.

"Oh, wow," he said.

"What?" Miryam questioned.

"That is such a trip."

"What is??"

"You saying that right now. *Earth to Joey… come in, Joey.*"

"Well, you're doing it again. You've got that far away look you get when you are thinking heavily about something." Joey turned around to face his bride and kissed her. He kissed her deeply and meant it. He kissed her as if he had loved her forever and hadn't been allowed to show it. She smiled up at him.

"Sit with me," he said. Leading her over to the couch, they sat intertwined.

"The fire is nice," she relaxed.

"Jackson said that to me. The night of the shooting, Jackson saw me staring at you and said, 'Earth to Joey…come in, Joey.'"

"Oh, wow."

"Yeah, and that is what I was thinking about as I was looking at the fire, so you saying it just now is a trip."

"That *is* a trip, whoa."

"Yeah. I was thinking about the fire and the way it looked in your eyes that night on the beach."

"Aww," she oozed. "That's so sweet."

"Miry, do you remember that night we had a burger in the diner? The night that you were probing me about what I was thinking about at the beach?"

"Yes! I do now."

"Do you remember how I said–"

Miryam sat up and interrupted, "–how you said you would tell me what you were thinking someday if we were still friends, and it still mattered." Joey chuckled.

"You remember."

"Of course, I remember!"

"Well, that night, Jackson was giving me a hard time because... somehow, when I looked at you, I knew I was going to marry you."

"You did not."

"I did."

"But you couldn't have known what was going to happen with Manny. And you would have never gone for someone so much younger."

"No, not at the time," he answered, "but I knew. Jackson had heard me murmur something out loud about marriage and–" Joey laughed with embarrassment. "Ho- man. He wanted me to take advantage of all the single ladies there." They both laughed.

"Jackson!" Miryam scoffed. "Tryin' to get my man off the trail!"

"Oh, no," Joey corrected, "there was no getting me off the trail." He looked lovingly into her eyes. "I've always loved you." Miryam leaned in and found sweetness in her husband's kiss. He was the only one for her, and she felt it with every ounce of her being. "Your lips drip nectar, my bride. Honey is under your tongue." Joey said deeply. Miryam felt a warmth come over her. She paused to feel the Essence of the Creator. It was as if he was with them on the couch, right between them, in the midst.

"Joey," she whispered.

"Yes, my love?"

"It's time," she answered. Joey looked her in the eyes and smiled. Without a word, he kissed her again and led her upstairs.

CHAPTER 10:

THE LUCKY ONES

Joey and Miryam were thinking they may end up staying at the cabin forever. It was as if time was suspended for them there. The sensation was that the whole universe was holding its breath before releasing their son into the world. But here, he was free to discover butterflies, go fishing, and play in the mud. They missed their parents, and Joey was itching for a whole business of his own, but there was no denying the sweetness of this season. Two years passed. Their marriage had the makings of a well-oiled machine with the two finishing sentences and communicating without words. They had a single goal of seeing Manny develop and grow in safety.

One evening after dinner, Joey turned on the news. Miryam was puttering around the kitchen, listening but not watching. "I don't know how you watch that stuff," she hollered. "It's so depressing. I get about three stories in and wonder why I even bothered." Ironically, the third story began with the newscaster's announcement.

"And tonight, the death of a long-time political front runner, Governor Mashaka Mondo. In confirming the Governor's passing, leaders from all over the region are sending condolences and, indeed, already vying for his position. Sources say Mondo struggled with severe anxiety and stress, which led to a battle with heart disease. Hounded for years because of his selfish ambitions and failure to produce much good for the community, the words of Aristotle are appropriate to mention here, 'For what good would their prosperity do them if it did not provide them with the opportunity for good works?' Mondo succumbed to his struggles this afternoon at 3:17 pm."

Joey turned and looked over into the kitchen. His eyes met Miryam's. "I wonder if Sibyl has seen this." Sibyl had kept in touch over the years and informed them of Mondo's ill intent. That night, Joey had a dream. He was standing in a glorious workshop. Every tool imaginable was at his disposal. Just looking at them made him want to start a new project. Joey ran his hands over the instruments. He caught a glimpse of himself in a window. He was older. He turned, and there were five young men around the shop, all skilled in using the tools. He was overwhelmed with love for these men. He noticed a huge sign that read, "Paladin & Sons Carpentry and Construction." Joey lost his breath. These young men were his sons. Five!! He started to approach them when he heard the greeting, "Hello, Joseph." Turning toward the voice, he saw the copilot sitting on a workbench.

"Long time no see," Joey said.

"I'd ask how you've been, but I already know." They both laughed. Joey turned back toward his sons. "Like what you see?" the copilot asked.

"So much," Joey gushed. "It's amazing. It's overwhelming. My boys!"

"They're something," the messenger agreed.

"And the shop– our shop– it's everything I have ever wanted. Look at this guy," Joey pointed to one of his sons, "he looks so much like Miry!" He laughed, "That is crazy. And this one; wow. He looks kind of like my dad! Unbelievable."

"It's time to go back now, Joseph."

"Oh, not yet...." Joey contested, "This is too wonderful."

"To Netzer. Take the young child and his mother and return, for the ones who sought his life are no longer a threat."

Joey could hear Miryam's voice in the distance. He turned to see three female figures through the window. They were headed toward the shop with what appeared to be food. Joey became emotional. He knew one was Miryam and anticipated seeing her face advanced in years. Were these with her his children too? Daughters? *How many kids did they have?*

"Joseph, gather your things. It's time to pack up," the copilot instructed. Joey waved his hand as if to say, 'all right, all right,' but was solely focused on the face of his beloved. The door opened, and the young men rushed towards the women. Two were young girls– lovely, lovely girls. Their hair flowed and shined. Their eyes sparkled. For a moment, Joey wondered if this was heaven. He moved slowly toward the group. He ached to throw his arms around the lot of them and see the look on their faces as they saw him.

What a life. His boys, his wife, his daughters, all the picture of health and prospering.

"Joseph," the copilot warned, "It would be best to gather your things."

Joey did not stop his forward motion to embrace the group. As he approached, not one of them turned to notice him. Not one paused or looked him in the eye. He touched the back of one of his sons, greeting him and wanting a hug. The young man did not respond. He was not offended. Love was the only emotion he felt. He waited for Miry's eyes to look up and meet his; they did not.

"Honey," he said, but she was busy setting out food and preparing paper plates. He wondered what his children's names were– and then, he just knew them: James, Joseph, Jude, Sim, and Manny, of course. He looked to the girls, Joy and Eva. He started calling each of them by name, but none paused to acknowledge him. It was almost as if he weren't there, and then he realized– he *wasn't* there. Turning to seek the copilot, he was gone. Joey turned back to face the group who had engaged in eating and sharing stories. One of them mentioned Dad– finally! "I'm here," he said. No response. Joey realized their speech was in the past tense. Dread set in. They couldn't see him. They didn't know he was there. The revelation caused him to drop his head. When he looked up again, there was one set of eyes locked on his. Manny was looking right at him. Joey cocked his head. Manny held his gaze. Manny could see him. He sighed, thank the Creator, Manny could see him. Wait. *Only* Manny could see him.

Manny was beautiful. His eyes were the same– bright and wise. His hair was full and curly. He had a five o'clock scruff. He wasn't exceedingly handsome, but he wasn't ugly. To his father, he was beautiful. "My boy," Joey whispered.

"Dad," Manny replied.

"I'm not going to make it," Joey realized.

"It depends on your definition." Manny smiled.

A bright light started to appear in the corner of the room. It grew brighter and brighter until Joey couldn't see his clan any longer. Covering his eyes, he woke up in the bed next to a young Miry and Manny snoring in the next room. Relieved, he leaned over and kissed his wife's cheek. He got up and quietly started packing. When Miry awoke, he would tell her everything. Well, almost everything.

Ten Years Later

Finally, the day had come. It was a lovely spring day, just perfect for a road trip. Every year, the Commemoration of Trials festival took place in Government City to honor ancestors who had endured and been delivered by the hand of the Creator, Theos. To some, it was a sacred event, and to others, merely a traditional family reunion. There were games for the kids and family food favorites. Certain uncles always drank too much, and certain aunts would always complain, but overall, it was a celebration dated so far back that no one questioned whether or not to go– they just went. Nestled in a small valley of the Watch Mountain Foothills and overshadowed by a beautiful antique steeple, this location had become as familiar to them as any. They had seen these hills in every condition; flush and green to dry and full of weeds. Manuel, as he was now usually called, tended to look to the steeple. It was a steadfast, constant, and faithful companion. It witnessed countless family gatherings; if that steeple could talk– the tales it could tell. No matter what the event– a touchdown, perfectly landed horseshoe or fat lip– Manuel would turn and look at the steeple as if it was watching and sharing the moment.

Miryam and Joey, her parents Anne and Joaquin, Zach and Liz, with Sally and her husband Zeb, always held the day with great significance. The business of life rarely allowed for them all to be in the same place at the same time, but this annual tradition was a guarantee they would have the chance to catch up. The boys had all shot up so fast and with few incidents. How could it have been 12 years since Liz's miracle of getting pregnant and the gossip of Miryam's pregnancy? Sally's boys had come much later than Liz and Miryam's, but the big boys didn't seem to mind playing with five-year-old Jimmy and two-year-old Jack at all. They seemed to enjoy showing them how to skip rocks and wrestle. Granted, it sometimes caused pre-teen humor to infiltrate Sally's young boys. Like the time they drove all the way home, making farting noises on their arms because the jr. high schoolers thought it would be funny to grant them this remarkable talent. Still, it was a treasured thing to spend time together.

Sally especially treasured the day with her sister Miryam and cousin Liz. They were ahead of her in the parenting game, and she liked to glean from their successes and perceived failures. Letting her mind wander, she remembered a trip when they all stayed overnight after the reunion– sitting outside as the twilight turned into night. The boys were down, and she was big pregnant with Jimmy. They felt thoroughly fortunate in the face of some of their relatives' issues. Hearing of drug abuse, physical attacks, divorce, and more– they had looked around at their small sect and verbalized their appreciation for the others. It was an uncommon communion of mutual respect. They had laughed and teared up at some of their relations situations. After a bout of laughter, a solemnness came over them, and Zach lifted his glass. "We really are the lucky ones." With complete agreement, the group sipped and felt the pause.

"Here, here."

It was a good memory and one that they had since referred to from time to time with the phrase, 'the lucky ones.'

"Mom!" Snapping back into reality, Sally heard Johnny implore his mother, Liz, for permission to eat a piece of cake. From birth, Zach and Liz had kept Johnny from indulging in too much sugar and rarely cut his hair. They were free spirit's in that way. The scene was interrupted by a crashing. All eyes turned to see old Gulliver losing his balance from intoxication and bringing down the whole table of home-baked goods. Gulliver's wife rolled her eyes and started publicly ridiculing him. No one cherished the thought of living with that woman. She was like a constant dripping that wouldn't cease no matter how tightly you might turn the knob. Some rushed to help Gulliver up, and some tried to shush his wife. Other's laughed right out loud, but everyone felt the shame. Zeb looked over at Zach and simply lifted his glass, indicating, 'the lucky ones.' Zach nodded.

The crowd became restless as some were still cleaning up Gulliver's mess. Complaints were rising about desserts that took much time to prepare. No one needed dessert, but needless to say, it was what everyone wanted and looked forward to. When the issue started to settle, Miryam looked over to Manuel. He met her eyes almost instantly. He always knew when she was seeking him. Lifting her hand up between their locked eyes, she beckoned him to come to her with a gesture. As he approached, he had a sense of what was about to happen.

"Manuel," Miryam started in a slightly lowered tone, "didn't we bring extra deserts in the back of the car?" She looked around inconspicuously. Manuel looked up to meet his mother's eyes.

"No, Mom. We didn't."

"Manuel," Miryam said again in a firmer tone, "Are you *sure* we didn't bring some extra desserts?" He looked at her and pursed his lips, half smirking. "Manuel," Miryam instructed, "Go get the extra desserts we brought from the back of the car." Manuel slapped his hand to his forehead and shook his head, running his hand down his face. He sighed and headed toward the car.

Manuel reached the car and called out to one of the other older boys. Careful not to tempt his cousin Johnny beyond what he was allowed, Manuel asked the boy to help him carry desserts from the back of the car to the reset-up table. Upon approaching, the boy exclaimed, "Holy cow! What the what?!"

"Help me carry some of these to the table, man."

"Oh, it's going to take more than you and me, man," the boy responded with eyes wide open. "I'm not going to lug desserts all day. Hey! Hey, you guys! Come help us out for a minute!" A group of boys, including Manuel's brother Joseph, made their way to the rear of the car and started shouting with whoops of cheer.

"Right on!"

"Oh, yeah!"

"Dibs on the berry one!"

Smiling to himself, Manuel simply started stacking up piles of dessert. Joseph looked at his brother inquisitively.

"I didn't see these get loaded up. We had luggage back here– didn't we?"

"Hey, man," the first boy interrupted, "why would you guys bring so many desserts?"

"Ask my Mom," Manuel answered.

The day seemed to pass quickly. After the food was gone and extra desserts passed out to take home, the crowd started to disperse. Many families had rooms in the area and would gather in smaller circles for breakfast before heading out, while others insisted on hitting the road early to return to their own beds. On this particular occasion, the 'lucky ones' had all decided to swap passengers and cars. Joey had to be back first thing in the morning for a business meeting, but Miryam didn't, so she decided to stay over with Liz while Zach hitched a ride with Joey to get back sooner. Zeb caravanned home, but Sally decided to stay over with the ladies for a girls' breakfast. Anne and Joaquin said good-byes. Kids were loaded up with Zeb, and everyone went their separate ways.

Left on their own, the girls were footloose and fancy-free. They enjoyed eating rich cultured food that never went over as a viable choice when the guys were around. Minutes turned into hours as they shared situations and struggles. Even though Liz was older, there was no division among them. Every opinion was valued, and every hurt was shared. Always vowing to get together more often, each woman knew these times were precious. After a fulfilling evening and a tad loss of sleep, the girls finally crashed in anticipation of the drive home in the morning.

The guys made excellent time. If it weren't for the need to stop for gas, Joey might never have paused. He heeded prompts from Zach for bathroom breaks but was an assertive trip taker. It was a relief to Miryam not to have to make the ride back with him. Love him as she may, Joey was a regimented traveler. He often packed a week in advance of a trip and had all of the stops mapped out. He preferred to pack meals and drink as little as possible to reach the destination as swiftly as feasible. However, with kids in tow, this was rarely possible. For this very reason, he was glad to be heading off with just Zach. He hoped it would ensure the ability to stop seldomly. No distractions, no hindrance. His mind was already on to the business meeting he had upon return, and knowing Zach would sleep part of the way, he was free to focus on the road and his plan of action. All of the boys piled up into Zeb's car, so they could play games and goof off. Zeb was much easier going in this regard, and if they had to stop, it wasn't a burden. Zeb was pretty easygoing in most respects.

Breakfast for the girls was a delight. Almost every meal tastes better when prepared by someone else. It was divine not to have anyone tugging at them or stating their preferences. They discussed possible stopping sights on the route home: that antique mall that always seemed to be for another time, the shoe outlet just a bit off the beaten path, or even that fantastic Mexican food restaurant on the ladder part of the stretch. Perhaps two of the three could even indulge in one of their Cadillac margaritas.

After driving the better part of the day, Miryam's phone rang. Seeing it was Joey, she answered, prepared to assure him that all was well and the whereabouts of their current location. The first words out of his mouth were, "Hi, honey. Don't panic." A shot of adrenaline ran through her body.

"What's happened?" Fully expecting to hear that one of the boys had broken an arm or gotten sick from travel and road food, she listened.

"Is Manuel with you guys?"

"Is Manuel with us? No, what are you talking about? It's just us girls; you know that."

"Well, I thought I knew that… but he wasn't in Zeb's car with the other boys, so–"

"What do you mean he wasn't with them? I thought all of the boys were in Zeb's car?" Sally's ears perked up at the mention of her husband's name, and she wondered where he might be guilty.

"I mean–" Joey responded, "the boys all stayed over at Zeb's last night, and when they came home today, Manuel wasn't with them. I thought, perhaps, I had missed something, and he stayed over with you guys."

"No." Miryam's head started swimming. "Why would he want to stay with a bunch of women?" She began to grasp the situation. "Wait a minute, wait a minute. You're telling me– no one knows where Manual is? What did Zeb say?" She shot a look at her sister Sal. Sally put her hand up to question, 'what?!'

"Zeb didn't say anything. He had a car full of boys. One missing was not his main focus. He said he did ask the boys about Manuel last night but had gotten mixed answers. He figured he must be home like the boys thought. He focused on feeding the brood. He is feeling pretty bad, actually."

"Feeling pretty bad?!" Miryam was starting to panic.

"Where are you guys now?" Joey asked.

"Close! We're close. I can be home in 20 minutes."

"Okay, just come home, and we will make a plan to head back. I will call around. It's going to be okay." Miryam responded in kind, but deep in her gut, she didn't know so. She flashed back on Governor Mondo and the hitman he had sent when Manny was a baby. The feeling of him being in danger terrified her.

By the time the girls dropped her off, and they all went inside, Joey was on the phone to the Watch Mountain police. Miryam started transferring her bags into their car and giving instructions to the other boys. Sally offered to take her nephews to her house until they returned with Manuel. Poor Manny… where could he be, and why hadn't he called home? That's it. The boys each needed a cell phone of their own. It wasn't like him to leave his family concerned. Of all the boys, he was the last one they would have imagined doing anything like this. Maybe he had been kidnapped. Dear Creator, let him not have been kidnapped. All of them had thought it, but no one had spoken it out loud. Not yet. The police were not convinced there was a problem just yet. At that age, a boy may be feeling neglected after such an event, wanting to teach his parents a lesson or rebel, could have just slipped away. All of that was foolishness, and both of his parents knew it. They would have to head back. They would have to retrace their steps. Since it had been 24 hours, the police would begin an investigation, but Joey and Miryam were determined to head back immediately.

CHAPTER 11

LOST, FOUND, AND DELIVERED

Three days passed since Manuel had last been seen. Miryam was beside herself. Joey had the confidence he would be found. He reminded Miryam that the boy's purpose had not yet been entirely revealed or fulfilled. It didn't stop her heart from feeling the loss of his presence. Joey thought that when he found him, he might wring his neck. This was unlike anything Manuel had ever put them through before. He was always the most considerate of his brothers and never needed to be told anything twice. Joey remembered him as a baby putting his toy tools away. Being obedient was in his nature. How, then, could he have caused his mother such worry? Even though they had been there twice upon their return, Miryam wanted to go once more to the reunion site in the foothills of Watch Mountain. She asked Joey if she could be alone. Sitting on the bench of a picnic table, Miryam began to speak to the Creator. Talking out loud to Him wasn't something she always did. For her, it was as if everything between them was unspoken– a deep understanding where every thought was before Him. Speaking didn't have to enter into the equation. He knew. She knew He knew. She pondered things, and He led her to the answers or direction. They were in constant communication. But today, after three days, she needed more.

Looking up, Miryam simply shook her head. "I'm sorry," she began slowly. "I'm sorry, I don't understand." The sky was still with a few slow passing clouds. The frustration she had been feeling the last few days was turning to anger. "This is quite an honor you've given me, and I don't mean to seem ungrateful. But what is this about?" Hot tears started flowing down her cheeks. "Joey and I, we have… sacrificed. We have danced around questions and protected at all costs. I know you have something planned, something we can't– but this can't be it. Twelve years of raising him, and then he's just– gone? No. No." Doubt and fear crept into her soul. "Did you change your mind? Do you want someone else to take over now? Is there a reason that you would choose to remove him from us? But why? Why like this? Why not give Joey a dream? Why not send us a word? How can you be so cruel?"

A wind blew and cooled her tears. "Something is wrong here; something is at play. Is there someone new who seeks his life? What would be the point? When he first came to me, your messenger said Manny would be great and called the son of the Highest Deity. Your son. He said his purpose would fulfill *all* of the strivings of the world and that his sphere of influence would know no end. Well, that hasn't happened yet." Miryam could feel the anger rising. She could feel her tone being less than reverent. "I still see strivings. I still see pain. His sphere of influence hasn't even reached outside of our family! What is going on?! Where is the *efficient source of power* now? Where is the spirit of your essence?" Dropping from the bench onto her knees, Miryam lowered her head into her hands and pleaded, "Where is my boy?"

"Whose boy?"

Miryam thought she heard thunder rumble. It was a reasonably clear day. Looking upward, she repeated in a whisper, "Where is my boy?" The thunder clapped.

"Whose boy?"

A quickening came into her spirit. She stilled herself and wiped her tears. Closing her eyes, she waited for the Essence to give her guidance or direction. There was nothing. Only calm. Sighing, she opened her eyes and again shook her head. As she did, she spotted the steeple. The steadfast, constant, and faithful companion that Manuel loved so. 'The steeple,' Miryam thought. 'THE STEEPLE!'

"Joseph!" Miryam yelled as she started running towards the steeple.

Joey saw Miryam running full steam and panicked. Did she see him? What was she doing?

"Joooooseeeeeph!" she screamed as she continued her stride. Joey started running after her in the same direction. Although he didn't know where she was going, he knew she was on to something. Reaching the place of gathering, Miryam flung open the doors. Joey was right behind her. Briskly walking down the aisle, their hearts were pounding from the run. Miryam's eyes dashed to and fro, seeking her son. There, in a group of men and women sitting to the side of the front, was Manuel. Engaged in deep, thought-provoking conversation, Manuel did not notice his parents come in. They were astonished upon finding him so casual.

"Manuel," Joey said in a scolding tone. "What are you doing?"

"Son," Miryam joined in, "Where have you been? Why didn't you call us? Dad and I have been anxiously searching for you!" She rushed toward him and grabbed him in a desperate embrace. The men and women around him were confused. They didn't know he had been apart from his family or missing.

"I've been listening to these teachers and asking them questions. We've been sharing perspectives and learning from one another," Manuel answered calmly.

"What were you thinking?" Miryam admonished, "It's been three days. We couldn't find you. Didn't you think we would be worried? Freaking out?"

"Mother," Manuel checked, "Why were you searching for me? Didn't you know I would have to be in my *Father's* house?" Manuel gave his mother a convicting look. He was not there on his own agenda but that of the Creator. "I didn't mean to worry you."

One of the men stood to introduce himself and shake Joey's hand. "Sir, my apologies. Mike Benson– we didn't realize your son was anything other than a local boy who was wandering in each day. We really have had some incredible conversations. I'm sorry now that you and your wife weren't here to partake of them." Joey reluctantly shook Mike's hand. It wasn't him they were upset with, but the ordeal had wearied them both. Miryam started checking Manuel from head to toe, his arms, his face; she ran her fingers through his curly hair. He seemed to be okay.

"Have you seriously been here the whole time? When did you eat? Where did you sleep?" Manuel looked at his mother and slowly shook his head as if he didn't want to answer in front of everyone. Miryam read the look and silenced her probing.

"Sir," Mike started, "I want to commend you on an incredible young man. I'm not sure how you've taught him the depth of all that he grasps, but he has our wheels spinning for sure. Quite frankly, we have been amazed at his level of understanding for someone so young."

"Well, thank you," Joey obliged. "He is very discerning, it's true. But I think now– we ought to take our very discerning son home."

Mike and some of the others hugged Manuel goodbye. Some wanted to exchange social media information and stay connected. They were eager to see what would become of such a young man. Miryam thanked them for their kindness and ushered Manuel out by her arm around his shoulders. As they reached the door, Miryam started to cry silent tears. She was thanking the Creator and apologizing for her episode earlier. She realized a shift was coming and that things would not always be the way she hoped. Manuel was someone *other*. She wouldn't be able to keep him in her grasp at all times, and she wouldn't be able to protect him. She had a glimpse of life without him, if only for three days. She did not look forward to a time when he stepped out fully into the required tasks ahead of him. Tasks that would offer an end to all striving and create a sphere of influence that would change the world. For the first time, she considered the greater ramifications of such a call. She felt a dread that would suggest devastating sacrifices and further episodes of Manuel's unexplained behavior.

They all walked silently to the car. They called home to let the others know they had found Manuel and that he was well. They drove for quite a way before Miryam broke the silence. Turning sideways in her seat, she looked back at her son and asked: "Manny, what just happened?"

"Mother, there are going to be things I must do. I'm not always going to be able to stop and explain them to you."

"Oh, yes, you can," she combated. "We are not here to stand in the way of your calling, Emmanuel. But we have a calling, too. To watch out for you, to parent you, to walk beside you in this thing. What is this thing– do you know? Do you know what you are facing?" Miryam became a bit more selfish and curious, "Do you know what we're facing?" Without speaking it, she wondered if they would have to let Manuel go. Joey looked in the rearview mirror at his son. Manuel simply looked out the window and sighed. Miryam wrestled with every conceivable notion in her heart. She allowed his silence for the moment. Sometime later, she turned back around to her son, "Manny," she decided it was a safe time to return to her examination, "Where did you eat and sleep?" She knew he would not withhold an answer from her now.

"Mom, I have food and rest that you can't perceive. What felt like three days for you felt like a few hours for me. I don't mean to scare you, but it's like the desserts at the reunion. It's like pulling on what you need from someplace else. It's sustaining. There's an abundance of everything you could ever need. Or want. If you pull with the right motive, at the right time…anything is possible. Food and sleep…" Manuel shrugged his shoulders like they were not that big of a deal.

"Son," Joey was putting on his captain's hat, "We know it must be difficult for you. We can't possibly understand everything you walk through or will be walking through as time goes on– but we can ask that you try to keep us in the loop. At least as much as possible. We have a responsibility too and are accountable for you." Manuel understood and agreed.

~~~

Five Years Later

News spread around Circuit High School of a pretty major party. Joey and Miryam's second son, Joseph, wanted to go. He had seen the handmade flyers with a map going around school all week and was scheming how he could get out of the house without his parents knowing his destination. Joseph was a sophomore to Manuel's senior and had no business attending a party, but he was just sneaky enough to make it happen. By Friday, Manuel was positive that his brother was up to something. Known to his younger siblings as an informant, Manuel did not enjoy it when they were up to no
~~~

good. He would usually just handle things himself, but when necessary, he would clue his parents into things that needed their attention. Manuel had become quite adept at ushering them to conclusions they believed they had come to all on their own. When harmless, he would sit back and watch the consequence of his siblings' choices take place for the sake of their growth. Parties, however, were seldom harmless. Drunkenness, drugs, and even sexual activity could happen if the event became pervasive enough.

After dinner Friday evening, Joseph asked his parents if he could go over to a friend's for the night. Joey and Miryam wondered whether the boy's parents had given permission. Oh, they had, he assured them. As usual, they required the address and phone number of the home and offered to drive him over. Meeting the parents was always preferred, but things had lightened up a bit in the high school years. The Paladins raised their kids with integrity and trusted that they were following through for the very most part. Joey headed to the car with Joseph trailing closely behind him. Manuel stood beside the front door and made clear, direct eye contact with Joseph as he passed. Joseph knew if Manuel found out where he was going, his plan would absolutely be foiled. He always knew somehow. Joseph had become a pro at covering his tracks and being honest, without giving the whole story, to accomplish his intentions. With a weighty stare, Manuel simply said, "Have fun." Joseph knew his tone. He was on to him. How did he always know? He had most likely seen the flyers at school as well. How could he have missed it? They were everywhere.

Joseph did go to his friend's house for the night. But from there, they headed to the rager. Kids were everywhere. One could tell right off that this night could not last long. Neighbors were sure to call the cops. A thick cloud of cigarette and marijuana smoke hung in the air. The music was kicking, and people were dancing. Joseph was excited. He and his buddy went into the kitchen to find a beer. There was a keg with a guy charging three bucks for a cup. They gladly paid and filled up. As they perused the scene, they each picked out a girl they would like to approach once the optimum level of liquid courage was reached. Things were getting a bit fuzzy. The slamming of dice cups was heard randomly, followed by loud bursts of laughter or whoa. As the evening progressed, Joseph felt a brief sense of guilt. His parents really would be saddened to know he was here. But what they didn't know couldn't hurt them. And what could it hurt to party a little? Sitting on the couch surrounded by strangers, Joseph looked up to see Manuel leaning against a wall with eyes locked in on him.

"No, really?" he said out loud. "Manny! Man– it's my brother! Come here, Man– come here." Manuel came and sat down. "What are you doing here, Man? I can't believe you're here." Joseph was drunk.

"I'd like to say, 'I can't believe *you're* here,' but…" Manuel replied. Joseph laughed.

"Duuuude. You're not going to front me off to the folks, are you? Dude, that would suck. You got me, right? Manuel– Manny, my brother. You got me, right?"

"Oh, I've got you," Manuel informed.

"Have a beer, dude. Let me get you a beer." Joseph tried to stand but stumbled backward, returning to his seat. "Whoa, oops."

"No, I'm good, man. I'm good."

Manuel looked around at the sea of teenagers. The house parents left for the night, having permitted this amusement. Their only rule was that no one touches their personal stash of marijuana plants in the master bedroom closet. Their daughter was under strict instruction to guard it and allow no one near. Youth were coupling off and making out. Some were losing their virginity, and some were passing out. Gradually, boys started lining up along the hallway wall. It didn't seem to be anything unusual, just guys hanging out and leaning against a wall. It was near the bathroom, so at first glance, it might seem they were waiting their turn to relieve themselves. Manuel caught something in his spirit. Something black-hearted. Something beyond teenage play. He stood, telling Joseph he'd be back. He passed the lined-up guys and did use the restroom. Upon coming out, he could see that the line led directly to a bedroom. Manuel reached to open the door. A kid at the front of the door said, "Hey, man… wait your turn. There's a line, yo," and directed with his thumb to the back of the line. Manuel opened the door to find a young girl, no older than 15, in bed with a guy on top of her. The front window was open, and a boy who had been watching jumped out upon Manuel walking in. The guy on top of the girl did not stop. Manuel's eyes were opened, and he could see a room full of demons prancing. They were having a party of their own. One of the demons was placing a black iron collar with chain links around the girl's neck. They were snickering and hissing. Every boy that came in added a link to the chain. It would be years before this chain would be broken, if ever. Manuel's anger rose. He grabbed the shoulder of the guy in bed and pulled him off the girl.

"Hey, man…" the kid disputed, "back off. I'm busy here." Manuel bypassed him, pulling the girl out from under him. "What the hell, dude?" The guy rose. Without touching him, Manuel lifted his hand in a stop position and knocked the kid back. Continuing to gather the girl, he was searching for her clothes on the floor.

"Oh, hey… it's okay," the girl said in a drunken slur, "I liked that one." The line at the door began to disperse as they saw Manuel deliver the girl.

"All it takes is one chump to spoil a good time," one of them snorted.

"It's time to go home," Manuel told her.

"What? No, I'm not ready to go yet," the girl argued.

"You are. Come on. I'm going to take you." Gathering her belongings and seeing her dressed, Manuel took her arm and led her out. The girl even flirted with him a bit, trying to convince him to continue the party. It wouldn't hit her until much later, all that transpired that night and the salvation that was hers. Manuel made eye contact with Joseph across the room and waved him over. "We're going," he mouthed. Joseph didn't want to leave but saw the look of seriousness in his brother's eyes. Manuel could rat him out and spoil the whole night if he didn't go now. Upon exiting the house, Manuel told Joseph, "Call the police."

"Dude, no way, are you kidding?"

"Right now, Joseph. Call the police. We're taking this girl home and getting out of here. Call them. Now." Joseph pulled out his cell phone and reported the party. He hoped no one would catch on to the fact that he was the one who had turned it in. "This place is a wasteland."

CHAPTER 12:

A VOICE IN THE WASTELAND

13 Years Later

Johnny had grown to be a strapping man. Healthy and full of charisma, he was a vegetarian who rarely ate sugar and never drank alcohol. Johnny kept himself set apart from the ways of the world that so easily entangled. He had become a radical online celebrity with a following that reached millions of people. His channel's political tone was often upsetting to those who held office in both the religious and governmental arenas. The government was striving for an authoritarian system but was still met with opposition by the religious sect, who preferred their totalitarian practices. But what they all agreed on was that extremists were bad for business.

Governor Gale Tetrarch of the tri-state Region of Circuit, Watch Mountain, and the City of Peace secretly never missed one of Johnny's posts. Whispers of the Governor's sexuality pervaded his term, and being married to his dead brother's wife seemed too convenient to resolve the issue. Governor Tetrarch lived in a luxurious home and surrounded himself with soft things. He could be savvy in the Legislative Building but was as weak as a reed in the wind. Easily swayed, he seemed to allow anyone who flattered him a voice in his ear. He liked Johnny, even if he couldn't openly support him.

Military Superintendent Dirk Pontius was constantly managing conflict in the City of Peace just within Governor Tetrarch's tri-state influence. M.S. Pontius was from an elite family. He earned his undergraduate degree and was an officer in the Military. His wife, Aislyn, was the niece of a Vice President, so he married into power as well. Aislyn was known to be intuitive and insightful. She made her husband aware of Johnny's channel, indicating he was someone to watch, but M.S. Pontius was not one to make time for such things. As the local authority for the Union Empire, his focus was to 1. Keep the peace with the religious sect, and 2. Bring in the money.

Speaker of the Church, Sabeen Smith, was the appointed moderator over the Conservative and Liberal branches of the Church. She had seen some of Johnny's posts and kept her eye on him as an influencer with a religious following. Handpicked by the President of the Union Empire to be an officer of the state, Sabeen represented the religious sects with pride. Whereas the Union Empire had not become entirely authoritarian, the swing was in full force to practice keeping radical individuals under the state's subordination and authority. Speaker Smith's charge was to manage her people while maintaining harmony with political matters and leaders. She often met with the Military Superintendent on the grounds of squashing potential rabble-rousers.

Johnny didn't give a rat's ass about any of them. His was a voice in the wasteland crying out. He stayed very near the Slide River but moved around the region as he felt led. Johnny would not be bound to any person, place, or thing. Continuing in the free-spirit vein of his parents, Zach and Liz, Johnny posted thought-provoking videos on political leaders, signs of the times, and encouragement to be productive in keeping with a good conscience. Johnny spoke of someone who would come. A great leader who would change the world. Someone who would end the days of big brother and the growing vapor of totalitarianism. Johnny taught with boldness. He called out Union Empire leaders as a brood of vipers. He warned that if the Empire continued along this same path, it would be cut down like a tree and thrown into the devouring fire. Much of what Johnny prophesied was frightening to people, but there had always been radicals who spoke of gloom and doom throughout the ages. Johnny was different. A miracle child himself, Johnny had the Essence of the Creator upon him his whole life. He often flowed in long orations for the betterment of humankind. He encouraged his followers to wait for the One who could lead them into the next triumphal phase of existence.

Johnny would sometimes plan events and invite his followers to the Slide River for ceremonies of immersing themselves; it was a symbolic gesture of cleansing from the Union Empire's wicked ways and life itself. Lives were changing, and some of Johnny's followers became radical devotees to his message.

"I immerse you with water for cleansing and purification as a symbol of dying to what was and rising to what can be. But One is coming who is so much greater than I am." In a whisper, he continued, "I am not even worthy to… carry his boots." Returning to the crowd, he projected, "He will purify you with the Essence of the Creator and Fire." The group whispered among themselves.

"The *what?*"

"I don't know about the fire thing," one guy questioned a friend. Sometimes Johnny could be a bit radical even for his most devoted followers. But they liked his overall message and chose to believe. He had a voice that affected the culture. When he said someone was coming, they hoped for him and looked forward.

Who could this One be? Johnny always said that when the One came, he would separate the hypocrites from those with true integrity. The reprobates from the moral. He explained it like the process of purifying gold.

"Unrefined gold is submerged in a mixture of nitric and hydrochloric acids that dissolve the ore and separate the gold from the impurities. Once this is accomplished, the filth can simply be… washed away. The remaining substances will be water and pure gold. So it will be for all who follow."

Oh, how a society without defilement sounded good. But how could any single person do all of that? Journalists reported Johnny's followers as having 'drank the Kool-Aid.' But for those who had been in his presence, it was apparent he carried more than just charisma. There was a truth that they could hear behind the hype. Johnny was sincere and sold out to his beliefs, causing them to want to be too.

Members of both the conservative and liberal church parties ventured out to see what this voice in the wasteland was pushing. The crowd was pulsating with conviction and a desire for change.

"What can we do to avoid being cut down and consumed by the fire?" the crowd pled.

"Become a people of consideration," he began. "We see the beggars on every corner– if every one of them had one person to pour into them, one person to extend themselves and be uncomfortable, we wouldn't have the homeless in number as we do. I know. 'They're on drugs,' you say. Well, maybe they are. I'm not saying give them drugs. I'm not saying contribute to their habit. I'm saying CARE. What does *caring* look like for you? What would you want someone to do for that person if they were your son? Your brother? What does it cost to carry a box of protein bars in your car to hand out at the stoplight?"

People from every class came to see Johnny and be immersed in the waters. Police officers, church leaders, blue-collar workers, and real estate moguls. Johnny's message was the same for them all.

"Don't extort money or accuse people falsely. Learn what it means to be content and work hard. Everyone is so selfish in this world. Everyone wants something for nothing. It's a sickness that has infested and rotted the whole of humanity. No one owes you anything, and nothing taken without working properly for it will ever be enough."

People were hungry for change. The oppressive rules of the religious right and the liberal left-wing leaders of the Union Empire had exhausted the nation.

~~~

Johnny was causing quite a stir. Draco Conti, an international televangelist of the conservative sect, had been encouraged to watch Johnny's channel. Draco had far-reaching arms with feelers on the ground in every region. If this young man were indeed something of note, perhaps Draco would have him on his show to share his message. Anything that promoted Draco or brought him into the view of potential followers interested him. He ordered one of his attendants to watch Johnny's channel and give him a report on the situation. He also wanted the temperature of the local leaders checked regarding the impact Johnny may be having. Anyone with that many followers online was worth examining. But Draco had created a brand for himself and didn't want to bring on any riffraff that may cause more trouble than they were worth. He had a strict formula of living by the law, shaking hands with as many conservative political leaders as possible, and judging those who didn't share his views. It was working for him. Independently wealthy by the donations given to his religious organization, Draco lived the life of an international superstar. Homes, cars, a private jet, and a trophy wife– none could contest that his higher power favored him.

Draco's attendant reached out to Johnny through the comments on his channel. Soon, they were sitting face to face. Johnny hated the show that Draco put on, but if this opportunity might spread the word of the leader he knew was to come, it was worth investigating. Johnny made no attempt to impress the attendant. Welcoming her to the Slide River, where he held his immersion events, they sat on a park bench.

"Thank you for seeing me," she began. "Mr. Conti has taken note of your ministry and would like to commend you on your followers."

"My followers are seekers of truth," Johnny replied. "They don't belong to me. They follow the promise of hope. Draco should not be impressed with the number of followers on my channel but the Truth to which they are responding."

"Are you the promise of hope? Are you the truth?"

"I am not. I bring the promise of hope. I am making a straight path, a landing strip, for the Truth to come and land. Are you ready?"

"Me?" the attendant asked.

"Yes, you. Are you walking in a manner pleasing to Theos, the Creator?"

"I work for Draco Conti."

"I didn't ask you who you work for. Do you think working for Draco Conti is going to save your immortal soul?" The attendant's eyes grew wide.

"I would hope so," she responded. "I'm a good person, and I– wait. This isn't about me."

"And yet you're talking about hope. Hope- that you're doing things well enough, that being a good person will qualify you for– what is it that you believe?"
~~~

"Okay… Sir," the attendant was getting defensive.

"It's just Johnny."

"Fine, Johnny, I am here to see if perhaps you might be a candidate for Mr. Conti's program. So, getting back to you– Are you a prophet? What do you say about yourself?"

"I am the voice of one crying out in the wasteland. This jungle where commonplace is to miss the mark and call it acceptable. But if you're asking me who I am, then you haven't heard my messages at all." Johnny leaned forward on the bench and looked deep into the attendant's eyes, "I am only a messenger to tell the world about the anointed One who is to come. He will have the answers. He will make the change. He is going to turn this place upside down, man." Johnny started laughing with a gleam in his eye that struck the attendant as a bit maniacal. At that moment, she wasn't sure he was right for Draco. Draco was about order and control. There was no guarantee that Johnny would play by those rules.

"So, this immersion ceremony that you perform, what do you think is being gained by those who partake?"

"It's not a performance," Johnny corrected. "I guess you could call it a ceremony of sorts in that there is a solemnity to it. It's not a show or parade. But it does commemorate the cleansing of one's life and a choosing to turn and walk in a new direction. A better direction. A direction of consideration and intentionality. We've lost that. It is so dog-eat-dog out here." Johnny felt a wave of grief flood him and his eyes watered. Now the attendant knew he was not Draco Conti material. Still, there was a distinct principle in his passion– an unwavering, gut-wrenching pull about his speech. "Aren't you tired?" he questioned her. "What is your name again?"

"Amy." She whispered.

"Aren't you tired, Amy?" He was pulling on her heartstrings now. She *was* tired. For the first time, she saw beauty in this wild man. He had a brutal delivery, but the truth was certainly what he brought. Amy let her shoulders drop. She hadn't even realized she had been holding them so tightly. How long had she been holding them that way? Johnny could see the drop and the look on her face; in fact, he had seen that look countless times.

"You are tired," he observed. Amy started to tear. Now she felt like *she* wasn't Draco Conti material. She was questioning everything just by sitting with this man for 20 minutes.

"What are you doing?" she questioned. Letting go, she laughed. "Uuuugh. Who are you, man?" They both laughed. Amy found herself sharing things with Johnny that she hadn't spoken of in years. Things that she had put away long ago and vowed never to bring up again were floating in the air between them. After several more minutes and personal revelations of the hope to come, Johnny again leaned forward.

"I have an idea," he said with a gleam in his eye. "What would you say to maybe getting immersed?"

"What? Oh, no way…" she refused, but she wanted him to come in after her. She wanted him to insist this uptight, self-righteous follower of the law be torn away.

"It's pretty simple," he contested. "You just go under, let go, and come up new. Embrace it. The Truth is coming. This is just water. He's going to bring a counselor that will never leave you and a purifying fire that will burn away the dross." Amy found herself wanting truth in a way she had long ago settled to live without. "Whaddya' say?"

"I don't have any other clothes with me," she hesitated.

"Really??" Johnny laughed. "You're going to let getting soaked stop you from freedom? Amy– it's a rental car! Who gives a flying fig if it gets wet? You've got clothes somewhere, don't you?" He stood and extended his hand. Amy stood and took it. Leading her to the water, he began to speak out loud. He was addressing the Creator, which Amy had never experienced before on such an intimate level. She had seen Draco appeal to the Higher Power many times on his program, but it was nothing like this. Johnny was so bold. So free and intimate. It was intoxicating. They started to wade into the water, fully clothed. Johnny didn't flinch. These were his waters, his personal sanctuary. Amy giggled and held onto his arm as well as his hand.

She flinched, "Ahhh, it's cold!"

"Suck it up, buttercup," Johnny chided. "It's a momentary discomfort for the hope of an eternal reward."

"Hope of??" Amy gasped, "You mean this doesn't guarantee a reward?" She was still laughing at the whole event.

"Immersion doesn't bring the reward," he said, "The One who is coming will do that. This is your willingness to show him you're ready and that you want to be made clean." Turning to Amy, he stood beside her. "Amy," he became solemn. "Turn from your old ways now, for the kingdom of great promise is at hand. Are you ready?" Amy nervously nodded her head. Johnny laid her back with smooth grace and immersed her in the water. The cold washed over her face.

It was oddly refreshing and freeing to not care about her hair or make-up. In light of this new hope, she didn't care what someone might think. That alone was worth the dunk. As Johnny pulled her back up to the surface, she let out a little, "Woo!" It wasn't intentional, and it wasn't about being cold. It was as if something had left her. Something she didn't even know she was carrying.

"Good riddance," she said quietly.

"Exactly," Johnny agreed.

~~~
~~~

Johnny was sitting in his recording studio. A few friends were socializing just outside the door in the next room. Some of them were devout and had followed Johnny's posts from the beginning. Some were seeking and not quite sure about being sold out on every word Johnny taught, but they liked the idea of it all. Some just wanted to be near the 'latest thing' and took advantage of the notoriety Johnny had gained. Jack, however, sat on the couch, cleaning his glasses with the bottom of his shirt and thumbing through a magazine. Jack was the younger son of Sally and Zeb's two boys. He was a second cousin to Johnny and had a lifetime of holiday memories with his magnetic cousin. Jack could almost always be found within the vicinity of his older brother Jim. But today, he thought he would just go hang out with Johnny. Little did he think about his cousin's groupies being ever-present.

Johnny was recording live. He was in the middle of thanking his followers and most recent subscribers when stillness came over him. It wasn't the adrenaline rush he usually got before a post or going live. It wasn't nerves. It was the familiar warmth of the Essence of the Creator. What wasn't familiar was the weight that entered the room, a knowing, a presence so strong that he wondered if anyone else in the studio felt it. As he looked up and around, he saw Manuel in the doorway of the studio. Johnny stopped. Frozen. Hand to his chest, gripping, he said, half to Manuel, half to his live followers, "I didn't know who it would be until right this moment." Overcome by emotion, Johnny stood and walked swiftly to Manuel, embracing him. It was a deep, robust hug, filled with the culmination of all his passion and work. *'This is it. This is Him, of course, it is Him!'* It was as if a light turned on, and Johnny understood that Manuel was the leader he had long-awaited. The One. How could he have known Manuel his whole life and not *known* him? How could he have not seen him clearly for who he was– or who he would become?

"I'm so stoked! Come on, man– come on." Johnny excitedly led Manuel to the computer camera and microphone, where his followers were still watching live. "Have a seat, have a seat…" he directed. Turning his attention back to his viewers, Johnny breathed deep and embraced the moment he had dreamed of so many times. The introduction of the leader who would redeem the world. "This is so surreal," he said, shaking his head and looking at Manuel; Johnny could not stop grinning. With amusement, he addressed his viewers, "Guys!" Johnny placed his hand on Manuel's shoulder. Manuel sat perfectly calm but with a huge closed-mouth grin. He had longed to reveal himself to Johnny and loved that his cousin was finally having his moment of revelation. Manuel knew the work Johnny had been so diligent in doing and loved him for it.

Jack was already texting Jim, telling him to turn on Johnny's channel. "Guys!" Johnny repeated. "This is it. This is actually it! Here is the One I've been talking about for so long! Here is the One I said would come after me but ranks before me because– He *was* before me." He didn't seem to be making sense. Johnny's excitement stilled to a solemn pause, and he continued, "Just now, as He entered my studio, I saw the Essence of the Creator descend upon him and remain. I have felt the Essence my whole life, but I have never *seen* it. It's– He's covered with– is the camera picking this up?" Turning to Manuel with all of the understanding of their whole lives coming into clarity, he edified, "He's the One. He's the One who can–" Johnny finally took his eyes off of Manuel and intently returned speaking to the camera, "I've been telling you how to get cleansed, make your lives new with turning from old ways and immersion, but…" his eyes returned to Manuel. With a perfectly still, silly grin, steadfastly calm, he repeated, "He is the One who can cleanse you with the Divine Spirit; the Essence of the Creator." Tears filled Johnny's eyes unashamedly. "I have seen and can attest that this is the One we've been waiting for. All of it is true– all of the prophesies, all of the hopes and preparing. This is the Son of the One True Creator."

Instantly, the newsfeed on Johnny's channel lit up. People were commenting with both adulation and skepticism. All Johnny could do was laugh and hug Manuel. Manuel said not a word but looked directly into the face of millions, waved, and chuckled with Johnny.

CHAPTER 13:

TEMPTATION

Johnny was in shock. He couldn't stop grinning and hugging his cousin. Alone after the groupies had left, Johnny, Jack, and Manuel sat in the silence of the empty studio. "I can't believe this," Johnny said. "Dude, how could I have not known?"

"Don't beat yourself up, man. It wasn't time for you to know." Manuel was calm and collected. He had grown into a diligent and solid man. At 30, he was now the eldest brother in the Paladin and Son's Carpentry and Construction business. Sturdy but not overly substantial in size, Manuel had an intuitive business sense and compassion for everyone he met. Not one to be taken advantage of by contriving customers; he was a just and considerate businessman. Manuel and his brothers had run the business in almost equal parts since Joey's death years before. Being the oldest of Joey and Miryam's seven children, Manuel was ordinarily seen by his younger siblings as the leader. He had an innate ability to attend to their mother as well as wisdom beyond his years. Manuel carried himself with slightly lowered shoulders, and his head often seemed to be looking up from a bowed position. Never one to attract attention to himself, he was generally soft-spoken; however, when Manuel was intent on making a point, he spoke with direction and unrestricted confidence.

"How long have you known?" Johnny asked. "Have you known your whole life? Or was it revealed to you in pieces? I mean–" he sighed with a bit of frustration, trying to wrap his head around the weight of his cousin's position and purpose.

"Have you known who *you* are your whole life?" Manuel asked. "You have been anointed since conception for certain tasks. We all have. Did you know that, or did it come to you gradually?"

"Well, some of it I knew because my parents told me of the miracle of my conception. I also abstained from sugar, meat, alcohol– all of that. So, I've always walked in a certain direction, but the revelation of purpose came gradually. But you're different."

"Somewhat," Manuel responded. "But in most ways, I am the same. There were things I knew and things I had to experience."

"Your dad would be so proud."

"He is," Manuel replied.

There was a knock at the door, and Jack spoke up, "That will be Jim." Having watched the live video of Johnny announcing Manuel as the long-awaited person who would bring a solution to the current political climate and more, Jim was curious to get to the bottom of things himself. Even though they were cousins, Jim and Jack were several years younger than Johnny and Manuel. Jim was young and vocal, while Jack was even younger and more of an observer. Entering the studio, he put his hands on his hips and addressed Manuel directly, bypassing Johnny.

"So… you've come to change the world? You? Mr., 'I disappeared and freaked my parents out for three days when I was 12?' Mr., 'Let me just go my whole life without any political standing or preparation ever' to suddenly, 'vote for me, I'll change the world?' How are you going to break into the political arena at 30, Manuel? What are you guys trying to pull? Most politicians start in high school with legislative aspirations or military service. They are intentional in college with resumes that will impress voters later. Is this a joke? Or do you sincerely believe that because you have run your dad's business for oh-so-many years now, that you have what it takes to stand up to Government City leaders? Where is this coming from?"

"Hello, Jimmy," Manuel answered. "Good to see you, man." Manuel stood and hugged his cousin. "Who said anything about me running for office or becoming a politician?"

"Johnny! On his channel." Manuel looked to Johnny with a furrowed brow and back to Jim. Cocking his head.

"Did he? Is that what he said? I think that's what you heard."

"No, he said, 'you were the long-awaited One who would bring redemption and end the– he said you were before him, even though you were after him, and that you ranked higher than him,' or something." Jim paused long enough to observe the look on Manuel's face. His eyebrows were raised, and he had a half-grin. "You're making fun of me," he challenged his cousin.

"No," Manuel said, shaking his head. "No, but what you were expecting and what Johnny said was coming were two different things. You expected someone to come in with political stature and change the climate from within the system– takedown the leaders. I'm coming for the people, Jimmy. I've come to bring hope and the truth from outside of the system– to change the leaders. I didn't come to change the law but to fulfill it, do you understand?" Jim dropped down into a chair for the first time since coming in.

"Not really," he answered. "How can you change the world and bring redemption if you don't do it from a political platform?"

"What is your definition of redemption?" Manuel asked.

"The same as everybody else's," Jim insisted. "Conversion of the state of the Union."

"Conversion of the state of the *people*," Manuel corrected. "The state of the Union would be secondary as a result of the first." Jim looked at his cousin's expression again. The grin was an understanding beyond his own. His raised eyebrows were patiently waiting for him to get the revelation. His eyes were compassionate, with no judgment for having been so single-minded and missing the bigger picture. Suddenly, he didn't see Manuel as his cousin whom he had known forever but as someone different. Someone new. Maybe he *was* the One Johnny had been teaching would come. But how could he be the Son of the Creator any more than any of them were?

"Are you with me?" Manuel asked.

"With you?"

"Yes, will you come with me, Jim? You and Jack both. I'm going to need some good men about me."

The family didn't usually refer to people as young as Jim and Jack as men. Something puffed up in each of their chests. Jack jumped up and chimed in immediately.

"I'm in!" Looking to his brother, he waved him on, "Come on, Jim. Don't be so rigid." Jim was having a tough time, not being so dogged.

"What are we supposed to do? Leave our jobs and just follow you on the road or something?"

"Something like that," Manuel chided. "… might be fun. Might be… life-changing."

Jim squinted his eyes. Even though he didn't want to, he felt compelled to jump on board. It might end up being a crazy train, but he was confident it would be something he didn't want to miss.

"I'll give you three months," he answered.

~~~

Scout Nikkos had been writing for the Tri-State Triton for 12 years. He had a free hand to write whatever stories of interest intrigued him. Scout saw the video of Johnny's announcement of this guy who would redeem the people and claimed to be 'the Son of the Creator.' Scout wasn't a follower of Johnny's or a believer in any creator, but he could sniff out a good story. With as many subscribers as Johnny had, there was certainly an audience for this report. Based out of the City of Peace, Scout headed north to Netzer to snoop around and interview some of Johnny's followers. He also hoped to speak to Johnny himself to get a background on the whole 'redeemer of the world' concept. Scout packed a bag of his standard gear; two pairs of jeans, six t-shirts with sarcastic statements or beer advertisements, a carton of Karelia cigarettes, and toiletries. Not one to waste time or resources, he reached out to several people who had commented on the revelation video. He wanted to capture both the skeptical and believer views. Always willing to put a sucker to shame, Scout looked forward to meeting the key players in this game.

~~~

Manuel let the guys know he would go away by himself for a bit before launching out in all that he was called to do.

"Let us come with you," Johnny suggested. But Manuel insisted Johnny's work was not yet done, and he needed to continue for now.

"I need to spend some time with Theos on my own and get my head on straight. We're about to walk into a lot."

"Like a Silence and Solitude," Jim thought. "I get it. But just know that this time is coming out of your three months."

"Jim," Jack protested, "Come on, man. Don't be a jerk. You can wrap up work and request your time off while he's gone." Turning to Manuel, he continued, "Where are you going? Do you think you'll be back pretty quick, or…?"

Manuel had one place in mind; the cabin where his parents had fled to when he was a baby. But he didn't want to divulge his destination. "I'm not sure how long I'll be gone, but I'll hook up with you guys when I get back.

We have a lot to prepare. I suggest you spend time wrapping up your affairs and packing a few things to go on the road."

"We're going on the road?!" Jack chirped. "Sweet!"

Manuel let his mother, Miryam, know that he would be at the cabin but encouraged her not to tell anyone. Miryam had become accustomed to heeding her son when he confided in her. Starting the long drive to the cabin, he rolled down the window and let the fresh air blow his hair. Manuel loved almost everything about creation. The smells, the colors, the way it flourished and flowed. Heading to the cabin was one of his favorite drives. It was the perfect way to start this time of focus for direction. Uninterrupted time with the Creator was one of his favorite things, but with his dad's business and taking care of his mother, there hadn't many been long, concentrated times to get away. With the commencement of his purpose around the corner, this one was much needed.

His purpose. Whereas many men didn't know the reason for their birth and life, Manuel knew before coming to the world how his life and work would change it. All of it. He was overwhelmed by his love for humanity and grieved at the way they embraced hatred for one another. Racism, apartheid, murder, and greed– it was never intended to be this way. Why had love become so complicated? Simply because the flesh desires what is contrary to the Spirit, and the Spirit what is contrary to the flesh. They are at war with each other, and people tend to do whatever seems right in their own eyes. Trials had become too much to bear: death, famine, stepfamilies, and adultery. How could they find joy when facing such difficulties? Why had they not believed the Ancient Writings and asked the Creator for wisdom? He gives wisdom generously to all without reproach. No one is less than loved equally in His heart. But instead, the world was living in a state of doubt, being driven and tossed by the wind. This same wind brought refreshing and peace to Manuel's soul. Men were double-minded and unstable in all their ways. How differently they interpreted the wind depending on their circumstance.

So, he came. For the joy set before him– the redemption of this beloved humankind– Manuel knew he would endure great suffering for their sakes. But if it led to them having an opportunity to learn peace and the steadfast love of the One who had created them, it would all be worth it. Nerves rose in his stomach. There was much he knew, but plenty he didn't. But he did know that he would scorn any shame and brave any opposition to bring the truth and show them the way to deliverance. Part of him wished it was already over, that he could wake up years from now with humanity understanding the path to redemption. He wished they could escape the consequence of their choices with just a word but knew that the process was in the journey. And he knew what it would cost him.

Pulling into the familiar driveway, Manuel got out and paused, leaning on the hood of the car. He took several deep breathes, remembering summers and swims in the lake. The sun was on his face, and he immediately tuned in to the Creator.

"Hello, Papa," he sighed. "My life, my source… the designer of all things. Thank you. Thank you for originating and imparting life. Thank you for being the artist that has animated us who seek you by infusing your Spirit into us. Thank you for looking out for us. Thank you for your supernatural messengers. Thank you for meeting me here, today, and always, Papa. I honor you."

Manuel headed to the lake. Maybe he would swim later. He had already decided he would fast from food as an exercise of disciplining his body and tuning into the frequencies of the elevated realm. Food could be a distraction, and he wanted none. He wanted only to spend time in the presence of his wellspring and gain a divine understanding for the days ahead.

"Hello, there…" a voice came from behind him. Turning, Manuel saw a handsome man with salt and pepper hair. His eyes were steel blue, and he wore a perfectly tailored suit that matched them. "I've been looking forward to our time together," he said. The hair on the back of Manuel's neck stood up. He felt darkness creep into his mind. He knew instantly that this was the adversary of the world, a fallen creation who tormented the souls of men for his twisted pleasure. He couldn't conquer the Creator, but he could antagonize His favorite creation by granting them every selfish desire and pleasure they could imagine. For, each person is tempted when he is lured and enticed by his craving. Then desire, when it has conceived, gives birth to man being misled, and misguidance, when fully grown, brings forth death, and this pleased the adversary very much.

"Hello, Teivel," Manuel stood from his squatted position of gathering stones to skip. Dusting his hands off on his jeans, he quipped, "Enjoying your king of the hill status?"

"The hill?" Teivel quipped. "Don't you mean the world?"

"Seems like a hill in comparison to the multiple universes we both know exist." Teivel grinned from ear to ear. He was going to enjoy this. Manuel came to be in unity with his Papa, but Teivel had come to lure him in every other way.

"So, you're going to *save the world*, are you?" Teivel's laughter sounded like a deep comfortable sip of whiskey. Warm with a hint of sting, followed by a lack of care that allowed judgment to drift away. His laughter caused a pull that invited freedom from confinement. "Tsk, tsk, tsk. Don't you know they don't want salvation? They're having a grand ol' time with me. You're going to waste your energy."

"You're going to have to do better than that, Teivel. Do you think I'd sway so easily?" Manuel headed into the house to settle in. He knew it would be a long stay and that the adversary had no plans of leaving. 'This is just the beginning,' he thought. 'I know You're with me, Papa. I know You have given me everything I need to resist him. I thank You for the opportunity for victory and trust You in advance for equipping me for whatever comes next.' Manuel lit some candles and sat to meditate with the Creator. The adversary blew them out and sat directly across from him in distraction. Manuel opened a window to let in the fresh air; the adversary brought the aroma of dead animal carcass wafting through the breeze. Manuel prepared for bed but knew he would get no sleep. For 40 days, Manuel sought the Creator and resisted the adversary. It was exhausting, and he was growing weary from not eating. Confident that it was working to prepare him for his future endeavor and journey, Manuel faced every challenge and temptation with steadfast confidence. Finally, one night Manuel was sitting on the couch. As ever, the adversary sat near him with his piercing eyes upon him. Manuel met his stare and did not look away.

"I know you're hungry, Emmanuel." Manuel did not look away. "I could whip us up some filet-mignon or fresh salmon. But you're a simple guy, aren't you? How about a pizza?" At that moment, a fresh, hot, perfectly baked pizza with all of Manuel's favorite toppings appeared between them on the coffee table. Manuel could identify each topping without a glance. He could smell the cheese and spices in the sauce. The warmth from the perfect crust seemed to be an inch under his nose. He was so hungry, and it would be so easy to eat a slice. "Not the right choice?" Teivel teased, "How about a hamburger? If you are the Son of the Creator, tell this stone to become a burger. Go on." They both knew he could do it. And Manuel knew the adversary knew he wanted to. Manuel closed his eyes.

"The Ancient Writings tell us that man does not live by food alone, but by every word that comes from the Creator."

"Oh, that ol' thing?" Teivel quipped. When Manuel opened his eyes, they were both sitting on the top of The Venetian Hotel in Las Vegas, Nevada. With telescopic vision, Manuel could see everything in detail. He saw beautiful women dressed in revealing clothing. He felt the pull towards using them. He saw alcohol flowing and became thirsty for both drink and escape. He saw through the walls to the casino and people playing cards. They were laughing and even winning. Manuel felt a desire and lust rise within him; he could easily embrace them. Teivel leaned in and put his hand on Manuel's shoulder. With his face an inch from Manuel's ear, he said, "I will give you all earthly authority and splendor. You know it has been given to me, and I can give it to anyone I choose. Nothing and no one would resist you. If you worship me, it will be yours." Manuel looked around and felt the full weight of the offer. Turning, he looked at Teivel as if he would accept.

"I will revere the One True Creator alone and serve Him only." Teivel squinted and shook his head in anger.

In the next moment, they were standing on the highest building in the City of Peace. This is where Manuel was born, and he could feel the roots of Joey's family coursing through his veins. It caused him to want to end this incessant temptation and rest. Walking to the edge, Teivel challenged, "If you are the Son of Theos, throw yourself down from here. Don't the Ancient Writings say that 'He will command his celestial beings concerning you to guard you carefully?'" Teivel was being sarcastic now and prancing around, acting as if he were a divine messenger, "Won't they lift you up in their hands so that you will not strike even your foot against a stone?" He began laughing and taunting Manuel. How dare he suggest that Manuel might not actually be the Son of the Creator. How dare he linger day after day trying to break him down! 'I could show him,' Manuel thought. 'I could think one thought and wipe this joker off the face of his little hill.' Manuel felt the heat of the Creator's dunamis power rising in his fist. Upon lifting his hand, Teivel froze. His eyes widened, thinking he had finally won and accomplished defeating Emmanuel.

Manuel looked at his hand and said, "Do not put the Master of the Universe to the test." Irritated by this final declaration, Teivel vanished, leaving Manuel on the roof. Manuel knew it was just a matter of time before he saw him again.

CHAPTER 14:

HOLD ON, BOYS

Manuel was grateful that the time of temptation with Teivel had passed. Although it exhausted him, he came out of it with a new authority and confidence. He knew that by resisting Teivel's offers of dark power and worldly success, he had stepped into his calling to walk in the light of the Creator and all of the authority it would take to accomplish the tasks set before him. There would be a greater temptation and enticement to walk away all together when the ultimate sacrifice became required. Also, the temptation to use the miraculous gifts he was given for personal gratification. To Manuel, the thought was incomprehensible. He was devoted to the plan that would allow every man to walk in their gifting from the elevated realm. Humankind had become numb and undiscerning to everything available to them. Manuel came to bring vision and light into the darkness. Not only was he going to illuminate a path to the Designer of all life, but he would intentionally bring His Kingdom to earth.

Manuel thought of Sibyl and how she had always seen and known he was outstanding. Every year on his birthday, she sent a gift and often called. Sibyl could see Manuel for who he truly was. It was comforting to have someone look into his soul and understand the weight he carried. So few did. Even his beloved parents, Joey and Miryam, caught up in the day-to-day routine of life and raising kids, often failed to see where Manuel was in his supernatural development. How could they? Chosen and precious as they may be, they were not tuned in to the Creator the way Manuel was and could not possibly know every moment what was happening in the spiritual realm. Of course, they knew of his giftings and witnessed his wondrous abilities, but Aunt Sibyl, as she had become, always looked at him with reverence and carried the depth of who he was on the surface.

It had been over a month since Manuel had seen his cousins. Johnny continued his message of directing people to the now revealed One, who would make all things new. Johnny had always been bold in calling out what was wrong with the world, but since announcing Manuel on his channel, he had a new level of confidence. Calling out Governor Gale Tetrarch for his adulterous relationship with his brother's wife and marrying her after his mysterious death, Johnny made blatant accusations regarding the dysfunction of their situation. He also challenged the Governor to acknowledge the rumors of his sexual orientation. Governor Tetrarch was not amused and instructed authorities to watch Johnny and arrest him upon any slight offense that would get him off the airwaves. It wasn't long before they succeeded. With trumped-up charges, officials took Johnny into custody.

Scout Nikkos could taste the story. "Influencer Incarcerated," the headline would read. It was perfect for Scout; now, he wouldn't have to search for Johnny but could go directly to the source in jail. Having interviewed some of his devotees, he could simply reach out to them for follow-up quotes regarding their precious *voice in the wasteland* now. Manuel was saddened by his cousin's confinement but knew that this was just the beginning of powers opposing the mission. He also knew that he would need friends and supporters directly with him to accomplish all of the details of these appointed days.

Calling Jim and Jack, Manuel told them to prepare for a road trip. "We're going to need a few more guys," he said. Being led by the Essence of the Creator, Manuel already knew where to look for the men. Starting at the docks 40 minutes from Netzer where Jim worked, he went alone to find someone who would be a rock for him. Someone who would be strong and bring passion to every situation. Manuel walked without issue or resistance straight past all security and protocol into the office of the owner of Simon's Seafood, Inc. Heading straight for the door, the executive secretary tried to stop him.

"Um, Sir… excuse me! You can't go in there!" Manuel smiled at her and just walked in. Simon was behind his desk. Looking up, he growled.

"What the hell is this?" His secretary came rushing in.

"Simon, I'm sorry… this guy just…"

"Who do you think you are?" Simon seethed.

"Simon," Manuel looked at him with deep love in his eyes. No one looked at Simon with deep love in their eyes. Simon was a gruff fisherman turned businessman as his single fishing boat turned into a fleet. Solid Obsidian Magazine had awarded him the most successful black man of the year– twice. He employed both Jim and Jack, although Jack was just a seasonal employee. Surrounded by success and yes-men, Simon was not used to people simply walking into his office without permission or doing anything else without his permission. Just then, Simon's brother Andrew came into the office with files of paperwork for Simon to sign. He didn't look up from the papers or notice the tension in the room.

"So… I have the current NOAA reports for your review and told Judy I would have an answer for her by noon regarding the–" Andrew looked up to see Manuel standing in the room. He knew him immediately. Dropping the papers, he scrambled to pick them up but couldn't take his eyes off of Manuel.

"Hello, Andrew," Manuel greeted.

"How do you know Andrew?" Simon barked. Turning to his brother, he inquired, "Who is this guy, Drew?" Andrew halted when his eyes met Manuel's.

"Hi," he whispered.

"Drew!" Simon snapped, "Snap out of it! What the hell is wrong with you?" Manuel bent down and started picking up the scattered papers. He began putting them in perfect order. Andrew didn't move to help but noticed the order in which Manuel was arranging the pieces.

"It's true," he muttered.

"What's true? What is this?" Turning to Manuel, he barked, "Would you like to explain to me what's going on here?" Simon's secretary quietly backed out of the room.

"Andrew," Manuel smiled, "Would you like to explain to your brother what's going on here?"

Andrew cleared his throat, accepting the ordered papers Manuel was handing him. Looking at Simon and shaking his head back to reality, Andrew wondered how to begin. He had never shared with his power-driven brother the online musings of the Influencer, Johnny. Looking into Manuel's eyes, a calm came over him. Suddenly, it didn't matter what Simon would think. He felt such assurance that everything Johnny shared was genuine. It was a presence he had never experienced before.

"This," he began, "is the Redeemer of the world."

"The redeem– the what? Oh, Andrew, what the hell?" Simon was disturbed. He had work to do. Manuel walked over to Andrew and embraced him. Andrew clung to Manuel, careful not to drop the papers again. "So, you guys know each other from where?" Simon pressed.

"We've never met," Manuel answered.

"You've never met," Simon repeated sarcastically.

"Nope," Manuel grinned. "But I know you both very well."

Simon was tired of the games. "Well, I assume you do. Anyone who's read a business magazine from the Tri-State Region in the last decade would probably know plenty. But what brings you barging in here today?"

"Was I barging, Simon?" Manuel teased. "It was more like a stroll."

"Simon!" Andrew interrupted, "Seriously, this is the Redeemer. He's come to change the political climate and grant deliverance to the world."

"Deliverance to the world? Do you hear yourself, Drew?"

Simon knew of the prophecies. He knew that many people lived in the hope of One who would come and liberate not just their region but the whole world from big brother and the like. It all sounded too good to be true, but

he hoped in the recesses of his soul that somehow it could be. Simon was tired. Hustling in the fishing industry since he could hold a rope, all he knew was the physical labor of earning a dollar. He was fortunate to be doing alright with a successful business and kept his family well above water with his passionate pursuits.

"Simon, son of Jonah, I've come to bring you with me." Simon was starting to lose it.

"Alright, lunatic, time to go. I don't know what my brother has shared with you, but obviously, knowing my father's name is not going to make me believe you are some messiah." Picking up the phone, Simon called security.

"Simon! Listen to him…" Andrew opposed. Manuel hung his head and chuckled.

"See, this is why I love you, Simon. This is why I need you."

"The only thing you need is a straitjacket," mumbling under his breath Simon continued, "barging into my office…strolling, he says–the nerve– Yeah, Simon here. Get security up to my office pronto. We've got some whack job spewing nonsense." Andrew fell at Manuel's feet and embraced his legs. Simon halted. What had gotten into Andrew? How could he be so unmanly?

"Please, forgive him," Andrew pleaded. "He's worked so hard for so long; he doesn't understand who you are. He provides everything for all of us and doesn't stop to know what's going on outside of this dockyard." Manuel patted Andrew's shoulders and encouraged him to rise. Simon was dumbfounded. He really didn't know what was going on outside of this yard. He looked again at the man standing in his office. His eyes looked into Manuel's for the first time. Manuel looked at him with such compassion. He had actually said he loved him, and stranger yet, Simon believed him somehow. He could feel it. What was this warmth flooding him? He shook his head and set the phone down.

"What's going on here?" he softened.

"I'm going to call you my Rock," Manuel said. Something in Simon's chest puffed up. He was a rock. He was always the one to rush to the rescue of anyone in his family that needed it. "I see you, Simon. I see how hard you work and your innermost desires. I know about your wife and the sickness her mother has endured. I know all that you've sacrificed to make this business successful even though your real dream would have been to go to school." Simon was speechless. He never told anyone about his dream to be educated formally. No one. Ever. "I know about your difficulty sleeping and how you envy men who don't carry such weight." Simon felt himself choking up. He coughed, commanding his body to conform.

"Who did you say you are?" Simon asked.

"I am Emmanuel Paladin. I have come to bring an end to the tyranny of the world and show the way to peace. It's going to be quite a task, and I need a man like you beside me. Will you come?" Just then, security barged into the office and reached to handcuff Manuel, escorting him off the premises.

"Wait, wait," Simon interrupted. "Just wait." Looking at his brother, he could see the hope and excitement in his eyes. He looked back at Manuel and saw love and a different kind of leadership. "Just…leave him alone. Never mind." Returning to his brother, he asked, "You knew about this guy?"

"I saw him online, but I never dreamed he would walk through our doors."

"Why didn't you mention it? This whole redemption plan thing– and someone who could– why didn't you say something?"

"When, Simon?" Andrew defended, "Things are so driven around here, and you demand perfection from all of us. When would I have told you about something I had been following online? When would you have listened to it?"

Simon took a deep breath and sat down behind his desk. He looked at all of the papers and stacks of things that needed his attention. He couldn't wrap his head around leaving on some unplanned trip, as much as he would like one. Who would he trust to run things? How could he stay on top if he left? How could he even be considering– Looking back at Manuel's face, seeing him grin like he knew everything Simon was thinking, Simon paused.

'His rock, huh? Well, that was something that made sense. But I'm not sure this guy is actually…' Looking at Manuel, it was hard to deny his presence. He stood relatively silent, almost swaying in a carefree manner.

"Here's the thing, Simon. I know your soul is craving an adventure. I know you ask yourself every day if you have what it takes to stay on top of the business world. You are so exhausted by this rat race that you would trade it all in a minute if you could know that your family would be okay." Simon could not believe the depth of understanding this man had of him. It was as if he saw directly to the depths of his being and read them like a book. "I assure you, brother, coming on this trip will not only answer all of your unspoken questions but meet your deepest desires. Granted, you'll face your greatest challenges– but you are created to rise to these challenges, Simon. Most men never get the opportunity to step out and embrace them. Come, or regret it for the rest of your life." Simon sat in silence for what seemed like forever. Andrew was so envious but secretly hoped his brother would throw all caution to the wind and grab the moment with both hands.

"You're insane," Simon concluded.

"Some will say so," Manuel agreed.

"How long is this *adventure*?"

"Now, Simon, you can't put these things on a clock."

Simon squinted his eyes. He couldn't help but like Manuel. He had cajones. Simon was used to being the mightiest force in the room– but this guy. This guy could be some fun. Simon sighed at the thought of actually having any fun. How would he tell his wife?

'She probably won't mind,' he thought. It had been so long since they had engaged in their marriage. She took care of her ailing mother, and Simon was obsessed with the business. Simon started slowly nodding.

"All right," he said. Andrew's mouth dropped. "I will inform the board that I will be taking an extended leave. Andrew, I'm giving you the final word on issues that cannot be resolved in-house, and I will have my phone on me at all times." Oh, how Andrew longed to go also. Manuel knew it.

"Andrew," Manuel comforted, "Don't think that your position here is any less important than one out on the road. Simon couldn't go if he didn't have someone he trusted here. He wouldn't have received me the way he did if it weren't for you. You have a role to play. You're a part of this team."

"If you need me at any time–" Andrew responded.

"I know, friend. I know. Thank you." Returning to Simon, he said, "Pack your things, Rocko." Manuel chuckled and headed for the door. "I'll call you when we're ready to take off."

"Let me give you my number," Simon said.

"You've got much to learn," Manuel said and left. Simon turned to Andrew with a puzzled look on his face.

~~~

Johnny's followers wanted to hear from Manuel. Little had been seen of him since he was introduced. Word spread, and people wanted to hear more from him, not merely of him. Manuel knew that the time was coming but had not quite come for him to go universal with his spiritual revelation and leadership. He knew that once he revealed himself entirely, the political wolves would be at his door, nipping at his heels. He knew that everyone who chose to be associated with him would suddenly become a target. He did not look forward to the harassment they and their families would endure.

The Paladins had a wedding to attend in the Region of Circuit. Manuel picked up Miryam and some of his siblings that were available to go. He knew Jim and Jack would be there. He invited Simon as a light-hearted opportunity to get to know each other better in a feel-good environment. Simon brought his wife, who was grateful for a day away from the worry and affliction that came from caring for her ill mother. When Jim saw his boss, Simon, walk in, he became uneasy. After all, he had just requested an extended leave of absence and was now going to be seen by the top dog living it up at a celebration. "Don't worry," Manuel assured him. "He's going to be coming with us on our trip. I wanted him to begin to feel at ease with us."

"Coming with us?!" Jim balked. "My boss? Are you kidding?! Why him?" Manuel put his hand on Jim's shoulder and took a deep breath, encouraging him to mimic.
~~~

"Look, Jim, you're going to have to trust me. You're going to see me make a lot of decisions that won't always make sense, and I need you to loosen up and calm down." Somehow, even when Manuel was firmly direct, he had a way of speaking that made others want to comply.

"All right. It's just– dude, you could have warned me."

"He's nobody's boss on this trip, Jimmy. He's just a guy. Don't worry. He's one of us."

"Simon? One of us? Oh, man, sometimes I wonder about you, Manny." Manuel laughed and greeted Simon and his wife. The wedding reception was grand and went into the evening. Miryam loved having family about her and wished that Joey could be there to enjoy it. She imagined dancing with him and sharing cake. Looking at her boys and their father's likeness in them brought warmth and comfort in his loss. Miryam noticed that the parents of the bride were in a heated discussion. She tried not to pry but couldn't help watching the frustration between them. What could be worth getting upset on a day like today? She saw some servers scrambling and then saw the mother of the bride shrug her shoulders in defeat. Miryam grabbed a passing server.

"What's going on over there?"

"Oh, I'm sorry, Ma'am. They've run out of wine, and I think the parents are upset by that."

"I see." Miryam knew that this party was far from over. Even though wine wasn't a must for a good time, she could see that the hosts wanted to provide their guests with every courtesy. Miryam started searching the room for Manuel. By the time her eyes found him, he was looking straight at her. He began to head in her direction before she could even summon him.

"You rang," he teased.

"They have run out of wine," she informed.

"Woman," Manuel objected, "what does that have to do with me?" He knew what she wanted him to do. Manuel remembered the deserts at the family reunion the summer he was 12 years old. He knew his mother well. She hated for anyone to be disappointed. "My time hasn't come," he told her.

Miryam didn't speak a word but looked at her son. Manuel looked around the whole room, avoiding his mother's eyes. He could bear no more than 15 full seconds of silence before looking over at her. Miryam was giving him the Mom look. A grown man or not– she knew he would not disregard her.

Grabbing the next server that walked by, Miryam said, "This is my son. Do whatever he tells you." Manuel rolled his eyes and walked with the server towards the kitchen. Jack saw Miryam and Manuel talking, and then Manuel walking with a server toward the kitchen. Sensing something was going on, he rushed over to follow his cousin into the server's area. Manuel told the server to fill the empty wine barrels with water. The server looked at him sideways. "Dude, please, just… fill these barrels with water." Jack pulled out his phone and started video recording.

The servers were hoping the food service manager wouldn't catch them fulfilling this ridiculous request. They figured, 'the customer is always right,' and weren't going to argue with the people paying the bill. Jack caught their expressions and then filling the barrels with water. He got a shot of an empty wine barrel and the spout from the sink they were using to fill them just for good measure. Manuel noticed Jack but said nothing. The servants filled the barrels to the brim. When they finished, Manuel instructed, "Now draw some out and take it to the father of the bride." They thought he was crazy and felt sure to lose their jobs for this prank. They took it. As they poured the beverage into the father's glass, a rich red wine flowed into his glass. The father looked surprised but tasted it. With relief, he raised a glass to the caterer and toasted the bride and groom.

"At most events, the best wine is served first. When everyone has had their fill, and people feel good, they start serving the lesser wine to save a buck. But tonight, we are receiving the best wine last! Let's celebrate! To the bride and groom!"

Jack couldn't believe what he had caught on camera. Manuel looked over to Miryam. Miryam stood smiling with a sense of satisfaction. Jack showed the video to Jim, Simon, and his wife. They were amazed and looked over at Manuel. Manuel said, "Hold on, boys. This is just the beginning."

CHAPTER 15:

WOUNDED SOULS

Scout Nikkos was granted a 20-minute audience with Johnny. Not much time for the average reporter to pull out enough for a substantial story, but Scout was not the average reporter. He had already written his back story with supporting testimonials. Now, he just needed to hear from the radical himself. Scout wanted the bottom line on why Johnny would threaten his prominent position and followers to muddle himself with trash topics like Governor Tetrarch's sex-life and controversy surrounding his dead brother's wife. Who was this "*redeemer*" supposed to be, and what was the truth to these cooked-up charges he was facing?

Johnny continued to do what Johnny did best; he pointed to Manuel. "Let me try to put it as simply as I can for you, Nikkos. None of that crap matters. The only thing that matters is the One who has come. See, now– just– stay with me. Before anything existed, before earth as we know it, this One existed. He existed with the Creator of all things and *was* the Creator of all things. Big bang theory, eternal inflation, the oscillating universe, or whatever– it was all started with Him. He was there at the start of all things, and all things were done through Him, by Him. Okay? In Him– was life. And that life was the light of humankind. He is the light that will shine in all the darkness of this wasteland we have come to know. Government, deceit, murder, manipulation, selfishness, and greed. The light of the universe and beyond has come to bring life and light to this dark world!"

"Okay," Scout allowed trying to make sense for his readers. "So, you… you are a part of the light?" Johnny buried his face in his hands. Feeling the frustration of so much to tell and a limited time to tell it, he corrected Scout.

"No, no. I came first merely to act as a witness to the light. To the Truth. The true light, redemption, and answer. He gives revelation to everyone."

"Everyone?"

"Yes, Nikkos. Everyone. Anyone who seeks the Truth and isn't bound by darkness and the wickedness that ensnares so easily."

"Wickedness that ensnares– that's good."

"No, that's bad."

"Right, right, but I mean– it's good. Never mind. So, you've announced on your channel that this guy, your cousin, in fact– Emmanuel Paladin– you're saying he is the *One.* He's going to bring the revelation of *Truth.*" Johnny felt the Essence of the Creator land heavily upon him. He relaxed and allowed himself to lean into it. Time didn't matter within the presence. Twenty minutes or two felt like a calm refreshing. Prison bars could not hold love out or rob him of the peace that the Essence brought. Johnny started foretelling.

"The true light has become flesh and lives among us. He came to us because we are His, but not all will receive Him. Those who do receive Him will be given the right to become *children* to the Creator. Theos Himself. Children that haven't been born by the will of a man or by the lust of the flesh. But by divine love. Children…who can run to their papa. Children who are embraced and forgiven for the most horrendous things."

Scout could see that Johnny had slipped into another state. He didn't dare interrupt him, but he was also confident that either Johnny had lost his mind or tapped into something completely other.

"His importance will be seen," Johnny continued. "His importance as the only Son of the Maker of all things, full of grace and truth. This is it. *This is it.* From the fullness of this One, we can all receive grace upon grace upon grace. Unearned and unmerited favor." Johnny was stirring now and walking about his cell like a caged animal. He wasn't hysterical but calm and definitive. "We've all been slaves to this law that we could not possibly live up to or fulfill. The law was given by those who came before, 'Don't do this, make it like that,' but… *grace.* Grace and truth will come through the One. Through Manuel." Johnny was crying now, and Scout felt as though he was in someone's private inner sanctum. Cell or no cell, this place was sacred. "No one has ever seen the Creator. The ONLY Creator, Theos… but He is making Himself known. Now. In this time."

"Through Manuel?"

"Through the One." Johnny allowed his head to drop back. He appeared to be having a love fest with someone Scout couldn't see. It was intimate and real– for Johnny, at least. Scout could swear that he felt a warm embrace enveloping him. For a moment, he allowed himself to breathe it in. This guy was right. Or completely spun. Maybe it was all an act to get out of the charges pressed against him. Scout felt the sincerity of the moment and decided right then he needed to interview Manuel Paladin. His cell phone started buzzing on silent and broke the moment. The notification read, "Mother of missing kids arrested! Cease all other articles. Tickets waiting for you at airport. Flying to Government City."

Scout was torn. Everyone in the Union Empire had been following the story of Stacey Dreggs, a mother whose three children had been missing for months. Originally from Government City, the woman had relocated with her three children to pursue a relationship she started online. After the mysterious death of her new lover's wife, the couple was found in the Bahamas with no children in tow. Further investigation showed that no one knew where or when the children had disappeared. Neighbors had last seen the children with the couple at least a month before being tracked to the Bahamas. Scout, like many other reporters, had covered the story at length. He was ready to rush to the airport but found himself truly invested in Johnny. Shaking his hand through the bars, he wished Johnny well and said he hoped they would meet again. 'Why would I say that? I never say that.'

"Tell the fortunate news," Johnny pled. "Tell it well, Nikkos." Scout just nodded, not knowing when he would be allowed to publish with this latest Dreggs development.

~~~

After his ordeal with Teivel at the cabin, Manuel returned to Netzer, walking in a new level of dynamic power. Jack posted the video of the phenomenon at the wedding to a mixed response. Most people thought it was doctored and believed special effects were used. Even so, it caused enough of a reaction that Manuel was developing a following of his own. Johnny's followers were quick to convert. New eyes were skeptical and wanted more evidence. Manuel knew it was time to head out on the road, but he had one stop to make first. Sunday morning, he headed to the church that Joey and Miryam had raised them in. He sat through the service and slipped into the back, where he knew the board, elders, and pastors gathered once a month for lunch. Most of them knew Manuel. He had gained a loving reputation over the years as a devoted son and a dependable member of the congregation. Manuel had worked with the youth and was always available at the most critical times. As the men settled and readied to start the meeting, Manuel asked the Pastor if he could share something with the group. This was uncustomary, but having known Manuel since his youth, he trusted it wouldn't be anything outlandish and decided to grant the boy's request. Some of them had seen the video from the wedding, while others wondered if it would be an announcement about Johnny and his arrest.

Manuel took a deep breath and picked up a book of the Ancient Writings. The men quieted. Manuel didn't say a word but opened it to a familiar section and started reading. Instantly, the men knew the passage from one of the most esteemed prophets to have ever lived.

"The Spirit of the Creator is on me,
because He has anointed me
to proclaim good news to the poor.
~~~

He has sent me to proclaim freedom for the prisoners
and recovery of sight for the blind,
to set the oppressed free,
to proclaim the year of His favor."

Manuel closed the book and paused. The room respectfully waited with all eyes fastened upon him. Manuel looked up and began, "Today, this prophecy is fulfilled in your presence." Some of the men were puzzled, and a couple appalled that he had been able to just walk in and speak. Those who had seen the video and heard the buzz about him knew exactly what he was saying. He was claiming to be the long-awaited Redeemer of the world. God incarnate. Manuel Paladin- contractor. The room started to bustle. They were whispering to each other under their breath and questioning.

"Is he saying what I think he's saying?"

"Isn't this Joey's son?" Manuel addressed them again.

"Hearing this, I'm sure some of you are going to want to me show you some sign or wonder. Like, *do here what you did at the wedding*. But I'm telling you the truth– no prophet is accepted in his hometown. It wouldn't matter if I did."

The Pastor stood and attempted to settle the group. "Now, Manuel… you asked me to let you speak today, and as a kindness, in faith, I trusted you to do so. But what is this nonsense you are suggesting?"

"I am right here among you, but you doubt that I may be who I say I am. There are people online and in other towns who are quick to accept me, but you, who've known me my whole life, are whispering among yourselves and doubting the video to be true." At this, the men became indignant.

"What is this?" an elder seethed.

"Who are you saying you are, exactly?" the Pastor questioned, although he feared he knew the answer.

"I'm not suggesting anything, Pastor. I'm telling you that today, this prophecy is fulfilled. I am the anointed One, sent by the Creator, to save humankind. I am His Son. The Son of Theos."

"Do we look like we need saving to you?" One board member objected.

"Look, young man, some of us have been on this board since before you were born. You have the nerve to come in here– unannounced– and claim to be a prophet? A savior? Savior from what?"

"From the consequence of your choices that lead you to a separation from the Creator and to torment beyond what you can conceive. Not just after death but here, now, in this life."

The group grew furious. Some men rose and headed towards Manuel with the intent of physically removing him. Those with more level heads blocked them.

"Why are you so upset? You've read the same Ancient Writings that I have. You knew that someone would come. Didn't you? Or did you not actually believe what you've taught week after week? What you claimed to live your lives by?"

"Are you serious," one man piped up, "Who do you think you are, speaking to us this way?"

"Who do the Ancient Writings say I am?"

"That's it. We have legitimate business to attend. Pastor, if you don't have this con artist removed, I will." Several men felt insulted and rose more than willing to get rid of Manuel. As the group reached the front to drive him out, they found themselves grasping only each other. Looking around, they slowly realized that Manuel had disappeared. Looking under the table and behind each other's backs, they rushed and even checked the door. Manuel had vanished.

"What the?"

"You don't suppose–"

~~~

Manuel bought a used white eight-passenger R.V. and started to gather his guys. He picked Jim and Jack up first. Simon had his wife drop him off to meet them. They decided to stop at Walmart to grab some snacks and drinks for the road. Manuel was fortunate to have saved some money knowing that he would be taking this journey someday, but he didn't have enough to pay for everything, always, for as long as they would be gone. Still, he decided to treat the guys to this first round of food for the road. He wasn't worried. His trust in the Creator secured the fact that there would always be enough for everything they would ever need; the guys, however, would be stretched in learning this. Jack was like a kid in a candy store. This was an adventure, and heading out with a group of guys was right up his alley. Jim was less than thrilled that his boss was along for the ride but was looking forward to a much-needed break and time with his brother and cousin. Simon, on the other hand, still wasn't sure what he had signed up for and why, exactly, he had agreed to come.

The guys each gathered their supplies and found themselves assembled on the chip aisle. As they joked around and debated between flavors, a sort of hissing distracted them all. Once the sound had their attention, they turned to see a man coming directly towards Manuel with a look of possession in his eyes. He hadn't showered in months. His hair was matting, and Simon instantly thought, 'drugs.' He was curious how Manuel would handle him, but Manuel didn't *handle* him at all. Instead, he turned directly toward the man and stepped away from his cart. Jack whipped out his phone and started recording. Manuel made eye contact, and the man became bothered.

"I know who you are. I *know* who you are. I know. I know. I know who *you* are." The man was almost dancing in circles in the aisle. As he did, his eyes never left Manuel's. "GO AWAY!" the man yelled. People were starting
~~~

to stop now and watch. "What do you want with us, Emmanuel? Have you come to destroy us?"

The guys were exchanging glances, and Simon had decided he wouldn't put up with much more. This guy was obviously crazy and on drugs. He needed to be sent away or swatted like a gnat. Manuel put his hand up towards Simon, knowing what he was thinking. The man continued.

"I KNOW WHO YOU ARE! The Anointed One of Theos!"

"Be quiet," Manuel said sternly. "Come out of him!" The man was thrown to the ground and started dry heaving. People were gawking and judging him. He coughed several times, and Manuel stepped to him, bending down to help him up-; the man looked at him with clear eyes.

"What… what did you just do?" he asked. Smiling, Manuel put his arm around the man's shoulders.

"Oh, you know… just got rid of those soul suckers that were running the show." The man looked at Manuel and then down at himself. Noticing the filth he had become, he was suddenly embarrassed.

"Oh, wow… I– I think I– gosh." Putting his hand to his forehead, he rubbed it as though remembering how he came to be in such a state. All of the people were in awe and whispering to each other. This man had been walking the local streets for as long as some of them could remember. Now, here he was, speaking clearly, unlike his usual mumbling self.

"I would encourage you to take a shower," Manuel said, "and call your daughter. She will be relieved to hear from you." The man nodded in agreement and started to cry. "Hey, hey," Manuel comforted. "You're going to be okay now. Just call your daughter, all right?" With a final hug as though the man didn't even smell, Manuel returned to his cart. He acted like the crowd that had gathered didn't even have to do with him. Jack ended the video and followed Manuel out of the aisle. The other guys did, too. Before they hit the check stand, Jack was uploading the video to YouTube. He called the channel Redeemer Roadtrip and decided he would upload anything more that might happen. Returning to the R.V., Simon was the first to speak.

"Okay, man. Spill it." Manuel was putting his groceries away.

"Spill what?"

"No, no, no. You don't get to act nonchalant. That guy was crazy, man, and you just…"

"He wasn't crazy," Manuel corrected. "He was tormented. Don't be so quick to call people crazy, Simon."

"People who aren't crazy bathe themselves and hold jobs."

"That's your definition." Manuel turned toward the guys and their questioning eyes. "We have a body, a soul, and a spirit. All of them need care. Our soul– our mind, our will, and our emotions– gets wounded. We experience trauma, and then we aren't operating from a healthy place. Everything we experience after that filters through this wound. We see things differently as a result, and we don't make the right-minded choices we normally would because… we are walking wounded. Do you understand?" The guys nodded but only somewhat followed. It made sense when he said it, but they hoped he wouldn't ask them to repeat it. "I have come into the world to resolve it of its wounds. I will make way for people to not only be forgiven of all that's gone wrong but *restored.* Truly. Restored." Jack grinned from ear to ear. He looked at his brother like a kid on Christmas morning. Jim was processing what was said, and Simon was surprisingly clear on the matter.

"I'm sorry," Simon said. "I've never… I've never thought about that or looked at people as having been wounded in some way."

"It changes everything," Manuel enlightened. "We've all been wounded in some way. Some of us recover, and some of us– don't. That man didn't."

"So, you just told him to be quiet and then…" Simon was at a loss for words.

"I told the demons to come out of him." The guys got quiet and looked at Manuel. He was completely serious.

"The demons," Simon repeated. "Like… evil spirits."

"Yes, Simon. When we miss the mark or break the spiritual laws in some way, demons are given the legal right to torment us. Even when someone else commits some offense against us and we are caught up in the wickedness of it all in our thoughts, intentions towards them, or bitterness lasting years later– that opens the door to them coming in. Everyone deals with it. That man is not special."

"You're saying… I have demons."

"And me?" Jack chimed in.

"A great man once wrote,

'There is no one righteous, not even one;
there is no one who understands;
there is no one who seeks the Higher Power.
All have turned away,
they have together become worthless;
there is no one who does good,
not even one.'"

"But that's not true," Simon disagreed. "There are plenty of good people who don't know or believe in the Creator."

"Their throats are open graves;
their tongues practice deceit.
The poison of vipers is on their lips.
Their mouths are full of cursing and bitterness.
Their feet are swift to shed blood;
ruin and misery mark their ways

and the way of peace they do not know.
There is no reverence before their eyes."

Manuel looked discerningly at his new friend, "Sound like anyone you know?"

"Sounds like a lot of people I know, but… that doesn't mean they aren't good people."

"I'm not saying they're not good people, Simon. I'm saying everyone has fallen short and missed the mark in life. That causes wounds. Everyone is worth the opportunity to be healed from those wounds and understand a better way."

Simon couldn't argue with that. He, for one, would be glad to lay down some of the anger he struggled with, and if this guy had the way to do that, he wanted to find out how. There was something about Manuel that Simon, well, loved. He was so honest and straightforward but not brutal in his delivery of anything. Simon wondered if he might come to a place someday when he could flow in the knowledge that Manuel had and even help set people free from their wounds. Simon was always so zealous. His delivery almost always hit like a punch, even when he didn't mean for it to. He didn't want to ask at that moment; he was still finding his way in this lot, but he wanted Manuel to kick his demons to the curb, too. He wondered how he would do it and if he would feel any different afterward.

CHAPTER 16:

AND THUS, IT BEGINS

Simon's mind was processing the information Manuel had given them and playing the scene of the man in Walmart over and over. He was curious about any operating demons in his own life. Simon wanted to know more but wasn't willing to go after his demons quite yet. He still wasn't sure that he had any and how that worked, but it did make him wonder about his mother-in-law and the illness that kept her impaired for so long. Manuel knew Simon was processing. He started the R.V. and began to drive. Jim and Jack were in the back, already digging into some of the snacks.

"Hey, guys, we're going to be eating pretty quick. Don't eat too much," Manuel warned. Simon sat contemplatively in the passenger's seat.

"So, these demons," he began, "they made that man… sick."

"Yep," Manuel replied, knowing where Simon was going.

"Do they cause any other kinds of illnesses?" Manuel smiled and glanced over at Simon.

"Yep." Manuel wanted him to say it. They drove for another mile or so before Simon spoke again.

"So, you made them go with just a word…" Simon was beating around the bush.

"Yep."

Jack was checking the status of his most recent post. "Whoa! Guys, check this out!! I just posted the Walmart deal, and it's already got 157 views! I posted it like 25 minutes ago. That's crazy."

"How many did the wedding post get?" Jim asked.

"It's still getting hits, but that one has caused a lot of controversies. Arguments about whether or not it's real."

"Manuel," Simon dared, "My mother-in-law has been sick for several years. My wife– well, she stays home to care for her, and it has really caused her a lot of grief and stress." Simon softened and looked out the side window, "It's affected our marriage. My wife is exhausted all the time, and doctors don't help." Looking up, he realized they were turning into his neighborhood. He shot a glance over at Manuel.

"You were saying?" Manuel encouraged him to continue. Simon didn't continue. He watched as Manuel made every correct turn until he pulled up directly in front of Simon's house. Simon's heart beat faster. Things had suddenly become very personal.

"How did you know where I live?" he asked.

"Simon, really? Are we still there?" Manuel took a deep breath and looked at the house. "Would you like to give your wife a head's up, or are we good to just go in?"

"Why don't you give me a minute?" Simon responded. Heading into the house, he wondered how he would explain to his wife. She had dropped him off not an hour earlier, and now here he was, back again. She would most likely think he forgot something. Should he go into the whole story about the man at Walmart? She had been present at the wedding, but Simon wasn't sure she caught the whole of what happened. Simon's wife was upset that he was leaving her alone to care for her mother for who knew how long, and now he was bringing a group of guys home unannounced. She was startled to see him. Coming out of her mother's bedroom, she closed the door as softly as she could. Puzzled, she looked at him but didn't even speak. Words had become so few between them that looks did most of their communication.

"Honey, I have Manuel in the car. He'd like to come in and talk to your mom for a minute."

"Talk to my mom? Simon…" her tone was exasperated. It was as if their conversation hadn't just started but was the continuation of a million disagreements they had had before. "I just got her to sleep. She had a rough night, and you know that means I had a rough night. What is this about? Why would he want to meet my mother? What are you thinking?"

"I know, I know… I'm sorry. But look. Something is going on here– something I don't know how to explain just yet but– Manuel. He's…"

Simon didn't have the words, so he just went straight to the point. "Look, Manuel has some sort of gift. He produced wine out of nothing at that wedding we went to, and just now, at Walmart, he made this crazy guy sane. Well, he wasn't crazy, he wasn't crazy." He was losing her. "Honey, Manuel claims to be sent by the Creator to redeem the world."

"Oh, my god, Simon–"

"No, wait. I know. I know it sounds crazy. But he has this theory about demons, and I watched him bring this guy from– *torment*– into clarity." Simon's wife began to tear. She was exhausted beyond her ability to cope with even an ounce more, and now her rock, her husband, was suggesting what? That some guy come in and kick demons out of her mother?

"Demons, Simon? Seriously?" She shook her head and knew that he wasn't going to quit until she let them in.

"Honey, I know that your mother is in torment. I know that you have struggled, and I know that, as a result, we have. I'm just saying, why not give this guy a shot. It can't hurt, right?!"

"So, you want to wake her up?" Throwing her hands up, she gave in. "Go ahead. Whatever. You're going to do whatever you want to do anyway." She waved him on, "But so help me, Simon, if you make a mess for me to deal with and then run off with your new buddies, I swear–" Simon wished he could say that wasn't exactly what he was going to do, but he honestly had no idea what was going to happen. He went to the front door and waved Manuel in. Jim and Jack came bounding in behind him.

"Look, guys, look–" it was clear to Jim that this wasn't the same man he had seen at work day after day. This man was broken and troubled. This man was tender and concerned about his wife. "Please be quiet. My wife is frayed, and it's been a rough night. Well, it's been rough for years. So just, don't go bounding up there, okay?"

"Jack, I want you and Jim to wait down here," Manuel instructed. Jack looked like a little kid who had just had his balloon taken away, but he respected Manuel. Opening his phone to the camera, he clicked the video mode and handed it to Simon. Simon wasn't comfortable with the thought of filming whatever was about to happen. It felt far too invasive. Still, for their family history, it would be incredible to have something miraculous on video. He refused Jack but secretly decided to use his own phone. Simon led Manuel up the stairs and to his mother-in-law's door. Looking at Manuel, he began to speak, but Manuel just placed a hand on his shoulder. "Simon, don't worry. Open the door."

Stepping into the room, it was overly warm. The woman was easily chilled and looked to be about 100 years old. Manuel stepped to the side of her bed and sat down on its edge. Simon could feel his heart pounding out of his chest. His wife came in and anxiously stood on the other side of the bed. If her mother opened her eyes, she didn't want her to see the face of a stranger first thing. Simon started recording. Manuel looked up and closed his eyes. He looked as if he was seeking something or someone. Laying his hand on top of the woman's hands, she opened her eyes. Looking at him, a look of joy came over her face. "Oh, hello…" she greeted him. Her voice sounded as if she had known him her whole life. Simon's wife looked to him and then back to her mother.

"Mama, this is–"

"Hello, Carolyn," Manuel greeted her. Carolyn smiled. She suddenly looked like a five-year-old girl inside an old woman's body. Her face lit up, and she put her second hand on top of Manuel's. "It's time to get up now. Are you ready?" Carolyn nodded and closed her eyes in anticipation. Manuel simply spoke to the fever and commanded it to go. Upon the rebuke, Carolyn opened her eyes. She looked at Manuel and smiled a huge toothless grin. She looked at her daughter and did a double-take as though she had not seen her in quite some time.

"Oh, baby," she said, "You look so worried." Dropping to her bedside, her daughter searched her face. She could not find any part of the ailing woman who had been their companion for these last years. Instead, Carolyn seemed to have had a facelift in a matter of moments. Manuel stood and offered her his hand to help her rise. "I don't need that," she quipped. "I can do it." Throwing off the covers, she stood to her feet. A bit embarrassed at wearing her pajamas, she announced, "Well, I don't know how you did it, son, but I thank you. Now, go downstairs and let me get dressed. I'll fix you all something to eat!" Shooing them out of the room, Carolyn started bossing people immediately. Simon's wife ran to him and threw her head into his chest, weeping uncontrollably. Simon stood in silence, phone in hand, still recording. Manuel simply patted him on the back as he passed behind him out the door and down the stairs.

"What just happened?" Simon's wife asked.

"He rebuked the fever. And– it left." Simon clicked his phone off.

"Oh, Simon… you have to go with him." Looking up to her husband with gratitude, she insisted, "You have to. And it doesn't matter how long it takes. I think he is who he says he is. I think you have to help him in any way he needs you." Crying again, she tried to get the words out, "You've been my rock for so long– I couldn't have survived without you these past years. Now, I want you to do the same for him. You can call me and tell me everything that happens. Mama and I will be here waiting to hear from you. Oh, Simon– I've missed you so much." Simon wrapped his arms around his wife and held on tighter than he could ever remember having done before. Kissing her on the top of the head, he realized he was stepping into a whole new season of life. All his anger and frustration seemed to melt away with the delivery of these two women from their bondage. Simon went downstairs and fell at Manuel's knees.

"You don't want to take me with you, Boss. I've been missing the mark for so many years. I am the worst of all we've seen." Manuel placed his hand firmly on Simon's shoulder.

"Don't be afraid, Rocko. I know exactly who you are. From now on, instead of seafood, you're going to fish for men." Manuel turned and headed to the restroom.

After Carolyn had changed, she bounded down the stairs to find Jim and Jack standing in the living room. "Well, I don't know who you two are, but you're probably with the other one," she greeted. "Go wash your hands. I'm going to see what we've got in this place to fill your bellies." Manuel stepped out of the restroom.

"Rose soap. Mmm. See, I told you we were going to be eating soon."

Heading into the kitchen, he sat and enjoyed Carolyn telling stories and explaining where she had been for these years. Simon and his wife were in a bit of a haze but could not be happier. They gazed lovingly at each other and touched as the other passed. "Well, don't just stand there, girl; I raised you better than that. Set the table and pull out some drinks for our guests." Jack was always up for a meal and bounced into the kitchen.

"Did you get it; did you get it?" he asked Simon.

"Did I get what?"

"The video! Did you get it?" The video. Simon hadn't even thought about that aspect of the event.

"Oh… yeah," he said, "I did. I did get it."

"Can I post it?"

"Oh… I don't know, Jack. I mean, it's my mother-in-law and–"

"What's that?" Carolyn snooped.

"Mom," Simon discouraged, "I took a video of Manuel with you upstairs, and Jack wants to put it on the internet. But I don't think it would be wise to–"

"You want to make me famous?" Carolyn asked vivaciously. "I've waited a lifetime to be famous, and you don't want to do it, Simon?" She teased and instructed the lot, "Put it up, or post it, or run it…whatever you kids do. I want to see it!"

"Mom," Simon cautioned.

"Dagnabbit, Simon! I've been half dead for years, and now you're wanting to put a damper on me becoming a celebrity? Maybe Johnny Carson will want to have me on his show when he sees it!" The room erupted with laughter.

"What?" Jack asked, "Who's Johnny Carson?"

"Mom," Simon informed, "Johnny Carson is dead."

"What?" Carolyn's face dropped. "Ah, poor old goat. All right. David Letterman, then." Again, the room burst with laughter.

~~~

Jack posted Simon's video on the Redeemer Roadtrip channel. Followers and subscribers started coming out of the woodwork. Carolyn did become a celebrity. She started doing little clips, and people were remixing her words to digital tunes. She started her own YouTube channel and was teaching people how to cook. Carolyn would often add tidbits about how she had been healed and credited Manuel for her new life. Simon and his wife were sending loving texts and video chatting a few times a week. Word spread about Manuel throughout the Tri-State Region and beyond. People were amazed and talked about the authority with which he could give orders to impure spirits, and they would obey. Wherever they stopped and whatever they did, people would approach them with all kinds of sicknesses and issues. Laying his hands on each one, Manuel healed them. Moreover, demons came out of many people shouting, "You are the Son of the One True Creator!" Manuel saw Teivel around every corner and behind every demonic assignment. He loved people so much, and it pained him to see the suffering they endured simply by a lack of knowing how to get their souls healed. Frequently, he would stand in the midst of the gathering crowds and teach them. How hungry they were for hope. How desperate they had become for an answer to the pain and suffering life brought.
~~~

Some mornings, Manuel would rise before daybreak and walk to a solitary place. People would always be looking for him if they saw the R.V. in the area. They would try to get him to stay and not leave their town or region. He would always inform them, "I must tell others about the kingdom of Theos, too. That is why I've come." He and the guys would move on, and he would keep teaching to all who would listen. Jack was recording every word, healing, and impromptu enlightenment and posting them. Manuel was touching people right where they were. There was never any judgment in his delivery, but he didn't shy away from hard-hitting topics. Some people decided to quit their jobs and follow Manuel. They would caravan behind the R.V. and hang on every word he shared. Manuel encouraged them to return home and share what they had learned with others. Some would, but others insisted on driving whatever distance just to be near him. Manuel's fame was rising, and multitudes of people were commenting on the channel wanting him to head to their regions. People were posting their videos about how Manuel healed them and how their lives had changed. The revelation of demons tormenting people while having a legal right caused people to rethink how they were living, and communities were changing as a result.

People wanted to start supporting the men on their journey. They wanted to know where they could send funds that the men could access for food, gas, and any repairs to the R.V. Manuel knew that accepting money could become a slippery slope, so he insisted they bring someone in that would handle the money.

"Where do you just pick up a guy that handles money?" Jim asked.

"Where else?" Manuel replied, "The Internal Revenue Service." A wave of disgust rolled through the R.V.

"You can't be serious," Simon retched.

"I'm completely serious," Manuel replied.

"You're just going to stroll into the IRS and tell them you need a guy to handle donations." Jim scoffed.

"Well, not exactly," Manuel laughed, "but something like that. Jack! Google the closest IRS office."

"What… your spidey powers don't just let you know where the closest office is? Like you did with Simon's house and everything else?" Jack bantered.

"Yeah, I do," Manuel taunted. "But I thought I'd let you feel useful."

"Ooooh, ouch," the guys cracked up. "Burn, brother… burn."

"Whatever!" Jack snorted. "I'm not the one who farts in my sleep and stinks up the whole R.V.!"

"Heeeey!!" Jim knew that was directed at him, "Low blow! Low blow! Don't make me come over there and break your nose again." The guys continued laughing.

"What?" Simon asked, "When did you break his nose?"

"It's not important!" Jack detoured, "Jim! Don't, man. Don't you dare."

"When Jack was seventeen–" Jim started.

"JIM! Dude…" Jack was rushing towards his brother. Manuel pulled into the Internal Revenue office and parked.

"Ooooh, saved by the bell," Jim snarled. Manuel informed the guys that they'd all be going in. "Don't you think that would look a bit odd?" Jim asked.

"Since when do you not look odd?" Jack injected.

"Okay," Manuel conducted, "Let's go." Walking in, Manuel took a number for service. Sitting down, they all wondered why they were there. Surely, Manuel didn't need them when he got to whichever window would call him up. They were, however, curious about what he would say. While they were waiting, a man covered with eczema spotted Manuel and knew who he was. Falling with his face to the ground, he begged, "Kyrios[1], if you are willing, you can make me clean." The men had never heard this term before and were unsure what it meant. Manuel, however, replied without skipping a beat. Reaching out his hand, he touched the man.

"I am willing. Be clean." Immediately, the eczema vanished, and the man was healthy. Before he could let out a yell of delight, Manuel stopped him. "Shh, shh. Don't say anything in here. Go home to your family and local church. Let them know what has happened to you. But, right now, we have some business here." The man nodded and hugged him.

"Thank you. Oh, thank you, Kyrios," he whispered and rushed out of the building.

"Coo-ree-ahs?" Jim asked. Manuel shook his head, indicating it wasn't the time. Eventually, someone called their number. All four men shuffled up to the window. Levi greeted them and brought them back into his little cubicle.

"How can I help you…*all* today?"

"How's it going, Levi?" Manuel shook the agent's hand.

"Juuust fine, Sir. What am I helping you with today?" Levi feigned consideration.

Manuel knew there were cameras all over the office. He knew that one of them would have caught the healing in the waiting room. He knew it was only a matter of time before someone, somewhere in the building, would come rushing in, wanting him to heal someone else. In this minute, however, he was focused on letting Levi know who they were and gaining the two most important assets the IRS had to offer.

"Levi, I'd like to invite you to come with us." Levi looked at the group of guys and back at Manuel without so much as lifting an eyebrow. In a seamless motion, he placed his hand on a panic button under his desk and recited the mantra taught to all agents on day one of working in the Internal Revenue Office.

"IRS agents do not keep cash on the premises. If you have a dispute with the IRS and are seeking retribution, please be aware that we have cameras on you at this time and that an assault on an agent of the IRS can lead to imprisonment of up to–" By this time, each of the guys were laughing, and Levi realized he had misjudged the situation. Manuel was not laughing, but he was smiling. Levi removed his hand from the panic button. "What is this about?"

"Levi, my name is Emmanuel Paladin. I guess you haven't seen–" just then, a light came on in Levi's recognition, and he gasped.

"You're the YouTube guy."

"Well, there are a lot of YouTube guys, but, yeah, I mean… I guess I am the YouTube guy."

"You don't have an issue with the IRS?"

"Well, not specifically."

"Wait- you said you wanted me to come with you."

"Yes! Now we're talking. Levi, I'd like to invite you to come with us."

"Come with you."

"Yes, Levi."

"You mean… in the R.V. On the road trip… with you."

"Yes, Levi."

"With all of you."

"*Yes*, Levi."

"Me?"

"Yes! Levi…"

"Why me?"

"Why not you?"

"Because… I work for the IRS."

"And?"

"And… I don't have friends, I mean, people don't usually want to– is this some sort of gag? You can't post any footage of this, you know. You can't film inside a government office."

"We aren't filming," Jack said, "I'm the guy who films."

"It's not a gag, Levi. Look, you're a tax guy. We've got some tax questions– how to handle donations and all. We need a good tax guy."

Jim whispered to Simon, "Do *good* and *tax guy* go in the same sentence?"

"You're serious. This sounds fishy." Levi questioned.

"You mean it smells fishy." Jim corrected.

"No," Jack piped up, "That's just Simon. You get used to it." Jim smacked Jack on the back of the head.

"If you're seeking to discuss business, we can do that here in the office."

Manuel looked at Levi and cocked his head. He could see the overweight, insecure, lonely heart of this man. He sighed.

"Oh, no," Levi said, "Don't do that. You're doing that thing. That thing you do on the videos where you just kind of look at someone and know what's wrong. Oh, please, please don't do that." Manuel smiled warmly at Levi. "You can tell, can't you. You can see it. Drat. I know you can see it." Manuel said nothing but continued watching as Levi spun slightly out of himself. Levi was starting to murmur under his breath and dig in drawers as a distraction. 'For some unknown reason, you just want me to go with you. Just drop everything and go with these YouTube celebrity guys in their freakin' R.V. on a road trip.' The guys wondered why Manuel wanted this guy. He was socially awkward and a bit bumbling. Did they really need an in with the IRS? It wasn't like they planned on doing anything wrong with the donations. Manuel started to instruct Levi.

"We want to be upright in every way and be accountable for every dime donated. I want you to be my financial advisor and our accountability with finances. Can you do that, Levi? Will you be my money guy?" Levi suddenly felt very important. His chest puffed up a bit. Manuel was speaking to him in a way no one did– like he was a person. With worth. Suddenly, Levi didn't care if he ever sat behind this desk again. Here was a challenge to accept a new position, as unknown as it may be, with a group of guys on an adventure of a lifetime. At least, for Levi. "We won't be paying you; it's strictly for the good of the people. But you will have what you need."

"You really want me?"

"We really want you," Manuel smiled warmly. Levi turned a corner and shifted gears.

"Okay! Okay, I'm in!" He knocked a pile of papers off of his desk and clumsily began picking them up. "Oh, oh, I shouldn't have left those there. I'm just going to– okay! Okay!" The guys started chuckling. Jack was already thinking of all the ways he could tease Levi on the road. "I'm going to give my notice! Geeze, I *hate* this job! I mean– I'm good at it. I'm like, really, good at it. But I hate it. This is going to be good. Change of pace, yeah. This is going to be– I'm going to throw you a dinner!" Levi was bouncing all over. "I'm going to throw you guys a dinner! Do we have to leave tonight? Because by tomorrow night, I can have a gathering of really elite people together! You could get more donations. Yeah– you could make some good connections. I could hook you up." Manuel smiled. He didn't need Levi's help getting hooked up. But he would allow it to play out as it should.

"That would be great," Manuel agreed. "Tomorrow night, then."

CHAPTER 17:

ALL EYES ON MANUEL

Levi invited a large crowd of tax collectors, local leaders, Liberals, Conservatives, and lawyers to his house for dinner. Some of the lawyers even brought full-service escorts. It was last minute, but upon hearing that this latest miracle-working YouTube sensation was the guest of honor, people were interested. It was a great spread. Levi lived with his mother in a palatial family home. There were servants and beautiful gardens. The R.V. seemed utterly out of place, pulling into the circular drive. The guys stared at the house with jaws hanging open.

"Oh, crap," Jack said. "All of a sudden, I don't think I am wearing the right clothes."

"Don't worry about your clothes," Manuel instructed. "Just put on the nicest whatever you brought."

Simon pulled out a three-piece suit. Jim put on a golf shirt, and Jack pulled out a t-shirt that read, "This *is* my dress shirt." Manuel put on a white button-down shirt and a nice pair of jeans with white converse. A butler greeted them and ushered them into a large room where the attendees had gathered. Some greeted, and some whispered, but everyone watched. Cocktails and hors d'oeuvres were served. Levi greeted the guys with excitement. He was an odd fellow but came from a well-connected family. He lived alone with his mother. An only child, his father had passed years ago. A bit spoiled, Levi never had very great friends. As a child, he always had more than the other kids and tried to buy friendships. As a teenager, he was never the good-looking one and hadn't mastered his intimidation of peer groups or girls. As a young man, he completed his education and became an employee of the Internal Revenue Service. People left him alone to do his job, and he was used to not being accepted. Intelligent and skilled with numbers, he found a comfortable routine between home and work. His mother was excessively proud of him and catered to his every whim. Levi wanted for nothing. Nothing but true love and companionship.

The crowd was watching Manuel's every move and judging him. They waited for him to work a miracle or produce a creative wonder. He knew all eyes were on him and precisely what they expected. But Manuel's mission was not a party trick. He hadn't come to show off or entertain the masses. Manuel only moved when the Creator motivated him to. He certainly had discernment and supernatural knowing, but he wasn't going to predict the future or answer any personal love life questions. Some of the religious leaders were judging him on everything from his attire to his choice of company.

"Why do you eat and drink with tax collectors, whores, and sinners? You must have something in common with them," they insinuated.

"Everyone needs a job," Manuel coolly answered. "At least they're working. Besides, it's not the healthy people who need a doctor, but the sick. I haven't come to the righteous, but those who have missed the mark." Manuel was a bit facetious. As he had told his guys previously, '*All* have missed the mark. None are completely righteous, not even one.' In their false piety, it was evident they had separated themselves from anyone who was perceived to have missed the mark in any way.

"A doctor goes to sick people, and a savior goes to sinners." He knew as well as the religious leaders did in their hearts that everyone could do better and should. And they knew that he knew. Realizing that Manuel was calling them out without blatantly doing so, they challenged him.

"Johnny's followers often fasted and prayed. So do the devotees of the Conservative sect. But your guys seem to be eating and drinking whatever they want whenever they want. Do they exercise *any* spiritual disciplines?"

"Can you make the friends of the bridegroom fast while he is with them? The time will come when the bridegroom is taken from them by force; in those days, they will be deprived enough."

The priests, teachers, and local leaders were disturbed. Had he answered them? Some of them understood his claim but others were too publicly aware to ask him what he meant. The religious leaders were of the mindset that in order to be a super spiritual person, one had to deprive themselves; if it didn't look like suffering or sacrifice in some way, it couldn't possibly be pure. They bound themselves with legalism, and Manuel was painfully aware of it. He decided to tell them a story in hopes they could relate.

"There was a guy who had a couch since college. The throw pillows were missing, some of the springs had broken, the armrests were filthy and started to shred in areas. As a gift, someone came– free of charge– and gave him a brand-new couch. No one would take the new throw pillows, springs, and a piece of cloth from the new couch and sew it onto the old one. Some people assume that because they are comfortable with the old couch, that it's better. But I have come to introduce something entirely new. I haven't come to patch up the old ways; I've come with a whole new lifestyle. Likewise, when an acorn falls to the ground and dies, no one grieves the acorn. They look to the great oak that has fulfilled the acorn's purpose."

The local and religious leaders were here scoffing when a group of men came assisting a person with paralysis. The snobbish room was hushed. The small group's courage and faith moved Manuel. He did not rush to them but took pride in their every step in his direction. Once they reached him, he simply said, "Friend, your deficiencies are forgiven, and shortcomings are all restored." Before the man could be physically healed, his soul needed restoration. Manuel forgave him. The man felt his legs bulk up beneath him. Muscles grew to full size, and he could feel the renewal of his strength like a wave of tingling and heat. Dropping his elbow crutches, the man stood upright, allowing his legs to bear his full weight. He looked at Manuel and praised him. The crowd gasped and cooed. Some had the nerve to golf clap. The religious leaders began thinking to themselves, 'This man is speaking sacrilege! No one could forgive shortcomings, but Theos alone!' Manuel hugged the man and knew what the teachers and preachers were thinking.

"Why are you thinking these things in your hearts?" He asked. Dumbfounded that he could hear them without speaking, they were stunned. "Which would be easier: to say, 'Your failures are forgotten,' or to say, 'Let go of your crutches and walk?' I want you to know that I have been given authority on earth to forgive evil-doing." Turning to the healed man, he said, "Hey, brother. You're good, man. Bless you." The man picked up his elbow crutches with tears in his eyes. Thanking Manuel profusely, he went home praising the Creator. Everyone was filled with awe.

"That was amazing."

"I'm blown away."

The religious leaders were furious. If this guy thought he could come in and shift the hearts of the people away from all that they had put in order, he was crazy. The local government leaders were concerned. If this guy caused too much of a social upset, it could potentially lead to rebellion. Cell phones were out, and calls were made to authorities. No one with any legal or religious power wanted Manuel to walk freely for very long.

Everyone wanted to talk to Manuel. They had questions regarding their issues and family members. Levi thought it was all too good to be true. Without being told, the guys started to head back to the R.V. Simon stayed at the door watching for Manuel. Not even consciously, he had become a sort of bodyguard. Manuel instructed Levi to say goodbye to his mother and grab a bag. Levi hesitated.

"What is it?" Manuel asked.

"I can't leave my mom," he winced. "I'm all she has, and– really, it wouldn't be good for her." Manuel stepped closer to Levi.

"I understand, and I admire your heart for your mother. We should always honor our fathers and mothers. But are you sure this doesn't have to do with you? With the fear of stepping out of your comfort zone?"

Levi looked at Manuel with dread. "Wait, wait… I know a guy!" Running off into the next room, Levi left Manuel standing by the door. Simon looked at Manuel with a sense of urgency.

"We need to slip out. This room is getting tense, and these people aren't going to let you go."

"Thank you, Rock. We're almost finished. We just need one more thing." Levi returned with another man.

"Here… this is Jude. He works with me. He knows money. He knows the law. He can be your money guy."

"Hello, Jude," Manuel extended his hand. "It's nice to meet you. Do you know what's going on here?"

"I think Levi is volunteering me to take his place on a trip or something. Right?"

"Right, right," Levi confirmed. "Jude is super brave. He doesn't give a crap about authority or controversy. He's perfect for you. He can handle stress." Jude just laughed.

"Well, he isn't wrong," he confirmed. Manuel knew exactly who Jude was, the role he would play, and that he would, indeed, come with them.

"Well, that's all good and well," Manuel said. "Welcome aboard, Jude.

But Levi, I asked *you* to join us because I have much for you to do and learn. You don't even know who you are– I want to show you. I'm not letting you off the hook that easily." Levi was starting to sweat. He secretly wanted to leave his mother's hovering eye and learn what it was like to have a bunch of guy friends. But fear was gripping him.

"It's like the couch," Levi confessed. "It might be old and dysfunctional, but it's all I know. I'm comfortable with it, and the thought of the unknown just freaks me out, man."

"I know," Manuel soothed. "But I also know that you were created for this. You just don't know it yet."

"Don't be a wuss, man," Jude barked. "Stop sweating. Get a bag. Tell your mom you'll be back when you'll be back. The butler can comfort her." Jude walked past Manuel and headed toward the R.V. As he passed Simon, he shook his hand and introduced himself. "Hey, man. I'm Jude. I'm your new money guy." Simon held Jude's look.

"Is that so? You're not *my* anything."

Jude snorted and kept walking.

"Levi," Manuel invited. "You can do this." Levi wanted to do this. He didn't have the confidence, but he did want to try to be a part of something bigger than himself. He wanted to become who he always pictured himself to be; vital, masculine, confident, and brave with a purpose. He wanted an adventure to live, a beauty to fight for, and all of his questions answered[2]. Knowing the battle that was happening in Levi's head and what he was thinking, Manuel asked, "Do you know what the definition of bravery is?" Levi met Manuel's eyes. "It's been said that the definition of bravery is the ability to face adversity despite the fear and do it anyway." Levi sighed. "But… you're going to become *courageous.* Courage is having the quality of mind or spirit that enables a person to face difficulty, danger, pain, or whatever– without fear." Levi felt something rise within him. The look in Manuel's eyes made him believe it was true.

"I'm scared," he whispered.

"I know," Manuel whispered back.

"I'll get my bag and say goodbye to my mom."

"Atta' boy."

~~~

The guys had been trying to adjust. Six grown men in one R.V. would be tough enough if everyone were the best of friends, but six grown men who
~~~

didn't know each other was another story. Each had different grooming habits, and each a different perspective on sanitation. Levi left the money handling to Jude and focused simply on the social adjustment. Manuel decided to take them all fishing as a way to relax and start to bond.

"Fishing? Really?" Simon asked.

"Simon," Manuel insisted, "When was the last time you sat at the side of a lake with a pole and just relaxed. Not your corporate boom and boats, but just you, a pole, and a group of guys."

"Well, when you put it like that. It's been a while. Let's stop for a six-pack." The guys stopped for snacks, sandwiches, and bait. While inside, a follower of the Redeemer Roadtrip recognized them. Philip had been watching Jack's posts. Charged that he was seeing them, he ran the few aisles over to his brother Nathan.

"Dude! You'll never guess who's in the store."

"Nope, I won't." Nathan wasn't biting.

"Dude… seriously. You'll never guess!"

"Dude…seriously. You're right because I'm not going to try! If you want to tell me who's in the store, Phil, just tell me."

"Emmanuel Paladin."

"Who?" Nathan looked at his brother with no expression.

"Emmanuel Paladin! You don't know who he is? What, have you been under a rock? He's that guy from YouTube who heals people and teaches about the Creator. He's from Netzer!"

"Netzer?" Nathan quipped. "Can anything good come from Netzer?"

"He's traveling around with the guy from Simon's Seafood." Philip and Nathan lived in the same town where Simon had made a name for himself in the seafood industry. Nathan knew well who he was.

"Seriously? That's weird. I thought that guy was some sort of workhorse or something. He's just traveling around with a guy doing miracles?"

"In an R.V." Philip grinned.

"You've got to be kidding," Nathan chided. Philip shook his head.

"Okay, this I've got to see. The high and mighty Simon's Seafood with a traveling circus in an R.V.? It's too good to be true."

Without making themselves known, the brothers decided to follow the R.V. Dozens of others had the same idea. The lake was calm and beautiful. The guys got settled in and baited their hooks. Levi had never been fishing, so Simon took him under his wing and talked him through the steps. Levi wasn't thrilled to be touching worms or leeches, but he loved the male camaraderie. Manuel knew of the growing crowd gathering nearby, but none had been bold enough to approach. He knew it was a matter of time and leaned back in his folding chair. Allowing his head to fall back, he felt the sun on his face and sought the Creator for what steps would be ordered that day.

Eventually, the crowd started pressing in closer. Philip was beside himself and wanted the opportunity to speak with Manuel, but as he and his brother approached, without turning around, Manuel said, "Hello, Nathan." The men froze in their tracks.

"How did you– how do you know me?" Standing, he turned around to greet the men face to face; Manuel smiled.

"You are a true man of faith. There is no deceit in you." The brothers looked at each other and back at Manuel, who was now casually baiting his hook. "Before Philip ran into your aisle and told you about us in the store… I saw you. I saw you this morning in your prayer time. Sitting in your favorite chair, drinking your coffee, just like you do every morning. Hello, Philip." Philip practically skipped over to Manuel.

"This is fantastic! Do you mind if I get a picture with you?"

Nathan dropped to his knees and said, "Teacher… you are the Son of Theos. You are the King come to deliver us." Philip was clicking selfies while standing next to Manuel.

"Get up, Nathan. Because I said, 'I saw you on the aisle, and in your prayer time,' you believe I am the Son of Theos? You're gonna see more incredible things than that, man." Nathan rose and slowly approached Manuel. "I'm telling you the truth; you will see another realm open up and messengers of the Creator ascending and descending on me." Nathan felt like he had been punched in the gut.

"Me?" he murmured.

Manuel smiled and walked back towards the lake to cast his line. The full crowd was moving in. By the time Manuel turned from casting his bait, the shore was full of people seeking him to heal them of their pain and diseases. Manuel released the dunamis power among them. Those tormented by impure spirits were delivered, and people were trying to touch him. All who came were made well, and Jack was getting the whole thing on video. Hours passed in what seemed like minutes. Finally, people were settling and sitting. Manuel encouraged them to do so and began to teach them about the

Kingdom of Theos.

"Those of you who are poor now are becoming fortified in ways rich people never can be. You will experience the fullness of the Creator and His realm through hardship. The hunger and desire that consume you will not last. You will be completely satisfied. There is laughter coming for those who are weeping. A deep, all-consuming joy that will replace the depth of your brokenness.

"Don't worry when people hate you, post nasty things about you, or shun you, and insult you. When they reject you and say that you're evil because you have dared to believe in Me. I know it sounds crazy but celebrate that day! Because you are favored by the Creator and are gaining reward in a kingdom that most people don't know anything about.

"The saddest thing is the sorrow that haunts those of you who are rich because you find your contentment in money and this life only. You have already received your comfort. But the hunger for more and emptiness will torment you. You take your joy now and laugh at everything lightly. This is the only life you see. But grief and mourning will come when you realize there is more, and you missed it. Your fathers and grandfathers lived the same way, and none of them knew a true prophet."

Some in the crowd were crying, and some were taking notes. Individuals were recording videos. Jim and Simon were among the people comforting them. Jack was recording, and Jude was taking it all in. Levi couldn't remember the last time he felt so comfortable in a crowd and was grateful to be a part of it all. Manuel noticed a young woman sitting towards the front with an expression of anger. She was slowly and silently shaking her head in frustration. Knowing her thoughts and the pain she was carrying, Manuel continued.

"Love your enemies." The girl's head bolted upright, and her eyes widened. Looking directly at her, he said, "Do good to those who hate you. Bless those who curse you and intercede for those who mistreat you." The girl started weeping openly. Without ceasing, Manuel walked up and laid his hand on the top of her head. "Harassment only lasts for a season. Anger only keeps you bound."

"I know we have beggars on every corner. If you pass one and have something to give them, give it. How would you want someone to treat you if you found yourself in their position? Oh– you think you'd never *be* in their position. Careful. You don't know what led them there or how the wounds in their souls have crippled them. Do you think you're such a good person? Do you show that only by loving the people who love you– only caring for those who care for you? Really? Even wicked people do that.

"What if you loan money only to those you know will pay it back? How does that contribute to your character? Look, if you loan someone money and they don't pay you back– that's on them. You made the choice to loan them money, so don't treat them poorly, talk behind their back, or cut them off. It's not lost. Your reward isn't in the repayment of the money. Your reward is in being known as a child of the Creator. Children become like their parents. The Creator is kind, merciful, forgiving, and generous. Be merciful, just as your Maker is merciful."

Manuel could tell that this had been enough information for one day. These concepts were completely counter-cultural, and he could see their heads spinning. The sun started to set, and the guys had long since gathered up the fishing gear. Manuel blessed and loved on the people. When he returned to the R.V., the guys were packed and ready to go. As they drove off, many tried to follow. It would become only more and more difficult to escape the masses.

"We might need a bus," Jude said.

CHAPTER 18:

THAUMATURGY

Manuel's popularity was growing. Word was spreading, and side videos were going viral with people being healed. Clips of his teaching were posted and reposted. Jack started recording teaching segments in the R.V. apart from the crowds. He could get better audio, and Manuel could speak directly into countless homes about the Kingdom of Theos. Sometimes, just the conversations the guys had in the R.V. were worth recording; they were learning so much. Manuel was bringing a revelation of selflessness and love for your fellow man. He taught that judging someone was one of the worst things anyone could do. "If you don't judge others, you won't be judged. Don't condemn people– you don't even know the whole story. Don't condemn others, and you won't be condemned." Manuel often said, 'whatever you gave out in the world would come back to you, and when you gave generously, generosity would be returned.' It made sense and was pretty simple. But people didn't live that way, and the thought was revolutionary. People had been looking out for themselves for so long that life had become every man for himself.

Manuel would often teach in story format. He believed that even if people didn't get it in that minute that they would continue to think about the story and get the message at some point. He asked thought-provoking questions like, 'Can the blind lead the blind? How can someone who can't see lead someone else who can't see? Eventually, they will both fall into a pit. The student is not above the teacher, but anyone open to learning will eventually become like their teacher. Mature. Learned. Capable of leading others.' He would challenge people to quit blaming others and own their part in things. "Why do you look at the speck of dust in someone else's eye and call it wrong… when you've got a stinkin' log sticking out of your own eye and refuse to deal with it? What a hypocrite! First, deal with your own business, and then you might be able to see clearly enough to help someone with their business. Maybe."

The Redeemer Roadtrip was gaining followers and subscribers at a record-breaking rate. Manuel was receiving marriage proposals and invitations to speak everywhere, from Ted Talks to churches. YouTube even offered to start paying to place ads before their videos. Manuel wouldn't have it. "The Creator's message doesn't come with an advertisement first. He will provide all we need to continue this journey. We don't need to be paid for the message, no way." It was true. People were very generous out of the gratitude they felt from hearing the message Manuel brought. They would place money directly into the guys' hands, who would always instantly give it to Jude to keep safe on his person. Jude handled paying for all the gas, food, and any extra necessities that came up. Manuel was always encouraging Jude. He had a rough childhood, but Manuel always called him 'good fruit.' "Speak it until you see it," Manuel confided in Jack. The guys started calling him different kinds of fruit just to get under his skin.

"Ay, yo... peachie boy... wipe down the sink when you're done. It looks like a tidal wave hit in there." Jude was annoyed by all of it. So, they continued.

It started because Manuel said, 'No good tree bears bad fruit, and a bad tree can't bear good fruit. Each tree is recognized by its own fruit– what it produces. People don't pick figs from a thornbush or grapes from briers. But a good man brings good things out of the good stored up in his heart, and an evil man brings evil things out of the evil stored up in his heart. And good or evil, the mouth is going to speak what the heart is full of.'

Jude was not a bad man. He had just had a rough life. This opportunity with Manuel was unlike anything he had ever known, and the words he spoke were sinking into Jude's heart, just like everyone else. His favorite was when Manuel taught about the difference between wise and foolish builders. He encouraged people to listen to what he said and put it into practice, not just hear it, but do it. He said, "If you hear what I'm saying and put it into practice, it will be like a man building a house who digs down deep and lays the foundation on solid rock. When a flood comes, the torrent strikes the house but cannot shake it because it is well built on a solid foundation. But when anyone hears what I'm saying and doesn't apply it, it is like someone who builds a house on sand. The minute a storm comes, it will fall apart and face complete destruction." Jude wanted to be good fruit. He had never met anyone like Manuel. He was so down-to-earth and genuine that just being around him made you want to be a better person. He had an uncommon sensitivity. He looked at someone and saw their heart. He didn't look on the outside with its appearances but saw straight through to the root of who someone was and why. It was astounding to the guys how Manuel could be playful with them one minute and segue straight into powerful instruction in the next.

One day, Manuel had just finished teaching when a couple of uncommissioned officers approached him. Their Captain heard that Manuel was speaking nearby and sent them to plead for his help on behalf of a favored assistant. The assistant had become like a member of the Captain's family. He was highly valued and sick to the point of death. The Captain wanted to see him healed and restored to their family. The soldiers told Manuel, "Our Captain has done so much for all of us. He truly cares for us and deserves to have you help him. He loves our empire and has contributed so much to our country." Manuel, moved by their loyalty to their leader, went with them. When they were en route to the house, the officers called the Captain on speakerphone to let him know. Stopping them, the Captain addressed Manuel.

"Sir, don't trouble yourself. I don't deserve to have you come under my roof. Just say the word, and my assistant will be healed. I am a man under authority myself with soldiers under me. When I tell someone to 'go,' he goes. When I tell someone, 'come,' they come. When I command someone to do something, he does it. So, just speak the word, and I know it will be done as you have commanded."

When Manuel heard the Captain, he was amazed. Turning to his guys, he said, "I haven't heard anyone anywhere with faith like this guy. He gets it." Manuel turned to the officers and released them to go without him. When they got back to the house, they found the assistant perfectly well.

Manuel was traveling, teaching, and healing all around, but on this day, they stopped in a town called Nain. By now, people were following them everywhere they went. As they entered the city, they passed a funeral parlor with people lingering out front. Manuel saw a woman crying. She was being escorted into the parlor and barely able to walk on her own. "Stop," he told Simon and hopped out of the R.V. before anyone could park and follow him in. Rushing up, he took the other side of the grieving woman and helped escort her in. She looked up at him in shock.

"Who are you? Were you a friend of my son?" Others immediately recognized Manuel and answered her.

"No, Auntie… this man is a healer. How did you find us?"

"Don't cry," Manuel told her.

"Don't cry?! My husband died years ago, and my son was all I had. He was my only child! Now he's gone! What am I supposed to do?"

Seating her in the front row, Manuel looked at the open casket. All eyes were on him as he approached. The guys had parked and headed into the back of the parlor so as not to disturb. They knew that any minute, others from the caravan would intrude, and they couldn't guarantee their reverence.

Simon stayed by the door to dissuade them. Manuel stepped up to the young man in the casket and touched him.

"Get up," he said. The people near the casket heard him and froze. Was he crazy? How dare he? Again, Manuel spoke, "Young man, I'm telling you to get up." The young man opened his eyes. A woman who witnessed it shrieked with terror and backed away. Men nearby dropped their jaws and stood numb. The young man sat up and looked around. His eyes met his mother's, and she fainted on the spot. Manuel extended his hand and offered help out. People were freaking out. Some were recording video, some were running out, and some were screaming with delight. Manuel walked the young man over and returned him to his mother.

"Mama?" he greeted her. Family members were attending to her and embracing the man with tears. The woman clutched her son and wept uncontrollably.

"What happened?" She cried, "What just happened?!"

"A prophet has come!" Someone shouted.

"The Creator has sent someone to help His people!" Another declared.

The crowd flooded the front to embrace the young man and touch Manuel. Simon felt a wave of angst and rushed forward to help Manuel. Pushing through the crowd, people were grasping and pulling at him. When Simon reached Manuel, he observed the absolute calm in his eyes. He simply smiled and asked, "Did you catch that one, Rocko?" He moved back and forth by the people's demand. But in the midst of the chaos, Simon felt the Essence of the Creator. He saw life and death in Manuel's eyes. It frightened him even though he felt deep assurance that all was well.

"Man– uh…" Simon was suddenly unsure what to call Manuel. He felt the weight of him being something greater than a man. He wanted to say so in addressing him but had no idea what that would be. "Let's get you out of here." Manuel smiled and calmly walked out of the whirlwind. Jack, Jim, Jude, and Levi were already back at the R.V. with the engine running. They were able to get a couple of blocks away before followers started catching on to their escape. Inside the R.V. was a smaller version of what was going on in the funeral parlor. Jack was standing on the couch, whooping and praising the event. Jim was laughing as he drove. Jude was applauding and slapping Levi on the back. Levi was silent and in awe. Simon sat directly across from Manuel, who was covered with overflowing radiance. Simon just stared at him. Manuel looked lovingly at Simon and started to speak.

"Kyrios," he said. The guys continued to be giddy but were listening. "That's the word you were looking for, Simon." Simon recognized the word from when Manuel healed the man with eczema at the IRS office. He knew that Manuel had seen him searching for how to address him and was answering him now. "From the root word Kuros, which means supremacy." A light bulb went off in Simon.

"Yes," he agreed. "That's it. I have never seen such power and authority."

"I know, right?" Manuel threw his head back and laughed. He smiled at Simon with such warmth and brotherhood. Simon wondered how he had been chosen to sit where he was sitting. And to think he hadn't wanted to come on this trip. "Nor has the world, Simon. Nor has the world."

"And that's why you're… why you've come." Simon was piecing things together. Manuel nodded in agreement.

"Now, what's for dinner? I'm starving. That sort of thing takes it out of me," he said, chuckling and winked at Simon. Simon had a new sense of responsibility.

"We can't stop now," Simon warned. "The caravan is too close behind us; let's wait a bit." Manuel knew that Simon had shifted and was becoming his appointed rock.

"As the man says!" He conceded and laid back, folding his hands on his belly. Simon couldn't take his eyes off of him. How could he be so casual? They had just seen him raise a man from the dead. It would be all over the news. Videos would go viral. In his opinion, Manuel was about to become the biggest superstar the world had ever known, and he was sitting across from him in a used R.V.

~~~

Johnny was facing prison and felt like he was rotting in jail. He had a few devoted followers who would visit him regularly and give him reports from the outside. On one visit, when a couple of his devotees came, a discussion arose regarding his current position compared to before.

"We saw you," they said, "leading people to repentance and hosting immersion ceremonies. People of all ages were coming to you, and now you're– *here*. How is that possible, or right?" Johnny understood their frustration and was getting more and more frustrated himself as time went on. The false charges didn't seem to be fading but gaining ground to stand on. He knew that Governor Tetrarch had played his hand well. He wondered why his cousin hadn't been to see him in all his traveling or why he didn't work some miracle on his behalf to free him. Still, Johnny answered them with faithfulness to the cause he unswervingly held.

"Look, guys, I get your frustration. It sucks in here, for sure. But– no one can receive even one good thing unless it comes from the Creator. You guys have seen it– you've heard me say, 'I am not the Redeemer, but I was sent before Him.' The one who gets the bride is the bridegroom! I'm like the best man. I set him up, but he walks down the aisle and commits his life to his beloved. I mean, I did what I was supposed to do, and I'm– I'm happy for Manuel." Turning more introspective, Johnny felt a wave of sadness. "He must increase, and I must… decrease." Johnny's followers loved him. They still came to hear anything he may say to enlighten them. But this day,
~~~

they felt as if he was letting them go and encouraging them to seek after Manuel. They were a bit thrown by how he would explain things but understood that he was becoming depressed. Even if there was truth in what he said, he had lost his passion and platform.

"Manuel comes from the elevated realm and is above everything. I am of the earth; I had a purpose here and have spoken in earthly understanding. I spoke inspired words, but Manuel speaks the words of the Creator and moves in His Essence without measure. The Creator loves him." Johnny was starting to undo a bit. "The Creator loves His son and has given everything into his hand. Whoever comes to Manuel and believes that he is who he says he is will be given an indestructible gift."

"What gift?" they questioned.

"They will become immortal." Johnny's followers were convinced he had spiraled into a depression that caused him to slip in and out of madness. No one could be immortal. That was for novels and movies. "They won't be subject to death."

"Everyone dies, Johnny."

"No, of course," Johnny snapped back into the moment. "But… their spirit will become imperishable, everlasting, perpetual… do you understand? Whoever doesn't get on board with Manny and heed his teachings will not only miss out on imperishable life but will have to deal with the wrath of the Creator. How would you feel if you sent your child to someone with the greatest gift, and they were rejected? When all that child wanted to do was show them the way to– lack absolutely nothing. The world can't conceive it." Johnny knew that even then, these devotees could not conceive of it. He had lost all influence.

"Do me a favor," Johnny asked, "When you go to him– to Manuel– ask him something for me." Johnny's devotees leaned in to hear him whisper a question. They were shocked upon hearing it but agreed to ask, should they ever get close enough to Manuel.

~~~

Scout Nikkos published his article on Stacey Dreggs. Her arrest led to her conviction on three murder counts for her children and foul play regarding her lover's wife. Remains of her children, a four-year-old boy, a two-year-old girl, and a seven-month-old boy, were found buried on the property of her lover's mother. It was a foul business, and memorials were popping up in different parts of the country on behalf of the children. Scout stayed for the duration of the trial and wrote articles for the Tri-State Triton throughout. He also published his piece on Johnny and the controversy over his imprisonment, but his editors sold more papers over the murder of three innocents. His next goal was to speak to Manuel himself. Having become an avid follower of the Redeemer Roadtrip channel, Scout knew what everyone else knew; this self-proclaimed savior was traveling around, leaving
~~~

a wake of healings and resurgence in spirituality. The religious and political leaders, however, were threatened and watching his every move. Scout wanted to know more than the average citizen. He wanted to know if Manuel was a true prophet, as they said, or if he was a maniacal fraud. Johnny had undoubtedly believed he was genuine, but the fact that they were cousins looked a bit like a family plan for attention and power. If it was a plan, it wasn't working out for Johnny as well as it was for Manuel. Had their plan gone awry? Had Manuel embraced his fame leaving his cousin to rot in prison? Scout mapped the trail of the R.V.'s whereabouts and headed in their direction.

CHAPTER 19:

BIG QUESTIONS AND BIG ANSWERS

One evening the guys had all eaten and were hanging out in the R.V. It was warm, and opening windows was little relief. They placed a couple of fans to help move the air and were drinking cold drinks. Jim's cell phone rang with an unknown number. Not one to typically answer unknown calls, the call went straight to voicemail. When he noticed the caller had left a message, he immediately went to delete it, assuming it was spam. Instead, Jim received an inquiry from an assistant to one of the conservative sect's elite members. He listened to the full message and hung up in shock.

"Hey, Manuel. I just got a call." Manuel 'mm-hmmed' him and kept reading. Manuel had a phone, but only the guys and family had his number. "You just received an invitation to a barbeque." The guys laughed at any invitation that would come through Jim's phone. They weren't in the habit of accepting random invitations. Followers were always trying to find out where they were or get them to participate in parties of some sort. "No, I think it's serious." Manuel looked up from his reading. "It's some assistant's assistant to Draco Conti." The guys hushed and became thoughtful. "She said that they were inviting you to this barbeque where elite leaders would be. There is even a possibility that Draco might show. They want to know if you might be open to a pre-interview for his show. She said this would be a relaxed environment for casual introductions." Manuel leaned his head back and looked upward. He closed his eyes and waited. The guys waited for his response. They knew he was seeking Theos for direction.

"Well, they're going to have a pool," Manuel replied, "so, I guess we ought to go."

"Yeah!" Jack agreed and threw his hand up in the hang-ten symbol. "Thank Theos!"

"Did you hear that?" Levi asked. No one had heard anything. Again, there was a very light knock at the R.V. door. "Someone found us," he confirmed. Simon stood and was ready to defend. Opening the door, he saw a man with a sweatshirt hood pulled up over his head.

"Hi, forgive me… I'm sorry to intrude."

"Who are you?" Simon demanded.

"My name is Nico. Nico DeMos. I'm a–"

"Let him in," Manuel interrupted. Simon looked back at Manuel, who nodded. "Let him in, Simon." Simon stepped aside and invited the stranger in. The guys became uneasy. They had never let a stranger into the R.V. "It's okay, guys. This is Nico. Go back to your business. We're going to have a little chat." Manuel smiled at Nico and greeted him warmly. "Come on in, man. You found us."

"I'm sorry to intrude."

"Not at all. I knew you were coming. I wasn't sure when, but I knew. I didn't think about it being all creepy by night." The two men laughed.

"It is a bit creepy. The hoodie and all."

Manuel invited Nico to sit in the cab of the vehicle where they could share the driver and passenger seats. The guys were curious but went about their business. Manuel obviously knew this guy was okay, and they trusted that.

"So, if you knew I was coming, you probably know who I am." Manuel smiled and nodded, but Nico stated the obvious with an awkward chuckle. "So, as you know, I work in the upper echelon of the conservative sect. There is so much talk about you– who you are, who you might be, the threat you pose by the works you are doing. We know that you are a teacher and prophet that has come from the Author of the Universe. No one walks in the authority you do, and no one has ever healed so many people, rapidly changing so many perspectives and lives. I just had to– I wanted to see for myself– hear for myself– what–"

"Nico, here's the deal. Everyone wants to know the secret, but it's so simple people miss it. Before a person can grasp the kingdom I come from, they have to experience a shift in their thinking. A rebirth, if you will."

"A rebirth?"

"Yes. A regeneration. A personal revival. We were born, er– created, but we need to be recreated, change our characters from within– new thoughts, new habits, new… *birth*. Understand? It comes divinely. It can't be bought or earned. It is the work of Theos in our lives. The shift doesn't happen because your parents taught you something. It happens when each person individually hears the Truth and believes." Nico was slowly nodding. Manuel tried again.

"When someone believes and realizes that they are on the wrong path or unhappy because of their choices, they can go to Theos with that realization. Then, He is faithful and just to forgive them. See, people–*you*– need to be born anew. Because if you remain functioning out of the natural, your flesh, the human plane, then you won't hear the Higher Realm, and you won't enter into it. You have to listen to it and see it in the spiritual realm as a spiritual person."

"Okay…"

"A natural man– someone who hasn't shifted into this new perspective and spiritual reality– doesn't understand any of it. It's foolishness to him. But the person who flows in the Essence of the Creator understands– because he has the wisdom and discernment from the Higher Realm."

Nico was reeling. "You say it so matter of factly. You make it sound like it's simple. But how can someone shift? Be reborn?"

"You're one of the elite teachers of the conservative sect, and you don't know?" Manuel didn't say this to hurt Nico or cut him down. He was making a statement about the religious sects as a whole. They were so ruled and law-bound that they missed the whole point. "Nico, I have come to make alive all those who have died inside because they're bound to their religious ways. They are dead because they have missed the mark. I'm here to bring them new life. Infinite life. A life that won't end when they leave this body but enter into the next." Nico sat in silence for several minutes. Manuel sat quietly with him, saying nothing but letting him process.

"So, let me get this straight… The Maker of the Universe, the Creator of all things, loved humankind so much that he sent you– His Son– to earth. He didn't send you to condemn us for missing the mark and creating a mess for ourselves, but to *save* us from ourselves, from the consequence of our choices."

"Yes, exactly."

"And whoever chooses to believe that you are who you say you are– which is crazy evident by all your works and movement in this realm– will not be condemned or left in our mess. But– for those who call you fraud or don't believe– they are condemned already– by the consequence of their choices."

"Yes."

"You are a light for the world."

"Yes. I am."

"But… people love their ways. They don't want to be told what to do. We are rebellious and selfish by nature. So, those who love the darkness of their ways– won't be… redeemed."

"Exactly."

"But what happens to the people that don't believe?"

Manuel lowered his head and felt the pain of Nico's question. His eyes became moist, and he answered. "Everyone who does wicked things already hates the light. They hate me. They don't come to the light because the light exposes everything done in the dark. But those who do what is *true* easily come to the light, because there is no shame any longer for anything that has been done."

"But what *happens* to them?"

"They remain in the darkness, of course."

~~~

The day was perfect for a barbeque and swim. Jack was the first to check out the pool, although no one seemed to be swimming. The home was magnificent but appeared to be more for looks than living. Scout Nikkos managed to weasel his way in and front as a server to observe everything he could. Manuel knew Nikkos was there and what his plan was. Manuel was approached almost immediately by those wanting to associate with the latest thing. He took it all in stride. Jack was recording everything– the house, the pool, the grounds, and the people. He figured this was a once-in-a-lifetime gig. They were each wondering if Draco would make an appearance. His assistant's assistant greeted Manuel and invited him to make himself at home but carve out time at a specific hour for the pre-interview questions. The guys helped themselves to food, drink and took advantage of the pool. Simon stayed close to Manuel at all times. He truly had become his rock and self-appointed protector. After a while, some liberal sect leaders approached Manuel to dig deeper into his teachings and test him. The conservative sect zeroed in as well, wanting to examine him for themselves. If there was one thing that the two sects agreed upon, Manuel was bad for business.

"Mr. Paladin, hello," one of them initiated. "Oersted Hahn; liberal sect. Welcome to our little… *party*."

"Thank you for including me."

"Of course, darling, you are the man of the hour, are you not?" Oersted looked Manuel up and down like he could eat him.

"I suppose I am, yes."

"Laekker. Let's jump straight to the point, shall we? You are opposed to an authoritarian government, such as ours is headed, no?"

"That is jumping straight to the point. I'm opposed to anything that favors complete obedience and subjection to authority that isn't the true authority, the Creator. Individual freedom is divine and should be honored. It's not rocket science."

"Certainly not, but everyone knows that Government City, our own little Rome, is the source of both the wealth and some of the problems that occur in the Empire regions. So, our political reality is that of a dominant power overseeing life on a day-to-day basis. You resist this? Do you not think this life-threatening for you?"

"Have I made any statements saying I resist the authority in place?"

"Darling, your very existence and freedom-bringing ways threaten them. Let us not play stupid. You bring a whole new flavor."
~~~

"Flavor, yes." Manuel turned to address the crowd that was not so subtly listening to their conversation. He saw Scout busying himself nearby. "Isn't it sad that people even need a new flavor? The religious sects should provide all the flavor they need. But, if that flavor has lost its taste, how can it ever get it back? If it's no longer meeting the need, then it's not good for anything at all. You might as well throw it out." The crowd was shocked that he would be so blatant. Did he truly plan to dismantle the age-old way of doing things? One man? Fears of being superseded were no longer being hinted at but declared. "You were called upon to be the light of the world. A whole city lit up on a hill can't be hidden! Why aren't people finding comfort in the light, then? No one turns on a light and then wraps the light fixture with a blanket. It's supposed to help people see what they're doing throughout the whole house. As leaders, then– let your light shine before all men, so that they may see all that is good and true and right and celebrate the Creator who gave you that light." A leader from the conservative sect stepped to Manuel boldly.

"Do you think you can abolish the law and all that the ancient prophets set in place before you? Just throw out all the rules and skip off together like a bunch of hippies? The law brings order."

"I'm not here to abolish order or the law. I've come to fulfill it. I'm not suggesting we get rid of all that the ancient prophets taught– but I am here to complete it and give freedom where bondage has ensued. The law was designed to set men free. To show them where the lines were so that we could all live peaceably as a society. But instead, people are so bound by the 'thou shall nots' that they do one of two things. They ultimately rebel, causing them to miss the mark entirely and suffer from the consequence of their choices– or try to be so good that they become prisoners to a legalistic lifestyle that obliterates any hope of real intimacy with the Creator. Do you see?" Nico was there in the crowd with his peers. He was beginning to see and longed for the freedom of which Manuel was speaking.

"Tell us more," Nico encouraged.

"You know the ancient laws say that you shouldn't murder, or you'll be condemned. We get that. And yet, the world is full of murder. How's that working out? What I'm saying is that yes, we shouldn't murder. But even more so, anyone who doesn't even handle his anger properly will be liable to condemnation. Start at the beginning, the root issue. The root is what leads to murder and all kinds of poor choices. Deal with why you are angry, where that anger comes from, check out your family line and renounce any sort of generational bent in your characters that would *lead* to murder. How can you offer anything beneficial in this life if minutia binds you?

"If you've got some sort of a legal case with someone in court– don't wait. Come to terms with your accuser before stepping into the courtroom. If you don't, you risk him handing you over to the judge, then to the guard, and permanently binding you to the problem whether you're in a physical prison or an emotional one. I'm telling you– you will never have freedom until you have addressed the root issue and paid every last cent of debt in your soul." The crowd was settling in around him. They weren't arguing as much but starting to try and hear what he was saying.

"In the same way, you've heard it said, 'You shouldn't commit adultery,' but the world is full of adulterers." Heads started to turn, and people began to shift in their places. "I'm saying that anyone who even looks at another person lustfully has already committed adultery with them in his heart."

"Oh, come on…" Scout snarked. The elite looked at him, wondering why a server was even speaking.

"Bounce the eyes, brother," Manuel insisted. "When your eye lands on something enticing, don't settle there. Bounce away for the sake of your mind, your will, and your emotions."

"Our mind, will, and emotions?" Scout challenged.

"Yes, your soul. Your mind, will, and emotions. Staring will only cause you to have thoughts of engaging that person in a way that your emotions dictate. Letting those thoughts have their way leads to you wanting your will to be done with or to them. They are innocent in the matter. But taking those thoughts hostage and demolishing every pretension that sets itself up against what you know to be right and true brings honor and safety for everyone involved."

"Innocent in the matter?" Oersted snickered. "Really, Darling? Even when these innocents dress in such a way that begs for the attention they are receiving?"

"Or… maybe you don't know what is right and true. What do you think causes someone to dress in such a manner? Or speak out too often, or think they know it all? What causes someone to need that kind of attention? It's the wounds in their soul– *their mind, will, and emotions*– that have caused them to act out. It's fear and insecurity. Look, when someone is lured and enticed by his desire– it's a temptation. There's a choice there. When desire has conceived, it gives birth to misconduct, and when misconduct is all grown up– it leads to death. Don't be deceived. There is a better way." Manuel leaned in and made direct eye contact with members of the elite he knew had already given birth to such misconduct. "I'm telling you– when you choose to know the Creator and walk in the Essence that He gives, you won't have to gratify the desires of your flesh, be they drugs, sex, abuse, or self-mutilation. You can win the war between your spirit and your flesh; between the natural realm and the supernatural realm."

In this room of religious elite were those who had openly and secretly engaged in works of the flesh; sexual scandals, fits of anger, rivalries, excessive drunkenness, and the like. "Evidence of the light is love, peace, patience, kindness, goodness, faithfulness, gentleness, and self-control."

Some of the crowd started to dissipate. No one enjoyed having flaws pointed out publicly. The media had much-criticized one leader for divorcing his wife. This man stepped through and stood directly in front of Manuel with his chest puffed out.

"What about divorce?" he questioned. Manuel knew the story. This man had much power in his position and thought himself above the constraint of a covenant. He had tired of his wife and her nagging ways. Authority made him attractive to some of the most desperate of women. He liked it. He was not ashamed to have dismissed his wife, blaming her with insubordination. He would often beat her up with the ancient prophets' words about who a wife should be. Then using them as a weapon, he would justify his manipulative actions. He was one of Teivel's favorites. Manuel knew the demon operating in him.

"You know as well as I do that the Writings said divorce was permissible. But that was granted because of the arrogance and hardness in the hearts of man. It's obvious by how a man and woman fit together that they sync and become one unit. Divorce was *granted,* not *ordained.*" Manuel sighed heavily and sat on the arm of a couch. "Divorce is death. Death is never a good time. We know the Ancient Writings state that sexual immorality is grounds for a legitimate divorce." Addressing the leader, he confirmed, "Your wife has grounds." The man flared up. "But don't think that it is acceptable for anyone to endure any type of slavery. The Ancient Writings give plenty of evidence that the Creator does not condone or endure violence and oppression against his beloved. Their abuse has not escaped His eye. Vengeance belongs to Him, and He alone will repay it. It's a calamity to interpret Ancient Writings as permission to guilt people into enduring abuse. To condemn them by saying that their eternal destiny dangles on their ability to 'stick it out' is detestable. The Ancient Writings show us Theos Himself separated from His chosen people when they were faithless. We never support the strong trampling the weak by oppression. It is a gross injustice." The leader was seething but could say nothing.

Manuel left the circle and found a quiet place to recline in the backyard. A few of the religious affiliates and their henchmen followed and joined him.

"That was quite a display," one noted.

"It's exhausting," Manuel replied. "This stuff should be common knowledge, but instead, it's considered heresy." They sat for some time speaking on various topics when a woman who had come as a private escort to one of the elites slipped between them on the ground and started crying. She was touching her forehead to his feet and wiping the tears away with her hair. The leaders sitting with Manuel were appalled. When she started kissing his feet, they stood to remove her, but Manuel held his hand up to stop them.

"If you knew who this woman was and what she does for a living, you would not allow her to be touching you. You should hope no one even sees this," another snapped.

Manuel looked up to the man and replied, "Let me tell you a story." The man was stunned.

'A story? Didn't he hear the warning? Is he crazy?'

"Two people owed money to a moneylender. One owed $5000 and the other $500. Neither of them had the money to pay the lender. The lender– stay with me now– forgives both debts and lets the guys go free. Which of them is going to be more grateful?"

"The one who owed more."

"Yeah. That's right." Manuel reached down and placed his hand on the woman's head. She would not look up. "I came here today, and no one greeted me with genuine love. Everyone was curious and wanted something from me. But this woman has asked nothing of me, greeted me with genuine love, and has not stopped expressing it since she knelt. So, I'm telling you that her many failures are forgiven because of her great love. But whoever loves little is forgiven little."

The woman froze and could only hope he meant what she thought he meant. Could she truly be forgiven for all the places she had been and the corruptible acts she had committed? She didn't feel worthy of looking Manuel in the eyes. She had seen his videos. She knew who he was. She heard him say, "Your immorality is forgiven." The observing guests were whispering among themselves.

"No one has the authority to redeem morality and restore position. No one but the Creator Himself, and surely he wouldn't waste His energy on a whore."

"Do you know how many married men this woman has demeaned herself with? Isn't that something you would oppose?"

Manuel chuckled. "If there is anyone of you here who has not demeaned himself by missing the mark at one time or another, tell me now, and I will condemn her." No one spoke a word. A couple of the men walked away. "That's what I thought."

Slowly, she looked up and met his eyes. "Your belief has saved you. You can go in peace." The woman felt a reckoning in her soul. It was as if a warm flood came and washed away everything that had ever been true. She couldn't even imagine herself in any of the compromising positions. They were wiped clean. Her understanding was clear, and the desperation she walked with for years was simply gone.

"I– I–" she muttered, but words would not come.

"You're good," Manuel eased. "You're welcome." Pulling her to her feet, he hugged her fully. Again, tears came, and she cried on his shoulder. These were not the tears of shame as the previous ones had been but of gratitude.

It was the first time in her life she could remember being hugged by a man that didn't carry some sexual connotation. It was pure and trustworthy. Oh, how she loved this man. This man! How true and right and good he felt. She had never known anything like it. She hugged harder. Manuel looked over to Simon and nodded for him to come. "Simon, escort our friend safely to her car." Looking at her, he said, "You're going to be okay now. Change your phone number, Magdala." Her eyes grew wide. He knew her name! And the way it sounded coming from his lips was perfection.

Simon escorted Magdala out just as the assistant's assistant approached Manuel. "Sir, we're ready to sit down with you for the pre-interview. Would you follow me, please?"

"What's a guy got to do to get some food around here?" Manuel said under his breath.

CHAPTER 20:

DIVINE APPOINTMENTS

Scout tried to follow Manuel into the room that the assistant's assistant led him to but was blocked. After being seated, Manuel was left alone for several minutes. A door opened, and in walked Amy, Draco's attendant. She swayed in with ease about her.

"Well, hello," Manuel greeted her.

"Hello, Mr. Paladin. My name is Amy. I'm Mr. Conti's personal attendant. I've been looking very forward to meeting you." Manuel could see that Amy was nothing like the others. She was carrying the light about her.

"You believe in Me," he said.

With a bashful glow coming to her cheeks, Amy extended her hand and answered, "I do. I had the great fortune of meeting your cousin, Johnny. I was so sorry to hear of his imprisonment."

"Yes, well… as you know, this world is– unjust."

"Mr. Paladin–"

"Manuel, please."

"Thank you. Manuel– Mr. Conti has seen the rise of your celebrity on the Redeemer Roadtrip channel. He is grateful for this pre-interview opportunity to vet you for his show."

"It must be hard for you to work here," Manuel shifted.

"Sir?"

"You aren't like the others. You have found the Truth and are carving out a living in the dark."

"Well, I wouldn't say it's entirely dark. But– yes. It can be quite difficult. Every job has its difficulties."

"That's true. But Draco Conti."

Amy knew what Manuel was getting at but didn't dare breathe a word. Draco was far from the light. He had started with a good heart, but the glare of fame and fortune had twisted him. Draco made the Ancient Writings as easy to chew as bubble gum so that no one could be offended. Heaven forbid someone should become turned off and quit sending their support. Amy smiled, remaining professional.

"Well, it's a great honor to meet you, Manuel. I'm so deeply grateful that you've come." Manuel knew that Amy wasn't referring to the barbeque but earth.

"You are so deeply welcome."

"I could take all of your time picking your brain, but I have specific questions Mr. Conti would like addressed."

"Perhaps he could ask them himself."

"Oh, I'm afraid that isn't possible," Amy defended, "Mr. Conti has–"

"– just entered the room," Manuel finished. Looking up, Amy realized that Draco had slipped in, hoping to be unnoticed. Manuel swung his chair around to face the corner of the room where Draco stood.

"Mr. Conti," Amy stood to attention. "Forgive me; I didn't see you come in."

Manuel had felt Draco enter. Draco didn't want the suck-ups to know he decided to come and was only interested in meeting Manuel for himself. He dressed in a fine Italian cotton shirt that made his spray tan seem darker. With the pretense of respect for Amy, he thanked her and excused her all in one breath. As she exited, she looked for Manuel's eyes one more time. He smiled warmly at her and thanked her genuinely. Draco assumed Amy's chair across from Manuel and didn't speak. He sat, observing Manuel quietly, sizing up the competition. No one was greater than Draco Conti in the evangelical world. His was a household name that brought either devotion or disgust. Draco was trying to determine if Manuel was on the take with the intention of stealing his audience or if there could be something genuine in these healings. Reading people was one of Draco's many gifts. Manuel sat quietly, allowing Draco's process. Eventually, the man spoke.

"Like so many others, I have seen the videos." Draco didn't want to give Manuel even the slightest bit of Kudo but addressed the videos as inanimate. "They're very well done."

"Thanks. They're from Jack's smartphone." Draco ignored the implication that no one had altered them.

"As others have mentioned, I'm considering having you on my show. You realize this would be a larger platform than you could imagine, and my endorsement would catapult you into another sphere of influence. So, I want to make very sure that we are coming from the same place should I decide to make that happen." Draco's arrogance was astounding. The gleam of gold from his pinky ring was catching the light and shining in Manuel's eye. Manuel was sure he knew it. "We could say I discovered you, eh?"

"You know, Conti… you remind me of a story."

"What is it with you and your stories?"

"Well, you know as well as I do that they capture an audience." Draco huffed in response. "So, there was this farmer who planted his crop. As he was scattering the seed, some of it fell along the path. It was trampled on, and the birds ate it up. Some seed fell on rocky ground, and when it sprouted, it withered because it had no moisture to sustain it. Other seeds fell among some thorns and thistles. As it grew, it was choked and stunted. Finally, some seed fell on good soil, and when it came up, it produced a fine crop a hundred times more than had been planted."

"What is this supposed to mean?"

"Even though you have sight, you do not see. And even though you can hear, you do not understand."

Draco debated his response and then laughed. "I like you," he said. "You have guts. You will need that in this business. Explain your story."

"I am the farmer, and my words are the seed. Those along the path are the people who hear my words. But then the adversary comes and takes the word away from their hearts so that they don't believe and won't be redeemed. Those on the rocky ground are the people who accept my words with happiness when they first hear them, but they have no depth, no root. They believe for a bit, but when things get rough, they will fall away. The seed that fell among thorns represents people who hear my words, but as soon as they go on their way, they choke on life's worries, riches, and pleasures. They won't mature. But the seed that falls on good soil stands for those with a noble and good heart who will hear my words, retain it, and by persevering, produce a full crop. A life full of good fruit and provision for every need."

"You are clever," Draco observed.

"I am true," Manuel asserted.

Standing to his feet, Draco was satisfied. "I am going to have you on my show," he determined. "I will have Amy call you with the details. It would be beneficial if you could work one of your miracles there. The donations will pour in." Heading for the door, he did not wait for Manuel to agree to appear.

~~~

The guys had been to a myriad of towns and seen countless miracles. One evening as they were driving a long stretch of isolated highway, a storm that had been coming for days finally hit. The radio was warning of flash floods, and the guys were determined to get to the next town before pulling over. Manuel was sleeping in the back while Simon drove, and Jim navigated. The high humidity in conjunction with warm temperatures created massive
~~~

amounts of warm air rising into the atmosphere causing boisterous thunder and lightning to crack all around them. Jack was watching out the window, counting with each boom, "One-one-thousand, two-one-thousand, three-one-thousand…" BOOM. Levi was on the floor under the dining table that collapsed into a bed.

"You guys, this is serious. We need to pull over."

"We know that, Levi," Jude criticized. "We don't need you to state the obvious."

"We're trying, Levi, okay?" Simon encouraged. "We're trying to get there as fast as we can, but we can't just pull over on the side of the road. The rain will cause too much mud to pull this rig out of, and we would be like sitting ducks for a lightning bolt."

"But…" Levi was trying his hardest not to sound like the complete wuss he knew he was. "aren't we just like… driving ducks?"

Simon and Jim exchanged glances. Neither of them was comfortable with the situation. The wind was pushing the R.V. back and forth on the road. It was hard to stay in the proper lane. The rain started pounding on the roof, making an awful noise. At top speed, the windshield wipers were barely able to keep up. Jude looked back at Manuel, sound asleep. He wondered how the heck he could not be awakened by the thunderclaps and pounding rain. This was by far the most dangerous experience any of them had ever encountered. Jack kept counting and tried not to freak out. He was glad that Jim was there with him. He wished he could call his parents and thank them for all they had done for him. He was thinking the worst but didn't want the other guys to know it. Simon was definitely thinking the worst. "You're my Rock, he says. Always the one to protect him. Driving in the middle of God knows where." CRACK. Each of the men jumped and let out an expression. Even the R.V. seemed to jump.

"I don't see how we can make it, Simon." Jim knew there was no place to pull over but didn't see how they could continue driving. "Seriously, man. This is *beyond* bad." Simon was crawling along. The radio reported winds of over 90 miles per hour, and debris was blowing across the road. Jack started video recording in an effort to document their last minutes should anything happen.

"Alright," Simon agreed. "Wake him up. I don't know what to do." Jim headed to the back of the R.V., falling every other foot with the vehicle's unstable movement. As he reached Manuel, he succumbed to the floor. Pulling himself up, he got right in front of Manuel's face for fear he wouldn't hear him over the sound of the storm. How he could be sleeping was beyond any of them.

"Manuel!" he shouted. "Maaanueeel!" Calling right in his face brought no reaction. Finally, he grabbed onto Manuel's arm and started shaking him.

"Is he dead?!" Levi screamed. "He must be dead! Who could sleep through this? Oh, god! We're all going to die!"

"Shut-up, Levi!" Jude yelled. "If I am going to die, I'm not going out listening to your pansy-ass!"

"Manuel!" Jim shook harder. Manuel opened his eyes. "Dude! We are seriously going to die out here!" Looking around, Manuel observed the storm and the fear in the R.V. Manuel rubbed his eyes as if waking up from a pleasant afternoon nap. Standing, he placed himself in the middle of the chaos. He opened a window and breathed in, smelling the rain and wind.

"What are you doing?!" Jack cried as he shifted the camera to Manuel.

"Shut up!" Manuel yelled. "Be muzzled!" At that instant, the wind ceased, and the R.V. quit rocking. The rain stopped falling, and the thunder silenced. Simon halted the wheels. They could not keep their jaws from hanging open. Jack turned the camera towards the outside. Everything was calm. In fear and amazement, they looked at one another. Manuel simply walked back to the back of the R.V. and flopped down where he had been lying. The guys were in awe.

"What the–"

"What is wrong with you, guys?" Manuel asked. "Where is your faith? Do you really think the Creator is going to let anything happen to us? We aren't done yet." Jude got up and fell at Manuel's feet.

"Who are you? I've never seen anything like that, man. I mean– the wind obeyed you." Manuel put his hand on Jude's shoulder and leaned his head back while shaking it. He looked up in frustration and wondered how long it would take for them to get it. There was so much to do and so little time to do it in.

~~~

As soon as they came to the next town, they pulled into the first available lot to rest. Manuel, who had slept, took the wheel and drove to a cemetery on the town's outskirts. "What now?" Levi whispered, looking out at the gravestones and tombs. Manuel parked and looked across the grounds as if he was searching for something. His eyes locked onto something, and he rose to exit the R.V. As Manuel stepped outside, a demon-possessed man from the town immediately met him.

"Oh, this can't be good," Levi whined.

This man had gone without full clothing for years. Lingering among the tombs, he hadn't lived in a house or known the comfort of a bed. Although town members tried to hospitalize him, no one could bind him. He had broken chains, cuffs, and straitjackets while under guard. As long as he stayed in remote places, the townspeople agreed to leave him be. When he saw Manuel, he came running and cried out at the top of his voice, falling at his feet.
~~~

"What do you want with me, Emmanuel, Son of Theos the Highest?" Manuel addressed the impure spirit, not the man.

"Come out of him."

"I beg of you… don't torture me!"

When the demon didn't immediately depart, Manuel knew it was a significant spirit. "What is your name?" He questioned.

"Swarm," he answered, "for we are many." No matter how many there were, even they knew that Manuel had the authority to cast them out and torment them. They repeatedly begged him not to order them into the abyss of darkness and suffering. The guys were still in awe of the storm calming and realized that their leader had authority not only to forgive and redeem people but torment and condemn them as well. It was a whole new ball game. He held the power of life *and* death.

A large herd of wild boar was feeding nearby on a hillside. The Swarm begged Manuel to let them go into the herd. If they had to be disembodied, better into boars than the abyss. So, he sternly permitted them. Suddenly, the man looked as if he was being pulled off the ground by an invisible force. There were shrieking and guttural noises coming from him as he was delivered of the multitude of demons. The boar began making awful squealing noises and rushed into a nearby body of water, drowning themselves. The man fell to the ground, and Manuel approached him. Simon grabbed his arm in an attempt to keep him. Manuel looked him in the eyes and removed his hand. Approaching the man, he knelt and helped him to sit up. "Now," he repeated. "What is *your* name?"

The property owners where the boar had drowned hurried into town and reported what had happened. Before long, there were carloads of people coming out to see the man and verify what was true for themselves. When word spread that it was Manuel who was with the man, even more people wanted to investigate. As they did, they found the man sitting with the guys shooting the breeze as though nothing had happened. The guys gave him clothes, and he sat calmly in his right mind. The townspeople saw that the man was cured and became overcome with fear. This man had been wandering for years and anyone who could come and change that in an instant, killing a herd of wild boar in the process, was no one that they wanted around. They were so accustomed to the dysfunction that they would rather it remained than try to accept what was foreign and unknown.

"Look, we don't want any of that mumbo-jumbo around here. You all need to take your wonder wagon and get the heck out of Dodge." Jack tried to reason with them and offered to show them videos.

"Look, we stick to our own in this region. We don't need no outsiders coming in here, trying to fix nothing."

"Are you kidding?" Jude barked. "This guy comes in here and saves one of your own, bringing him back to life, essentially, and you would rather he stay that way? That's jacked up. Your solution for this guy was to lock him up or isolate him. But Manuel got to the root issue and healed him!"

"Now, that's enough!" One local threatened and pulled out his shotgun. "Pack it in, boys. The show's over. Ya'll get lost and don't ever think about coming back this way."

They insisted the guys gather their things and head out immediately. "Fear," Manuel told Levi. "It's a killer." Levi took this as a shot to the heart and saw himself clearly for the first time in the townspeople. He determined right then and there not to allow fear to rob him any longer.

The healed man rushed to the R.V. as they piled in. "Please, take me with you." Manuel hugged the man and understood his request.

"I'm sorry, brother. You need to return home and tell the people what's happened. They need you to reveal the Truth to them." The man's chest puffed up with pride. He had not felt purpose in years.

"I'll do it. I'll do it every day. You know, because of my intense anger and frustration, I would cut myself." He hung his head in shame, but Manuel was unphased. "It seemed to relieve my pain. I know that doesn't make sense, but for some reason, it released tension and brought me to feeling something instead of just– numbness."

Each of the guys encouraged him and said their goodbye's. They gave him Jim's cell number and encouraged him to let them know how he was doing. As they headed back onto the road, Jack spent time loading up the new videos of the storm and healing from the Swarm. Simon went straight to bed from the stress of the drive and day. Levi started making plans in his head regarding lifestyle change. Jim and Jude were chatting about their perspectives and personal revelations. Manuel stopped for gas and started the drive to the next destination. After about an hour on the road, Jude made his way to the passenger's seat in the cab. He didn't say much but sat quietly with Manuel. Finally, Manuel broke the silence.

"So, what did you think, Jude?" Jude choked back tears and refused to let them out. He was not one to express emotion, but after everything they had seen that day, something in him broke.

"Kyrios," he whispered.

CHAPTER 21:

TALITHA KOUM

Hanifa carved out a life for herself from home. She worked from home, enjoyed hobbies and entertainment for herself at home, and became accustomed to doing anything outside of the house quickly. For 12 years, she had been bleeding abnormally. It was not a menstruation issue. Doctors were unable to identify the cause and had tried a plethora of medications to make it stop, but none would cause a permanent cease. Hanifa had heard all of the bad jokes and never felt secure enough to enter any personal relationships with men. What could she say? How could she explain? Instead, she spent all of her income and effort searching for solutions to no avail. Her iron levels were low, which caused her to have low levels of red blood cells. Without proper hemoglobin, her tissues and muscles couldn't receive enough oxygen to function effectively. Anemia had become her constant companion. Whether she exerted herself or not, she was always tired. The color of her skin faded, and people would often ask if she was ill. Staying home was easiest in that she never knew when she would feel dizzy or get one of her debilitating headaches. Her heart would palpitate, her hair had all but dried up, her fingernails were brittle, and anxiety had its way of dictating her outings.

Hanifa cried out to the Creator countless times to fix her. She believed that He could but never saw any change. Visit after visit and medication after medication; she would hope and have her hopes dashed. When Hanifa discovered the Redeemer Roadshow, she became an avid follower of Jack's postings. She fantasized that she could meet Manuel. He would see her from across a crowded room and make direct eye contact with her. He would cross the room, ignoring all other people until He reached her. He would call her by name and lay his hand on her. He would speak some secret words and change her life forever. She would be able to stay out for long hours. She could go anywhere and do anything– maybe even a theme park! She would have the courage and confidence to date. Someone would love her deeply and honestly– if she could just meet Manuel.

Jack posted that the guys would be going to the Pine Valley Mall. He was curious to see how many people would show up if they knew in advance where Manuel would be. Word spread like wildfire. When they arrived, there were throngs of people everywhere. The crowd welcomed him and pressed in to be near him. Manuel pushed through and stood on a planter box.

"Well, hello!" he welcomed them. Crowds had never been Manuel's thing. He knew that it was a part of his calling to enlighten the masses, but he had a solitary demeanor. Speaking to crowds was a part of his sacrifice in coming. There were layers of sacrifice that no one could conceive of, but he willingly offered himself to them. The crowd cheered and called out to him. Shop owners left their registers to listen to him. "Thank you so much for all of your support and blessing," he started. Simon was standing in front of the planter box, watching the crowd diligently. Of course, Jack was recording, and the other guys stayed close by to intervene should anything go sideways. Levi had a new sense of self and was proud to be standing close to Manuel, helping with crowd control. "So, you guys have all been taught that you should never make a promise you can't keep or swear to something with no intention of following through. Well, you should *always* do what you say you will do. No matter what it is. If you say you're going to take out the trash– for pity's sake, do it! Because if you don't do the little things you say you're going to do– how will anyone ever believe your word when it comes to the big things? Like, 'I love you.' Or 'I will be there when it counts.' Right?" The crowd was calm. Even for the mass, a pin could be heard dropping. They wanted to listen to every word and not miss a thing. The mall's echo allowed Manuel's voice to carry, and people were standing along the second level railing to hear. Hanifa came and placed herself within eyeshot of Manuel. Surely, he would see her.

"Well, I say, don't swear or promise at all. Be a person of integrity and simply do what you say you will do– or don't say it at all. If you say *yes*, let it be a yes. And if you say *no*, let it be a no. Anything more than that becomes a form of evil when you don't follow through."

Everything Manuel said made so much sense. It was simple, but the people felt the lack of this truth in their lives. "Furthermore, we've all heard, 'An eye for an eye and a tooth for a tooth.' Like if someone does something to you, do that thing right back to them. Take from them what they took from you. But, seriously, I'm saying *don't* repay evil for evil. What will that get us? If someone offends you or insults you by smacking you– what would happen if you just turned away? Or stood your ground?" The crowd laughed at the absurdity of the thought. "If someone is determined to be a jerk, let them. What concern is that to you? Why lower yourself to their level? If someone is threatening to sue you for something you can replace– give it to them! And give them extra to blow their mind! Who cares?? You can get another one! Skip the lawsuit." Manuel was building upon each point, and the shouts of support began to wean.

"Or let's say your boss takes advantage of you– what would happen if you did more than he required? Do your best whether he's in the office that day or not. Don't ever give anyone the ability to speak poorly of you. If a co-worker or neighbor asks you for help, don't deny him if you're able to do it. If they ask you to help them move a pallet, offer to down stack it with them as well. Go the extra mile. I'm not saying to enable someone lazy continually. Have a boundary! But, if you're able to help– do it. And if someone begs from you, give them what you feel comfortable giving them. It doesn't have to be money. But give. You can offer a prayer for them, can't you? And while we're on the subject of people making you uncomfortable– we've all heard, 'keep your friends close and your enemies closer.' But I'm saying– don't hate your enemies. I know, I know. But look, appeal to the Creator on their behalf. Request the best for them so they can have a revelation of who they are and what they're doing wrong. Bless them, don't curse them. You very well may see them change. Your character in times like that will reveal your identity and what you believe to be true about the Creator. Think about it!! How are you any better than them if you act just like them? Do you only love the people that love you? Or is your heart big enough to show concern and care for those who don't even pay you any regard? Even the most twisted people do that. What credit is it to them? Since you are the creation of a perfect Creator of a Higher Realm, be effectual– just like He is effectual."

Authorities were starting to break up the crowd and encourage everyone to disperse. The people didn't budge but wanted to see Manuel do something miraculous. With the disruption, Jarius, a local synagogue leader, came and fell at Manuel's feet.

"Rabbi," he begged, "please, please come to my house. My only daughter is dying. She is just 12 years old." Manuel felt the man's pain and was willing to help. The authorities were breaking up the gathering, and he wouldn't be able to speak much more to the crowd. Simon couldn't believe the man's audacity to ask Manuel to leave all these other people and come to his house. He also couldn't believe the way Manuel responded to him.

"Yes, yes. I'm willing to help your daughter." As Manuel stepped down from the planter box, the crowds pressed in and almost crushed him. Simon and the others came around him and tried to push their way through. Hanifa had her eye on Manuel. She knew if he would just look at her, he would make his way to her so that her dream could come true, but the guys were leading him in the opposite direction. 'No!' she thought, 'No, he has to see me!' If he would just *see* her. Everyone was reaching to touch Manuel as he passed by them. Pulling at him and calling out to him, he was kind and gave a positive word to each as he passed.

"You're doing great, Rocko!" he hollered to Simon as he bulldozed through the crowd. Hanifa pressed through with every ounce of might she could muster. He wasn't going to see her. The mob was too large, and he was heading away. This was her only shot. If she could just touch his hoodie. If she could just get close enough to touch the cuff of his jeans. If she could just flick his hair with her fingertips– pushing through, she reached the verge of his sleeve and barely touched it. Suddenly, it was as if she was standing for the first time. She felt her uterus tighten up. She knew the flow had stopped. Her hair softened around her face, and her nails hardened and grew in front of her eyes. Her cheeks flushed, and she felt everything become fuller and renewed.

Manuel stopped in his tracks. He turned around and searched the horde. "Who touched me?" He questioned firmly. Simon also turned around. The other guys looked at Manuel in confusion.

"Are you kidding?" Jack asked.

"Someone touched me; I felt the dunamis power flow out of me." Hanifa felt a sense of fear, knowing that he was referring to her. *This* is not what she had imagined.

"Kyrios," Simon answered, "*everyone* is pressing in and touching you."

Hanifa stepped forward with her eyes lowered. She trembled and dropped to his feet and touched them with reverence. "It was me," she said softly. Manuel bent down and lifted her by the arms. Looking at her square in the eye, he smiled. He was so pleased with her courage and loved her for all of her struggles.

"Daughter, your belief has healed you. Go in peace. You are well." Hanifa hugged him and told him she loved him. "I love you, too," he said. She believed him. Manuel stepped away from her, and as he did, their hands slid down the other's arm until just the fingertips were saying good-bye.

Finally, the guys all made it to the doors leading to the parking lot. Jarius was ushering them and pleading with them to hurry. As they reached the doors, a maid from Jarius' house was rushing in to find him. With a look of sympathy on her face, she said, "Oh, Sir… I'm so sorry. You don't need this man to come anymore– your daughter didn't make it." Jarius fell to the ground, sobbing.

"No, no… he's right here! He agreed to come! No! Please– no." Manuel nodded to Simon to help Jarius up.

"Don't be afraid; just believe– like that woman just did– and she will be healed."

Jarius wanted to believe. The maid looked at Manuel with doubt. Maybe he hadn't heard what she said. The little girl was dead. The guys looked at each other, remembering what Manuel had done for the woman whose son had died and how he had restored life to his body. Jude looked at her and said, "Just wait."

The drive was not a short one, and Jarius was a nervous wreck. By the time the guys arrived at the house, there was a group of friends and family mourning and wailing. Manuel followed Jarius into the house. As they passed mourners, Manuel instructed them, "You can stop sobbing; she isn't dead but asleep." The mourners were offended. Did this man think they were so stupid that they couldn't tell when someone was dead? How insulting. How could Jarius allow someone like that into the house at a time like this? Jarius went into his daughter's room and found her lying lifeless on the bed. He dropped to her bedside and started sobbing quietly. She was beautiful, and the color had begun to drain from her cheeks. Manuel turned and asked Levi and Jude to wait with the mourners. Jim closed the door. Manuel touched Jarius on the shoulder, encouraging him to step aside. He knelt and took the little girl's hand. He kissed it and said, "Talitha koum." Jim and Jack looked at each other. They hadn't heard Manuel speak in a different language before. The color flushed back into the girl's cheeks. Jarius gasped. Her spirit returned, and she opened her eyes. She looked at Manuel and furrowed her brow. He chuckled at her response and stood up. "I think she's just fine, Jarius." Jarius rushed to his daughter and embraced her.

"Papa, who's this man?"

"My daughter, my love– this man is your savior!"

"Not just hers, friend. Everyones," Jim said softly. Manuel looked at his cousin and smiled.

"If the folks could see us now," he teased.

The little girl got up and wondered what the noise was coming from the front room. As she opened the door, the mourners gasped and screamed. One older woman passed out.

"Look who decided to wake up," Manuel said loudly. "I think she may need something to eat." The girl's mother rushed to her daughter and checked every inch of her being.

"What happened?" she begged. "What did you do?" Manuel shook his head from side to side and put a finger over his mouth.

~~~

Everywhere the guys stopped from then on had a crowd waiting for them. Individuals from different regions would report sightings, and some were permanently caravanning behind the R.V. Manuel knew that Scout was among those following and was publishing articles from each event. He could feel an inevitable interview breathing down his neck. One afternoon they pulled over at a rest stop to cater to the needs of any who would come. Manuel taught for a while and healed many who were sick, hurting, and
~~~

tormented by demons. People asked him how to remain healthy and avoid anything that could defile them and cause them to be sick.

"It's not so much what you encounter that can defile you but what comes out of a person that defiles him." This statement caused some confusion, so he broke it down for them. "Whatever goes into a person from the outside can't defile them. Too much cake isn't good for my health, but it doesn't go into my soul. It goes into my mouth, stomach, and then I get rid of it– if you know what I mean. But it's what comes out of the heart of a man that defiles him. Evil thoughts, misusing sex, theft, murder, coveting, deceit, envy, pride, and foolishness. These are things that defile a person." Teivel's face flashed through Manuel's mind. "Be vigilant because your adversary prowls around like a lion waiting to pounce and devour you. When you break the law or miss the mark, he enters in and causes all sorts of issues in your body and mind. For now, he holds the keys to death and isn't hesitant to use them."

Levi went to the restroom. When he came out, there was a blind man who was regularly there begging. "Hey, man, can you spare some change?" Levi reached into his pocket and dropped some coins into the man's hand. "What's all the commotion going on today?"

"Manuel Paladin is over there talking to people."

"Isn't he the YouTube guy?"

"Yeah, he is," Levi chuckled. The thought of a blind person at a rest stop knowing about Manuel struck him funny.

"He can heal me…" The man started to walk in the direction of the voices. "Emmanuel!" The man yelled. "Emmanuel Paladin!" Some of the people shushed the man. He was dirty and smelled.

"Hey, keep it down, old man. We're trying to listen here." But the man yelled even louder. He was determined to get Manuel's attention.

"EMMANUEL!! It's me, Bart!! I'm here, Kyrios! Have mercy on me!" Manuel heard the man and saw the people discouraging him. He told the very people who were shushing him to let him know it was okay to approach.

"Hey, cheer up, old man. He's calling you."

Levi led him to Manuel, who was tickled by his gumption. "What do you want me to do for you?" Throwing off his dirty sweatshirt, the man answered.

"Healer, I want to see."

"And I want you to." Manuel paused as if receiving some supernatural download. The man stood patiently, waiting. The crowd backed up because of his smell. "Your father… he was an idolater."

"Yes, he was all over the place. He put everything before us. He used to sacrifice his time and money to everything that was self-gratifying."

"That's a lot of iniquities to be born into. You've seen plenty. Now it's time to see more." Laying his hand on the man's head, he decreed, "Your faith has healed you."

Immediately, the man could see. He started pointing and saying, "What?! Look at that! Ah! Look at that!" He turned and looked at Manuel with gratitude. "Oh, thank you, Healer. Thank you so much."

"Absolutely! My pleasure, friend." The man looked at the clean attire that everyone else was wearing and down on his own. Levi saw the embarrassment come over him and stepped up to him.

"Hey, Bart… why don't you come with me." Leading him to the R.V., he showed him where to wash up and gave him some clothes. "They might be a bit big, but they're a good start." Bart gratefully accepted the generosity. After rejoining the crowd and listening to more of Manuel's teaching, he hitched a ride with some who were in the caravan. He wanted to go wherever Manuel was going.

CHAPTER 22:

THE QUEEN OF THE WORLD

The guys had been on the road for a year. In some regards, it seemed to have passed quickly, and in others, it seemed like an eternity since they had seen family, friends, and ran business firsthand. They decided to start looping back around toward the direction of home, stopping in regions they had not before. They were hitting bigger cities now, and the crowds continued to come. Authorities of both the governmental and religious sects followed Manuel's every move. They watched for any reason to catch him in something that could condemn him and mute him as a public voice. At all times, they had moles in the caravan, reporting back on what he had shared or done that day. Johnny was weary of his imprisonment and encouraged the devotees he had sent out to be bold in their charge to ask Manuel his question. Scout, too, had become more daring in his approach and was blatantly asking Manuel questions for his articles in crowd settings. One day while Manuel was speaking to a crowd and healing the sick among them, he called out Johnny's two devotees. "Go ahead," he welcomed, "Ask me your question." Scout perked up and was ready to record the transaction.

"Johnny has sent us to you to ask, 'Are you the one who is to come, or should we expect someone else?'" Scout liked the angle, 'Imprisoned Cousin has Change of Heart.' They had been witnessing Manuel heal people, cast out demons, and bring wisdom to the masses for months, so he replied to them, understanding Johnny's question better than they did. Johnny was discouraged. He had lived such an intentional life. He was faithful to his calling of being a voice to prepare the way for the season that Manuel was walking in currently. Even his parents, Zach and Liz, were faithful in his upbringing, knowing that he was a miracle and appointed by the Creator for something big. Manuel had never visited him in prison, and Johnny wondered why he had been abandoned and left for dead. He used to be somebody. Didn't he at least deserve to be visited or encouraged in these months of isolation? Manuel felt for his cousin but also had a greater demand for his time. Johnny knew the Truth. The masses did not. His call was to them so that they might yet be redeemed.

"You guys need to go back to Johnny. Report to him all that you have seen and heard: the blind are receiving their sight, the disabled are becoming whole, tumors are disappearing, people with skin issues see it cleared up, deaf people are hearing, the dead have been raised, and the needy are receiving the Truth. Theos will bless anyone who doesn't get tripped up on account of me."

They didn't quite understand the last part but would faithfully report it to Johnny as spoken. Manuel knew that Johnny was getting offended. He didn't want him to get bitter now, in this last stretch of his calling. He had done well, and Manuel admired him greatly. The two devotees left to head back to Johnny. They were pleased to have accomplished their task and trusted that Johnny would be relieved with the answer somehow. As they left, Manuel felt the weight of everything Johnny had sacrificed to be his living preface. Manuel began to speak to the crowd about him. Some of them had been Johnny's devout followers, and some had not come through him, so they didn't know all he had accomplished.

"Why did you go out to see Johnny? Why did so many people watch his channel and even travel to his immersion ceremonies? Was he someone who would just sway with the wind and bend to the powers threatening him? No. He was solid and consistent. Was he on T.V. and dressed in fine suits eating up a huge audience? No. He was just a guy out in the wasteland, releasing truth and opportunity to turn from the world's wicked ways." The guys could see that Manuel spoke with passion and frustration at the injustice his cousin was enduring. "Did you go to see a prophet? Yes. Seriously, John was more than a prophet. Theos appointed him before the earth's foundation, and there has never been a better man. And yet–even in this minute– the lowest person in the Kingdom realm is greater than he is."

Those who had been immersed and taught by Johnny knew that what Manuel was saying was right because they experienced firsthand all that he had revealed. Johnny, like Manuel after him, taught business, government, and religious leaders alike. But the religious leaders and experts in the law currently present and listening to Manuel rejected what the Creator was doing for them because they had not experienced the deliverance of immersion and the cleansing revelation it could bring. They had not yet turned from their self-seeking, power-hungry ways and possibly never would.

"How can I describe the people of this generation?" Manuel continued. "People who say, 'You didn't do what we wanted you to do when we wanted you to do it, so you're out!' A spoiled, microwave generation. Johnny came and didn't eat anything bad for him. He never drank alcohol of any kind, and you say, 'What a whacko! He has a demon!' But I come– eating and drinking– and you say, 'He's a glutton, a drunkard who doesn't know what he's saying. He hangs out with people from the IRS and whores.' Yeah– and? Wisdom is the parent that will be proven right by all her faithful children."

~~~

Governor Gale Tetrarch had heard enough. He knew that if his wife, Gailina, learned of one more person healed or miraculous event that she would become even more enraged. She hated that Johnny had started it all, spoken out against their marriage, and was the living embodiment of all that threatened their power. Never mind that Manuel was out there, making things worse. Johnny was the one who had called them out and threatened them personally. Tetrarch secretly feared Johnny's influence and somewhat protected him on the inside. He believed him to be a righteous and spiritual man. The Governor also worried that if anything more than imprisonment happened to him, the people who considered Johnny a prophet would rise against him. Tetrarch had watched all of Johnny's posts, and even though he was puzzled by them, he liked listening to him and found a passion he had never seen in a man. But if his wife, who wore the bona fide pants in the family, had even one opportunity to end his life, she would.

The Tetrarch's were hosting a soiree of their colleagues, officials, and military leaders for the Governor's birthday. Tetrarch dreaded any buzz in the room regarding Manuel's latest endeavors. He didn't want his wife to be provoked or make any public statement that would force his hand to take some action against Manuel or Johnny. The open bar was flowing. There was a den off the parlor where people could secretly bask in a hit from an opium pipe. Everyone was well into the cocktail hour, feeling its effects when the young and stunningly beautiful stepdaughter and niece of the Governor made her entrance. Alina's hand was sought after by many political leaders. Not only did she have a controlling political family but– that body. She invoked the spirit of lust among many a man. Alina was not naïve to her power over men. She was well educated and able to cause even the most decisive leader to stutter. Gailina enjoyed the power that her daughter possessed over men and encouraged her to wield it to her every advantage. Offers immediately presented themselves for Alina to share a drink or dance. Well known for her ability to weave a spell while she danced, Alina was pursued to do so whenever the mood was right. Indeed, the Governor had indulged in far too much wine to be of sober judgment, and when asked for Alina to dance, he wanted to gratify his guests. "Absolutely! Where is my niece, er, daughter– step-niece daughter. Hahahaha. Oh, my. Where is she?!"

Alina's gown hung on her like tiny crystal water droplets and nothing else. The music started, and she allowed herself to be saturated by the notes as
~~~

they danced through the air. Her gaze would fall upon one unsuspecting soul after the next, and each believed that she intended the dance just for him. Alina was mesmerizing, even to Gale Tetrarch himself. Not because she sexually attracted him but because he coveted her beauty and ability to hypnotize men and bend them to her will. Alina entranced the crowd. The men became lost in their desire and the women in their envy. When the music stopped, there was no applause. Everyone was numb by the experience. After several seconds, the crowd regained their senses and gave a full ovation.

"Reward her!" the men insisted. "Tetrarch! Honor the woman! Reward her!"

"Yes, darling," Gailina encouraged, "Do, reward her."

"Yes! Yes, of course. Lovely, Alina– lovely! You have pleased my guests, and so I will please you! How can we reward you, darling?" Tetrarch promised her with an oath, his eyes not able to focus. "Whatever you ask, I will give it to you!"

Alina's eyes widened. Slithering over to her mother, she entangled her arms about her. "Well, well. What should I ask for?" The two relished in the power of the moment. The room waited in anticipation. With a gasp, Gailina counseled her daughter.

"The head of our imprisoned Johnny."

Alina dropped her arms and took a step back from her mother, frowning. Gailina's eyes went from a sparkle to a command when she saw the hesitation in Alina's face. Alina did not want to be on the opposing side of her mother's drive. Begrudgingly, she announced, "The head of our imprisoned Johnny." The crowd gasped and cheered. Some wondered if Tetrarch would follow through. Political leaders and servants all, none would cross him if he did. The Governor's face dropped. He stuttered and asked her to repeat it. With her head lowered, she did. This was wicked even for Gailina.

"Come, come, Gale," Gailina chided. "You don't want to disappoint your guests, now do you?" Wriggling up next to him, she continued, "You don't want them to think you're a coward, do you, darling? Being outwitted by a young girl? What would they think if you didn't do as you said? Are you a man of your word or not?" Gale could feel the blood run out of his face. He was suddenly hot and cold all at once. He had made an oath in front of his guests and didn't want to refuse the worshiped Alina. Looking to his posted guard, he nodded in a 'make it happen' fashion. The crowd laughed. Half thought it was a joke and half salivated in anticipation of something so vicious. Teivel sat with legs crossed, swinging his top leg forward and back.

Tetrarch excused himself to the opium den and wallowed in his disgust. Gailina clapped her hands and ordered the music restored. "Friends!" She encouraged, "Please, enjoy the celebration!" Alina gracefully slipped into the corner of the room and hid before any could engage her.

~~~

Johnny's devotees returned and gave him the report from Manuel. He understood what his cousin meant and grieved that he wouldn't be coming at any time. Johnny had hoped that instead of the devotees, Manuel himself would have come to visit and answer the question they both knew the answer to. Still, he heeded the word of the Redeemer and turned from the distress that was causing him bitterness in his soul. Johnny spent time in true contrition and released any frustration he'd been holding. He knew that Manuel was in the midst of fulfilling all he was brought here to do. How Johnny wished he could be alongside him in the journey. He thought there might be a time when he could support his cousin and serve him faithfully along the way, not just beforehand. He envisioned pointing people to the Redeemer while He was actively redeeming. Still bound by the cement walls and cold bars, he wondered when, if ever, the restoration of his life and mission would come.

The devotees were leaving and planning to return to the Roadtrip caravan. As they said their good-byes, two large guards came in and started pushing them toward the door. Johnny stood and asked, "What is this?"

"It's time for your little friends to go," one answered.

"Am I being released? Has Tetrarch relinquished his stance?"

"That will be the day," the other barked. "You're coming with us."

"Where are we going?"

"It's not where *we're* going– it's where you're going." The guards bound Johnny with a belly chain confining his wrists and ankles with minimal ability to move.

"Where am I going? Is this necessary? Why the cuffs? Guys–"

The devotees started arguing with this treatment. The first guard grabbed each of them by the arm and ushered them out of the hall.

"Say good-bye to your little friend," he spat. "It will be your last chance." The devotees grew wild.

"Wait? What?! What do you mean? Johnny!! Johnny!!"

Johnny was confused. "Seriously, man, what is going on here? Haven't I always cooperated? Why are you chaining me and–"

"Don't worry about it."

Johnny felt the Essence of the Creator come upon him. He knew that what was happening was bad. Everything seemed to go into slow motion. The devotees were screaming.

"Joooohn! They're going to kill you! John! John!" Johnny felt the weight of their words; they resonated as truth.

"Stop! Stop!" Johnny commanded. The guard ushering the men out stopped. He didn't know why he stopped, but he felt his body obey.

"Tell my brother, tell Manuel that they've taken me. Tell him what's happening. Thank him. Tell him... *I was honored.* Tell him I'm sorry that I
~~~

questioned him. Tell him– tell him I'll be the first one welcoming him home."

The devotees calmed and nodded with commitment. The guard felt his legs let loose and continued to shove the devotees out the door.

The guards took Johnny into a medical room. They lifted him onto a metal table and laid him out in one swift motion. They strapped his arms and legs to the table. Johnny was trying to remain calm but could feel the adrenaline coursing through his body. Everything in him screamed to fight and try to escape. Still, the Presence of the Creator was ever with him, and he knew there would be no escape. In his mind's eye, he was screaming, "Just tell my cousin. Just tell him I'm here. Tell him what they're going to do!" He hoped against every odd that the door would burst open, and Manuel would come in. He envisioned a supernatural force sweeping the guards to the side like rag dolls and breaking the chains that bound him. Instead, he took deep breaths and spoke directly to the Essence in the room. He spoke in a language that no one had ever heard. With a loosed tongue, he communicated with the unseen. The guards felt the Presence, too, and were spooked. A doctor came into the room and put on her gloves and mask.

"Hey, hurry it up; this guy has cracked his nut."

The doctor hooked Johnny up to an I.V. and proceeded to manipulate the paraphernalia. Johnny stayed focused on the Presence. Tears of joy and pain were silently streaming from his eyes. He had done all he could. He had been faithful. He had given his all. He wished he could call his mother, but he knew she would learn soon enough. What a servant she had been, as well. In a flash, Johnny opened his eyes and spoke. "Don't I get some last words?"

"Sure," the doctor answered without looking over. "Go right ahead."

"I forgive you." The doctor stopped her movement and looked at the guards. The men seemed to shrink to a fraction of their size. The room grew cold, and each of them felt the chill.

"I don't want you to think you're taking anything from me that I haven't already given. I've given my whole life in service of what I believe. And this, even this– it's– not what I would have planned," he laughed nervously. "But I willingly depart from this world to join my beloved Theos in a greater one. And I strongly encourage you three to examine your lives and come to the full understanding that you can still be redeemed. You can seek the One who has come into the world and is, even now, showing people how to be saved from all of their torment."

The doctor could not get the barbiturate, paralytic, and potassium solution injected quickly enough. She just wanted him to stop. She also didn't trust that if he kept talking, she would have the ability to continue to do her job. The liquid reached Johnny's veins and brought a swift sleep upon him– then he was gone. The guards stepped away from the table. One found himself on the floor blubbering. The doctor checked for a pulse, declared the death, and removed the I.V. She then picked up her saw and prepared for the decapitation.

~~~

The soiree had lulled into an intoxicated haze. Guests coupled off and were gluttoning themselves on the smorgasbord of delicacies. A servant rushed into the room and approached Governor Tetrarch, who had all but forgotten the order he'd given because of his haze. The servant whispered in his ear, informing him that Alina's reward had arrived. It took Tetrarch a moment to regain comprehension, and when he did, he felt suddenly sober. Standing to his feet, he made an announcement. "*Ladies and… gentlemen.* Let it never be said that I am not a man of my word. Let it also be said that I am not one to be crossed. Ever." With that, he waved the servant away to bring in the reward. "Alina! Gailina! Come to me." Gailina sashayed to her husband's side in arrogance. Alina refused to come. "Alina! Now, woman." Slowly, Alina emerged from her corner and placed herself beside the Governor. Everyone stood at attention, waiting to see what the grand gesture would be. The doors flung open, and in walked a servant carrying a silver tray with Johnny's head in the center. The crowd gasped. The servant walked straight up to the threesome and presented the head. Tetrarch stood frozen with a new sense of loathing and power. Alina ran to vomit. Gailina smiled and imagined herself the queen of the world.
~~~

CHAPTER 23:

ON THEIR OWN

When word that Tetrarch had Johnny executed reached Manuel, he felt the need to withdraw. Grief struck him to the core. He knew his family would be planning a funeral but didn't believe it would be wise to attend. Anywhere Manuel showed up, a crowd followed, and he didn't want to dishonor the day by taking any attention away from Johnny. Not only had a warrior for their cause died, but he lost his cousin and couldn't honor him the way he would want. Manuel loved and deeply admired Johnny. He had started it all, and now he was gone. He did not deserve his end, but Manuel knew that he would see him again in the Higher Realm when he returned to his Kingdom. This was a double tragedy for Manuel. Thinking about the cruelness with which his cousin had suffered for the cause of redemption brought thoughts of Manuel's own end and the inevitable way that authorities hunt anything that threatens their power. He saw his cousin's death and sacrifice as a foreshadowing of his own.

Manuel gathered the guys and told them he was going to sneak away for a bit. The men had no idea what they were supposed to do during these days without him.

"Where could you possibly go?" Jim asked. "Are you going home for Johnny's funeral?"

"No, that wouldn't be fair. Don't worry. I am perfectly capable of being unseen."

"What are we supposed to do?" Jack wondered, "Should we each go home for a bit?"

"No," Manuel instructed, "No, the work isn't done. As a matter of fact, what you have seen until now was just the beginning. The world has me right now, but it won't always, and people need to understand that they can have the power and grace that I operate in."

The guys looked at each other with confusion. How could others operate in this same power? There was only one Redeemer. He was the One. He wasn't making sense to them. They thought that Johnny's death was making Manuel morbid. He was already thinking about the days when he would be absent from the world. Why would he even bring that up?

"I'm going to send you guys out while I retreat."

"Wait– without you?" Levi gasped.

"Yes. I'm going to release to you all that I carry to drive out all demons and cure all diseases."

The guys became divided. Jack was stoked and eager to think that he might be able to heal people the way Manuel did. Jude was interested in the power but wondered if it was true. Simon believed and felt the burden of following in Manuel's footsteps. Jim thought of himself more as an adviser than someone who would go out into the crowds. But he wanted to be pleasing and serve the cause well. Levi wondered if he had what it took to do it.

"You don't," Manuel interrupted their thoughts. "But I am going to give you what it takes. I will fill you with authority and the dunamis power that allows people to be healed and become pristine in their souls. It's the same power in which I flow. It is the power to perform miracles. Are you ready?"

"Wait, wait…" Levi struggled against becoming afraid. "How will we– when will you rejoin us? How long will you be gone? Are we going to continue on together? In the R.V.? What about the–"

"Levi…" Manuel laid his hand on his friend's shoulder. "Stop. What do the Ancient Writings tell us about worry?"

"Oh, geez, um… I'm not…"

"Do not fear, for I am with you. Don't be agitated, for I am the Designer of all things. I will strengthen you and help you; I will uphold you with my righteous right hand."

"Yeah, right," Jude joked, "that was right on the tip of my tongue."

"Guys, you can do this. People need you to do this. Look, don't worry about taking anything with you just– go. Wherever you go, stay where you are welcome. If people don't welcome you, then shake the dust of that town off of your feet and move on." Manuel could feel their discomfort, so he sat down and went deeper into their purpose.

"Look, don't be anxious about anything. Don't spend all of your time thinking about what you're going to eat, what you're going to wear, what you're going to do, how things are going to work out. Look at– birds, for example. They don't plant fields, harvest crops, store up food for the winter– and yet they are entirely provided for by their Creator. Everything they need is available to them as they need it. Don't you think He cares more about what you need than what a bird needs? Does being anxious add even an hour to your life? Um, no. It wastes an hour. Don't get hung up on things like what you're going wear, eat, get, or whatever. Johnny didn't. The Creator of the Universe knows exactly what you *need.* Just– before anything else– pursue Him and His Kingdom, and absolutely everything else you could ever possibly *need* will come. Do you understand?" The guys nodded. They weren't thrilled about being out on their own, but they understood his point.

"Just don't be anxious or worry about tomorrow. There's enough stuff to deal with today. Take it one day at a time."

Manuel closed his eyes and lifted his head toward the heavens. Each of the guys followed suit and shut their eyes as well. A light came into the R.V. and filled it to capacity and then ceased. When they opened their eyes, Manuel was gone.

~~~

Governor Gale Tetrarch was feeling pretty full of himself. He couldn't shake the shame of the order for Johnny's death, but there had certainly been a new level of fear and reverence shown to him since the event. Even his wife treated him with more regard, but Alina made herself scarce. News reached the Governor that not only was Manuel's popularity growing, but now his groupies were out healing people. Rumors arose that Johnny had risen from the dead and was among them working wonders. Although Tetrarch had dreams of that very thing, he knew it was impossible. He saw the head himself. He gave the order. His next order was to keep close tabs on this Redeemer person so that he, too, didn't get out of hand.

~~~

The guys headed out in hesitation and determination to make Kyrios proud. They wondered where he had gone and when he would return. When the caravan realized that Manuel was nowhere to be found, they dwindled and eventually returned home. One Sunday, the guys were driving past a church gathered for prayer. They noticed a man who had been crippled since birth sitting outside the gate. The sign above it read, "Beautiful," and he sat beneath it as a picture of anything but. He was weary and seemed to have given up hope. He was barely groomed and sat begging for money and thinking churchgoers might be willing to give. One after another, they passed by him. Only a few offered him help, which he was reluctant to receive.

"Why don't you come inside?"

"Just money, thanks. Just money."

Pulling over, Simon and Jack hopped out and made their way over to the man.

"Spare some change, guys?"

"I don't have money to give you, man. But what I do have, I willingly give to you." The man looked up at him like he was some loon. "In the name of Emmanuel, I command your soul to be restored… walk." The man laughed as though Simon had lost his marbles. But then, he felt the fullness of his legs come to him. Jack extended his hand and helped the man up. Instantly, the man's feet and ankles became strong. He jumped and then began to walk. Together they walked into the church's courtyard. The man was hollering and jumping. The people saw him and recognized him as the beggar at the gate. Many were filled with amazement and wondered how and what had just happened to him. They believed that a miracle created the universe and that miracles used to happen, but few thought they were still possible. Many wondered if the whole thing was a setup, and the man had been faking all along just for money. Simon and Jack blessed the man and rushed back to the R.V. to tell the others.

Four weeks went by with no Manuel. However, they could feel the Essence of the Creator and were learning much by operating in it on their own. They missed Manuel and hoped each day that he would return, but they stepped out in faith of what he had told them. Each time they saw the physical and spiritual intertwine in his absence, they were blown away. They were learning that their mission wasn't just for physical healing but for spiritual guidance as well. They were teaching, just as he had done at each event, simply by pointing to the Creator, speaking His Truth, and letting them know how they could be redeemed; by believing that Manuel was Kyrios. It was a two-fold revelation. People needed spiritual healing before the physical healing could take place. The guys were humbled that they would be trusted with such a mission and knew that they had much to learn before fully carrying its weight. They were grateful that Manuel had said he would be back. They were digging deeper into the Ancient Writings themselves. They even studied together in the R.V. at night, wanting to be well equipped and always prepared to give an answer for the hope they embraced. They tried to be both gentle and respectful, which wasn't easy in some crowds.

Finally, one evening after reading together, they all went to bed. In the morning, Levi got up first and started to make coffee. He looked over and saw a bulk laying in Manuel's spot. He looked around and noticed that each of the guys were in their respective places. Either someone had snuck in during the night, or Manuel was back. "Kyrios!" he announced and waited for the lump to move. Each of the guys stirred while Jack jumped up and rushed, leaping directly onto the lump. Manuel let out an 'oomph' and rolled over to greet his crew. They each greeted him and were abundantly happy to have him return.

"I'm so glad you're back, Man. Something serious is going on with Jim's butt, and we can't cast it out."

"Stop it!" Jim retorted. "Seriously?"

Manuel laughed. "Yeah, some demons will only come out after fasting and prayer."

"He needs to fast those tacos." The guys were all laughing and roughhousing. He was back. Kyrios was back. Levi returned to making coffee, and they all sat around catching up.

"You should have seen it," Jack delighted, "even the demons submit to us in your name. It was awesome." Manuel sat up and almost recited.

"'I saw Teivel fall like a thunderbolt from the Higher Realm. In an instant, he was kicked out of the Kingdom.' I have given you authority to stomp on snakes and scorpions and to overcome all of the power of the enemy. *All* of the power of Teivel and his minions. Nothing will harm you." The guys exchanged gladiator glances. "But… don't celebrate the fact that spirits submit to you. Celebrate the fact that you have been redeemed and that your names are written down in the annals of the promised Kingdom. The Creator knows you."

Manuel became overwhelmed with gratitude. He was refreshed and full after his time away. Opening his arms wide, he spoke openly to the Creator, "I honor You, Papa! Almighty Maker and sustainer of every realm, because in Your wisdom you have allowed even common everyday people to know the mystery of You. But Kings, Presidents, the learned, wise, and power-hungry are clueless when it comes to You. It's just what you have been pleased to do." He lowered his head and arms and looked at each of the guys intimately, "You guys… you guys are so fortunate. Do you know how many wise men, powerful people, and world leaders have wanted to see and taste what you have? To hear what you have heard and know what you have learned? They'd kill for it."

"We do," Simon sighed. "and it is so good to have you back, Kyrios." Jack jumped back on him, and one by one, each of the guys dog piled.

~~~

Manuel said that there was somewhere he wanted to take them. They did stop to address crowds on the way, but Jack also recorded Manuel in the R.V. and posted a couple of powerful teachings along the way. At one gathering, an expert on the Ancient Writings and law stood up and challenged Manuel.

"Teacher, what do I have to do to get this *immortal life*?" He knew other writings that taught how one had to earn passage into a Higher Realm. Manuel knew the man's heart and that he was trying to test him.

"What is written in the law?" Manuel replied. "How do you read it?"

"Love Theos [the Creator] with all of your heart, all of your soul, all of your mind, and all of your strength. Also, to love your neighbor as you love yourself."

"It seems you've got the answer. Do all of that, and you will live well."

"And so… who is my neighbor?"

"Are you asking me who falls in the lines of the requirement for good treatment?" Manuel asked not for the man's sake but all those who were listening. The man smirked.
~~~

Manuel leaned back and propped his feet up. "There was this guy who was traveling through a sketchy part of town. Robbers attacked him. They beat him up pretty badly, took his wallet, stripped him of his jacket and designer tennis-shoes, leaving him half-dead. A priest drove by and saw the man in a lump on the side of the road, bloody. He kept driving but prayed that Theos would send someone to help him. A minister jogged by and saw the man. He crossed the street and sped up in fear the same might happen to him but determined to call the police as soon as he reached his destination. Then, a foreigner who had only been in this country for a short while and barely spoke the language came upon the man. When he saw him, he immediately took pity on him. He wiped down his wounds, checking for anything life-threatening, and loaded him into his vehicle. He gave him his own jacket and shoes and took him to a local hospital. With no I.D. for the hospital, the foreigner offered to pay the medical bills himself until any family might be located."

A woman listening to the allegory was already crying as she could identify which of the passers-by she would have been out of fear. Another man found himself angry, because he too, knew that he would have kept going. 'It's a dangerous world,' he thought. 'You have to take care of yourself.'

"Which of these three do you think was a neighbor to the man who was robbed and beaten?"

"The one who had mercy on him, of course," the expert answered.

"Alrighty then. So, you know to do the same."

"So, I just need to be a good person," the man pushed. "Don't all ancient writings state this?"

Manuel knew of the path needed for people to be genuinely saved. He knew that it was more than a story that would do it. "Believe in your heart and confess with your mouth that you believe I am Kyrios, the son of Theos, and in all that will be accomplished through me– and you will be saved."

"What will be accomplished through you?"

"Total restoration."

This wasn't a concept people easily grasped. The crowd whispered among themselves and questioned what he meant. Would souls be restored? Would the earth be restored? Life as they knew it– restored?

It had been a long stretch, and the guys loaded up into the R.V. Jude made sandwiches for everyone and passed the bag of chips around. Manuel drove into the night to reach the destination he had planned. He pulled over and slept for a few hours before pulling up to the house of a woman named Marta. Manuel went to the door alone. When she opened the door to see the Redeemer Roadtrip R.V. outside and Manuel himself standing at her door, she grabbed her stomach and dropped to her knees.

"Hello, Marta."

"Hello, Kyrios."

"I don't mean to impose, but I thought maybe we could crash here for the day."

"Oh, my– you can– you are welcome to– I would be so honored."

Manuel waved the guys in and apologized in advance. They could be a bit overwhelming when all together. Marta asked if she might invite some friends and family over to enjoy his presence.

"Absolutely," he joked, "That's usually the way it works."

Before they knew it, Marta's brother Lazer, sister Maria, and many of their friends were all packed into their home and backyard celebrating. Marta wanted everything to be perfect. How many people have Emmanuel Paladin knock on their door? She was a type-A personality already, so she wasn't concerned about the state of her home. Still, Marta expressed love through acts of service, so she took hospitality very seriously and wanted everything to be perfect. Recruiting friends to stop for items before they came, she had a full spread in no time. Staying on top of the dishes and making sure the right utensils were out, Marta was going non-stop. Her sister Maria was sitting at Manuel's feet in the back yard, soaking up every word that came out of his mouth. Marta was trying to wave her sister in to help with all of the preparations and upkeep, but Maria would not respond. She knew Marta. She knew that she would be given six tasks to accomplish the minute she stepped foot in the house. *Emmanuel Paladin* was sitting in their backyard! There was no way she was going to miss the opportunity of gleaning some wisdom or seeing someone healed in some way. Finally, Marta walked straight out to the center of the gathering.

"Kyrios, I'm sorry to interrupt. Maria– come into the house; I need you."

"No," Maria dared. Smiling like the perfect hostess and not wanting to cause a scene, Marta tried again to influence her sister.

"*Maria…* Please come into the house. I need you to do something."

"No. I don't want to. Get Lazer to do it." Maria knew that she would be invoking the wrath of her sister but– *Emmanuel Paladin.* Marta sighed in disgust.

"Kyrios, don't you think that my sister should come and help me? She is leaving me to do all of the work myself. Please, tell her to help me." Manuel chuckled and took Marta's hand.

"Marta… sweet Marta. You throw a great party. But you are worried and upset about too many things. There are only a few things that are truly needed. Only one thing, actually. Maria has chosen that one thing, and I won't take it away from her." Marta felt like bursting out in tears. She turned quickly and returned to the kitchen. She started running water and rinsing dishes for the washer. Manuel came in and stood beside her.

"Oh, are *you* going to help me? Absolutely not. You're the guest of honor."

"Marta… my friend. You are choosing to get upset. You've done so much already; everything is great. Who cares if there are dishes in the sink? It's a party. Let it go. Come and join us. Sit with me." Marta started to cry.

"I can't. It will pile up."

"And who will die when that happens?"

Marta laughed and set her towel down. "Okay, but… if Maria doesn't help me when this is over, I'm going to be *really* pissed."

CHAPTER 24:

THE SON OF MAN

The guys parked the R.V. in a remote location. They thought they would spend a couple of days resting and enjoying the outdoors. It was rare that they could break from the caravan, but people hadn't followed them in such large numbers since Manuel's departure. However, it seemed that they might be starting to catch on to the fact that he was back. Even Scout Nikkos had quit following them long enough to go home for a bit.

Upon waking, the guys made coffee and started to stretch. They discussed a possible hike and wanted to find water nearby to try their hand at fishing again. Jude was the first to open the R.V. door. With six guys in one R.V., he felt the need to relieve himself quicker than the one restroom would allow. When he opened the door, there were many people within a close radius of the vehicle.

"Whoa," he observed and closed the door again.

"What?" the guys inquired.

"There are *a lot* of people out there."

"Aw, seriously? They found us." Jack was disappointed. He wanted the fun downtime with his brothers.

"How many people is *a lot*?"

"I don't know… a lot. Hurry up; I've got to use the john." The guys gathered themselves and stepped out to greet the crowd. Manuel stepped out and welcomed them. People immediately started to surround him and seek his attention. Simon rushed to his side.

"Holy cow," Jack gasped.

"Oh, wow…" Jim agreed. "This *is* a lot of people."

"How did they find us? We are in the middle of nowhere?" Levi wondered. "There must be at least five thousand people here."

Manuel climbed up on a rock and did his best to address the people. There was a greater number of people than they had ever seen before. Manuel knew that being in a bit of a valley would allow his voice to carry and echo off of the hills. He spoke to them about the Kingdom of the Creator and healed those who needed healing. A man in the crowd called out, "Teacher! I beg you to look at my son. He will be fine and then suddenly scream and go into convulsions. He foams at the mouth, and it's destroying him. I think he's possessed– I begged a few of your followers to heal him, but they couldn't." Levi remembered the man and his son from their time without Manuel.

Manuel sighed with frustration. "This generation is so depraved and unbelieving. How long will you need me to be right by your side before you start understanding what I'm saying to you? Bring your son here."

Manuel had been giving crowds the tools to cast demons out and take authority over sickness, but they still clung to him to do it for them. If his own guys, knowing all that they knew and seeing all that they had seen, lacked the faith to cast out the different ranks of demons, how would anyone else? As the boy was walking forward, the demon threw him to the ground in a convulsion. Manuel rebuked the impure spirit, healed the boy, and returned him to his father. The crowd again stood amazed at his authority. The father wept with gratitude.

The morning slipped into the afternoon, and Manuel was still pouring himself out. Levi approached him with water and encouraged him to eat something. The crowd was growing weak and needed to eat something also. Then, the early afternoon slipped into the late afternoon, and still, no one had left. Levi again approached Manuel and encouraged him to rest.

"Send the crowd away so they can drive and get something to eat. It will take some time to get anywhere nearby for food. We need to go get something, too."

Manuel looked at him and said, "You give them something to eat."

Levi wondered if the heat and no food were getting to Manuel's head. "Manuel, there's no way we could feed all these people. We're six guys in an R.V., man. Where do you expect us to get that kind of food?" Levi turned to Jack, who had come up alongside them. "Manuel wants us to feed the people."

"Which people?"

"*All* the people."

"Feed all these people? All of them?" Levi nodded. The others saw something happening and joined.

"What's going on?" Simon asked.

"Manuel wants us to feed all these people."

Simon looked at his leader and met his eyes. "What's the plan?"

Manuel smiled and asked, "What do we have?"

"Not a lot. I think we have about five boiled eggs and a couple of loaves of bread." Jude offered.

"Perfect," Manuel replied. "Have the people sit down and let them know we're going to eat. Get the eggs and bread."

Half wondering how the guys planned to serve them all a meal in these circumstances, the people sat down. Taking the five eggs and loaves of bread, Manuel looked up into the glory realm and thanked the Creator for the provision. His praise and spirit of gratitude rose in worship to the divine expanse causing a portal to open where the provision could be multiplied. When he lowered the food, it was pouring out from the small basket he had lifted. He began passing it out to the guys to hand out. Each time they came back, he had an abundance to give. It wasn't cheeseburgers and pizza, but it was more than enough. When everyone had eaten something and were content, Manuel had the guys go and pick up any remaining leftovers. They came back with twelve plastic bags of bread and eggs. It was strange and wonderful.

Manuel wrapped up the day and let the crowd know it was time to go home. He encouraged them not to follow on to the next town but find their way back to their lives and where they needed to be. He expressed gratitude and encouraged them to live by the teachings they heard that day. Each of the guys loaded into the R.V. Manuel told Jim to drive them out of the gathering. As they pulled out, Jim was sure that some would follow despite Manuel's request they stay. But as he pulled around, no one moved fast enough to follow. They were able to get all the way to the closest road and pull out without a caravan on their tail. "That's a miracle in itself," he teased.

Manuel sat and started praying. As incredible as these days were, they did drain Manuel. He needed the quiet restoration of being in the Creator's presence to restore, renew, and refresh him. The guys had become accustomed to his silence in these times and stayed reasonably quiet in reverence of them. When Manuel finally did look up, he asked the guys, "Who do the crowds say that I am?" The guys exchanged glances, and each answered separately.

"I actually heard someone say that you were Johnny; escaped from prison."

"I've heard people call you a prophet. Like maybe the great prophet, Elijah, come back to life. Or some other great prophet, you know?"

"Who's Elijah?" Levi asked.

Jim's eyes widened. "Elijah was one of the greatest prophets in ancient times. The Writings credit him as the one who led the people out of corruption and suffering– sound familiar?"

"And you guys?" Manuel asked. "Who do you guys say that I am?"

Simon answered, "You are the Anointed One. The long-awaited Redeemer and Son of the Theos."

"Simon… my Rock. You are favored. The coolest part of you knowing this is that my Father, from His established realm, has revealed it to you. You didn't learn that from a book or any human being but by His Essence, as you believed. I'm going to give you the keys of the Elevated Kingdom. Whatever you forbid on earth will be forbidden in the Higher Realm."

"Me, Kyrios?"

"Everyone… but you first."

Jim was getting tired and found a secluded place to pull over. He joined the others in conversation. These were some of their favorite times; late at night, they would all sit around and process everything they were witnessing and learning. Manuel would often break things down for them or clarify a point he had made that day. Manuel became somber on this night and warned them not to share what he was about to say with anyone.

"Who would we tell?" Jack asked.

"Gee, I don't know… the internet?" Jude said, throwing a pillow at him. Jack frowned and made a face at him.

"The Son of Man must suffer many things and be rejected by the government leaders, teachers of the law, and both religious sects. He will be killed but will come back to life."

"Who's the Son of Man?" Jude questioned. Jim shrugged. They knew that Manuel was the Son of the Creator, but they didn't know who this Son of Man was.

"Listen," Manuel continued, "anyone who wants to be a pupil of mine–learn to do all the things I do and gain the knowledge that I have–has to be willing to sacrifice daily. They have to be willing to follow me. When people cling too tightly to their life, they're just going to lose it. But whenever someone loses their life for my sake– they'll find it saved."

"What are you talking about?" Levi asked. "Of course, people want to hang on to their lives. Are you saying people have to die to follow you?"

Manuel chuckled, understanding the confusion but was discouraged; everything always required so much explanation. "I'm saying, if someone insists on seeking their life, their way, their desires first– then true life, the redeemed life, and enlightenment I am offering– will be lost. But, if someone is willing to let go– seek the Kingdom of Theos first, His ways, His will, His desires– then there will be so much freedom that they will have a full and truly satisfying life. They must die to themselves, not to life itself."

"Spiritual, not physical." Levi grasped.

"I mean, what good is it if someone works hard and gains everything they could ever want but doesn't have peace in their mind, will, and emotions? Why forfeit your soul when you could *truly* have it all?" They understood this. "I'm telling you guys, whoever decides he is embarrassed by me or the things I'm saying, the Son of Man will be ashamed of later in the Kingdom surrounded by the Creator and His sublime messengers."

"Kyrios…" Simon questioned, "Who is the Son of Man?"

"I am," Manuel smiled.

"But… you're the Son of the Creator. How can you be the Son of Man?"

"Simon– I don't have authority on earth because I am the Son of the Creator. I have authority on earth because I am the Son of Man. I faced off with Teivel and gained my authority. The original man was given the authority to speak life and death with his tongue. He was given authority to rule, reign, have dominion– create. But he missed the mark and made some poor choices– so I am here, as a Man, to regain that authority. For all men, not just myself." A light bulb was going off in some of their minds.

"You mean– we're all 'sons of men' and can– through–"

"Sanctification–"

"Sanctification– walk in every way that you walk in?"

"Absolutely. I'm telling you guys, some of you here in this R.V. won't even taste death before you see Glory from the Higher Realm."

~~~

Not all of the guys were clear on the whole 'Son of Man' thing. They knew Manuel to be human: their cousin, friend, and leader. But they knew that he was also the Son of Theos, the Creator. How else could he know the things he knew and understand how to operate in the spiritual realm? They spoke in private about their confusion regarding Manuel having to suffer, and did he say, 'die?' That would be insane. The Ancient Writings foretold the Anointed One would come in power and that he would carry the government on his shoulders. Manuel was here to overturn the corrupt ways that Government City and the Union Empire had become accustomed to and reveal a new way of leading the people. It would be a sanctified way that would allow for a happier and healthier society. Wasn't he? How then could he say that he would suffer? It had to be a part of a bigger picture. He must have meant to suffer and die figuratively. Like when he told them people had to die to themselves to gain true freedom. Still, they were eager to see the turnover of power and the Glory from the Higher Realm come to be.

Several days had passed since discussing these things. As he often liked to do, Manuel wanted to get away and take a hike to clear his head. He brought Simon, Jack, and Jim with him. Jude opted for a nap, and Levi was working their numbers. Manuel found a beautiful spot high on a mountain ridge and started to meditate and commune with the Creator. The guys lingered nearby, enjoying the quiet and sunshine. Jim had his eyes closed when he felt Jack smacking him repeatedly on the arm.

"What, what, what? Geez–" Opening his eyes, he saw his brother standing with his jaw wide open. He had stopped smacking Jim but was holding on to his arm for support and connection. Simon knelt and couldn't remove his eyes from the sight. Turning, Jim saw that as Manuel was meditating, the appearance of his face changed. His clothes became as bright
~~~

as a flash of lightning. He was standing with two other men. Somehow, without a word among them, they knew that these two men were Jekuthiel, the author of the first five books of the Ancient Writings, and Elijah, the prophet of old who came to deliver the words of the Creator and lead His people out of corruption. Manuel– his cousin and friend– was standing on a ridge lit up so bright that they could barely keep their eyes open, but they couldn't look away. It was some glorious splendor, and short of not being able to move, Jim understood why Simon had knelt and felt that he should probably be kneeling too. Having been tired beforehand, they were all fully awake now. Simon wanted so desperately to acknowledge his reverence for them that he called out to them.

"Masters! I am so grateful to be here! Let me prepare a place for you somehow. One for each of you to relax and– be here."

Jim was embarrassed for him but lacked the ability to speak and tell him to shut up. It was painfully obvious he didn't know what he was saying. They were witnessing something wholly otherworldly, and Simon was shouting to these men who obviously could produce anything any of them may need without his clumsy offer. A cloud appeared and covered the guys. They started to feel anxious when a booming voice seemed to come from every direction in the midst.

"This is my treasured Son, with whom I am well pleased; listen to him."

When the guys heard this, they fell on their faces. This was unlike anything they had ever imagined. The voice penetrated every cell in their being. If they had covered their ears, they would have heard it coming out of their beings. It was like a bass that vibrated their entire person. It would have been disturbing had it not come with a weight that would not lift. They were terrified. Manuel approached them and encouraged them to get up.

"Don't be afraid."

When they lifted their heads and opened their eyes, the other glorified beings were gone, and they saw only Manuel standing before them. He turned without a word and simply started walking down the mountain. As they were able, they got up and started to rush after him. When they caught up, Manuel casually instructed them.

"I wouldn't tell anyone about what you just saw until after the Son of Man is raised from the dead."

Raised from the– there he went again! And why did he keep referring to himself in the third person? Was it a way of compartmentalizing what was going to happen? Why was he talking about his death?! There was so much to do yet! They hadn't even made it to Government City for the upheaval of current methods. That was enough, things were getting unbelievable, and the guys needed some answers.

"Kyrios," for there was no other name for him at this point, "the Writings say that Elijah must come before the Anointed One. Was that it? That was

Elijah, right? Back there? With you– so, does that fulfill the Writings that he will come?"

"No, no, no… but I can see why you might think that." Manuel didn't pause or even look back.

"So, when will he come again?"

"I know it's confusing, but… Elijah already came. He came, and no one recognized him, so they did to him whatever their sick souls pleased. They will do the same to the Son of Man. I will certainly suffer at their hands."

They deduced that Manuel was talking about Johnny. He had been the modern-day Elijah and suffered at the hands of the authorities. They killed Johnny, and Manuel kept talking about how they would kill him. Jack stopped dead in his tracks. He hadn't conceived of a world without Manuel in it. Ever. He knew there was much that hadn't happened yet, so he couldn't– and wouldn't– think about that until he absolutely had to.

CHAPTER 25:

KNOCK IT OFF

Simon, Jim, and Jack had not told the others about what they saw on the ridge. They wanted to talk about it but strongly felt the Creator's presence and had a new level of reverence for both Him and Manuel. Manuel told them not to bring it up– and they didn't. They did, however, discuss the Son of Man suffering and dying thing with the other guys. They all found it hard to believe. Manuel had authority over life and death; they had seen it with their own eyes. They couldn't imagine anyone being able to get their hands on him, let alone cause him to suffer. Simon would never let it happen. While Manuel was out on one of his meditative walks with the Creator, the guys tried to process and make sense of it all. They discussed when the world would be in the right order, and everything was finally accomplished. They fantasized about what that would look like and what they would all do with themselves.

The conversation expanded into the coming time after they had each transitioned from this realm into the Kingdom. They imagined how it would be to live in the presence of the Creator at all times and in His established dwelling place. Each of them felt honored to have been chosen to walk with Manuel in these days on earth and believed Theos would honor them in the Higher Realm as well. They started arguing a bit about who would be regarded most in the Kingdom to come. Jack was convinced he and Jim would be honored more than the others because they were family. They had known Manuel their whole lives.

"Family won't be the same up there," Simon spat. "I'm the one he said he was giving the keys of the Kingdom to. Hello. Don't you think that means a bit more than DNA on earth?"

"Maybe," Levi chimed in, "one thing I know, it won't be me. I mean, I will be greater than the average Joe, but I don't think I'll be the highest-ranking. That wouldn't make sense."

"There's still time," Jude argued. "Shoot, I could do something in the next bit that puts all of you behind me in line. I'm going to sit up there and breathe in all the goodness that Kingdom has to offer, man."

Just then, Manuel opened the R.V. door and came in. The guys went silent with a bit of perspective on how they were behaving. Manuel's presence always brought a naturally convicting element. He didn't have to say anything, and he never condemned anyone, but his just being there made them realize the pettiness of their argument. Manuel knew their thoughts.

"You guys should get ready. People are waiting, and we have work to do. Nobody's going to be lapping up the seat of luxury anytime soon." Manuel hopped into the driver's seat and started to head out. Jack popped up next to him in the passenger's seat and changed the subject.

"Hey, Man. We saw someone driving out demons in your name the other day. Can you believe that? We tried to stop him because he's not one of us."

"Why did you do that?" Manuel scolded. Jack was surprised. "Hey, there is a lot of work to be done out there… if that guy wasn't against us, he was for us. That guy gets it. Let him help. We're going into all these towns, teaching every place that will have us, and demonstrating the Kingdom's authority by healing every disease and sickness. There are plenty of people who need help, but not many of us to help them. You should be praying for more men like him."

"Sorry."

"Don't be sorry, just… always check someone's motives before you try and dictate what should happen. Be careful not to judge anyone too quickly. The thing is, the same judgment that you use on someone else is going to be used when you are facing judgment. Does that make sense?" Manuel loved Jack with a special love. He felt more like his little brother than a cousin. Jack was younger and quick to jump. Manuel wanted to tuck him up under his arm and protect him from all that would come.

"Be careful, Jacky. Don't give dogs what is sacred, and don't throw your most treasured goods in with the pigs. They'll just trample on them and then turn and attack you." Jack couldn't help but chuckle. Manuel always reverted to some sort of analogy. "Do you get what I'm saying?"

"Yes," Jack answered like a reprimanded teenager.

"Do you?"

"Yes!"

"What am I saying?"

"I should always treat someone with the same respect that I want to be treated with and not judge them in any way that I don't expect to be judged myself."

"Right, and?"

Jack sighed. "And… I shouldn't take what I know and wallow in the mud with those who are just going to miss the whole point and bite me in the–end."

Manuel laughed. "10 points for the big guy, ladies, and gentlemen!"

~~~

Manuel had become a hot commodity. Jim's phone rang daily with Draco Conti's people wanting to schedule a time he could come in. Scout Nikkos was back in the caravan and seeking a one-on-one interview. Side channels had popped up with the Redeemer Roadtrip as the theme. It was growing beyond any of their control. There were followers of the channel on different continents. Some were even translating all Manuel taught into other languages. Jack would always announce when he found a new video in a foreign language. There were still those who didn't know of him, and Manuel loved it when they would encounter such people.

They entered into a town that everyone knew by name. It was a town famous for its crime and killings. People who lived there were considered the dregs of society and not worth the interaction. It was often dangerous and undeserving of an encounter. The guys tried to drive around the town, but Manuel insisted they go straight through. They wanted to get some food and headed out to get some. The guys could go into more places without being recognized, so Manuel often stayed behind and took the time to be alone. Manuel put on a baseball cap and hoodie and took a walk. He ended up in a rough part of the city where drugs and prostitution were rampant. As he passed a convenience store, he saw a woman putting money into a vending machine for bottled water. She was beautiful but had seen some rough miles. Her clothes were too tight. The curls in her hair were long and flowing. Her nails were long with a bright color, but one had broken; she didn't have the funds to repair it. She would by the afternoon. She had regulars that would be coming around anytime in the next couple of hours. Manuel's heart went out to her. He approached her, standing to his full height.

"Excuse me; I was wondering if you would be willing to buy me a bottle of water."

The woman looked him up and down. She noticed his clean clothes, his new-ish converse, and his trimmed facial hair. The expression on his face was warm and casual.

"You ain't from around here, are you, baby?"

"I'm not."

"If you knew who you were talking to– you wouldn't be asking me for nothin'."

Manuel didn't budge or change his expression.

"Or *do* you know who you're talking to, and *that's* why you're here?"
~~~

"If you knew who *you* were talking to and the gift that stands in front of you, you'd be asking me for a drink. Only, the water I give is living water."

"Living water? All right, baby. You need to move along. You done lost your mind, and mama don't have time."

Manuel chuckled. "No, I'm quite sane."

"Okay, I'll bite. You don't have any money, and you're asking me to offer you some refreshment. How you gonna get this life-giving water? Are you a better man than any that came before you?"

"Anyone who gets water from this machine is going to get thirsty again. The refreshment that I give will become like a constant spring of water welling up inside them, leading to infinite life."

The woman paused and looked into Manuel's eyes. He didn't seem crazy. As a matter of fact, he seemed sharp. It sounded like he could play verbal volleyball with her all day– and possibly win.

"All right, baby. Give me some of this water so that I won't ever have to come here again." The woman was referring to the streets and life that she was living.

"Absolutely. Go call your husband and come back."

The woman huffed, squinting her eyes, and shook her head. "Now, you know I don't have a husband."

"You're right. I do know you don't have a husband. You were married five times and have lived with several other men, but of the men you sleep with now– none are your husband."

The woman's eyes grew wide. She was not offended but suddenly saw Manuel for the prophet he was. She stepped closer to him and latched her arm in his. Leading him on a walk, she sought his counsel.

"Now, I have read the stars, and I have talked to lots of palm readers, but none can give me what you just did in two minutes. Baby– er, Sir– I perceive that you are a true prophet. My family always searched for truth in this town, but most religious leaders say that Government City is the true mecca. Do I *really* have to go all that way just to find the truth? What do you say? 'Cause, brother, I need some truth. You know what I'm sayin'?"

"Woman, believe me, the hour is coming when it doesn't matter if you're here, Government City, in a church, or on a hill. Everyone idolizes what they know, whether it's their job, some religious protocol taught to them by their parents, or their lifestyle. But the time is coming– and is now here– when those who've experienced a genuine revelation will offer true adoration that honors the Creator in spirit and truth; because that is who He is seeking to honor Him."

"Well, I've had revelations by spirits."

"Yes, but Theos is The Spirit, and those who honor Him must honor Him in genuine spirit and truth."

"Hmm. I know that someday the Anointed One will come. When that happens, He will straighten us out on everything. I can't wait until that happens. What do you think about those prophecies?"

Manuel stopped walking and turned to his new friend, "The man speaking to you right now is He."

The woman threw her head back and laughed. "Oh, you good. Ah, baby." Manuel did not say another word but revealed to her who he was in her spirit. As the revelation came, her face dropped, and her mouth opened. Her face softened, and all of the years of pain melted away. Manuel just nodded at her and removed his cap. Just then, the guys came by and pulled the R.V. over.

"Where've you been? You ready?" None of them acknowledged the woman. They were surprised that being who he was, he would be speaking to a prostitute. They tried to get him into the van before anyone recognized him. They wanted to ask him what he was thinking but didn't dare. The woman slowly backed away from him, speechless. For all of her searching, Manuel loved giving her the revelation of the real thing. He didn't see her for what she had done but for who she was created to be.

"We aren't leaving just yet," he hollered to the guys. "Estancia, we're going to be at Ada Park for the next while." He hugged her and hopped up into the ride. As they pulled away, some locals spotted the R.V.

"Hey! It's the Roadtrip guys! Hey, hey!! Hey!"

Estancia was numb, "He told me everything I've ever done."

"Huh?"

"They're going to be at the park."

A woman refused her, "Hey, sister go peddle your trade somewhere else." Women didn't give her the time of day.

"No…He…" Estancia dropped her water bottle. She was coming out of her haze and started broadcasting what had just happened to anyone she came across. "Hahaaaah! Come to the Park! Aye! Come see the prophet who told me stuff nobody knew! Aye! Go to Ada Park to see a true prophet! I think he's the Anointed One!"

People in the area knew Estancia, but she usually kept to herself. Her face was all lit up, and she was openly engaging passers-by. She seemed different. She rushed home to change her clothes and headed back out again to go to the park and let others know. As it always did, word spread quickly that the Redeemer Roadtrip R.V. was in town. The guys were trying to get Manuel to eat some of the food they had picked up, but he declined.

"I have food you know nothing about."

The guys figured he must have grabbed something for himself. They wondered what he had.

"No, you dorks. My *food* is to do the will of the One who sent me. I fill up on seeing His work accomplished. You know that saying, 'Good things come to those who wait?' Well, this is not the time to put things off. Someone is always telling the other to, 'Relax! Be patient.' But look around! These people are ready to receive *now*. We can't put off telling them about the Kingdom." The guys exchanged glances. Manuel knew their thoughts and became stern.

"Knock it off. Since the minute we came into this town, you guys have been wallowing in your misconceptions about the people here. You assume because they have succumbed to their lifestyles that they are not worth saving or that it would take forever before they could understand who I am and what we bring. Look, I'm training you guys to be my emissaries, my ambassadors. You've got to stop seeing cultural division and looking at the outside appearance. Don't get pulled into the junk of the day. Stop being prejudiced! You have to dismiss your thoughts and issues and represent the Creator; represent Me. I am here to bless everyone. *Everyone*. If you can't handle that, then you're on the opposite team."

"Sorry, Kyrios."

"Don't be sorry. Just change your thinking. I've been telling you guys not to judge others because you're going to be judged in the same way, and yet– Look, you don't know where you are in the lineup of someone coming into the Kingdom. This may be their first encounter or the one right before they step out, and trust me. Let's just give everyone the same opportunity regardless of what you see on the outside."

"Yes, of course."

"Okay."

"The seeds were planted by those that came before us long ago. All we have to do is go and reap the harvest. You didn't even have to work for it– just go, share the Truth, and watch what the Creator will do. Ready?"

The R.V. pulled up to Ada Park, and people were already gathering. Manuel met the crowd and began loving on them by healing them and casting out demons that had long been causing torment. People became clean and sober. He delivered some of them from trauma they suffered that caused them to choose their lifestyles, and others were relieved of the burdens they carried that were not their own. The people were in awe when they listened to Manuel. How could one man come and radically change the lives of so many if he weren't the Son of Theos?

Many people sat around Manuel, reclining and enjoying his presence. One of the guys, convicted by their judgment earlier, asked him, "Kyrios, will you teach us to commune with the Creator the way you do?" The crowd silenced. Was it even possible for them to have a relationship with the Creator of the Universe? How could they possibly tune into Him the way Manuel did? They sat eagerly waiting to hear his response.

"I thought you'd never ask." Manuel smiled from ear to ear and loved the look of anticipation in the eyes of the people. "It's simple– and yet there is so much to it." They chuckled nervously. "When you want to speak to the Creator, come to him as a kid would. When you believe in Him and Me, you become His child. Kids don't get all hung up on their words when they speak to their parents like they have a million times– they are bold in their requests! They just lay it out. They are simple and sincere, authentic. Don't be like the religious leaders who act like they have some connection with the Creator that you can't possibly understand or have. They are dramatic and long-winded. They want attention. Be the opposite of that. Simply come to Him– in private– and make your requests known. You could say:

'Abba,' which is like *Daddy*… and don't get hung up on the daddy thing. The Creator is not like your earthly father, who may have hurt you or abandoned you somehow. He is entirely Other. He is the Father you've never had. He created fatherhood.

'Abba– we honor you.

We proclaim that Your Kingdom shows up, and what you designed will be done here– in our bodies, minds, and wills– and on earth, as it is in Your Higher Realm.

We ask that You provide for us today.

Please redeem us from the ways that we have missed the mark,

And help us to forgive those who have hurt us as they missed the mark.

We know there will be temptations, so please help us not to surrender to them. But have a healthy plan of action so we don't hurt ourselves or others.

Thank You for always providing a way out when the enemy comes to tempt us.'

"Do you hear it? We open with relationship to Him. He loves that. Acknowledging that He is 'Our Daddy' shows that you are not alone in this family. He is *our Daddy*. Just talk to your Abba. Stand in awe of Who He is. Honor Him. Take time to worship because you've got Him wrapped around your little finger when you worship Him. He loves it– it's like music to His ears.

"When you decree His Kingdom occupy the earth, you're saying you surrender your thinking. Surrender everything you think is right, admit that there is a better way, and you welcome it. We want the Elevated Kingdom to operate here on earth. We need it. It changes everything.

"It's perfectly acceptable at that point to make your requests known to Him. Petition Him for the best outcome in personal and collective situations.

"And then, petition Him to give you a plan to avoid the evil one and his emissaries. Because they will trip you up and rob you of His provision every chance they get. Apologize and turn from everything you've done that is displeasing and enter into the rest that He brings in His perfect plan.

"And finally, know that practice makes perfect. He never gets tired of hearing from you– so, just talk to Him. Talk to Him like you'd talk to me."

Before Manuel could finish speaking, there were hushed whispers all around them. People didn't want to wait to enter into this personal relationship with Theos as Abba. A sweet smell rose from the crowd. It smelled of Lilacs in the hot sun and quickly permeated the area. People looked around to find where it was coming from, but Manuel knew it emanated from their communion with their Celestial Father.

CHAPTER 26:

ONE HECKUVA INTERVIEW

It had been a long, sweet afternoon. The people were generous with Manuel and the guys by giving them food, drinks and making sure they had everything they might need. The people asked them not to move on. They wanted to show their gratitude over the next couple of days with barbeques and celebrations. Manuel agreed as it would honor them to do so. It would also give him time to be stationary enough to meet with Scout Nikkos.

Scout was thrilled when Levi delivered the invitation to join Manuel. Grabbing his notepad, recorder, and camera, he shuffled into the R.V. and greeted the guys.

"Wow… the inner sanctum," he teased. Each of the guys stepped out of the R.V. except Simon. Scout set his equipment down and asked if the seat across from Manuel was okay. Simon sat a respectable distance from the two men. He didn't want to interfere with the conversation but did want to access Scout quickly should he need to be urgently escorted out. "At last, we meet," he teased again.

"Nervous much?" Simon said under his breath.

"Nikkos, you're good, man," Manuel welcomed.

"Great, well, thanks for seeing me. I've wanted to interview you for quite some time."

"Oh, we've read your work. It seems you've been doing just fine without an interview."

"Yeah, well… firsthand is always better."

"So, you met Johnny…"

"Yes! Yeah, I had the chance to interview him– it seems like ages ago now."

"And you interviewed the woman who was convicted of killing her three children."

"Stacey Dreggs– yes. Man, that's a crap show."

"Do you think she did it?"

"Absolutely she did it. No doubt. What a mess. Her lover's wife mysteriously disappears then her kids do. Then, they're tracked to the Bahamas– no shame there, eh? Geez."

"I'd like to talk to her."

"Really? Ah, she's going down. There won't be any talking to her for anyone."

"Well, even so… I'd like to speak with her sometime."

"If you ask me, they'll give her the tree." Scout was referring to the tradition of 'cursing someone with the tree.' It meant that she would hang for her crimes but not before being brutally tormented. "Alrighty! Shall we get started?" Manuel nodded and patiently waited for Scout to start his recorder and flip to the right page of his notepad. "Well, thank you for having me today. On behalf of the Tri-State Triton, we appreciate your time and transparency. Blah, blah, blah– That was quite a show yesterday."

"It wasn't a show."

"Interesting, I think your cousin was quoted saying something along those same lines once."

"Johnny was a good man."

"He was. Highly regarded– until he wasn't. Would you care to comment on his execution?"

"I don't see the point. The powers that be know they were in the wrong, and the cowards that allowed it know they were also. Johnny brought the beginning of true revelation, and they condemned him for it."

"Do you feel condemned? Do you feel that what happened to Johnny might happen to you?"

"One step at a time, Nikkos."

Scout chuckled, "Yeah, that was a bit much right out the gate. Let's back up. Yesterday was really something. People responded as people always seem to when you're around; hungry, grateful, changed. What is your secret?"

"It's no secret; I've been announcing it publicly everywhere I go. You know that. You've been there for much of it. I want people to know how to be healed of the trauma in their souls and walk redeemed through personal communication with the Creator. I want people to know they don't have to be slaves any longer to the consequences of their handicaps, pain, and poor choices."

"So, that's why you responded yesterday to the request of teaching them to pray."

"Communicating with their Divine Daddy; yes."

"Do you want to expand on that at all?"

"Sure. Let's say you have a friend, and you go to him at midnight and knock on his door. You're like, 'Hey! Give me some groceries! Some of my family just arrived from out of town– the stores are closed, and they're hungry. I don't have enough for them– help me out!' Suppose the friend doesn't even come to the door but yells out the window, 'Don't bother me! It's late. My house is locked up. My kids are in bed. I'm not getting up to give you anything.' Even though he won't get up and give you anything based on your friendship, because of your shameless audacity, he will eventually get up and provide you whatever it is you need."

"Oookay. So, you're saying that's what it's like when they communicate with their *Celestial Father?"*

"No, I'm saying that Our Father *isn't* like that. I'm saying He is the exact opposite of that. I'm saying it doesn't matter what time you go to Him, and it doesn't matter what the circumstance is; you don't have to hound him because you aren't bothering him. He's not going to reluctantly give in because you keep hounding him. I'm saying just ask, and it will be given to you. Look for Him, and you will find Him. Approach Him, and He will answer the door to you. Anyone who asks receives, the one who seeks finds, and to the one who knocks, the door will be opened."

"Always?"

"Always."

"Every time?"

"Every single time."

"No matter what we ask?"

"You're so human, Nikkos."

"No, seriously. I want a Maserati. If I ask the Creator for a Maserati, He will give me one?"

"Which parent, when their son asks for a sandwich, gives him a snake instead? Or if he asks for an egg– who gives him a scorpion? My point is, if you, being merely human and bent in your character, know how to give your child a good gift and what he truly needs– how much more will your Divine Parent give you what you really need when you ask Him? He will give you His Essence, wisdom, and all that comes with it when you seek Him in sincerity and truth."

"I don't hear that I'm getting a Maserati out of that deal," Nikkos snarked.

"If it's going to bite you in the end– probably not. Good parents know the art of motivation behind the request and when to say *No.*"

"Great. So… certain religious leaders don't believe that you are sent from the Higher Realm. They insist that you're a fraud leading people astray from the one true religion. They claim that any magician can heal people and that you are driving out demons by the power of Teivel."

Manuel laughed. "Any kingdom divided against itself will be ruined; a house divided will fall. You've heard that, right? If Teivel divided against himself– was operating in his own interests and I was operating in his interests– we couldn't both win. It would split up the winnings; how could his kingdom stand? And if I'm driving out demons by the power of Teivel, then what power are the religious exorcists using? That's crazy. Be consistent. But listen– if I drive out demons by the hand of Theos and dunamis power, then the Elevated Kingdom has come. Why not embrace that? Maybe because– okay– When a strong man, fully geared up, guards his house, everything he owns is safe. But when someone with more strength and better gear attacks his house and overpowers him– he rips off the gear the first guy had like it's nothing, and everything he trusted in is gone. The stronger man easily takes everything he owns and divides up the stuff."

"Um– okay."

"He does that," Simon chuckled.

"Do you mind breaking that down for me, buddy?"

"That was broken down," Simon offered.

"Simon."

"Sorry, Boss."

"I'm saying the only way someone strong can be overcome is if someone else is stronger. I am stronger. I have gone into the house of Teivel and stolen souls that were his property. The only logical conclusion is not that I did it in *his* power– but a power *greater* than his. The hand of Theos. A greater Kingdom is at hand, and it scares the wits out of Teivel *and* the religious leaders."

"I see."

"Whoever is not with me is against me. Anyone who is not on the side of gathering and healing is on the side of scattering and breaking down. There is no neutrality in the Kingdom. There won't be any leniency in that matter."

"Even if someone is basically a good person?"

"There won't be any leniency in that matter."

"Okay. When a demon is cast out, where does it go?"

"Well, if a person isn't careful, it can come right back. Not only that, but it can bring several of its buddies with it."

"Wait– what?! Then, what is the point of kicking it out? Don't you think that is kind of cruel?"

"Cruel? To deliver someone? Um, let me see, how can I put this– NO! When a demon is kicked out, it goes to dry and arid places seeking a place to rest, but there is no rest. So, it determines to try and re-enter where it has been kicked out of, and if it is given any grounds to do so– it will. But not only that, it might return stronger."

"What the heck? How can someone be sure that doesn't happen?"

"By cleaning up the vessel that was housing it, to begin with. Do the work. Getting healed is a beautiful thing, but it comes with responsibility.

It's not a clean slate and new free ticket to go out and do all of the things you did before that allowed the demon legal right to torment you. It is an opportunity to be free from the torment long enough to get to the root of the issues that caused the behavior that gave them–"

"–legal right to torment, right."

"Exactly."

"This is hardcore stuff, man."

"It is."

"I mean, if the world could actually catch on to this– everything would change."

"Hello."

"I heard a woman yesterday blessing the woman who gave you birth. Is your mother living? And if so, what does she think of all of this?"

"More importantly, blessed are the people who hear the truth I'm bringing and embrace it."

"Okay, doesn't want to talk about his mother. The crowds are increasing everywhere you go. Does it bother you that they always want to see one sign after the other?"

"This is a wicked generation for sure. Nothing is ever enough; they consume everything that is given and want more. But they will have the ultimate sign; that of the prophet Yona."

"Yona, Yona… I don't know that one. What does that mean?"

"Have you ever read the Ancient Writings, Nikkos?"

"You could say I've dabbled. Like most people."

"Yona was a reluctant prophet. He was given a message to save an entire people group and didn't want to give it to them because he didn't like who they were. Filthy, rotten people. So, he refused to go to them. Let's just say– you should read the story– but it caused a lot of trouble for him and for everyone who came into contact with him. He ended up thrown overboard from a ship and swallowed by a great whale."

"This sounds more like a fairytale."

"Then you're not a very good journalist, friend. There are documented stories of men being swallowed by whales. Check it out."

"I definitely will."

"So, Yona was swallowed by a whale and was in the belly for three days before being vomited out. He wasn't in great shape– you can imagine what the digestion tract would do to someone– but needless to say, when he emerged, he made it to the people whom the message was for with a new perspective."

"I bet!" Scout laughed.

"So, as Yona was to the Ninevites, so I will be to this generation."

"You're going to be in the belly of a whale for three days?" he continued to chuckle.

"Not a whale. Likewise, the Queen of Sheba traveled 1200 miles to hear the wisdom of Solomon. Here is a Queen who was accustomed to people traveling hundreds of miles to honor her, but when something better was available, she is the one who traveled because it was of great worth. I'm saying something better has arrived, and people should make whatever journey necessary to reach it; get out of their comfort zones. Something better than the richest and wisest king has arrived."

"You are greater than anything the world has ever seen, then?"

"I Am."

"That's a pretty bold claim."

"It is."

"So, what about the people who can't get to you? If they can't make the trip, how will they be *redeemed*?"

"Are you kidding? With everything available to them? Every video posted grants them the opportunity to find the Truth and believe. The Ancient Writings lay the breadcrumbs, and Theos has opened the door to His Kingdom. I'm not in hiding. I'm out and available. The light is right in front of you. You've heard people say, 'The eye is the window to the soul,' right? The eye is where the light comes in. When your eyes are healthy– when light is getting into your soul– your whole body is healthy. But when they are unhealthy, light doesn't come in, and your body is full of darkness. So, be careful that what you're letting into your soul isn't the darkness but the light. If your whole body is full of light and no part of you partaking in the darkness, then you'll be well. It is written, 'You will prosper and be in health, even as your soul prospers.'"

"So, there is no excuse not to know the Truth, er– the Light."

"No, there's really not. No one hides a good thing. It's just that the religious leaders of today don't see me as a good thing. And, I'm saying that if someone can't see good here then–"

"Then, they are full of darkness, right?"

"Well, their rejection of me is not a reflection of any evil in *me*."

"Oh, this is so good. This is really going to piss some people off."

"That's not why I'm doing it."

"I know, I know. But it will, just the same."

"Well, I'm trusting you not to embellish what I'm saying, Nikkos. Put it straight just as you and I are talking now."

"Thank you for trusting me."

"I didn't say I trusted you."

Nikkos laughed. "Johnny trusted me."

"Johnny had no choice. I am choosing you; do you understand?"

Scout felt a sense of pride well up within him. It was true. This guy could be speaking to anyone he wished at this point.

"Speaking of which– word on the street is that Draco Conti has invited you on to his show. Can you confirm that?"

"I won't confirm or deny it."

"Yer killin' me, Honcho. Any last points you'd like to make to our readers?"

Manuel paused and took a moment with Theos. Nodding, he smiled at Nikkos and continued. "Yes. People are so concerned with their stuff– shoes, clothes, cars, houses, boats, and purses for pities' sake. But these aren't the things they should be treasuring. Instead, they should be concerned with storing up treasures in the Higher Realm where moths and rust can't destroy it or thieves can't break in and steal it. Wherever your treasure is, your heart is. So, why not build up that which can't be taken from you? Things of value beyond what you can afford."

"Got it… and?"

"Back to the eye being the lamp of the body– so, if your eye is healthy, your whole body will be full of light, but if your eye is bad, your whole body will be full of darkness. So, if the light in you is darkness, how great is the darkness?!"

"Yeah, I think we covered that. Thanks."

"It bears repeating. But we didn't cover this: No one can serve two masters. You're going to either hate the one and love the other or be devoted to the one and despise the other."

"Meaning?"

"You cannot serve Theos and your desire for money and belongings at the same time."

"Let me guess; there is no neutrality in the Kingdom."

"Nice. Last thing: Please warn them to beware of false prophets. Mediums, oracles, palmists, and seers. Some have genuine gifts, but there are always those out to deceive in these ways, leading them further from the Truth. Those people can always be recognized by what they produce. You don't get good fruit from a bad tree."

"Got it. Thank you, Manuel. So, in summary– and please correct me at any time: It's no secret that people can be healed in their souls and then their bodies. It is possible to have a relationship with the Creator of the Universe, and He is not bothered by us coming to Him at any time,"

"No, He loves it."

"Loves it. Right. Uh… oh, yes; you are from Theos and not operating in the power of Teivel. Something about three days in the belly of a beast, and there is no excuse for a true seeker not to find the Truth because everything has been made available to us. And finally, people shouldn't store up treasures here on earth but in heaven, if you will, because that is where the true worth is."

"Not bad, Nikkos."

"I hope you look forward to reading it."

"I may or may not read it. I was here for the real thing, so…"

"Look, uh. On a personal note…"

"We're off the record now?"

"Yes, definitely off the record. Uh," Nikkos looked over at Simon and hesitated.

"Simon, can you give us a minute?" Simon stepped outside the R.V. and waited right by the door.

"Oh, thanks. Uh… I'm just, I mean– I've seen a lot of things in my time, you know? I've traveled all over and met all kinds of people, but I've never seen anything like what you've got going here."

"I understand."

"It's crazy. I look forward to doing follow-up interviews with some of these people whose lives have changed. Like those that received radical healing. I've even heard you raised people from the dead– is that true?"

"Nikkos– *Scout,* I'm so glad you're on this journey. I'm grateful that you have been present to witness miraculous things, and I hope you do follow up with those people. My question for you is– what do *you* need?"

"Me? Oh, no, no– I'm not talking about me. I just meant–"

"I know what you meant. I understood you. Now I'm asking the questions. What do you need?"

Scout laughed nervously. "Oh, I don't need anything. Thank you, though."

"Scout."

"Yeah? No, no, really."

"Scout. Do you believe that I am who I say I am?"

Scout sighed and looked about nervously. Manuel was leaning forward with his hands folded together, watching him intently. Scout could see that he wasn't going to relent. Leaning back, he sighed and wondered for a fraction of a second what it might be like to allow himself to be one of those people.

"One of *those people*?" Manuel asked. Scout's eyes shot across to Manuel's. How did he–

"Do you think this is all trickery?" Manuel pressed. "Is there any part of you that believes what you have been following? Even chasing. You've been following us for months, man. Months. You've seen it all, and you haven't wrapped up your story. You want to believe. What keeps you from becoming one of those people?"

"Do you really want to have this conversation?"

"It's what I want most at this moment."

"All right." Scout set his items down and propped his feet up. "The thing is, I wasn't raised in a religious household. My mom and dad broke up when I was young, and they never taught me anything about 'a higher power' or 'higher realm.' I've always thought that people who think like that just need some sort of crutch. The bits and pieces I did catch over the years seemed a lot like nonsense to me. When I got into college and started truly forming my own opinions on things– well, there was just too much pain in the world for there to be a 'God who cared.' At that point, it felt silly even to consider entertaining a Creator who might be interested in anything down here, let alone me personally. I mean, if He cared– why is there so much wickedness in the world? Why would He allow little kids to get cancer and good people to go to some burning place of torment forever just because they didn't choose to acknowledge Him for 80 years on earth? That doesn't compute."

"Yeah, I get that. You're not alone in thinking that way."

"Right. And excuse me, but what kind of *higher power* would create something as great as sex and then tell people not to do it unless they were married? Seriously? 'Oh, here's this knob standing out from your body that is affected when the wind blows but don't touch it! Just deny that it's there until you're ready to make a lifetime commitment,' that probably won't even last a lifetime because everybody is so blasted selfish that heaven forbid they learn how to communicate and give up anything for the betterment of the institution or someone other than themselves." Scout realized he had hit a nerve. All of the bitterness he kept tucked in on a daily business was pouring out all over. He looked at Manuel, who wasn't chiming in but simply listening with compassion. Scout wiped a tear from his eye.

"Hey, you don't have to look at me like that." Manuel briefly looked down, honoring the raw emotion but looked back as a symbol of his presence. "See, I told you– you didn't want to have this conversation."

"And I told you that I was greater than anything the world has ever seen." Scout took another deep breath. "So, answers."

"Huh?"

"That's what you need. Answers."

"Yeah, I guess so. I want some answers."

"I'm really glad you came today, Scout." Manuel took a deep breath. "Have you ever asked someone for something, and they didn't come through?"

"Yes, of course."

"Who?"

"Who hasn't?" he laughed to cover the pain. "My folks, different friends. A woman."

"Okay, so when you really needed it, and when you made yourself vulnerable enough to ask for it, they failed to help you out or come through."

"Yeah, but so what? Everybody has experienced that."

"Yeah, most people absolutely have experienced that. But we aren't talking about everybody. We're talking about *you*. We're talking about the way it affected *you*." Scout let out another heavy breath and shook his head.

He didn't like the tables being turned. "Isn't it possible that all these years as a journalist, you've been seeking answers to all these questions? I mean, you made a career out of getting answers and piecing things together. Isn't it possible that if you could find an answer to why 'Theos is real,' that you could have something in your life worth living for, something that even helps you when you make yourself vulnerable enough to ask for it?"

"I don't know, man."

"Sure, you do."

"I don't know."

"I'm sorry, Scout. I'm sorry that those people didn't come through for you. I'm sorry that you experienced rejection at such an early age and felt abandoned to get any kind of solid answers on your own. I'm sorry that when you tried, when you really tried, you were met with disappointment and pain."

"Yeah, well, you know."

"The thing is, they didn't have the answers either. Hurt people– hurt people. Your parents would have done better if they knew how. If they had any kind of faith of their own or had experienced dependable support from a Higher Power, they would have passed that on. But they didn't have that to give. So, when you started questioning and found nothing but what looked like a god that didn't care, you decided you wouldn't care, either. But Theos isn't like your parents. He has all the answers, and He wants to share them with you. As a matter of fact, if you lack wisdom, you can ask Him for it, and He will give it to you generously without reproach.

"And why *would* a loving God allow kids to get cancer? Have you ever considered all the chemical pesticides and poisons that are used in our foods now? Have you ever considered that there are cures for these things but that the pharmaceutical companies would rather keep people sick by profiting from their illness than heal them? Have you considered that the iniquity these babies were born into has not been properly addressed and dealt with, so it carries down into the family bloodline until someone pays a terrible price? Do you think that Theos caused that? Why is it that people want to live by their own moral code in life, but when tragedy strikes, He is the first one to receive blame? They think that the original law was given– thou shalt not murder, steal, covet, etc.– as a boundary to control everyone. My God! It was given to keep everyone safe and give freedom! But the selfishness you referred to keeps everyone from wanting to do anything other than what they deem is right! And *that*, my friend, is where the trouble comes."

"Go ahead," Scout chuckled.

"The sex?" Manuel continued. Scout nodded and chuckled.

"Truth- sex is a beautiful thing. The expression of love through sex, when shared with the one person who is intended to have it, cannot be compared to anything else. Magical. And there is nothing wrong with that. The problem comes when you think that person is forever, so you have sex, and things don't work out. Now, you move to the next person, and the same thing happens. Etc. Etc. Now, you've got a world full of people who are walking wounded because they didn't handle this beautiful thing properly, so it causes damage instead of intimacy."

"Specifically–"

"Specifically, it causes damage mentally, emotionally, and physically."

"I don't know. Physically it feels pretty good, and mentally it blows off a lot of steam."

"Mentally, it's damaging because it was intended for one person. When you have sex with multiple people, you have memories of each of them. Then one day, when you are with the right person, the one person intended to have this gift, you flashback to doing certain acts with other people because the mind remembers. Mentally, you can recall what worked with this person and try it on that person– when it was intended to be a uniting force between your true life partner. You have to carry these things mentally, and it was never intended that you should have to do so."

"Okay, okay. That makes sense. I get that."

"Emotionally, it's damaging because you opened up and let someone into your world. You exposed everything about yourself, physically and emotionally. Then, when things don't work out, you've left a piece of yourself on this person that you may or may not ever see again! Emotionally you learn that you shouldn't trust people as much or let the next person in– so you don't– and then the right person intended to have that gift pays the price of all those who came before. Theos never designed for you to have to go through that. The pain worsens with each encounter until you are calloused and unable to feel anything deeply because of your thick skin protecting you."

Scout sighed. That was accurate and all too familiar.

"And physically, well… ugh. Look at how rampant sexually transmitted diseases are. Countless people walk around with permanent illnesses because a partner gave them something they can't give back. Even if they were good, but their partner wasn't. Or if they were less than wise and gave it to a partner that didn't deserve it. You can't take that back. It's physically damaging because anytime you literally let someone in or enter into another person's body, there are consequences– good or bad. Look at the youth who are dealing with unplanned pregnancies because the natural result of their actions led them to something they weren't mentally, emotionally, or physically prepared to handle. Then there are abortions and people dealing with emotional carnage and PTSD. It just goes on and on.

"So, encouraging marriage wasn't a rule for control. It was to enable freedom from all the rest of it. I'm sorry no one ever explained these things to you, and you just heard it as a, 'Don't touch!' kind of deal."

"This is just– it's a lot to process, man."

"It is, but it shouldn't be. It's so simple, really. Don't overthink it. If you only have intellectual truth, you become hardened and proud. Freedom comes by grace through faith."

"Alrighty then. Thank you, um, Manuel. I think I have what I need for today."

"Thank you, Scout. I hope you'll stay with us and come to believe."

"I'm not saying I don't believe– I'm just–"

"I know."

"Alrighty, then."

"Rocko!" Simon opened the door, "See to our friend."

CHAPTER 27:

PROPHECY AND FULFILLMENT

Two days passed, and the guys prepared to leave the townspeople. In just two days, they had shown Manuel more hospitality than his hometown had. All who came for healing received it, and revitalization had come to the streets. Fellowmen practiced consideration, and people started cleaning up areas of the town together. Judgment and pride were put away. Those who had stolen, killed, and destroyed property apologized, and everyone allowed forgiveness to prevail. Some people were even offering to rebuild what they had taken as an offering of restoration. What was lost for generations was in the process of being restored in just a few days.

"It's amazing what can take place if people are open," Manuel praised. As they left, the people begged them to return. The guys knew that one, if not all of them, would revisit someday.

"Where are we headed, Kyrios?" Simon asked.

"You know, Draco's people are feeling snubbed by you," Jim interjected. "I'm not sure where we're headed, but maybe you should consider heading their way."

"I never said I would do the show," Manuel replied.

"Did you say you weren't going to?" There was a long pause.

"All right, then. Government City, boys." The R.V. went silent. Everyone knew that Government City would bring heat from the religious sects and pressure on Manuel. "Jim, let Conti's people know we are heading into town and schedule something."

There was a twinge of excitement. The guys had been on the road for so long and were wondering how long this might go on. With each chance they had, they would swing back to Netzer to visit family and friends. Simon's wife had been supportive but missed her husband. Miryam was always grateful to see her eldest son but understood more than anyone the calling on his life. Jim and Jack were in consistent contact with their mother, Sally, as Jack would video chat with her weekly. She was one of the Roadtrip's most faithful supporters financially and wanted all her boys to do well. Even though Lazer, Marie, and Marta lived reasonably close, the guys avoided Government City when visiting. They also continued to stop for impromptu events and speak to crowds delivering people from all kinds of illnesses.

This visit with Lazer and his sisters brought two familiar faces into the caravan. At one of the gatherings, Philip and his brother Nathan reemerged. With his brother's persistent nagging, Nathan agreed to join the caravan and become a more permanent devotee of Manuel's. They wanted to help and be of service in any way they could, as well as glean and grow from hearing him regularly. All the guys enjoyed having them around, but Jack and Philip got along best. They were both into video games and techie gadgets. Even though each of the guys believed in Manuel as Kyrios, there was a significant reverence from Nathan. Having come from much, the brothers could have been spoiled and unconcerned, but Nathan had always taken the Ancient Writings to heart and was well aware of the prophecies leading up to Manuel's arrival. He knew that the King would come and bring a new arrangement. No longer would the original law of Jekuthiel be the ultimate structure. Jekuthiel had been the only known mediator between Theos and man, but that arrangement was being amended and updated with this One true Redeemer. Now Manuel would be the mediator between men and Theos. The Ancient Writings explained believers of the Creator experiencing His interaction by speaking, acting, providing, redeeming, and judging. He was present with them through visitations. But this mediator would bring a permanent habitation of His Essence and personal path to eternal redemption.

Manuel knew that Nathan was a scholar where the Ancient Writings were concerned. Nathan longed to have a private conversation and ask Manuel a million questions regarding the fulfillment of all the prophecies. He kept a journal with each of the signs written out on the left and planned to record as he saw them fulfilled on the right. Nathan knew that Manuel's probability of fulfilling a large percentage of the prophecies, let alone all of them, would be improbable– if not downright impossible. But he was eager to watch and learn.

One afternoon, as the R.V. stopped to grab food, Manuel instructed Jack to swap places with Nathan and hang out with Philip for a bit in their car. Within minutes Nathan was knocking on the door. Jude let him in and patted him on the back.

"Well, well," he greeted. "If it's not the Sacred Writing thumper of the bunch."

"Nathan– come and join me," Manuel welcomed. He was in the back lounging in his sleeper. Nathan slowly walked back to where Manuel reclined. Looking around in awe, he gradually lowered himself with his journal in hand. Manuel couldn't help but chuckle. He loved how serious Nathan was. He loved the reverence he had for the Ancient Writings. It was refreshing to know that someone had sought the Creator as fervently as Nathan. "I love that you're here."

"You do?" Nathan asked.

"Yeah. I love that Philip talked you into caravanning, and you finally agreed. I know you've wanted a chance to talk but that you would never have been so bold as to ask for it."

Nathan laughed nervously. "Well, I just wouldn't want to–"

"I know. You're very considerate. But you have questions."

"So many."

"Well, let's eat and talk. You cool with hanging in the R.V. for the next stretch?"

"Of course, yes… thank you, I'm… thank you."

"Absolutely. Fire away."

"Well," Nathan flipped his journal open and wanted to work his way through the list systematically. "I'd like to ask you about the prophecies…"

"Mm-hmm." Manuel took a bite of his sandwich.

"Being the Anointed One would mean certain things would need to come to pass."

"Yep. That's true."

"So… they have?"

"They are coming true every day."

"Okay, but– forgive me–"

"Go for it, Nathan."

"Well, your mother… she would have had to have been…uh,"

"Chaste."

"More than chaste…"

"Untouched."

"Yes!"

"She was."

"But– why wouldn't we have heard about that? 'Virgin gives birth!' That would have been news."

"They didn't advertise it. Everyone in our family knew. I wasn't born in a hospital, so it wasn't like anyone reported anything other than normal. It was quite known; they didn't want every– she was only 16 when she became pregnant."

"Oh, wow. Hmm. Okay. And your name fulfills prophecy."

"It does… Emmanuel, meaning *Theos among us.*"

"You were born where?"

"I was born in Breadville but was raised in Netzer."

"I see…" Nathan knew that a ruler would come from Breadville, who would lead the people. This was accurate as far as the prophecies went, but there was a part Manuel hadn't mentioned. The Ancient Writings said, 'He would be called out of the Double Straights.' How did that match up with the other two places? Manuel waited, but Nathan didn't bring it up. He knew what he was thinking.

"So… the prophecies speak of an eternal kingdom. They say that the Redeemer's lineage would be from the founder of our faith and the greatest king to have ever lived…"

"These things are true. I guess I could pull up ancestery.com and prove it to you." They both laughed. "But it goes pretty far back. I am of the lineage of David, who reigned in the City of Peace, and I know the founder of our faith well."

"You *know* him…"

"Mm-hmm. Well." Manuel was still eating casually.

"But– he,"

"I'm telling you, Nathan. Before Abraham existed– I did." Nathan felt a combination of things. First, he wanted to rush out of the R.V. for fear of the ridiculousness of Manuel's statement, and next, he wanted to fall on his face in reverence with the hope of this proclamation being true.

"I know the work you have been doing fulfills prophesy. The healings and astounding feats. Also, that you are destroying the work of Teivel by doing so."

"Oh, his work will be obliterated. We're getting there."

"What will that look like?"

"You'll see."

"The world has gotten so out of hand. I can't imagine, but I can't wait either. On that note– the Writings speak of sacrifice. I mean, I know there are many sacrifices to living this way; on the road, people always want something from you as a public figure. But– a *perfect* sacrifice."

"Yes. It does say that. You'll know that one when you see it. Trust me; you won't miss it."

"If there is anything I can do to help? I'd be honored to be a part of history."

"Just be with me now, Nathan. You're helping me now."

"Okay. I know you are teaching righteousness; that's prophetic fulfillment. I know you use stories a lot; that's fulfillment. I know that even though they are profound, they often fall on deaf ears– that sucks, but it is fulfillment. I know the Anointed One will cause some people to stumble. I've never understood how someone good could cause that. Can you explain that?"

"Sure. They stumble because I am messing up their game. They'll get hung up on that and embrace bitterness and jealousy. They stumble because they disobey the message. But they were destined for that, so…"

"That makes me want to talk to you about predestination."

"It's the perfect segue– but we'd be here for hours," he teased. "Still, we can get to that in another conversation. It's always worth discussing."

"It causes so many divisions."

"And it shouldn't."

"Right. So- I know the Anointed One's mission would begin in the Region of Circuit. That was fulfilled."

"Yes. 'The people walking in darkness have seen a great light;'"

"Yes! '…the Way of the Sea, beyond the Slide River, O' region of Circuit– the people living in darkness have seen a great light; on those living in the land of the shadow of death, a light has dawned.' Beautiful."

"Nice! And the fulfillment?" Manuel tested.

"Well, I've heard you teach, 'Turn from wickedness, for the Kingdom of the Higher Realm has come near.'"

"That's exactly right."

"Another fulfillment is that you have drawn all people to yourself. I mean, it's not just this religious group or that– you've– it's like you've broken down all the walls of division. No people group, race, or organization is excluded. No individual left behind."

"That was one of the easiest ones. It should have been happening all along."

"Another prophetic fulfillment– 'Eyes of the blind will be opened and ears of the deaf unstopped. The lame will leap like a deer, and the mute tongue shout for joy.'"

"And Water will gush forth in the wilderness and streams in the desert." Manuel finished.

"Yes… what is that?"

"I bring refreshment in the chaos and uncharted regions of the soul. Streams of living water are coming to the driest places. The flood will come when the Essence of the Creator is released to bring His counsel, comfort, strength, and guidance permanently."

"It sounds like a whole new world."

"If people will embrace it, it truly is."

"The voice of one calling out in the wasteland… that was Johnny, right?"

Manuel lowered his head and sighed. "It was, yeah."

"He was the fulfillment of Elijah?"

"You know, Nathan, if everyone took the time to learn what you have learned– my job would be so much easier." Nathan smiled, honored to be thought of well by Manuel.

"Oh, I could go on and on. I love this stuff. I can't believe that I'm living in the time of restoration. Not only that, but it's also insane that I would– I mean that I could even… know you."

"Everyone can know me."

"Yes, I know. But I mean…"

"I know what you mean, man. I'm just teasing. It's my great pleasure to know you, Nathan. And to bring the perfect sacrifice that will make way for your redemption. All redemption."

"Nate." Nathan offered. "You can call me Nate."

"Theos has given."

"That's right! That's what it means."

"Theos *has* given."

"Yes… that's right."

"No, Theos really *has* given. You're an impressive guy, Nate. I appreciate you. As far as the prophecies go, I appreciate, encourage, and challenge you to keep up with their fulfillment. Someone will need to be documenting that for future reference, and I'm grateful that you so willingly take it on."

"I suppose we could talk all afternoon about each of them."

"For days…"

"Right. But one last fulfillment." Manuel chuckled again at his admirable persistence. "He was despised and rejected by humankind. A man of suffering and familiar with pain. Like one from whom people hide their faces, he was despised, and we held him in low esteem."

"From the great prophet Isaiah."

"At the rate things are going, I can't see it. I mean, I just can't see how everyone who is so enamored with you and drinking in every word you say could despise you and turn to rejection. What could you possibly do that would deserve that? No one could hold the works you do in low esteem." Manuel paused and thought about his future. Knowing what Nathan could not in any way know and not wanting to give him more than he could carry for the time, he simply smiled warmly.

"You know, Nate, we have a way to go yet. Did you ever hear the story that Corrie ten Boom's father told her about her train ticket?"

"No, I can't say that I have."

"So, Corrie had witnessed the death of a baby and was traumatized. It made no sense. It started her thinking about death and loss. She cried to her father that she didn't want to lose him at some point. His response was brilliant and is the same response I give you now.

"He asked her, 'Corrie, when you and I go to Amsterdam, when do I give you the ticket?' She replied, 'Why, just before we get on the train.' 'Exactly,' he encouraged her, 'and our wise Abba in heaven knows when we are going to need things too. Don't run ahead of Him, Corrie. When the time comes that some of us will have to die, you will look into your heart and find the strength you need, just in time.'"

Nathan knew the prophecy regarding the Anointed One's deliverance to the congregation of the wicked for judgment. He knew that though these days were bright and full of enlightenment, the perfect sacrifice had to take place somehow. He didn't know how to piece it all together, and clearly, Manuel was not going to reveal anything before its time.

"Don't run ahead of Him, Nathan. Each day has enough to carry." Nathan nodded. The two men shared a knowing glance and almost put the subject to rest. "Double Straights."

"Huh?"

"Double Straights," Manuel repeated. Nathan knew the reference was to the part of prophesy Manuel had left out in speaking of his youth. He *did* know it. "Out of Double Straights, I called my Son." Nathan nodded and smiled with relief. "When I was a baby, my life was in danger. Let's just say it wasn't a secret to everyone that a new regime was coming. The powers at that time wanted to squash it before it could, so my Dad– my earthly Dad– took us to Double Straights until that leadership had died, and he received word that we would be safe to return home."

"He received word? From who?"

"Who else? Abba. In a dream."

~~~

That night, Nathan had a dream. He was standing in an unfamiliar place that felt like home. It was dazzling and full of light. Surrounding him were people he had never met but knew by name. Just by thinking of it, he began to fly. He wasn't afraid of dropping low or being pulled down by weight. He had the full ability to control his direction. He flew over green fields and stunning waterways. Animals he had never seen before ran beneath him. He felt as though he could go on this way forever. Then, he came across a property that drew his attention. He couldn't pass it. He had to circle and land there. Walking the grounds, he felt warmth and peace. He knew that this property belonged to him. As he walked, he had the intense sensation that he had seen these grounds in every season. He had walked here a thousand times and knew each step by heart. He understood that it was representative of his life and known intimately. There was a well of life-giving water that was sourced from a stream. Everyone there had a similar well. As he passed, he looked down it and saw a rainbow of colors so exuberant that he thought it would bubble up and overflow at any moment. There were animals he had known before but had long since passed away. He sensed loved ones were just a thought away. He had never seen such beauty. It was a wonder he could take it all in. The desire to sit and absorb it was equal to the desire to go inside the structure standing in the distance. He headed toward it with a relief he never knew he needed. It was as if he
~~~

was breathing for the first time. The air was cleaner, and the temperature was perfect. He had no aches or pain in his body and felt almost weightless. As he approached the few last steps to the structure, he heard a voice.

"Well done, true and steadfast servant. You have been faithful with what you were given. I will now put you in charge of much more. Come and share your Creator's happiness." The voice was so clear and strong that Nathan turned to see who was speaking. Upon turning, he saw Manuel standing before him. He was wearing a white t-shirt and blue jeans, as always. He was barefooted and grinning from ear to ear. The love he felt for Manuel at that moment overwhelmed him, and suddenly nothing else in this place mattered. He rushed to Him and landed in His firm embrace.

"Welcome home, brother." Nathan felt completely loved. "You didn't think I would leave you down there, did you?"

CHAPTER 28:

IF YOU HAD BEEN HERE

Leaving Lazer, Marta, and Maria was never fun. The gang loved them, and Manual had unique camaraderie with Lazer. Marta was always the perfect hostess, and Maria, in her innocent devotion, caused everyone to want to be better people. At breakfast, Nathan told the group about his dream and of his disappointment upon waking. Manuel smiled and said nothing. Later, he said quietly to Nathan, "Wait until you see the inside of your place." Nathan wanted to ask more, but Manuel announced, "Let's do it! We've got a drive ahead of us, and we need to stop for gas."

Heading toward Government City was more than just another destination on the trip. For Manuel and each of the guys, it was heading straight into the fulfillment of his destiny. He sighed heavily and gazed out the window for a bit. The seasons were changing again, and it felt as if they had lived in the R.V. for an age. Finally, he interrupted the idle chatter among the guys and said, "You know… this leg of the trip is going to be different." They all paused, understanding the tone that they had come to know so well. Manuel wanted them to take note.

"We are going to Government City, and everything prophesied in the Ancient Writings about the Redeemer will be fulfilled." Nathan and Philip were traveling in their car, so the guys couldn't glean information regarding the prophecies' specifics from Nathan. They knew the Writings, and they knew that Manuel had a crucial action to accomplish, but they didn't realize the weight of all they headed toward. Manuel could sense their uncertainty and said outright, "Guys, I'm going to be delivered over into the hands of those who don't believe I am who I say I am. They're going to be pretty harsh in mocking me. They will insult me, spit on me, beat me, and ultimately kill me." The guys shot looks at each other and then at Manuel. Jack was driving and instinctively put on his indicator to start pulling over. "No, no," Manuel instructed. "Don't stop. Keep going."

"Kill you…" Simon clarified.

"Yes. Kill me. But don't worry. I'm not going to stay dead."

"Oh… You're not going to stay dead," Simon repeated sarcastically. "Oh, okay, then…"

"Simon," Manuel gently corrected in his tone. The guys didn't understand any of what he was saying. There was no way that everything they had worked for in these last years could just stop. There was no way the political leaders could ever get away with ending such a significant movement without an uproar. They couldn't get away with doing it to Johnny *and* Manuel. They couldn't.

"Never," Simon argued. "Kyrios, I will never let this happen to you. You know that. I will put myself between you and anyone who dares to approach you."

"Teivel!" Manuel yelled at top volume. At this, Jack did pull over. "You can get out of this R.V. right now if that's how you're going to be." Simon was confused. So were the others. "Don't you dare cause me to stumble now! You're not thinking about my mission or anything Theos has planned for the world's redemption through it. You're thinking about yourself! You're thinking about your gig as my frontman and how it would look if something happened to me on your watch."

Simon shrunk back in bewilderment. He hung his whole world on the fact that Manuel told him he would build the future through the things done by him and that he would be his rock. He had nearly abandoned his own business to be in this stinking van with the other guys. Was he supposed to step aside? Was his role here done? What was Manuel saying?

"I– I've left everything for you. *We've* left everything. Are we just supposed to–"

"Look. This is just the beginning, and I'm just letting you know. These days are going to take a quick turn and be brutal. But you cannot try and stop what is purposed."

"You dying?"

Manuel returned his gaze to the outside. The days were turning colder. "I'm telling you guys, there is going to be a renewal of all things. I'm going to return to Theos and operate from splendor. You guys– you precious brothers of mine– will also be operating out of sublimity. Anyone– everyone– who has sacrificed by leaving their wives, mothers, and families or businesses for my sake will receive a hundred times as much and gain immortality. It's not like you think. Those who were humble here and last in everything will become first in all things. And those who always gained everything first and had it all in this realm will be last in the Kingdom of the

Higher Realm. You can't wrap your heads around it, really. But you will. You will."

They sat in silence for several minutes. Jack's cell phone started ringing. It was Philip and Nathan wondering why they had pulled over and if everything was okay. "Yeah, no, we're good. We're going now. It was just– we're moving." Pulling back out onto the road, the guys were less than eager to speak again. Levi wished Jim hadn't pushed to go to Government City. They were not sure what was going to happen, but they were not looking forward to it. Surely, Manuel was speaking in one of his analogies. He wasn't actually going to be *killed*. But he said he would. And he said he wouldn't stay dead. They saw him raise that little girl from death, and then the young man– but how could he do it for himself? Is that what he meant? Or did he mean, in theory, the word of him would never end? It was all too much.

After some hours, the guys were just miles from Government City. Jack's phone rang again. This time it was Marta. Lazer had started not feeling well swiftly upon their departure and, within no time, developed a fever and chills. It became severe fast enough that they took him to the emergency room. It was so sudden that they wanted the guys to know, in case he could have passed something on to them. They asked Manuel to pray for him. They wondered if it were possible for them to turn around and return to his bedside as a personal favor.

"We aren't going back," Manuel determined. The guys knew how much Manuel loved Lazer and how serious Marta said things were. Still, they followed Manuel's lead, knowing he knew what was best and what they were determined to accomplish in the city. Manuel encouraged the guys to stop just short of their destination and rest for a few days. They camped outside of the city, but there was no hiding from all of Manuel's followers and the prying eyes of cameras. The media was ever watching to catch him in the act of doing something that would discredit him. Marta continued to call and give reports on Lazer, but he wasn't getting any better. Manuel told the guys that this illness wasn't going to end in death but allow recognition to come to the Son of Man. Again, they didn't grasp all he was saying; they were used to that. Finally, the call came that Lazer had slipped away. Shocked, Marta wanted to speak to Manuel directly and let him know that her brother wouldn't have died if he had chosen to go back. She was hurt and angry. She thought they meant more to him than to allow Lazer to spend his last days suffering. The guys were also surprised that Manuel hadn't chosen to return upon any one of the reports, especially in that he had explicitly said he wouldn't die. Things were getting strange. What was going on with Manuel?

It had been four days since the news of Lazer's passing when Manuel announced, "Okay. Let's go see the girls, and then we'll return to the city." Marta and Maria were well into planning Lazer's funeral. Their brother had been the primary breadwinner in their household, so with his death came the fear of how they would be able to maintain everything.

"Are we going to stay for the funeral?" Jack asked.

"Funeral? Lazer has been sleeping, but I'm going to wake him up."

That was it. They thought the stress of the last years was taking its toll. Manuel knew that Lazer had died. Marta called days ago, letting them know.

"Kyrios," Levi dared, but Manuel interrupted him.

"Yes, Lazer has died. I haven't lost my mind. But for your sake and for those that will be there, I'm glad I wasn't there. Now, maybe you'll believe what I say. Let's go."

When they arrived back at Marta and Maria's home, they found several people there offering help, meals, and support. Marta saw the R.V. pull up and rushed out to meet Manuel face to face.

"Kyrios… if you had been here, my brother would still be alive! But even now, I trust you. You can do whatever you want, and I know that if *you* ask Theos, He will give you what you want." Manuel looked at his friend. She was always so busy and worried. She was speaking that she believed, but the underlying anger and fear still existed in her voice.

"He's going to live," Manuel replied.

"Yes, I know. I know that in the end, he will be restored and live in the Elevated Realm."

Manuel sighed. "I Am Restoration. If anyone believes in me– even if he dies– he will live. And anyone already living who believes in me– won't ever die. Do you believe what I'm telling you, Marta?"

It was hard. But looking in Manuel's eyes, she knew that there was truth in what he was saying. "Yes, Kyrios. I believe that you truly are the Son of the Creator who has come into the world to redeem us."

"Alrighty then," he said. "Where's Maria?" Maria was slower to come than Marta. Mimicking her sister when she saw him, she fell into his arms.

"Kyrios, why didn't you come? We called and called you! If you had been here, Lazer would still be alive." Maria had instantly believed in Manuel's love with her whole heart. She took it personally when he didn't jump to their call.

Hugging her, he became deeply moved by her tears and asked, "Where is he now?"

"Lazer?"

"Yes, of course, Lazer."

"He's at the morgue."

"Let's go."

"To the morgue?"

"Yeah, to the morgue. I want to see him."

"Kyrios," Marta intervened, they don't allow people to see bodies at the morgue. He's been embalmed and kept cold until funeral and burial arrangements can be made. Will you be here for the viewing? You can see him then."

"No, no… we'll see him today. Let's go."

Reluctantly they piled into the R.V. along with several people from the house and caravan following behind them. There were whispers among the followers. 'If he has caused blind people to see and sick people to healed, why couldn't he save one of his closest friends?' Upon arrival at the morgue, Marta went to the front desk to speak to someone about seeing Lazer's body. The worker expressed that her request was impossible and simply never done. Manuel gave her a half-smile and tilted his head. She went into the back and reemerged, confirming that this would not be possible. The lobby filled with followers and even a couple of media people. Manuel put his hand on his forehead and silently wept. The people were whispering about how much he must have loved Lazer. Deeply moved, Manuel lifted his head.

"Bring him out," he said.

"Sir," the attendant resisted, "It has been four days, and he has been chemically treated. There's an odor, as he's not yet prepared for burial nor been seen by the mortician for appearance."

"I guess we really can't," Marta agreed.

"Marta, I told you that if you believed, you would see the glory of Theos through redemption." Manuel looked up into the Elevated Realm and invoked the Creator. "Abba, thank you so much for hearing me. I know that you never fail to hear me, but for the sake of those around me, I acknowledge this so they will believe." Turning toward the door that led to the backroom, he cried out in a loud voice, "Lazer!" Everyone went silent. Some froze, and some even started to chuckle. Was he mad? He was calling out to a dead guy! "Laaazeer! Come out here, man."

"Sir," the attendant declared, "I'm sorry, this is absolutely unacceptable. You will need to take this band of people and disperse immediately. We are not set up for–"

Just then, a woman came from the backroom, screaming with her hands stretched out in front of her. Pushing her way through the crowd, she headed straight for the front door and out as fast as she could. Behind her came Lazer with a body bag zipped around him.

"Unbind him," Manuel instructed. The attendant's face went as white as a sheet. She fell back against the wall and couldn't bring herself to reach for the body. Slowly she grabbed the phone to call for security and someone who might help.

"I said unbind him," Manuel repeated. "Let the poor guy out." A couple of brave followers stepped forward to unzip the bag. Marta and Maria stood holding each other in fear and anticipation. They wanted to rush him but were too stunned. Finally, the body bag was unzipped and dropped. Before it could hit the ground, Manuel grabbed it.

"Hey, hey, now," he said, "There's no reason to give away the goods. What's up, my brutha?" Lazer, looking pale and fragile, put his arm around Manuel's shoulder for support.

"What the heck?" he asked. People were snapping photos.

"Long story," Manuel replied. The crowd went crazy. Shrieks of joy and celebration rose. The attendant stood speechlessly. Marta and Maria finally rushed their brother with relentless affection. Security came and offered Lazer some used clothing. Manuel was grinning and said, "Let's get the man something to eat. Marta, what– you didn't bring anything with you?"

"Kyrios!" she screamed and hugged him as well.

Many religious and political moles became believers, but some went directly back to their leaders and reported what Manuel had done. The chief officers and leaders gathered together to counsel. They were concerned about their power being overrun by him. They went over stories of the miracles and signs he had performed and determined that his road trip had gone on long enough.

"If we allow him to go on like this, everyone and their brother will believe in him. You know that we can't have that. It could take away our place and our nation."

Sabeen Smith, the speaker of the church, was present. She rebuked them. "You fools. You know nothing at all. Think about it. It is better for everyone that this one man should die rather than the whole nation comes to ruin." The room was hushed in silent agreement that he should be stopped once and for all. From that day forth, they made plans to put Manuel to death.

CHAPTER 29:

GOVERNMENT CITY

Manuel knew that it was nearly time for the annual Commemoration of Trials festival. This would mean a larger population in Government City. The good news was that as a hub for all things political and religious, Manuel could reach more people for redemption. The bad news was that he would be under a hotter spotlight than usual. Authorities were patrolling the streets in increased numbers. Scout Nikkos's article in the Tri-State Triton had brought unprecedented attention, and on the road, things were running at full speed. Jim scheduled the taping with Draco's people for Wednesday but pulling into town on Sunday evening gave them time to connect with the citizens. It was harder and harder for the R.V. to pull into any town without a follower of the Redeemer Roadtrip channel spotting it and sharing its presence. The first night, they were able to stay pretty low-key, but the crowds started gathering by Monday morning. Both religious sects and the government leaders had additional plants reporting Manuel's every move to them.

Manuel gathered the guys first thing in the morning with an odd request. "Jack…go and grab Nathan for me. I need him to run an errand for me."

"Sure, boss, what is it?" Jack quipped, eager to get out of the R.V.

"Just grab him, man." Soon, Jack was back with Nathan, who was ready to run whatever errand was needed.

"Nathan, I need you to take your brother and start heading out of town. In about ten minutes, you're going to come to a ranch on the left side with a huge blue barn. You'll find a donkey tied to the railing outside. I need you to borrow the farmer's trailer and bring it to me."

"The trailer?"

"No, the donkey."

"You want us to bring you a donkey."

"Yep." It took Nathan two clicks before he knew where Manuel was going. When it finally struck him, he understood why Manuel requested *him* and why he wanted the beast. The Ancient Writings read, 'Behold, your King is coming to you, humble, and mounted on a donkey…' Nathan knew the prophecies better than any of the others.

"Are you saying…"

"You know what I'm saying. Grab it for me, yeah? The farmer won't give you any trouble."

"Absolutely, Kyrios." And he left.

Within an hour, Nathan and Philip returned with the trailer and donkey. They lowered the animal and led him to the back of the R.V. Manuel came out and threw a blanket on its back. "Are you ready, boy? You're about to make history." As odd as it seemed to the guys, Manuel rode the beast out to where the crowd had gathered. A hush came over the multitude. Some people were moved to bow as he came by. It was an intuitive way of honoring him as he entered the city. Some knew of the Ancient Writings, and some were just caught in the magnitude of the moment. They called out to him, "Kyrios!" "Save us!" "We trust you… teach us." They showed him love and adoration beyond measure. They threw daffodils at him to show respect and symbolize new beginnings. They threw chrysanthemums to symbolize their hope for the future. Ironically, they didn't think it odd at all that he was riding a donkey. They simply accepted him for all the miracles and wonders he had performed over the last few years.

Simon always stepped out first and scanned the crowd for anything abnormal. Today, he led the donkey. Manuel got down and was greeting the crowd as if they were his long-lost friends. "Good morning!" He called out so the furthest person could hear. For such an average-sized guy who was often a bit soft-spoken, the guys were always amazed at the way he could project his voice in a crowd. If nervous authorities didn't break up sessions, they could go on for hours. People had started bringing sack lunches or backpacks with snacks because no one wanted to leave long enough to grab food for fear that he would not be speaking by the time they got back. Sometimes they would all sit down to eat simultaneously, making it easier to resume the teaching and healings afterward, which they chose to do on this day. Everyone was sitting anywhere they could find and eating as they discussed all they heard beforehand. One of the plants for the conservative sect asked Manuel to join him for lunch. The traditionalist was surprised when Manual did not rewash his hands before eating. The conservative sect was all about ceremonial acts and practices. They made a show of every little task as a way of advertising their righteousness. Manuel knew who the plant was and what he was expecting him to do.

"You know what the problem with you conservatives is?" The man was startled; Manuel knew who he was. "You guys clean the outside of the cup and dish, so it looks good, but the inside is still filthy and stained. What does it matter if you wash your hands a million times if you are still full of greed and wickedness on the inside? Pure filth."

"Well, I… I mean, we don't– wickedness? How can you call us wicked? We are the leading carriers of religion in the world. We honor the ancient ways."

"And how has that worked out for anyone other than yourselves? Wasn't the soul made by the same Creator that made the outside of your body? Why do you keep only the outside pristine? It's foolish! Clean up the inside by taking care of the truly needy and poor. Get your minds off of yourselves and see the difference it will make."

"Sir, we have many programs for the poverty-stricken and offer–"

"And I'm sure everyone knows it. What do you do that is unknown? What isn't for show or sale? You systematically give your Higher Power a tenth of all your produce but neglect justice and His love. You should have practiced His love before becoming a slave to the tenth."

"But the law states that we *should* give a tenth of everything to Him first."

"Yes, to honor Him and receive a blessing on the 90% that's left; to learn gratitude and discipline. The ten percent was to fill community resources so that none would go without, not checking another box to show how good you are.

"You guys love the most important seats in the house and to receive praise when you're out and about, but you will walk over unmarked graves without caring or knowing it. Where is the reverence when it counts?"

The political leaders were sitting nearby and overheard the conversation. They were pleased to think that the religious sect was being put in their place but took offense at the similarities in their own offices.

"Teacher, with all due respect," one interrupted, "when you pinpoint caring about what the public thinks, you insult us, also." Manuel turned to the eavesdroppers.

"You *experts in the law*… shame on you. You guys load people down with burdens they can hardly carry and don't lift a finger to help them. You don't care about the people. You call yourselves 'public servants,' but all you're serving are your interests while lining your pockets."

"That's not true. We recently spent big money to build monuments of remembrance for great leaders and prophets of the past. We want people to recognize and recall all that their government has done for them."

"Monuments? Or tombs? Your predecessors killed those leaders and prophets, and you honor them for it. Theos, in His wisdom, sent you prophets and people to guide you, even knowing that you would kill them and scorn their message. It's been going on since the beginning of the world.

Listen up, friends. This generation is going to be held responsible for all of it."

The leaders and conservatives exchanged fearful glances. Manuel didn't flinch but sat twirling a blade of grass between his fingers. They felt that Manuel had just threatened them with the coolest of deliveries.

"Look, *Sir…*" the political plant retorted, "This *generation* has gone to great lengths to be responsible! We have built schools and provided economic programs for aid. We have environmental, animal, gender-sensitive, and health insurance for–"

"Shame on you!" Manuel sat up and looked the man in the eye, "You have raped the people and told them it was for their good! You have taken away the key to knowledge and have not given it to them! You yourselves have refused to enter into true justice and righteousness and hindered anyone of them who tries to get there. Don't talk to me about all you have done. We see all you have done, and there will be a reckoning."

Instead of *feeling* threatened, the group *knew* he had threatened them. Not so graciously excusing themselves, they each rushed off to report to those who had sent them out. Manuel knew there would be retaliation. Turning first to his guys, he said, "Be on your guard against the yeast of these religious and political moles. They are completely hypocritical. Nothing you may say is safe. They revel in the opportunity to expose any secret you may have. Anything done in the dark will come into the light. Anything you may have *whispered* will be heard. They have eyes and ears everywhere. And so does Theos."

The guys knew of the constant snooping around by the powers, but this warning of Manuel's felt more threatening. Returning to the crowd, Manuel continued his cautioning.

"Friends… Don't be afraid of those who can kill you and take the life from your bodies." There were so many people present that they thought he was talking about the threat of trampling each other. A hush fell over the group. "I will show you whom you should fear. Fear the One who, after your body is lifeless, has the authority to throw you into the abyss. He is the only power that deserves your reverence."

The people had never seen Manuel this way. His messages were typically uplifting while encouraging people to love one another. This day, he was straightforward about darker powers at work. He was full of warnings and words to the wise regarding hypocrisy, death, darker realms, fear, and reverence.

"I'm telling you… Theos knows you intimately– each and every one of you. He sees everything; He is everywhere. Not like the government sees and knows everything, but inwardly. He knows what you are thinking in your heart. He knows why you do what you do and don't do. He knows how many hairs are on your head! He doesn't miss a beat. He intentionally keeps your heart beating! He values you beyond anything that could be bought or sold." Some had never heard anyone tell them they were of value and sat in the weight of it. Others didn't quite believe him, although it sounded nice. Still more thought that the depth of the Creator's love must be for everyone else but not for them specifically. If Theos knew what was in their heart, then surely He wouldn't love them the way Manual was talking. Knowing what they were thinking, he said, "He loves you with an everlasting love. It's not fickle or conditional. It is constant without fail."

"What about that woman who killed her kids?" someone shouted from the crowd. "How can He love someone like that?" Many quickly agreed.

"Stacey Dreggs wasn't always a murderer. There were a series of events that led to her misfortune."

"Misfortune?" another shouted. "She had everything! I've had three miscarriages. I wish I had her kind of misfortune!"

"Don't do that. Don't ever wish for someone else's situation. You don't know anything about it. You don't see behind the scenes or what they've endured in coming to where they are. Good or bad. You don't know their childhood; you don't know their sacrifice. You don't know what demon whispered in their ear that caused them to believe it was their only choice. You don't know the pain she feels every day as a result. You don't know anything. You only know what the media feeds you, and you think you have a right to judge? You don't. Don't judge by appearances. If you follow Theos and me as His son, then you are certainly called to judge situations that demand your attention within the community. But you are not called to judge individuals or their situations. All judgment must be done in love. It's a fine line, and wisdom dictates you don't cross it."

The guys thought they should probably pull Manuel aside and check-in. The day may have been going too long, and that it might be wise to call it. Manuel simply looked at Simon and indicated, 'No.'

"Even Stacey Dreggs is loved by Abba." The crowd was quiet. One woman started weeping openly. Those around her began to comfort her. She thought that if Theos could sincerely love someone like Stacey Dreggs, then maybe He could love her as well; *truly* love her. The hope was overwhelming.

"I publicly acknowledge His love for not only people like Stacey but for *each and every* person. We acknowledge those we love. We recognize and support them. In that, whoever publicly acknowledges me, I will, in turn, acknowledge before the supernatural messengers of Theos. But whoever chooses to disown me will be disowned in the Higher Realm as well. Speaking against me can be forgiven– but anyone who dares to speak against the very Essence of the Creator will not find forgiveness."

"You safeguard us with Theos, but how are we supposed to defend ourselves to the officials and authorities here on earth? It's one thing for Theos to know us, but when they accuse us of something here–"

"When you are brought before authorities and accusers, don't worry about how you will defend yourselves or what you should say. The Essence of the Creator will go before you and teach you at that time what to say. Stay calm. He will provide all the evidence."

Just then, a man pushed through to where Manuel was standing. "Teacher, my brother is the Executor of our parent's estate. He isn't fair! He's here. Will you please tell him to share the estate with me evenly?" Manuel shook his head and rolled his eyes, wondering if this guy had heard one word he just said.

"Man, who appointed me a judge or arbiter between you?" Addressing the crowd, he continued, "Watch out! Be on your guard against all kinds of greed and selfishness; life is not made up of how much stuff you own! You are not defined by your abundance of possessions or lack thereof." Simon stepped up and ushered Manuel to a park bench so he could stand higher. Manuel launched into an allegory.

"There was a wealthy farmer who had an abundant crop one year. He knew he didn't have space enough to store it all, so he decided to tear down the barns that had served him well for years and build bigger ones to hold the surplus. Because he had so much stored up, he decided to take it easy. Eat, drink, and live the good life. There was nothing he wanted he did not get. But Theos spoke to him and said, 'You fool! If you died tonight, who would gain from all your stored-up surplus?' This is how it's going to be for anyone who clings to their wealth but isn't rich in spirit."

The crowd was beginning to feel conviction for each of the things they had hoarded when they knew they could have invested in the well-being of others. The perspective started to shift from a focus on themselves to a communal concern.

"I'm telling you! Don't be so hung up on, 'What am I going to eat? How can I look good; what should I wear?' Life is about so much more than food, your body, or the style of clothes. Of course, take care of yourselves but don't worry about everything so much. Think about it– rabbits, let's say, they don't store up food in their little refrigerators or go to work each day, but they always find what they need. Theos knows about them. He provides for them. How much more valuable are you to Him than *rabbits*?" The people chuckled. The animal activists were a bit ruffled.

"Or what about something as simple as wildflowers? They don't labor to be beautiful. They just are what they are created to be, and in that, they are beautiful. So are you. Even the richest, wisest king in all his splendor can't achieve the beauty those flowers achieve just by being themselves. If Theos cares enough to make sure that the wildflowers, which we pass by without any thought, have beauty enough– don't you think He cares enough to clothe you with appeal as well? Where is your faith?? Don't set your heart on where you're going to eat and what you'll wear– the twisted run after that stuff. Abba knows what you need, and He'll provide it. Don't worry! You'll still look cool!" The crowd laughed and related.

"Look," Manuel felt enough had been said, "Don't be afraid. Abba is more than pleased to give you His very Kingdom. Let everything else go. Don't be weighed down by stuff. Simplicity. *Simplicity*. Seek Him and His kingdom before any of this stuff, and I assure you– everything you need, and then some, will be given to you. Think of the poor and provide for them. When you do, you'll see that your own things will never wear out or fall short. Trust in things that come from the spiritual realm, not the earthly one. Nothing can be stolen there or destroyed. Your heart is attached to this stuff. I love you guys." Manuel looked at Simon, who cleared the way for him to head back to the R.V.

"It's still early," someone shouted. "Will you come back out later?" Manuel was tired. It had been a heavy session. Looking around, he saw the hunger on their faces and knew even better the desperation in their hearts. He knew he was going to need to rest up and prepare for the Draco taping on Wednesday. Simon started to shoo them as they pressed into him.

"No," Manuel said softly. "Let's stay a bit longer."

"Kyrios," Simon advised, "You can always come back for an evening session if you feel up to it."

"No, no. Let's knock this out now. They're here. Look at them– they're so hungry. The Essence will sustain me."

Looking around, Manuel could see the sky opening up and dozens of messengers flocking to support the crowd and bring healing. He had empathy and stayed. "The Messengers are here to heal," he said. "Press in and feel remorse for any time you ever mistreated someone you could have helped or stockpiled your belongings. Theos wants to clean things up. Don't be afraid. Just express to Him that you know you should have helped and didn't. He is slow to anger. He doesn't want to punish you in your vulnerability. He wants to heal you and bring you up to the next level. Be better. Do better." Simon helped Manuel back to the park bench. "Sit down, at least, come on, guys. Let's sit down." The crowd settled in, and Manuel continued to teach. He told a story about servants who weren't ready when the Master of the house returned from a business trip. They squandered away their time and were not prepared when the boss arrived. "Always be prepared. Purpose a course of action in advance so that when the Master shows up, you won't be caught off guard but be well equipped."

"But there's nothing wrong with resting and having a good time, right? I mean, that's not what you're saying…" a girl asked.

"Almost anything in excess is bad," Manuel replied.

"'A little sleep, a little slumber,
a little folding of the hands to rest,
and poverty will come upon you like a robber,
and scarcity like an armed man.'

"No, I'm not saying don't rest. Rest is crucial. But don't let rest become an excuse for not accomplishing anything else. The thing is, anyone who takes advantage of his situation and thinks there will be no consequence is wrong. If you know what you ought to be doing and don't do it– you're missing the mark."

"To whom much is given, much is required," the girl quoted the Ancient Writings.

"Exactly. And,

'The one who has been entrusted with much,
Of him much more will be asked.'"

"What's the difference?"

"One is a gift, and one is a deposit." The girl furrowed her brow and nodded. He smiled and gave her a side hug. "One is for you, and one I'm going to want a return on."

CHAPTER 30:

LIGHT IN THE DARKNESS

It had been a long day, and it had taken its toll on Manuel. He was quick to fall into bed after eating something. The guys let him rest and tried to settle themselves down, but they couldn't help but talk about the difference they saw in their leader that day. He was sad and burdened. He seemed full of sorrow for everything the world had become. His delivery was harsh. Manuel woke and heard them talking softly. He went out to join them.

"I love you for your concern," he greeted them.

"Kyrios– we didn't mean to wake you."

"You didn't wake me. The Essence of the Creator woke me. You need to process; let's process."

Although he was tired, Manuel was always willing to give. He knew how to separate himself with boundaries but most often chose compassion and sacrifice. The men sat together, feeling what seemed to be the weight of the world. Manuel asked Jim to text Nathan and Philip to join their late-night discussion, and soon they were tapping on the R.V. door.

"What happened today?" Jack asked. "You seemed… mad."

"I wasn't mad. I was irritated. I'm sick of these so-called leaders not fulfilling their purpose. It's a privilege to serve, and they've only served themselves. It's gross negligence, and it's disgusting."

"I guess we just aren't used to our days going that way, so we felt strange about it."

"Things are going to get a lot stranger. Look, guys, I have come to cleanse the world with a refining fire. I wish it were already fully lit. I told you; it's not going to be all good times. There will be more confrontation and plenty of admonition. It's like I'm in a pressure cooker until– Do you think I'm here to bring peace? On the contrary, I am here to bring clear division."

"But… you're all 'peace and love! Love your enemy…'" Jack said in a sing-song way. The guys chuckled.

"Absolutely. But from now on, there will be families taking different sides; father against son and son against father, mother against daughter and daughter against mother, mother-in-law against daughter-in-law and daughter-in-law against mother-in-law."

"Well, there's nothing new there," Jude said under his breath.

"The point is people are going to have to choose Who they're going to serve. Either they will choose to walk in the ways of family and society, or they will see the truth in the light and choose it. You can't be entangled in the ways of this wicked generation and expect to find the true reward. Whoever isn't with me is against me, and whoever does not pull things together… just scatters everything."

"You make it sound so black and white. Aren't there always shades of grey? Isn't it possible to be a good person and just not fully understand what it is you're bringing and choose to stay in the ways of their family?"

Manuel sighed and hung his head. Shaking it, he said, "No. No, it's not. There will always be shades of grey to muddle the lines. But lines are there to keep good things in, not just bad things out. Boundaries aren't for suffocation; they're for freedom. Don't get muddled."

It turned into a long conversation through the night. As tired as they all were, these times were when their intimacy grew. They trusted Manuel with their whole hearts and were willing to walk with him through any adversity. Or so they thought. Finally, Nathan asked, "Kyrios, what about this place of agony that becomes the consequence of choosing the chaos? How will people know if they're on the right side?"

"People are such hypocrites," he moaned. "anyone can see a cloud rising in the west and quickly say, 'Oh. It's going to rain.' And it does. And when the wind blows from the South, they say, 'It's gonna be a hot one.' And it is. How is it, then, that anyone can interpret the weather and say what will happen, but they cannot wrap their heads around what's going on in this present time? The signs are all so clear. Why can't they judge for themselves what is right? It's like– let's say someone has an issue and finds themselves headed to court. They should seriously do everything they can to settle out of court because once you are standing before the judge, you might be turned over to the officer and then thrown into prison. I'm telling you– no one is getting out until everything they owe is paid."

"How can someone pay if they're in prison?"

"They can't. That's why they need to accept the ransom paid for them in advance because everyone is going to stand in front of the Judge at some point."

"What's the ransom?"

"If there be for him an angel,

a mediator, one of the thousand,
to declare to man what is right for him,
and he is merciful to him, and says,
'Deliver him from going down into the pit;
I have found a ransom;
let his flesh become fresh with youth;
let him return to the days of his youthful vigor'".

The guys regretted not paying more attention to the Ancient Writings. They knew he was quoting them but were too embarrassed to ask him what he meant.

~~~

Wednesday morning came with an eleven o'clock call time to be at Draco Conti's studio located in his megachurch in the hub of the city. The guys slipped away from their location early in the morning so as not to be followed by the majority, but few were always savvy and followed wherever they went. Scout Nikkos was one of them. Camera-ready he took shots of the guys as they stopped for breakfast, as they grabbed a few things at a market, and as they pulled into the multilevel parking garage that belonged to Draco's church. Scout parked before the guys and tried to be at the entrance before they arrived so he could get shots of them entering the building. The courtyard leading to the church entrance was large and had become an urban hang-out spot. There was a coffee bar with roasts from all over the world. There were food carts and a shop full of Draco Conti gear. People were wearing Draco Conti t-shirts and selling apparel. There were bumper stickers and coffee mugs for sale as well as a bookstore with every Draco Conti material ever published or printed. Any outsider would feel comfortable with contemporary music playing and oversized comfy chairs for lounging. If one didn't know better, they might think they had happened upon a mall. All that was missing was the movie theatre where you could watch *all Draco all day.*

Scout grabbed a coffee, smoked a cigarette, and watched to see from which direction the guys would enter. As they approached, Manuel looked to some as if he was entering with his entourage. The Conti people were accustomed to celebrities arriving with their posses, so the seven guys that accompanied Manuel didn't seem any different. When Manuel reached the courtyard, his pace slowed. The guys instinctively paused, following his lead. As he reached the center, Manuel was overwhelmed with passion by what he saw. The exchange of money, the casual contempt for what should be a place of reverence. The t-shirts and bumper stickers. There was a line of people waiting to give their monetary gift and obeisance. A religious leader stood to bless them and grant a ceremonial gesture. Rage rose within Manuel. Before the guys could follow what was happening, Manuel started roaring. He
~~~

rushed a food cart and flipped it over. The population turned to find the commotion. The guys were in shock. Jack instinctively reached for his phone to record but hesitated as he didn't think this is what the people should see. Others recorded, there was no avoiding it. Manuel moved on to those selling coffee mugs and t-shirts. He smashed the mugs and threw the shirts down, trampling them. He flipped the register over and began screaming. Somebody called security while chief officers and elders of the church rushed down. Manuel saw the marketplace as a mockery and was scattering the shameless whoring of Conti material. Nathan turned to the others and recited from the Ancient Writings, "Zeal for my Father's house will consume me." They began to understand. They had never seen Manuel like this but could feel his fury. People started running out of the courtyard. No one was taking any chances. Random shootings and people going mad were on the news enough.

Manuel's raid continued, and money was flying until security grabbed him and the chief officers and elders approached. "Who do you think you are?" they condemned.

"Quit making my Father's house a place of commerce!"

The officers and elders felt the sting of his words but were aware that they needed him for the show's taping that day. They ordered him released. "If you are who you say you are," one demanded, "what kind of sign or miracle can you do right here, right now to prove it? What gives you any right to come and destroy all we have built?"

"Destroy this frame, and in three days, I will stand it up again."

The officers and elders were dumbfounded. "Are you kidding? It took years to build this place into what it is today. You think you can just tear it down and build it up again in a few days?" But the frame that Manuel was referring to was his own body. Simon looked at Manuel and shook his head, 'No.' Manuel knew that the years of following him and plotting his demise would soon be coming to a head. They had long wanted to terminate his existence and operation, and he knew they were formulating plans.

"We're outta here." Manuel determined.

"Wait! The taping! Draco is upstairs waiting for you."

"Draco's going to be waiting a while. There is no way I'm going to be any part of this."

Nico DeMos had been among the elders and was secretly admiring Manuel in his stance. He longed to walk out with him and end his slavery to the trade. But he had a family and a mortgage, so the battle in his conscience continued.

~~~

After the scene at Draco's place, the guys headed to a local spot where people gathered freely to share music, poems, and opinions on an open mic. Near a lake with huge rocks and terrain, people regularly spread out lawn
~~~

chairs and blankets as natives and travelers alike came to enjoy the community amphitheater. Manuel knew things would get harder now as there were plots to kill both him and Lazer. Many people in every sect and walk of life had come to believe in him due to the miracle with Lazer. The religious leaders knew their influence was slipping as a result of the freeing ways he taught. Manuel was less about rules and regulations than he was love and honor for each other. Becoming a better person and following the laws of the land easily came when redemption flooded their souls. It was a natural transition to wellness and prosperity.

The guys laid out a blanket and listened to different people step up to the mic. It wasn't long before the focus wasn't on who was on stage but the members of the Redeemer Roadtrip lounging in the crowd. As Philip went to get food and drinks for all, he overheard some foreigners from Greece who had traveled to the Region in hopes of locating and experiencing Manuel's gifts in person. They studied his videos, read everything printed, and were determined to see him in person. "I know where he is now," Philip told them, "and I would be shocked if he didn't end up speaking." They followed him back to the spot and were in awe as they placed themselves nearby. Philip told Nathan and then Manuel about the people coming all the way from Greece to find him. Manuel knew all the signs of the time and that the days were closing in on him. He was troubled and wanted to ask, 'Abba, please save me from these final hours.' But he knew the purpose of his coming was for the very hour he dreaded. There was no other way to ensure humanity could be fully redeemed but to offer his own life as a sacrifice.

The crowd was cheering and hounding Manuel to take the mic. He stood, and as he walked to the front, the group began to cheer. The cheer became a roar, and the roar became silent as he raised his hand to calm them. "Hello…" he said calmly. There was so much on his heart. He was full of sorrow and love for them. Would they get it? Did they understand enough for him to leave them soon? It was what it was. Either they would get it, or they wouldn't. He was doing all he could for them. Overwhelmed by love and devotion, he began, "I know you guys have some expectations. Some of you have traveled from other lands with such hope. I'm grateful. My desire is for you to know the source of all restitution and abundant life." Softly, almost apart from the mic, he said, "Abba, show them who You are. Magnify your name." Just then, a voice came from nowhere and everywhere all at once.

"I have magnified it, and I will continue to."

The crowd shrieked. Some thought that thunder had shaken an open blue sky. Others searched frantically for supernatural messengers that may have spoken. They felt the rumble through their bodies, and some fell face down on the ground in fear.

"It's okay. It's okay," Manuel assured. "This voice has come for your sake… not mine. I know this voice as well as my own. Now is the judgment of this world; now will the ruler of this world be cast out. This very week the Son of Man will be offered and raised from the earth drawing all people to himself."

The crowd was scared and confused. This was certainly not what they were hoping to hear from him. They wanted to see someone healed or get something from him. This was just scary and bizarre. At the back of the theatre stood Teivel. In a sharp grey suit, despite the sunshine, he stood coolly observing. Manuel saw him and lifted his chin in a steadfast position. No one seemed to notice him or care. Typical.

A man called out from the crowd, "The Law and Ancient Writings have taught us that the Redeemer will remain forever and change the government as we know it. What do you mean then when you say that the Son of Man must be offered and raised up? Are you the Son of Man? Or– who is it?"

Manuel said these things as a clue to how he would die and the climax of the political struggle hunting him. The crowd started grumbling. They had thought more of this guy than seeing him in person was turning out to be. Knowing what they were thinking in their hearts, he spoke calmly into the mic. "I have–" the mic screamed with feedback. The crowd winced and became more irritated. He tried again. "I have brought illumination into the world to reveal the darkness."

Teivel chuckled and whispered, "They don't see you as a light. They see you as a vending machine. They only care about what they can get out of you for as little cost as possible. You know that." Manuel could hear him as if he were standing right beside him, whispering in his ear.

"I am the illumination," he continued. "I am the Truth. I am the Way to redemption, and I am Life." The grumbling started to grow, and Manuel knew he was losing them. The guys stood looking at each other in awe. They had never seen a crowd turn on Manuel before. What was happening?

"Get off the stage!"

"Work a miracle!"

"Show us something good. Come on!"

"Boooooo. Hisssssss."

"The illumination will be among you for a while longer," he said tenderly. "Exercise it while you can. Move forward while the path is clear. Darkness is all around and will overtake you if you don't. Anyone who walks in darkness has no clue where he's headed. While you have light, believe in it, that you may become Sons of the Light." Someone threw an orange on stage. Then a tomato. Then all sorts of objects started hurling towards the front. Simon ran up to grab Manuel, but he was gently backing away from the mic. Looking at them with heartache, he knew this was the beginning of the cruciality.

Simon reached the stage, but as he did, he noticed Manuel was nowhere to be seen. Checking every side of the platform, he didn't know how he could have made it any distance so fast. The crowd stopped throwing things but was still booing and grumbling. Teivel stood with a grin from ear to ear. "That's it, my pretties. How dare he not perform for you today. Spirits of Doubt and Betrayal I release you. Invade their hearts and minds. Spirit of Dissension- go." Things started getting ugly. Simon returned to the guys swiftly.

"Have you seen him?"

"You didn't get him?"

"No, he… slipped out somewhere. Let's get to the R.V. He'll be there." But upon their return, Manuel was not there. They had never experienced anything like this before and hadn't planned any sort of rendezvous point should things go wrong. People started coming for the R.V. with rocks and clenched fists.

"We're gonna have to get out of here," Levi said.

"We aren't going anywhere without him," Simon answered.

"He'll find us," Jack volunteered. "Come on; you know he can."

Pounding and screams of a challenge started. Philip was already in their car with the engine running, but Nathan pushed his way through the crowd and pounded on the R.V. window. He had watched Manuel disappear and knew he was nowhere to be found. "Go! Go!" He screamed.

"Nathan is screaming to go!" Jude chimed in.

"Their eyes have been blinded! Their hearts have hardened! Go, go!"

Knowing that Nathan knew the Ancient Writings better than any of them, instruction from him seemed superlative. Jim started the engine and spoke to Manuel as though he were sitting beside him. "We're headed to the other side of the lake. Meet us there, Kyrios." When Nathan heard the engine roar and start to pull off, he ran to the car to join Philip.

"These people," he complained to Philip, "if they don't see it with their eyes or touch it with their hands, they don't get it. If they would just turn and be open, the Creator would absolutely heal them."

Among the crowd were certain authorities who believed in Manuel despite the mob turning against him, but they didn't dare confess it because they valued their positions in the church more than the position they could gain as Sons of the Light.

Suddenly, Manuel was standing on top of a huge boulder. He cried out, "Whoever believes in me believes not just in me but in the One who sent me! If you see me for who I am, you will see Him! I have come into this world as a light so that whoever believes in me won't remain lost and floundering in the darkness. If you hear everything I've taught– all my words– and don't keep them, I get it. I'm not judging you! I didn't come to judge this world. I came to save it. But if you reject me and don't receive anything I have said, there is a Judge. The words you don't believe will judge you in the end. I haven't spoken any of this stuff to you on my own. Every single thing I have given and said was given to me as an edict. This edict is *eternal life*, people. What I say, I say as Abba has told me. If you're pissed, you're not pissed at me, but Him." As they rushed the boulder, Manuel disappeared because it was not the time for them to seize him.

CHAPTER 31:

ON THE WATER

The sun had set, so the guys were able to pull into a secluded spot behind some trees on the other side of the lake. It was hard to hide the R.V. anywhere these days, but Jim managed pretty well. How tired they had all become. The road trip was in its third year, and although the work was compelling, it could also be exhausting. Manuel had started carrying some darkness that was never fully expressed, and truth be told, they were missing home. Nothing compared to life with Manuel and radically seeing lives change before their eyes, but it didn't feel good to know that Big Brother was out for his blood. With the plot to kill Lazer, they knew there might be plots to kill each of them as well. No one could be this close to Manuel and not pay the price.

"I've got to get out of this stinking R.V.," Jude complained. Leaving the guys, he stepped out and walked down to the lake to clear his head. Simon thought it was a great idea and casually chose to do the same. Each of the guys took a few minutes on their own to breathe and wait for Manuel. Surely, he would find them.

Dusk was Simon's favorite time of day to go out in a boat on the water. It had been so long since he had held any boating gear or equipment in his hands, and suddenly, he couldn't think of any place he wanted to be more than in the middle of that lake. His eyes scanned the lakefront for a boat. Any boat. Large or small. He saw a man sitting on the bow of a midsize Bowrider. Perfect. Before he thought, he found himself in full stride towards the boat. The guys saw him walking with purpose, and one by one, started to follow. Simon reached the vessel and called to the man.

"Ahoy," he greeted. The man sat with his legs crossed. He was at perfect peace with a pipe in his mouth, watching the water. He nodded to Simon but didn't say a word. "She's beautiful. Had her long?"

"Long enough."

"Sir, my name is Simon–"

"I know who you are. You're the Fisher King."

Simon chuckled and lowered his head. "Yes, well. Thanks– I think. Sir, I was wondering–"

"You want to use my boat."

"Uh… well, yes. How did you know that? Kind of a crazy request at this hour."

"Some guy came and told me you'd come here and to please allow you to use my boat when you asked. Nice fella. Had a way about him."

Simon nearly cried. Kyrios. Not only had he gone before them so many times before, but he knew. He knew that Simon was going to find himself in this position with this desire, and he made way for it to not only be doable but *easy*.

"Yes. Yes, He does."

"Climb aboard. I'm gonna get some supper. You just tie her to the dock when you're done. Where are your buddies?"

"My buddies?"

"He said you'd have some friends." Simon's heart sank a bit. He wanted to be at peace. Glancing behind him, he saw the guys cautiously coming up the dock. He sighed.

"Yeah. Here they are now. Thank you– for your consideration."

The old man chortled. Each of the guys nodded or acknowledged him as he passed, but he didn't say a word to any of them. Supper was calling.

"Simon, what's up, man?"

"I'm going out into the middle of the lake. Who's with me?"

"It's getting dark," Jack cautioned. Jim smacked him on the back of the head, reminding him who Simon was. One by one, they awkwardly stepped out onto the boat. Jude was the last to straggle up the dock. Simon was already pulling out and moving when he fully decided to join and leaped onto the craft. They were tired and followed Simon's lead by not speaking to each other the whole ride out. They simply smelled the water, felt the wind, and released the cares of the day. At least they tried. Simon anchored and found a spot to recline with his feet up on the edge of the boat. No one approached him. They all sensed the need for space and decompression. Dusk turned into night and night into near dawn. They had fallen asleep when the wind rose and caused waves to start buffeting the side of the boat. The rocking started waking them one by one. Jack vomited over the side. Shortly before dawn, a figure started coming toward the boat.

"What's that?" Levi asked. "Do you guys see that?" Rubbing his eyes, he was trying to make it out.

"Where?" Jack asked. Levi pointed. Jude rose and walked to their side.

"What the–"

Simon started to stand and stretch. He wasn't concerned about whatever it was they might be seeing. He had seen all there was to see out on the water and didn't rush to their concern. When all four of the guys were standing on the same side, causing the boat to lean, Simon finally joined.

"Hey," he commanded, "Spread out. What are you trying to do?" He searched for their focus, and there, coming toward them, was a figure on a direct course to the vessel. It was tall and stood above the water. It was coming at a steady pace, but it was too small to be a boat and too tall to be any kind of jet ski. It wasn't leaving a wake, either. There was barely enough light to see anything clearly. The only sure thing was that it was definitely coming straight for them and getting more prominent with its approach. Levi started to freak.

"This was the dumbest idea! Who's flipping idea was it to come out into the middle of a lake! We don't know anything about this boat! Where's Manuel when you need him?! Do we have a weapon of any kind? Do we have a gun? Or a net?"

"A gun… or a net?" Jack laughed out loud.

"We are unprotected and vulnerable," Jude said. "This is kind of a stupid idea. Not to mention, I'm starving."

"Just relax," Jim cut in. "Wait. If I didn't know better– that looks like a person."

"No way."

"Oh, crud. It *does* look like a person."

"Get outta' here it can't be a person. Don't be– oh, shitake mushrooms! What the heck is that thing? It's a ghost. You guys! It's a ghost!"

"Simon, get us outta here!"

The vision was getting closer. The guys were scrambling and rebuking evil as they had seen Manuel do. Jack began to notice something all too familiar. This ghost was wearing a white t-shirt and blue jeans, just like Manuel always did. He stood among the chaos and squinted through his glasses. Hair: check. Stride: check. Mannerism: check. "It's Manuel," he whispered. The guys continued to scatter and insist Simon start the engine, to which he was ready to oblige. Louder, Jack said, "It's Manuel. It's Manuel!!" The guys froze and looked again for themselves.

"Don't be ridiculous!" Jude shamed, "It cannot possibly be…. Manuel?" Noticing that it did look an awful lot like Manuel, he concluded, "He must have died!"

"Oh, no! They got him!" Levi shrieked. The scene would be comical if the guys weren't so serious. Finally, they could see it was indeed Manuel. Simon was transfixed.

"What a bunch of wussies," Manuel called out. "Where's your courage? Don't be so afraid! It's me."

They knew it was Manuel's voice. But what was he riding? He was distinctly walking. How was that possible? For all the miracles they had witnessed, they had never seen anything like this. In all their adventures, everything had been incredible but tangible. He was defying the laws of gravity. Or was he? Was he walking on something? But it wasn't making waves. This was too far beyond what they could wrap their heads around.

As he got closer, Simon found himself practically hanging off the side of the boat, awaiting his arrival. "Kyrios!" he called. "If it really is you and not some apparition– let me–"

Before Simon could finish his sentence, Manuel was instructing him, "Come on." Simon looked down at the water. He looked back at Manuel. Manuel took two fingers and motioned them from his eyes to Simon's then, extended his hand and waved his fingers to come. He grinned, so pleased that Simon was fearless in his belief. Simon sat on the edge of the boat and flipped his legs around. His feet dangled in the water. He cocked his head and fought every ounce of knowledge he'd had about water since day one of his years on the water. He took a deep sigh. The guys were staring with eyes wide open and jaws dangling. Jack wanted to grab his phone and start recording, but he also didn't want to take his eyes off of Simon. He fumbled around his pockets, searching for his phone. He got it out in time to see Simon stand up. He stood up! He was standing! ON THE WATER. Jack panned from his feet to his head, then from his feet to Manuel with hand extended like a father waiting for a baby to take its first steps. Manuel nodded as if to say, 'Good job. You've got this.' Simon didn't even wave his arms as though trying to balance. He was solid and standing as if on a rock. He kept his eyes on Manuel and took a step forward. Manuel stood several feet out and waited patiently. Simon stepped. Then, he stepped again. He let out a breath and felt as if he hadn't breathed in several minutes. He took another deep breath and stepped forward. Another breath. Another step. Another breath. Another step. It was wet and cold but felt soft and stable under his feet. He kept his eyes on Manuel. Suddenly, a gust of wind came up and felt like it would blow him over. He considered blowing over and what would happen if he fell. Would he land solid or splash into the lake? As he thought these things, he became afraid and felt the solidity beneath his feet, starting to give way. He gasped, and before he knew it, he was dropping into the water. "Kyrios!" he screamed and slipped under the water. He pushed himself above the surface and cried out, "Save me!"

Immediately, Manuel reached out and caught him up. Wrapping Simon's forearm around his own, he placed his second hand on top of Simon's and asked, "What happened to your belief? Why did you start doubting?" When he spoke, it was as though there was no other sound. The wind, still blowing, made no sound. The waves, yet crashing, made no noise. Simon felt the steadfast firmness under his feet once more. Together they walked toward the boat. Once they reached it, Manuel let Simon climb in first. The guys helped him. Manuel then hopped over the edge and greeted them. "Hey, guys."

"What the–"

"How did you–"

Simon turned to him and simply said, "Thanks."

"Anytime."

Jack rushed to Manuel and threw his arms around him. His leader, redeemer, and cousin. "We thought maybe they…" Manuel wrapped his arm around his cousin's shoulders.

"Oh, little Jacky." He ruffled his hair. "Not yet." Looking back out toward the water, he sighed and repeated softly, "Not yet."

"Dude," Jack quipped, "You really freaked us out." Manuel started laughing.

"You should have seen your faces. A ghost? Really?"

"Well, what would you have thought?! Oh, wait– you know everything, you would have just remained perfectly calm, right? Some figure in the breaking light coming at you with no explanation."

Levi was grabbing towels and tossing them to Manuel and Simon. Strangely, Simon did not feel cold or bothered by the wet. The towel simply hit him and fell to the deck. He looked at Manuel, who smiled at him with his eyes. The guys were all talking, but Simon couldn't stop looking at Manuel. He didn't need to say anything. Manuel knew everything he was thinking and feeling. He could tell just by looking at him that Manuel was reading him. He wondered if he talked to him in his mind if Manuel would reply– but one earth-shattering event was enough for now. He felt so connected to him. He was overwhelmed with love for him. This man had become closer than any brother could ever be. Drew. Simon was flooded with missing Drew. How he wished he had been there to see it. Not just this, but *everything*. How could he have been so selfish to leave him behind in charge of everything? He had to make a call. Drew had to come on the road. The business could take care of itself. Drew could appoint somebody. Anybody. All at once, nothing mattered except this man. This mission. This reality. Not money, not personal gain. Just him and what he came to give the world. Simon knew that he would do anything, give anything, be anything that Manuel wanted or needed him to. Until the day he died. He felt guilty for having been so sick of it just several hours before.

As they returned to the shore, the guys were celebrating what happened and honoring Manuel. "You truly are the Son of Theos." Manuel chuckled that they were with him this long and still having revelation regarding that fact. As they reached the dock, the old man stood, pipe in mouth, tapping his foot and waiting.

"Well, now, you made me miss the best catch of the day," he said. He wasn't genuinely agitated but felt the cantankerous need to inform them. The sun was now fully up.

"Thank you for the use of your boat," Manuel greeted him. You have a full tank of gas and our gratitude.

"Full tank of gas?" he questioned, "Hey, I didn't see you with the group when they boarded." Manuel put his hand on the man's shoulder and looked him in the eye. The old man dropped his pipe from his mouth and lowered his jaw. "Oh," he remarked, "Kyrios." No word had been spoken, but Manuel revealed himself to the man in a manner which he would receive. The guys had long since stopped wondering *how*. How was for fools. How was for people who questioned. *How* was none of their business. Their business was to walk with assurance and not by what they could see.

CHAPTER 32:

SPIRITUAL DISNEYLAND

The guys were feeling closer than ever; their group had become the closest troupe of brothers. With the Commemoration of Trials celebration just a couple of days away, the city was overtaken by visitors. They knew it would be harder to maneuver, so they relished the times when it was just the nine of them. Philip and Nathan were always with them except when they slept. Simon had called his brother Drew to come to Government City and join them. Drew was on the next plane out and caught up to them. No one knew where he would sleep, but they had become extremely flexible on their journey.

Manuel still had so much to tell them and knew that the crowds would press in if they stopped. "Let's take a drive," he instructed. "We're not going anywhere… let's just go to the outskirts of town and drive."

"Aye, aye, Captain."

Philip and Nathan parked their car to join the men in the R.V. for the drive. Drew was excited to be with the group. Jim made their way out of town. As they drove, Manuel just started talking. He talked and talked, telling them all sorts of stories, each building on the point of the one before. He foretold of the destruction of all the systems they had come to know. Manuel informed them that not only would he be removed from them by force but that even when they thought it impossible, he would return to them. They wanted to know when these things would happen and what signs they could watch for to learn.

"Just watch out that no one deceives you," he warned. "Many will show up claiming to be the returned Redeemer. Some people will believe them. There will be talk of wars and actual war. Ethnicities will rise against different ethnicities and territories against territories. It's bound to happen. But that won't be quite the end."

"The end?" Of what? Of dissension? Of peace? Of– the world?

"There will be droughts, severe famine, earthquakes, and natural disasters. All of this is just like– a birth pain. Just the beginning that shows the true event is coming."

"The true event? This is getting creepy."

"It is creepy. It's been creepy. That's why Theos has chosen to make a way to cease all wickedness and grant a way of redemption."

"What is the way?!"

"I am the way." The guys became silent. They hated it when they couldn't understand what he meant precisely. Why didn't he just tell them straight out? "I will be handed over to the authorities as a resolution for all the destruction that has happened on the earth. Then later, you will be handed over to be harassed and tortured as well." The guys looked around at each other. "Did I fail to mention that when I invited you to come?" No one was laughing at his joke. "Look, people and authorities are going to hate you because of me. Many will turn away from everything we've brought them and hate each other. Shady astrologers, clairvoyants, and witches will appear deceiving people. Love will all but grow cold, and everyone will only listen to their own voice of reason. Salvation will come to those who are found standing firm in the message we bring. The whole world is learning this message even now but by then…"

The guys were confused. It sounded like there was a lot of gloom and doom in store for them, but– had he answered their question about when it would happen? Manuel knew what they were thinking and continued, "No one knows exactly when all of this will happen. I don't even know. Only Theos determines how long He will give people to come away from the darkness they've chosen and trust in the Truth and the Light. So, be vigilant. I mean, it's like– if the owner of a house knew what time the thief was coming, he would have kept watch and not allowed misfortune to occur. Keep watch. Be on guard. You live in a world at war and cannot retreat. Arm yourselves[3]."

Even though they had barely reached the edge of town, the drive already felt very long. Nathan pulled out a smart device and decided to take some notes. Levi had become more assertive in the course of their travels and found himself determined to rise to the challenges before them. Jim kept his eyes on the road and pondered every political aspect of all that Manuel was saying. Jude sat in the back, counting the money and listening while he wondered what he could do to avoid any suffering but still make money off the whole thing. Drew was in a bit of shock and curious if the entire trip had been this heavy. Simon sat co-pilot and felt prepared for anything that came their way. He had no doubt he would continue to be Manuel's 'Rock' until the day he died. Jack sat quietly at Manuel's feet with soft tears in his eyes. He pushed his glasses aside and wiped them. He had known his cousin his entire life and wasn't ready for the thought of a world without him, even for a short while. Jack had never heard Manuel speak like this. How he wished his mother Sally was there. He wondered about Aunt Miryam and when the last time Manuel may have spoken to her. Did she know everything that was going on? Did she know that Manuel thought things were about to get ugly? Had she always known?

"Let me see how I can put it…" Manuel continued. "Let's say a man goes on a journey," they all knew that Manuel was the man. "He leaves everything in his possession to his servants and assistants. He trusted each of them with different amounts of wealth and tasks according to their ability. One guy got just a simple amount, one guy got about twice that, and one guy got the bulk of the money and responsibility. The guy who got the simple amount tucked it under his mattress and decided he would just keep it safe until his boss returned. The guy with twice that amount made a couple of investments, spread some of it around to do good, and doubled what he had. The guy who was trusted with the bulk of the estate put it all to work with creative investments, implemented new procedures, tightened the budget, and created abundant wealth for the owner in his absence. After a long time, the man returns and calls each of them to settle accounts. He commends the guy with a modest amount for doubling what he'd been given. He sees the abundance created by his faithful servant and commends him for all his effort on his behalf. He tells them both, 'Nice work! You've been trustworthy with these few things; now, I will put you in charge of many things!' They beamed with pride. In comes the first guy, with only the simple amount. He returns the exact amount he was given with pride saying, 'See? I didn't lose a penny. This is the exact amount you gave me, and I'm returning it in full.' The boss winced and replied, 'You wicked, lazy man. You could have at least deposited my money in the bank and gained a modest interest! Take all that was given to you and give it to the most productive man.'

"See, whoever has been trusted with more will have an abundance, but whoever does not put to work even the little amount they have will lose it."

"I've got a cousin like that," Drew offered.

"We all know someone like that," Jim answered.

"Even worse," Manuel continued, "That worthless, selfish, lazy servant will be thrown out into utter darkness where there will be ceaseless weeping and loss beyond comprehension. Just as I have told you of the Kingdom of the Higher Realm– there is a place of agony."

"But… the guy didn't lose any money. I mean, he kept it safe," Jude mentioned.

"He was lazy and useless," Manuel insisted. "When I come back in full majesty– because trust me, at that point, there will be no doubting that I am the prophesied King– I will be bringing every kind of supernatural messenger with me. Every nation and ethnicity will assemble before me. They will be separated not by class or color but into those who were diligent, true adherents and those who were lazy rationalists. They will be judged. That's determined. The King will say, 'Come, you who have been favored by Abba and take your inheritance! The Kingdom of the Higher Realm is prepared for you!' but those who have thrown all opportunity away will hear, 'Depart from me, you who are cursed. There has also been a realm prepared for those who have chosen as you have. It was your prerogative. Here is the consequence of that choice."'

"Seems kind of harsh," Jude uttered.

"It does," Manuel agreed. "And completely unnecessary. So, let's solicit them to all be diligent and upright in their pursuits."

~~~

Manuel spent the next couple of days teaching. Each morning he would go out to Olive Ascent, a local clearing where an olive grove used to stand, east of the original Government City. It allowed crowds of people to gather easily and escape the hustle and bustle that downtown had become. They would come early in the morning and listen until dusk, when Manuel would call it a day.

The Commemoration of Trials was upon them, and everyone who was anyone made the trek to the city. Draco and his team were there planning a major stage event with celebrities and healers alike. Oersted Hahn was there making the rounds and acting as an unofficial representative for the authoritarians. The religious conservatives had their tents set up for street salvations spewing their obsessions with the Law and every rule required to achieve the hope of reaching the Higher Realm. The educators of the Law and elders of the local churches were out in droves with pamphlets, strong words of condemnation, and bullhorns. "Turn or Burn!"

The authoritarians were present with tents of their own, selling how Big Brother was out for man's best common interest and encouraging complete subordination to the state's power. 'There could be no other way to true peace and security.' The totalitarians had booths directly across, promoting the differing opinion of centralized government without tolerance of parties saying otherwise. Different churches had booths set up to invite the event goer with games, giveaways, and free food to entice a hearty attendance.

Speaker of the Church Sabeen Smith was on hand as the governor of all religious activity. She and her people were mediators between the groups. They held a firm hand in alignment with Government City's protocol office to maintain the peace at all costs. Military Superintendent Pontius was there as well but preferred to stay as secluded as possible. He was weary of the day-to-day management of constant conflict between communities and would be called upon for only the most significant events during the festival. Governor Gale Tetrarch rented the penthouse in the local luxury hotel. He hoped to catch a glimpse of Manuel at some point. Tetrarch brought his
~~~

entourage, wife Gailina, and daughter Alina to indulge in all the days had to offer.

Sabeen Smith was called upon to preside over the opening ceremony, and each organization had a time slot to share from the stage all they thought, believed, and were advocating. The atmosphere was like a carnival, complete with tours that would walk the public through the footsteps of the land's original settlers. They would follow the trials they had overcome to build the city and learn traditional beliefs. Theos was deemed The Creator, the Author of the Universe, The Ultimate Judge by different parties, all of which was true. But Manuel brought him as Abba, Father, and One Who desired true intimacy with His creation. The lights were bright, and the characters were even brighter.

Manuel knew that his hour was close at hand and no longer walked openly among the crowds. He knew that even then, leaders and officials gathered intending to find him guilty of some crime that would allow them to seize him and silence him from leading any more people away from their religious establishments. They expressed to each other their concern that the whole world had followed after this contractor from Netzer. The council, headed by Sabeen, did, in fact, gather immediately after the opening ceremony.

"What are we going to do? This guy has not stopped his traveling roadshow teaching counter-cultural vomit and his so-called healings. If we let him go on like this, everyone will believe in him. His crowds are insane! The Chief Governors will remove our authority and our place in the empire. We can't have that. We cannot allow one man to eliminate our power and influence single-handedly."

"Agreed. We need drastic measures. We're afraid that the people will turn on us! Surely by now, Sabeen has some plan that the majority of us have not heard. What is it?"

Sabeen lowered her eyes from the mad pack in front of her. She knew the plan, and she knew who else had taken steps to initiate it. They just needed one of Manuel's own. They needed an insider to get the information they couldn't quite get their hands on. Somehow, he always seemed to slip out of their grasp when they tried to establish any wrongdoing.

"A plan is in place," she assured them. "We have been devising an angle for quite some time and are in high hope that during these festival days, we will be able to execute it at last. Don't be overzealous and ruin what we few have determined. He will be found guilty, and we will eliminate him. We will not allow our whole establishment to perish."

The assembly agreed and applauded that there was an end in sight. Teivel stood in the midst of them, rousing the crowd to incite justice. He breathed in their direction and released venom to enter them. Men were planning to jump Manuel and beat him within an inch of his life. Others wondered where his family may be and if they might be brutalized as an incentive to cease his teachings. Where was he eating? Could they poison his food? Where were his guys? Couldn't one of them be turned? Repugnance grew with every suggestion, and Teivel loved it all. Finally, he slithered out to find the one he knew could be turned.

~~~

Jude sat with a beer and a corndog. He had been sent to get food for the group but decided to grant himself a breather before returning. Dangling his leg over a railing, he hung lazily, enjoying the crowds, especially a few young ladies. Teivel stepped up alongside him with a beer and corndog of his own. Wearing blue jeans and a black t-shirt, he swung his leg over the railing near Jude.

"This spot taken?" he gestured and took the spot without an answer. Jude winced and thought the man an inconvenience to his peace. "What a bunch of suckers," Teivel begrudged. "Coming down here to hear the same old crap from the same old hypocrites. It's exhausting." Jude stood upright and brought his leg back over the rail. He turned from the crowd and faced the opposite direction to finish his beer without interruption. Teivel mimicked him.

"It seems to me a good man, just wanting to earn a simple dollar, has to jump through too many hoops in this life just to get what's coming to him. Am I right? I mean, look at all these losers. Seeking some sort of spiritual Disneyland to give them all the answers they seek for life's mysteries. One guy heals their leg and another their ear, and they think there must be some higher power behind it all. Whatever."

Jude no longer resisted. "You don't believe in a Creator?"

"Why? Because the mountains are so majestic? I'm not saying there might not be some sort of higher power. But what has He ever done for me? What has he ever done for you?"

"Well, what about this new guy? This Manuel Paladin?"

"What about him?"

"Don't you think he has come with a different message than the rest? Don't you think he's genuine?"

"Don't tell me you've been suckered in, too. You think this guy is different from any other false prophet that's come over the thousands of years? And why now? Why would he show up now instead of years and years ago when we really needed someone like that?"

"Well, the Ancient Writings–"

"Ancient Writings? You're gonna listen to a bunch of dead white guys?"

"They weren't white; they were–"

"I don't care what they were. It's all a bunch of hooey. Hey, you want another beer?" Teivel handed Jude a fresh cold beer as if he had just come back from a booth. Jude found himself reaching for it. "Truth be told, I
~~~

think this guy, this… Manuel, did you call him? I think he ought to be turned over to the authorities."

"What? Why?"

"Think about it. All the ruckus he's caused. I bet the establishment is seeing red! I bet they'd be willing to pay good money to get him off the streets." Teivel turned and breathed toward Jude. Suddenly, Jude understood what the man meant precisely. "Just think," he repeated, "Big money. Easy money. Money that could eliminate a lot of bull in this life." Jude shook his head in a daze and ultimately agreed. "I bet if you went and found those leaders of the establishment, they'd have plenty to say on the matter."

"I wouldn't even know where to–"

"There's a green door on the side of the brick building on Perfidy St. Right at the double-crossing."

Jude didn't remember walking. He didn't remember ending his conversation with the stranger or deciding to talk to the establishment. All he knew was that he was standing in front of the green door on Perfidy St. He could see that there was security around, but none bothered to stop him from approaching. He turned the latch, and it opened without resistance. As he entered, there was a dark hallway. He could hear voices coming from the other end, so he decided to head toward them. He walked past several open doors with people inside, but none stopped him or asked what it was he needed. As he reached the end, he paused to remember what it was he was doing there. The door opened, and inside he saw many directors of the church and educators of the Law. The disciplinarians looked at him. There was silence. Then one of them recognized him as one of the Redeemer Roadshow clan. He rushed an attendant to get Sabeen.

"Hello," someone greeted him.

"Hello," he responded.

"Can we help you?"

"Hello," Sabeen interrupted. "Mr.…"

"Jude. My name is Jude."

"Jude. Hello. Funny meeting you here."

"Is it? Yes. Yes, well, I heard– I mean, I thought you might be interested in some information I have."

"Go on."

"Well, I mean, are you seeking information?"

"Mr.– Jude. Are you seeking a proposition?"

"I suppose I am."

"And what is it that you're hoping to gain?"

Teivel's words rang in Jude's mind, 'Money that could eliminate a lot of bull in this life.' "I want to– I mean, I'd be willing to–"

"Jude." Sabeen snapped Jude out of his haze. "Are you here to trade details and the whereabouts of Manuel Paladin for money?"

"I could be. How much money are we talking about?"

CHAPTER 33:

WILL YOU MARRY ME?

The Commemoration of Trials was in full swing, and the city was buzzing. Traditionally there was a large meal in the evening, and Manuel remembered fondly the years he and his family would travel to the Watch Mountain Foothills where the steadfast steeple was always watching. He closed his eyes and remembered wrestling with his cousins and the smell of barbeque. He remembered Joseph and the love he always gave so freely. He missed his mother and siblings. He gave her a call to touch base. Manuel let her know the time was near and expressed his deepest love and pride in her.

The guys were eating breakfast and catching up from the previous day's events. Manuel was sharing memories with Jack and Jim from their youth and Watch Mountain. Jack was laughing and recalling grass stains and injuries, trying to keep up with the big boys.

"What are we going to do for the celebration dinner tonight?" Jack inquired.

"I'm glad you asked. I want you and Simon to head into the heart of the city. Take Haven Place past the station. You'll find a man wearing a blue backpack. Follow him to the house that he enters and ask for the owner. When you meet him, tell him, 'The teacher asks for permission to use your formal dining room to eat the Celebration Dinner with his friends.' He won't be surprised. The Spirit of the Creator's Essence has already spoken to him in a dream. He will take you to a large room. Ask Jude for some money to buy the goods and make preparations there."

Simon was hesitant, "Do you think it's wise for me to leave you?" Manuel chuckled at Simon's challenge of his wisdom.

"Yes, Rock. I do. But thank you." They went and found things just as Manuel had described.

When evening came, the guys headed over to the house for dinner. It took Simon and Jack all afternoon to prepare, and Jack was like a little kid filled with anticipation for what they had arranged. Manuel enjoyed every childlike expression of, 'Look at this!' and 'We did that.' Jack so longed to be pleasing to Manuel. Manuel held a special love for his younger cousin and regarded him as one of his most cherished relationships. "You've done very well, Jacky. Thank you." The guys settled in at the table.

Before they ate, Manuel stood and made his way to the restroom. He returned with an empty basin and a pitcher full of soapy water. He had a large towel draped over his shoulder and an apron over his arm. Setting them down, the guys wondered what he was up to now. "Kick off your shoes," he instructed. The guys looked at each other with curious brows; this was an odd request.

"Our shoes?" Levi questioned. Manuel just looked at him like he wasn't going to repeat himself. Some began untying laces. Some flicked off their flip-flops and pulled off boots. Levi was self-conscious of his feet and hesitated.

"Pee-yu!"

"Dang, Jude, for real?" Jim pestered.

"Shut up," Jude flipped.

"Someone open a window. This is worse than the R.V."

"That's enough," Manuel calmed. He tied the apron around his waist and started to wash their feet one by one. It was awkward and lowly. The room fell silent. Drew silently held back tears. It was such a humbling thing for the Son of Theos to do. As Manuel knelt before Simon, he held up his hand.

"No way. You will never wash my feet." He slid his shoes over as if to put them back on.

"Simon," Manuel sighed, "If you don't let me serve you, then you have nothing to do with me." Simon's eyes grew wide.

"Kyrios, if that is true, then why stop at my feet? Wash my hands. Pour the whole bowl over my head."

"You're not that dirty," he replied, chuckling. "Always with the drama. Anyone who has been washed in the Truth doesn't need to be cleansed again and again. But you have all walked a great distance with me, and I want to show you my gratitude. You are clean. Well, most of you are clean." The guys exchanged glances. Manuel completed each man's feet and then removed the towel and apron. He washed his hands and resumed his place at the table.

"Do you understand what I've just done for you? You guys call me Teacher and Kyrios, and you're right. That's Who I Am. So, if I can humble myself to kneel before each of you and wash your sweaty, smelly feet– you ought to be able to humble yourselves to serve in whatever lowly manner is required of you as well. It was an example, and I trust you've received it.

"Seriously, someone who serves is not greater than the one who hired him, and neither is a messenger greater than the one who sent him. Do you know what I mean?" The guys were following and very aware that Manuel wanted them to understand they would be called upon to do humiliating things. "If you understand that no task is beneath you, then you will find favor for doing them." Manuel went strangely silent. He was almost visibly emotional. Throwing his head back, he took a deep breath and said, "One of you will betray me."

The guys shot looks around the table at one another. What did he mean by *betray*? Surely, none of them would have gall enough to betray him. They examined each other's faces trying to determine who he meant. Drew was the newest, but he had known more than the others before even meeting Manuel. Levi had been the weakest, but he had really grown in the last years and was dedicated now. Jack would never. Simon would never. Not Jim. Jude was moody but was too clever ever to consider– Simon nodded at Jack, who was sitting right beside Manuel. 'Ask him who,' he mouthed. Jack leaned over and could barely get the words out. He felt if he gave them air, it would be an admission of their validity.

"Kyrios," he managed to whisper, "who would do that?"

Manuel turned and met his eyes with pain. Sighing again, he replied, "The one who I give naan and hummus to." Taking a piece of buttery naan and dipping it into the hummus, Manuel handed it over to Jude. Thinking he was acting as a servant again, Jude took the morsel and popped it in his mouth in one bite. As he did, Teivel appeared in the corner of the room. He was not visible to anyone but Manuel. They locked eyes. As Jude swallowed, Teivel entered into him. Manuel said to him, "Go do what you're going to do quickly. Don't drag it out." Because he was the money bearer, the few that heard Manuel thought that Jude was being sent on some task. Jude left as the sun was setting, and darkness fell quickly.

Manuel turned to the remaining guys and said, "Now is the time. The Son of Man is going to be magnified, and Theos will be magnified in Him."

It was always so intense when Manuel spoke in the third person. They knew he was the Son of Man who lived as a man for these 33 years. They also knew that he had come to educate the world about Theos, not as some punishing Higher Power but as Abba, Daddy, wanting a genuine relationship with His beloved creation. Not as an earthly father who fails, but as a supreme being who knows everything and can orchestrate everything for their best.

"Let me tell you guys a story." They were all well used to Manuel's stories and knew to pay attention to the deeper meaning. As he began, he poured a large glass of wine in front of himself. "Back in the day, when a Jewish man was going to propose to a woman, he would buy the opportunity to sit with her and her family so he could propose. He would offer her a glass of wine, explaining that this was his offering, his covenant of marriage, and she would either accept him and drink or deny him and refuse the offering. If she accepted, she would drink and then return to her town. Instead of being called by her birth name, they would now refer to her as 'one who had been bought with a price.' The groom would return home and prepare a place for her to come and reside with him. The bride and groom endured a period of time where they didn't speak firsthand. The best man might run messages to her now and then. The groom would work on the prepared place in love until one day his father would come with inspection and say, 'It is finished. Go, and get your bride.' At this, the groom and his best men would ride into town to get his promised bride, blowing their horns. She would not know the day or hour he might come, so she always lived in readiness for the day he would return for her."

At this point, Manuel broke off a large chunk of bread. Holding both the wine and bread, he looked to each of his men and said, "Likewise, I'm saying to you guys, 'This is my offering, my covenant, my body, and what will be my spilled blood poured out for the redemption of many. I ask you to take it and always be in covenant with me."

Drew was fully wiping away tears now. Jim and Jack would go down any path with him no matter how crazy. Simon was the first to reach for the cup. As they each drank the wine and ate the bread, Manuel continued.

"I won't drink this again until you are all with me in Abba's Kingdom, and we celebrate." He paused. "Guys, I won't be with you much longer. Where I'm going, you can't come with me. *I'm* going to prepare a place for *you*. Make sure that you always love each other well, just as I have loved you well. That way, everyone will always know that you are my witnesses."

Simon was disturbed. "Kyrios, where are you going?"

"I just said, somewhere you can't come. But you will… later. When it's time."

"But why can't I follow you now? You know I would. You know I would die for you."

Manuel looked Simon in the eye. "Really? Will you truly be willing to die for me?"

"Yes, you know I will."

"Simon," he leaned in and whispered, "Before the sun rises, you will deny that you even know who I am. Not once but three times."

"That's crazy. Never."

Manuel held up three fingers, then softened them into a loose fist and brought it to his chest.

Some of the others began asking questions. They wondered how they could get to where he was going and when they could join him. None were willing that this journey should end. Manuel further explained, "I am the Way. You'll know when it's time which way to go. There is no way to Abba and the Higher Realm except through me. If you truly know me, then you also know Abba and won't have any issue with direction."

"Will you show us Abba? That will be enough for any of us," Philip asked.

"Philip, have I been with you all this time, and you still don't know me? If you've seen me, then you *have* seen Abba. Don't you believe that I am in Him and He is in me? We are one and the same. I haven't done anything by my own authority but by His intention and empowerment. In fact, whoever believes in me will also be able to do all the works that I have done. Even greater works." Their eyes grew wide again. Who could possibly do greater miracles and works than Manuel had done these last three years?

"If you love me, you will do all of the things I have taught you. Then, I will ask Abba, and He will send you the Essence of His Presence permanently. He will dwell in you and live in you as a counselor, a comforter, strength, and a guide. You will never be without us. Ever. Do you understand?" They did. And they didn't. "He will teach you everything you need to know and help you remember everything I have said in these last years. I'm leaving you with peace. Not peace like the world knows it, but true peace. No matter what happens– don't be afraid. I said I'm leaving. If you love me, you'll be happy for me because I am going to be with Abba. I've told you beforehand, so when everything goes down, you'll believe and understand. Don't freak out– because the twisted ruler of this world is coming for me. He doesn't have any claim on me, but I will go with him because Abba has allowed it so that the world can learn how much He loves them."

"But how?" Jack asked. "How does losing you cause humanity to be redeemed? How does that make sense?"

"Theos created the first Son of Man from the earth. He placed him in a place of perfection and gave him everything he would ever need for life. He gave him the companionship of a helpmate, and life was good. But Teivel came, still angry and obsessed with his dismissal from the Higher Realm, determined to deceive the first Son of Man and cause death to come into their world."

"How did he do that?"

"With the offer of being all-knowing and having the same power as Theos. Technically, with food, believe it or not. He's still using food as a stumbling block, but that's another story. The point is, the first Son was created in the flesh and allowed corruption in, so only the second Son of Man– created in the Spirit– can restore it to its original intent."

"It?"

"Relationship with Theos."

"Wait," Philip reasoned, "This sounds like the Ancient Writing story about Abe and his two sons. Ishmael and Isaac. Ishmael was the son of the flesh, and Isaac was the miracle son by the Spirit."

"Yes, Philip. Yes, that's exactly right. Well done."

"But Isaac was delivered! Theos provided a ram in the thicket so he wouldn't have to– my God."

"I am the perfect ram, Philip. Missing the mark leads to death. It is the natural consequence of misconduct. But Theos, in His perfect love and mercy, has delivered a ransom; a substitute. He sent me as a payment for that misconduct to be reunited to His beloved creation and grant them immortal life. There must be a payment, either by the individual or by a rescue. Only through payment can humankind be acceptable to enter into the perfect presence of Theos."

The night turned into late-night, and the guys were crashing out around the table, so they headed back to the R.V. Instead of going in, Manuel took Simon, Jim, and Jack aside. "Come with me." He led them to a grove of trees behind Olive Ascent. "This is where they used to press the olives." He seemed seriously distressed and troubled.

"Are you okay?" Jack asked.

"My soul. My soul is full of agony, man. It's like I'm starting to feel the weight of everything anyone has ever done wrong. It's... heavy. Look, I need you guys to stay with me. Just stay here and appeal to Abba for help."

"Help for what?" Jack asked. Manuel cupped the side of Jack's head in his hand.

"Just pray."

Walking further, he found a spot to be alone. Falling on his knees, he became afraid of all he was about to face. Shaking, he prayed, "Abba... Oh, *Papa*. I know that You are able to do anything that You want. If there is any way–" Hearing a crackle, Manuel turned to look behind him, searching for any possible predator. "If there is any way for the redemption of the world to be accomplished without me having to–" he didn't speak the words out loud. "Will you allow it to be done another way?" There was silence, and Manuel knew the answer in his heart. "Still, it's not what I want but what You want. I'll do whatever needs to be done. Abba?"

Feeling anxious and apprehensive, Manuel walked back to where he had left the three. Huddled together, he found them sleeping. Kicking Simon's foot, he woke them up. "Are you seriously sleeping right now? Simon. Dude. Couldn't you wait for even an hour?" Simon smacked the other two and acted ashamed.

"Guys, what the heck? Come on."

"I need you guys to be on the lookout. Watch and pray so that temptation doesn't overwhelm you! I know your spirit is willing, but your flesh is dropping the ball. Fight it."

Again, he left them to go to the spot where he had been alone. He asked Abba the same thing and got the same response. He returned to the guys to find them sleeping a second time. He felt like crying but knelt right next to Simon's ear.

"Rock."

Simon jumped up with fists in the air. The guys were so tired and their eyes so heavy. They had no excuse or way to answer him.

"Sit up."

He left them a third time and asked Abba one final time for there to be some other way to redeem the world except by his ultimate sacrifice. Again, no answer came. Manuel knew this wasn't the dealing of an unloving father but the most profound love a father could show. That He would be willing to allow His own beloved Son to come into the world, teach them, raise them, love them, and then suffer the sacrifice of his own life that they may know the Way to His Presence and life immortal. Instead of offering money, good deeds, or trusting that they were 'good people,' He would ensure that they would have a genuine way to be redeemed. By the blood and body of the covenant, He came to offer. If they would only believe in their hearts and confess with their mouths that He was the Son of Theos– they would be saved.

Manuel returned to the guys a third time to find them sleeping. Dropping to his knees, he simply stared at them. Simon felt his gaze and awoke. Jumping up, he tried to shake off the sleep.

"How was your little nap?" He asked. "Did you get a good rest?" Simon started kicking the feet of Jim and Jack.

"Get up, you losers." Manuel looked at him with the inner corners of his mouth drawn up, a hard blink, and head shake.

"Enough," He said. "It's time. My betrayer is coming." He swallowed hard.

CHAPTER 34:

APPREHENSIONS

The sky was pitch black. The trees covered any light from the stars or moon. The rustle of many feet sounded like a machine moving in the darkness.

"What is that?" Jack asked.

Manuel knew what it was, and as the sound got closer and closer, it became evident to the others.

"Let's get out of here," Simon said forcefully and grabbed Manuel's arm to leave. Manuel did not move but simply shook his head in slow denial. "This doesn't look good. Let me get you out of here." Manuel pulled back and regained his arm. They could see flashlights searching the ground and whispered commands. Finally, out of the darkness came the pack of Elders, Educators of the Law, Disciplinarians, deputies, henchmen, and attendants of high-ranking officers like Sabeen Smith, who couldn't be seen in the mob. They were holding various weapons and chains. Jude walked out in front of them all. Having known Olive Ascent and being led by Teivel, he directed the mob toward Manuel. Upon making out the four figures in the darkness, he greeted them.

"There you guys are. What the heck are you doing out here?" he asked casually. Manuel didn't respond but waited for the confirmation of his person. Jude hesitated.

"Go ahead. Do what you came to do, friend."

Walking up to him, Jude hugged him and kissed his cheek. Simon, Jack, and Jim were confused by such a show of affection. Manuel was not.

"Jude. You betray me with the greatest expression of endearment?" Jude didn't speak a word but stepped to the side. "Who are you looking for?" Manuel asked the men.

"Manuel Paladin."

"I am he." As the words left his lips, the mob fell back upon themselves by an unseen force. They scrambled to regain their position, and while they did, Manuel waited patiently. Again, he asked them. "Who did you say you were looking for?" The men were hesitant to respond in fear that they would be blown over again like rag dolls.

"Manuel Paladin."

"I already told you. You've found him. Why are you coming at me with chains and clubs like I'm some crook? I was available to you every day for any kind of confrontation. Now you come to capture me in the cover of night? Am I leading some sort of rebellion?"

"Shady," Jim muttered. Simon took out the blade on his Leatherman and lunged toward the crowd. He sliced off the ear of Sabeen's attendant standing nearest him. The group drew their arms.

"Stop! Stop!" Manuel intervened. "Enough!" Reaching down to the bleeding and moaning attendant, he put his hand over the missing ear. The man stopped moaning and looked at Manuel with widened eyes. The ringing had stopped, the pain was gone, and his ear was replaced. The man looked at his blood-covered hands. He felt his ear and realized it was made whole. He scrambled away in fear, not wanting to be any further part of the apprehension of this man. Manuel turned to Simon, "Rock. Put that thing away. I am going to fulfill every step Abba has ordered for me. If you live by violence, you *will* die by violence. Do you think I couldn't call on Abba and have six thousand supernatural warriors here to defend me? I *will* walk this out. I *will* see the redemption I've come for."

Turning to the mob, Manuel encouraged them to let his friends go. As they pressed in, they bound his hands and smacked him to the ground. The three guys scattered and ran for their lives. Jim raced back to the R.V. to inform the others, but Simon hid at a safe distance. He wanted to dial 9-1-1 but saw that in the mob were deputies and policemen. This betrayal was well coordinated. They led Manuel to the Speaker of the Church's Mansion, where he was presented before the Chief Priests and Speaker herself, Sabeen Smith.

Simon managed to get inside the gate and watch from a courtyard that was full of angry people. From where had they all come? How did they know this was going on? It wasn't even dawn! How long had they been plotting this? Where were the crowds who had loved them all and reached for an ounce of attention from Manuel? Jack found his way into the courtyard and was recognized by Sabeen's people, so they let him in to hear all that was happening. He went to the door and motioned for Simon to come in also. One of Sabeen's people said to Simon, "Oh. You're one of them." Simon gave her a scouring look. He had no idea what they were in for, so he said, "One of who? No, I'm not." Jack didn't hear and continued to move into a position that would allow them to see what was going on with Manuel.

Manuel stood in front of a crowd of elite council members with Sabeen at the center of them. They questioned him about everything; his teaching, the miracles, who people said he was and who he claimed to be.

"You know everything I've said," he answered. "I've never hidden anything. All of my teaching and works were done in the open. Why are you asking me? Ask those who have listened to me what was said. Anyone could tell you." At this, one of the guards came and struck Manuel alongside his head. He felt a throbbing, and his head spun. He thought he might fall but caught himself.

"Is that how you talk to authority?"

"What did I say? If what I said isn't true, then hit me for that, but if what I said *is* true, then why are you striking me?"

Simon wanted to rush out and grab the man, but he knew they far outnumbered him. A man near him saw his struggle and said, "You're one of his guys– the road trip guys. Aren't you?" Simon knew it wouldn't do him any good to admit it in this mob. What benefit could there possibly be? He had to remain nearby for Manuel.

"No," he answered and gave the man a dirty look. Jack looked at him without expression. Simon returned his focus to Manuel's inquisitors. But one of the gang members who had seen Simon cut off the ear of Sabeen's attendant heard the whole thing.

"Didn't I just see you in the grove with him? You're pretty handy with a knife."

Simon wanted to lunge at the man. "You don't know what you're talking about! I have no idea who that guy is." Just then, the first rays of light came from the morning sun. Simon saw them and remembered Manuel's words just hours earlier.

'*Before the sun rises, you will deny that you even know who I am. Not once but three times.*' He could see Manuel's tender eyes in his mind. He felt a punch in his gut and turned to look at him now. Standing like a criminal in front of all the local powers, Manuel noticed the sunlight and turned to find Simon in the crowd. Simon saw this and knew it was him Manuel was seeking. He slumped down behind the man beside him to hide from Manuel's eyes. Eyes that just hours earlier looked at him with such love and compassion. He couldn't bear to think of them seeing him now. What shame might they hold should they find him?

The council asked Manuel, "If you really are the long-awaited Redeemer, show us. Prove it."

"You won't believe me no matter what I say. But before this whole thing is said and done, I will be seated at the right hand of the Mighty Creator."

"So, you are saying you *are* the Son of Theos?"

"You've said that I am."

"That's it. Why go any further? This guy is full of himself and wickedness! He has insulted us in every way possible and now must be convicted!"

Although this crowd hated him and had plotted against him, they knew that the real power to destroy him lay in the hands of the Governmental Leaders. After harassing him for hours without gaining a single thing they could condemn him for, they determined to take him to Military Superintendent Dirk Pontius. In his ruthlessness, surely, he would find something that would throw the book at Manuel.

Pontius was no common Military Superintendent but was highly regarded for his rank both in family and profession. Because he had married into money and position, he was supported on all sides and could get away with murder should he choose. Pontius was the absolute highest authority in the region. Hand-selected by the Chief Governors to maintain peace in the area, he was constantly managing conflict between the communities. Known for being unbending and recklessly hard, Pontius had no issue being brutal when the situation called for it. The religious leaders were counting on him to solve their problem. But what they hadn't considered was the fact that Pontius had gotten himself into a bit of trouble with his own leaders. The Military Superintendent had ordered several lavish projects that had run out of money. He robbed religious sources for the money, and the religious sect sent brutal messages to the Chief Governors regarding him. He was instructed to keep the peace at all costs. Any threat or need for the Chief Governors to intervene meant severe punishment and removal for Pontius himself, so he wasn't thrilled when this mob came to him for resolution.

The offended leaders had Manuel led to the Military Superintendent's headquarters. The mob remained outside. Their religious practices dictated that the secular domain would defile them should they enter for justice. M.S. Pontius went out to them and asked the crowd, "What are the accusations against this man?" Having received a brutal beating on the car ride over, Manuel looked like a full-fledged criminal and victim. Pontius had no regard for his favor or condemnation. "Take him back to wherever you came from and judge him by your religious laws. Don't involve the Government."

"He's been traveling for three years, misleading the people by practicing witchcraft and evil. He opposes payment of taxes, incites rebellion, and claims to be a king! We wouldn't have brought him to you if he weren't a threat to all of society! He deserves the most severe punishment, but it is not lawful for us to put anyone to death."

"Death?" Pontius questioned. Manuel winced. He knew this was his fate but hearing the words from those he loved so profoundly cut deep. His physical cuts were burning, and his emotional ones were stinging. Pontius motioned to his men to bring Manuel inside. Standing almost alone, he came close to Manuel. He sniffed him. "You reek of sweat and blood." Manuel didn't respond but wiped the sweat from his brow with his still bound hands. "You can't be completely innocent, or they wouldn't have brought you here like this. Bound like a dog." Manuel stood silent. "Do you hear me talking to you, boy?" The few others in the room shifted, feeling that this might be a lengthy interrogation, but M.S. Pontius was not in the mood. He was hungry. It was lunchtime, and he didn't feel like giving this his whole afternoon.

"I've heard of you, you know. I've heard you called The Redeemer of the World, The Long-Awaited King, Kyrios– Are you the King of these people? These people who would see you condemned? Are these your loyal subjects?"

"It is as you have said. But my Kingdom is not of this realm."

"Do you hear them bringing all these accusations against you? What happened to the love?" Manuel did not reply. He didn't defend himself against even a single charge. Pontius was amazed. Normally by now, the accused would be begging in one form or another, especially when the word *death* had been used. Just then, a messenger brought a note in from his wife, Aislyn.

> "D–
>
> Whatever you do, don't have anything to do with this man's demise! He is innocent. I had one of my dreams, and I know this absolutely. You've seen the result of my dreams before. You know what I'm saying. I've been suffering since the minute they brought him into the house. Please. Don't do this. Wash your hands of it.
>
> –A"

At this, the Military Superintendent decided to send Manuel to another source. He wanted nothing to do with being caught in the Chief Governors' crossfire with the religious sect.

"Where are you from?"

"Netzer."

"Netzer? Well, then– this is out of my jurisdiction. You need to be sent to Governor Gale Tetrarch. He just happens to be in town. Lucky you."

Hearing the name reminded Manuel of his beloved cousin, Johnny, savagely beheaded by Tetrarch and his wicked wife. He longed for Pontius to get it over with, but the journey would last a while longer. It was announced that they would send Manuel to the Governor for a meeting with him. The crowd waited in anticipation outside M.S. Pontius's compound for the word of his sentence and demise. But the Directors of the Church, Elders, Educators of the Law, and Disciplinarians raced to the Governor's luxury suite to watch the trial in all its sickness.

Governor Tetrarch sat amidst a large group of yes-men. His wife lounged on a couch as if she was Cleopatra herself. She was barking at servants and watching for entertainment with her daughter Alina sitting obediently at her feet. Tetrarch was thrilled. He had wanted to see Manuel in person for quite some time. He wanted Manuel to perform a sign of some kind like a trained circus animal. The Directors and Elders started vehemently accusing him. Those guarding him ridiculed and mocked him.

"What's the matter, tough guy? Not so tough now? Cat got your tongue?"

Manuel would not speak or answer one word any of them threw at him.

"Oh, come on!" Tetrarch complained, "How disappointing! I've waited and waited, and this is all we get? Some roadshow you are." The people laughed. Secretly, Gale was saddened. He carried remorse over Johnny's death and hoped that this so-called Redeemer would not only acknowledge those days but forgive him somehow. He wanted to be alone with Manuel and confess it wasn't his fault but his wife and her spoiled accomplice. He wanted the private audience, but ever the flunkee of peer pressure, he played the part and succumbed to pleasing the crowd.

Governor Tetrarch ordered his men to place an elegant robe on Manuel. "Fit for a King," he announced. They teased him and taunted him with insults. When his toy simply wouldn't play, Tetrarch sent him back to Military Superintendent Pontius.

"Oh, send him away," he complained. "What a shame. That's an hour I can never get back. Still, I'm glad to have seen for myself that he is a fake and a waste of air. How ridiculous those who believed in him must be."

The Governor sent the Superintendent a note of thanks for including him in the fun and games. Before that day, they had been enemies for power, but Tetrarch considered this gesture to be one of camaraderie.

The twisted caravan yet again returned to M.S. Pontius's compound. Aislyn was sick to her stomach and pleading with her husband to find a civil way of exiting the situation. Pontius called together all the Directors, Elders, Educators, and Disciplinarians.

"Look, you brought me this man saying he was inciting the people to rebellion. I don't see that. Governor Tetrarch doesn't see it. He has been thoroughly examined, questioned, and harassed. Let that be good enough. There is no basis for your charges against him. You might disagree with whatever he's doing, but he certainly doesn't deserve death. There has been no heinous crime committed. If anything, he seems to have been helping people, so I'm not sure why you are all so set on disrupting his travels. Unless, of course, it has strictly to do with the fact that his power is increasing, and as a result, yours is diminishing. *By Jove, I think he's got it.*"

"No, no! He's guilty! He causes dissension and claims to be the Son of Theos! He's a madman. He's creating a cult that could send countless ignoramuses to their death. We can't have that. It is our responsibility to look out for them and pull them back from the ledge!"

"But haven't you all been waiting for a Redeemer? Don't your Ancient Writings foretell of One who will come and restructure both Spiritual and Governmental life? One who will justify many?"

"Why, Military Superintendent, you do amaze."

"So, why can't this maybe be the guy?"

"It is not *the guy*."

"Why not?"

"It is not."

"But… why not?"

"Sir– we assure you. This is not the prophesied Redeemer of the World."

M.S. Pontius sighed and accepted that they would not relent. Aislyn's words rang in his heart and head.

> *'Whatever you do, don't have anything to do with this man's demise! He is innocent. Wash your hands of it.'*

The group returned to the awaiting crowd in the courtyard. Pontius ordered Manuel brought out with his face now swollen and elegant robe. He had one last shot at avoiding being accountable for Manuel's sentencing. Tradition held that each year in honor of the Commemoration of Trials Festivities, an inmate be pardoned from his sufferings. The deliverance of his trials was a symbolic reenactment of the original settlers' delivery. The Military Superintendent addressed the crowd.

"In honor of the annual release of an inmate for the Commemoration of Trials Festivities, I hereby declare this man, Manuel Paladin, to be released with all of his charges dropped." Aislyn breathed a sigh of relief.

"Noooooo!" The crowd screamed. "Let us choose! We get to choose!" The religious leaders stirred up the crowd.

"There is no choice. Let this be done."

"No! Tradition states we choose! We choose– Stacey Dreggs!"

"Yes! Release the baby killer!"

"We choose Dreggs! You cannot deny us!"

"Dreggs! Dreggs! Dreggs!" The crowd was chanting and stomping. The rumble shook the pillars of the compound. Pontius looked to see his wife fervently shaking her head, 'No.'

"All right! All right!" Pontius walked over to Manuel. He wanted to put his hand on his shoulder but couldn't be seen as compassionate. In all his brutal years, he had never condemned a man that didn't deserve it. Still, with the Chief Governors breathing down his neck to keep the peace– it was this guy or him. "Are you truly a king?" he asked quietly.

"You call me a king. I'm saying that this is the very reason I came into the world– to bring the Truth. Everyone who is of the Truth listens to my voice."

Pontius felt chills rush up his spine. "But… what is truth?"

CHAPTER 35:

QUIETUS

The crowd grew impatient. It had been a morning full of back and forth, and the religious leaders wanted this issue resolved. Military Superintendent Pontius was growing weary of the situation himself. With pressure on all sides, he was caving.

"Away with him! Give us Dreggs!"

"Why? What crime has he committed?" the Military Superintendent argued.

"He's a demon! He's possessed!"

"He's claimed to be the Son of Theos! He's crazy!"

"Is he not your King?"

"King?! We have no king! Our rulers are none other than the Chief Governors! He undermines their authority!"

"What is it that you intend for me to do with this man?" Aislyn was watching from a nearby window and shaking with fear for her husband's life as well as this Redeemer's.

"Hang him!"

"Firing squad!"

"Curse him with the tree!"

Pontius's eyes grew wide. They fully intended him to die. "I find nothing he's done worthy of death. I will have him punished and then released. Be satisfied."

"Injustice! Injustice! Honor our tradition! Give us Dreggs and condemn this imposter!"

"If you release this man, you are not Tetrarch's ally!"

Pontius could resist no longer. He was tired of it and forced to stay on the people's side for his position's sake. He could see that he was getting nowhere. With loud shouts, the people demanded that Manuel be eliminated.

Their shouts prevailed. Pontius granted their demands and ordered the release of Stacey Dreggs. The crowd cheered and welcomed the murderer with open arms. As he surrendered Manuel to their will, he ordered a wet towel brought to him. He stood before them and made an announcement.

"I will not be held accountable for this man's blood. The whole thing falls on you." He washed his hands with the towel as a symbol of his innocence in the matter. "So, let it be done."

Suddenly, a shriek came from the back of the crowd. It was Miryam. She had driven the two hours to be near her son in his hour of need. "Nooooo!" She screamed. Beside her was Aunt Sibyl, whose face declared that Manuel would not be spared but face every inch of the measure of punishment assigned to him. She held Miryam up. "He's innocent! You can't!" Manuel's eyes fell on his mother. He hated that she was there. Why didn't she just stay home? But nothing could have kept her away. For the first time, Manuel allowed his eyes to scan the crowd. He saw many of the people who had greeted him so warmly just days before. He saw Jack and Simon. He saw Magdala, the woman from the barbeque, where he first met Conti. She was weeping and making her way toward his mother. Precious Sibyl. Aislyn. Those who had been healed and followed him in the caravan. How could they switch so readily? Sabeen Smith was there looking content, and Scout, who made it just in time. Manuel saw Jude. 'Poor Jude,' he thought. Manuel's eyes fell on Teivel, grinning like a Cheshire cat untouched by any filth in his pristine grey suit and steely blue eyes. He could see Teivel's emissaries planted throughout the crowd, rousing them toward the worst-case scenario.

"Whatever!" The crowd sneered, "Let his blood be on our children and us!"

With that, Military Superintendent Pontius gave the nod to his guards. Forcefully they drug Manual out of the view of the crowd. The Chief Guard was a sadistic man. He looked forward to making Manuel pay for whatever he had or hadn't done. He called together his whole battalion. They mocked him with cries of, 'heal this,' and 'heal that!' They laughed and took turns punching him. Manuel's eyelid split open and bled, blurring his vision. He dropped to the ground.

"You think you're a king? What country do you think this is? We don't need no stinkin' king!" They twisted wrings of barbed wire and stuck it on his head like a crown. Pressing it down, it cut into Manuel's flesh. He screamed, then whimpered silently. It felt as though razor blades had reached his skull and his head throbbed with every pulse of his heartbeat. He felt faint and didn't think he could stand again, but another soldier pulled him up and propped him against something hard. He couldn't see. They ripped his clothes off. How could this be legal? Where was Pontius? They spit on him and drug him out to subjugate him completely.

Tying him to a post, they lashed him with whips containing metal in the tips. They punished him until the flesh hung from his back and legs. The stripe-like lacerations stung in the air. The scourging cut through the subcutaneous tissues and tore into his underlying skeletal muscles. Manuel couldn't breathe. His body went into shock from the loss of blood, and his head was spinning. They struck him no less than 39 times. The soldiers had every intention of bringing him just short of collapse or death, taunting him every lick of the way.

"Let him down," the Chief Guard hollered. "Someone bring him the log."

"Wait, wait!" a young soldier called out. Rushing to him, he draped the robe around him. "Here's your royal robe, your majesty!" They cackled and coughed. The robe stuck instantly to the blood flowing from Manuel.

As was the cruelest tradition, the soldiers brought a log out to the victim. It was to be strapped to the shoulders and carried out to the gallows on which the criminal would hang. Government City was located in one of the only three regions that still allowed hanging as capital punishment. They reserved it for the worst of criminals guilty of heinous crimes and worthy of brutal death. Because Manuel had been such a public figure, the Chief Governors, Religious Leaders, and Educators of the Law wanted to be sure that all eyes would see what happens to those who think too highly of themselves. They leaked the event to the press so that cameras could air the whole thing in live time. It interrupted regularly scheduled programs and convinced countless people that Manuel had been just another false prophet. No power in this realm or the next would dare to override them again. Because this was the goal, they determined that Manuel would have to walk the length of six football fields before reaching the determined post for his hanging at Skull Hill. Outside of the city, Skull Hill was located where the smell of flesh would not be carried downwind and disturb the inhabitants who did not wish to watch.

Loading the log onto Manuel's mangled shoulders, they strapped it to his shoulders and underarms. He fell immediately to the ground from the weight of it. It was easily 100 pounds. How was he expected to carry it? How would he ever make it to Skull Hill? He didn't know. Maybe he would die on the way. Maybe he wouldn't have to go through the actual hanging. As the guards led Manuel out to start the trek, the crowd remained to watch him suffer and walk. When Miryam saw him bloodied and beaten, she didn't recognize him. She flashed on the memory of the old man in the hospital chapel when her son was born.

"Even you, sweet one, will experience a piercing through your own heart and soul. But, by such, the thoughts and intentions of many will be revealed."

She fell trembling, unable to sustain the weight of her body at this sight. Sibyl was on her right, and Magdala had joined the women uplifting her on the left. Together they started to follow Manuel as he clumsily carried his log just steps at a time.

"My son!" She cried out, "Beloved! I'm here! Mama's here, Manny!" Hearing her voice did strengthen him. But it wounded him as well. "We're with you!"

The lack of sleep Manuel had the night before was contributing to his inability to see straight. His one decent eye was soaked with blood, and he couldn't wipe it as the weight of the log kept his hands on the ropes in his armpits. When he did try to wipe it, it seemed to make things worse with the feeling of something scratching his eyeball. He kept squinting to try and force all fluid out, but nothing made a difference. He tried walking with his eyes closed, but the soldiers would scream, "Watch where you're going! Hurry up! Move it, move it." One soldier was designated to carry a sign to be posted above the criminal. It would state his name and his crime.

Manuel was taking too long. All but the sadist Chief Guard wanted this thing to finish up so they could escape the vicarious living of the awful scene. Women were shrieking from the sight of him. Men turned away in gut-wrenching disgust. Some threw rocks and always the spitting. Seeing that it would take him forever, a soldier called a man out of the crowd to help Manuel walk upright.

"No way," the man protested.

"Get over here now!" the soldier demanded.

"Absolutely not! Sod off!"

The soldier walked over with his club in hand and raised it to the man's head. "Get your ass over here right now, or you'll wish you had." Seeing that he meant every word and knowing that the guards were hungry for blood that day, the man obliged. Walking up to Manuel, he didn't know where to touch. He knew he was about to be covered in blood just by trying to help. Where would he grab the log? Manuel fell again to his knees with the log forward on the ground– his face in the cement, without a care for his face. Pain was pain at this point, none better or worse than the other. Reaching for the right side of the log, the man pulled Manuel up with his left arm and wrapped it around his shoulder, placing his head next to Manuel's right shoulder and grabbing the log on his own right shoulder. Instantly, he felt blood soak through his shirt and bring a flow of warmth to his skin. Queasy, he reflexed a gag. "Move it!" Nauseated, he stood smelling the scent of blood and sweat.

"All right, now," he said to Manuel. "I'm Simeon. You got this, man. I'm with you. Don't quit on me now." Glancing over, he could see Manuel's direct gaze from one soaked eye. The most horrible compassion he had ever experienced shot through him. At that moment, he would have walked him to another country. Simeon nodded in tacit encouragement.

'How appropriate,' Manuel thought. The old man Simeon had been present as a prophetic encouragement at his birth, and now, this Simeon to help him in his death. 'Just when I needed it. Thank You for your grace and mercy, Abba.'

Manuel looked up and saw Joey standing in the crowd. He did a double-take. His heart roused. Dad… *Dad.* Joey encouragingly nodded his head. It was just as he had done at any event he and his siblings had ever competed in. There was Joey, arms raised in victory, calling out to them in support. Manuel blinked, and he was gone.

After what seemed like an eternity, the two men arrived with the soldiers and crowd at Skull Hill. The soldiers approached them and pulled Simeon off of the log. As they did, he turned as if to say goodbye to this man he would forever be haunted by but couldn't as they swiftly propped Manuel up and yanked the soaked robe from his body, ripping open the wounds that had sealed with blood to the material. Manuel screamed. Simeon wretched. Jack came scrambling from the crowd.

"Emmanuel! Emmanuel! I'm here! I'm right here, cousin! *Manny*… Kyrios!"

Miryam, Sibyl, and Magdala made their way to Jack's side. They groveled as near to Manuel as they could while the soldiers held them at bay.

"Come on, man," Jack snapped, "She's his mother! *His mother*, you idiot!" The guards had no remorse.

Two other men were already strapped up onto their poles enduring their punishment. One had been tried and convicted of grand larceny– the other of petty thievery living a life in and out of prison. Soon, Manuel would be hung between them like any other common criminal. They placed the sign with his name and crime on the gallows that would be his end. But instead of reading his name and crime, it read, "The King and Redeemer of the World." A soldier rebuked his colleague who had carried the sign.

"What are you doing? It can't say that! He isn't actually the redeemer of the world, you half-wit!"

"Don't look at me," he rebutted, "The Military Superintendent wrote it and would not hear otherwise. It is what it is."

Sabeen was livid when she saw the writing. Scout took pictures and would write every word of it in his article. They took Manuel and bound his log to the gallows. The crowd half grieved him and half condemned him. Calling out, religious leaders sneered.

"Oh, you can save all these people, but you can't save yourself? Some *redeemer.* You're the Chosen One? Ha! The Son of Theos would never allow this to happen!"

Sibyl flashed on the vision she had seen so many years ago regarding the King. A rope swinging from a tree. The noose had blood on it, and with it came a flood of suffering– heavy, wicked torment. Today was the fulfillment of that vision. But there was more. Wanting to intensify the process, the Chief Guard, in all his sadism, declared that Manuel would not only be hung but spiked to the gallows with sharp iron spikes in his wrists and ankles. This way, when he tried to breathe, he'd have to pull himself up by the incisions, and his death would be even more brutal. Manuel could take a breath if he chose the pain of pushing himself up on the spikes to raise his body to a position where his lungs could take in air. But if he hung, he would only be able to take pitiful pants that would never satisfy. The pain or the breath. The pain… or the breath. It would be a choice. Every instinct is to breathe. By law, the guards were required to offer the dying man his last drink. It would usually contain a mild analgesic as an act of mercy. But to Manuel, they provided a vinegar mixture. He refused despite his desperate thirst.

Manuel was flat on his back in the dirt. Stretching his arms out, they held them in place while one soldier positioned the spikes. Miryam again shrieked. "This isn't necessary! It's too much! Haven't you done enough? He's going to die… he's already going to die!" Sobbing, she buried her face into Jack's chest. The soldiers didn't hesitate. An order was an order, and they were in league with the Chief Governors. Their loyalty was to no one else, and it paid well to stay in with their leaders. First, the left wrist, then the right, was spiked to the log. Once properly impaled, they lifted Manuel by the log. They mounted it up on the gallows and proceeded to position his ankles on either side of the post.

"Abba," Manuel whispered. "Abba, please… have mercy." The soldiers exchanged glances but did not look upward at him. They were used to condemned men begging at the last. "Absolve them of this abomination," their eyes grew wide as they realized he was not begging for himself but for them. "They have no idea what they're doing. I forgive them. I forgive them, Abba." Now, they looked up. One man dropped the spikes and hurried away. Another picked them up to continue.

"Let's go. Get on with it." The Chief Guard demanded.

Manuel wasn't just petitioning Theos on behalf of the soldiers but on behalf of everyone who had condemned him. With that, they hammered the spikes through his left ankle and then his right. Manuel could only breathe out with the pain. His energy to scream had left him. The soldiers stepped back while the crowd wept and wailed. One of the accused hanging next to him mocked him.

"I thought you were supposed to be the Redeemer. Why don't you save yourself and save us while you're at it?"

In disgust, the second man lashed out, "Have you no fear of Theos?! This guy has done absolutely nothing to be hanging here. We have. Oh, God. I have." Softer, he addressed Manuel. "Kyrios… I'm so sorry. We are getting our due justice, but you…" he whimpered. "Please, I know I don't deserve it, but… please. Please remember me when you enter into your Kingdom."

Manuel was moved to compassion. Turning his head toward the man, he said, "Brother, be assured. Not only will I remember you, but you will be with me in paradise."

Jack and the women hung on Manuel's every word. Looking at them, Manuel addressed Jack, "Cousin. Look after my mom. Like she was your own." Jack nodded in a committed agreement.

Jude hid deep in the crowd. He couldn't believe he had been the one responsible for this depth of punishment. He had been sure that Manuel would be perfectly capable of saving himself, and the guys would be none the wiser to his wallet gain. After all, they'd seen Manuel do countless miracles. How could the Son of Theos end this way? He would return the money. He would return the money and get right with the guys. They would never have to know.

Simon was nowhere to be found. Carrying the weight of his denial, he had rushed back to the R.V. to inform the others of the events. Lost and afraid of being arrested themselves, they all scattered.

It was around 3:00 PM. The clouds moved in at record pace, and the sun stopped shining. Manuel, with what little breath he had left, said plainly for all to hear, "Abba, that's it. It's accomplished. I release to You my essence." He let out his final breath. His head fell to his chest, and the thunder rolled. The sky went from dark to black. The earth shook, and the wind howled. People in the crowd shrieked in fear. They fumbled around, trying to leave. Sabeen was knocked down and scraped her knees and hands. The guard who had dropped the spikes and left became convinced that this man truly must have been the Son of the One True Creator. He pounded on his chest and tore off his uniform.

The soldiers had orders not to leave or remove the bodies until they were positive death had occurred. Wanting to flee and make their way through the darkness, they checked each of the bodies for signs of life. The first thief was still breathing, so they placed a noose around his neck and cut the ropes from his underarms, letting him drop and break his neck for a swift death. Approaching the second thief, they found him crying in silence. It wasn't for fear of death but for Manuel and the promise of redemption he had gained. He patiently waited as they dropped the noose around his neck and cut the ropes from his underarms, relinquishing him to death. They approached Manuel's body. Jack, Miryam, Sibyl, and Magdala all remained. As the soldiers examined him, they found him already dead.

"Pontius will want proof," one said. So, they took a fighting utility knife and climbed up to jab it through his ribs. Strangely, instead of blood, a steady stream of blood and water, entirely unmixed together, poured out of the opening. Manuel didn't flinch. Miryam did.

"That's it. Let's get the heck out of here," he confirmed.

Leaving the bodies, the soldiers started to go. Clean up was someone else's job. Grabbing the left behind tools, Jack ran to the body and started climbing to release him. Miryam, Sibyl, and Magdala all waited to catch him. As Jack reached the top, he couldn't help but weep. Hugging his cousin, he rested his head on the lifeless shoulder.

"I've got you. I've got you, cuz. Okay? I'm gonna help you. I'm gonna help, okay?" Dislocating each spike and using the ropes from his underarms, they gently lowered Manuel to the ground. Miryam sat, cradling her baby in her arms and rocking back and forth.

"Good boy. You're such a good boy, baby. You did it. You said you would, and you did, didn't you? That's my good, good boy. Papa would be so proud. Don't you worry. We're gonna take good care of you now. Don't you worry."

Present watching the whole thing was a man named Joseph. He was a member of the religious council but had not agreed with their decision and actions. Immediately upon Manuel's death, he called Pontius's office and requested permission to receive Manuel's body for burial. Being a member of the council, M.S. Pontius saw no reason to refuse. He wanted the whole thing put to rest. Literally. Solemnly, Joseph approached the four. Profusely apologizing, he offered his personal burial vault to place Manuel in. Being at a complete loss on how to proceed, Miryam agreed with gratitude even though it was not in their hometown of Netzer.

"He belonged to everyone," she said. "It's only right he be among his people."

"But remember, mother," Jack offered, "He said… I mean, he did say that– maybe he won't actually need it for long."

Miryam smiled at him and touched his cheek. She wanted with her whole heart for what he was suggesting to be true.

CHAPTER 36:

IT'S NOT POSSIBLE

Jude was seized with remorse. The money was burning a hole in his pocket, and he could not reach the council fast enough. Upon entering the temple courts of the brick building on Perfidy St., he found people scattered with sewing machines and tools of repair.

"What happened here?" he asked someone.

"The craziest thing. There was an earthquake, and the whole sanctuary cracked right down the middle. The tapestry at the front of the sanctuary split in two from top to bottom."

"The top to the bottom?"

"Yes, isn't that crazy? It's most precious as it symbolizes the holiest place behind the curtain, but now, it's ripped wide open, so we're trying to fix it."

"Why would you fix it? Don't you see?"

"See what?"

"Don't you know what just happened? With Manuel Paladin?"

"Yes, I mean… I heard. I couldn't watch it. But he deserved it. Calling himself the Son of Theos."

"He *was* the Son of Theos, you fool. If you had watched, you would truly know! Fixing that stupid tapestry is like saying you don't want access to the Holy of Holies, the Higher Realm. To Theos Himself! Oh, forget it. Have your stupid religion." Brushing past them, he headed straight into the council meeting room where the Directors of the Church and Educators of the Law were gathered. Sabeen sat tending to her bloodied knees and hands. "I don't want it!" he yelled.

"Well, hello, Jude." Sabeen returned smoothly.

"I don't want it," he held the money out in a bundle.

"Well, we had a deal," Sabeen answered.

"Screw your deal. This isn't what I signed up for."

"Oh, this is what you signed up for precisely. What's the matter? Afraid your boys will find out?"

"No… I mean, yes, but–"

"Keep your money, boy."

"No! I can't. I've betrayed innocent blood."

"That's not our problem, now is it?"

"It is! You're the ones who–"

"–Who what? Who silenced a false prophet misleading the people to damnation? We are to be commended. Every system is saved because of us."

"No. The system that brings damnation remains because of you. But it won't matter." Jude threw the money at their feet. "It won't matter because it's all bigger than you. It's all bigger than your stupid tapestries and laws. You'll see. He really was the Redeemer. He really was the Redeemer, and you missed it. I missed it."

"This is blood money. We don't want this."

"It's too late," Jude warned. "It's His blood and your money."

Leaving, Jude knew he couldn't face the guys. They would never understand or forgive him. He couldn't imagine ever getting past what had just happened, let alone by his hand. Maybe he could run. He could take the guys' money and– no! Enough dirty money. How could he change these circumstances? He couldn't. How could he face the guys? He couldn't. How could he ever be a part of the group again? He couldn't. Besides, there would be no group now. What had he done? And for what? Money? Jude saw with his own eyes all of the change Manuel brought. His words rang in Jude's head from the grove, *"Do what you came to do, friend. Jude, you betray me with the greatest expression of endearment?"* He had betrayed him. He had betrayed himself and robbed the whole world of redemption. Hadn't he? He couldn't take it. If Manuel had endured being hung, then he would too. It was only right. Buying a rope, Jude went out to a field outside of town. Throwing it up and over the branch of a healthy tree, he put the noose around his neck. Climbing out on a limb, he searched his heart and mind for any other way. Down below, Teivel stood happily.

"Go on," he pricked. "Jump. You deserve it. No one will ever love you now. Maybe if you jump, they'll feel sorry for you. At least you'd have that." Still lies.

Taking a deep breath, Jude slid off the branch. The rope strained and snapped his neck.

~~~

As evening approached, Joseph and Nico DeMos carried Manuel's body into the vault. The women washed him and clothed him in fresh garments. There were no professionals who dared be involved. Once he was dressed and properly loved, the group reluctantly departed. Miryam was numb. Was
~~~

this the fruit of all of her sacrifice? Of his? Had this truly been the plan all along? Like this? They sealed the door with an ABUS Granit lock. Renowned for being one of the world's most secure padlocks, they wanted no one to know where he was laid or be able to break in and disturb the body. Jack had taken the sign down from the gallows and placed it in the tomb with him for, truly, He was the King and Redeemer of the world.

The next day, some Directors of the Church and religious leaders went to Military Superintendent Pontius's office.

"Oh, what now? Will it never end?! Send them away. I'm serious. I'm over it."

Their persistence again dominating, M.S. Pontius agreed to see them one last time. "Sir, remember while he was alive, the deceiver insinuated that he would rise from the dead after just three days."

"I've about had enough of your madness. Have you not had enough? It's done. Leave it alone."

"Well, we'd like to, Military Superintendent. We'd love to. But see, we want to ensure that no lunatic devotee of this deceiver makes it possible to steal his body and say that he did, in fact, rise. You understand. This deception would be worse than the first."

Pontius sighed heavily. He was already in the doghouse with Aislyn. He dreaded any upheaval in his professional relationships as well.

"What more could you possibly ask of me?"

"We'd like guards placed at his burial site to ensure testimony of his death and remains."

"Guards? Plural?"

"Better safe than sorry, Military Superintendent. Wouldn't you say?"

"Oh, there's plenty I'd like to say. Fine. Two guards."

"So, you know where he's been taken."

"I do. You won't. Now, get out before I have you thrown out, and don't come back to me with any further *requests*."

The Military Superintendent gave two guards orders to find Joseph's vault and remain there with rations until further notice. For no reason were they to abandon their post. No matter what. Not only did he post guards, but he had a wax seal poured around the door to ensure that should it ever be opened, there would be evidence in the broken seal.

~~~

The guys were distraught. Levi wanted to return home to his mother almost immediately. Simon wanted to return to his business and bury himself in tasks, but Drew insisted they stay together. Jim and Jack had somewhat become surrogate leaders as family to Manuel. At least, the guys referred to them as such, but they certainly didn't feel like leaders in any way, shape, or form. After all, they should have believed him when he spoke of the day coming and done more in whatever way they could, although they didn't
~~~

know what that would possibly have been. Philip and Nathan were permanently in the R.V. now. They felt that nowhere was safe for them, and Jude was just gone. They adopted a guy who had been at the execution. He had been in the caravan for months, although none of them ever met him. He was a devout believer and made himself available now for any menial task needed. They needed someone like him to go out into public for food, supplies, or– whatever. Thomas, they realized, was more committed to the cause than they were at this point. Maybe it was because he hadn't been with Manuel as they had. Maybe it was because Theos knew they would need someone like him at the time. Or maybe, it was simply because none of them seemed able to function outside of the fear that they were next by association.

They spent two days locked up together in the R.V., overwhelmed with grief. They hid on the property of Thomas's uncle. No one would know they were there, they hoped. Miryam, Magdala, and Sibyl were welcomed into Thomas's uncle's house to stay until they felt strong enough to return home. Magdala had no desire to leave Miryam ever. Miryam called her sister Sally, who promptly made the trip to join her sister at the loss of her nephew and Redeemer. She longed to see her boys. The guys were concerned that until things died down, the religious leaders may be hunting them as well. If they could do such brutal things to Manuel when all he did was help people, then what would happen to them for having been his accomplices?

They missed their friend. They missed his humor and his wisdom. They missed his leadership and their purpose. They missed how much they learned from him, but most of all, they missed how connected to Theos they felt when he was around. They remembered specific events and laughed, recalling his bravery at Draco Conti's place. They had never known love or brotherhood as they had these last three years, and just like that– it was gone. Jack wanted to visit the vault, but Jim objected.

"You don't want to draw any attention," he warned. "Give him that."

The days were endless and full of despair. They would have to determine how to return to their lives. How would they ever be the same? How could they be? Should they be? The Commemoration of Trials was over, and the town was returning to its everyday routines. On the first day of the new week, Miryam decided she would go to the vault and pay respects before heading home. Magdala and Sally would go with her. They headed out before sunrise so as not to be discovered. As they approached the vault, there was another violent earthquake. Dropping to the ground, the ladies clung to each other.

"Whoa!" Sally exclaimed. "That was freaky! I didn't know where we could take cover!"

Miryam stood and felt a wave of peace come over her. It was a feeling she had known intimately for the last 33 years. Without speaking, she headed swiftly to the vault. Sally and Magdala rushed after her.

"We should be careful, sis. What if there's another one?"

Miryam didn't answer but kept heading toward the vault. Turning a corner, they saw the vault with the door swung wide open. Magdala gasped. One guard was slapping the other to wake him from a passed-out state. They shook like two frightened puppies, unsure of what they had just experienced. Miryam walked right past them and saw the lock still latched on the door. The wax seal did not look broken. It remained on the wall as if it was melted that way initially, smooth and clean, not violently ripped apart.

"What happened?" Magdala asked the guards. They looked at each other and shook their heads. They weren't sure they should speak for fear of getting in trouble later. Besides, how could they explain? "What happened?!" she repeated loudly. They did not speak.

Miryam entered the vault. Her son was not there. Neither was his body. Magdala and Sally followed. Suddenly, a supernatural being sat before them where the body had laid. His appearance was like lightning, and his clothes were as white as clean snow. At this, the guards ran off in horror to report to their commanding officers what was going on. Sally and Magdala dropped to the ground with their faces bowed down. Miryam smiled and remembered being 16, thinking that she was dreaming. The same wave washed over her. As she had then, she straightened up to the full measure of her person. The messenger spoke to the women.

"Gentlewomen, don't be afraid. Why do you come seeking the living among the dead? Emmanuel told that he must be delivered over to the hands of earthly authorities, be executed, and after three days be raised and rekindled." They remembered Manuel's words.

"He has awakened, just as He said. Now, when you tell His brothers, tell them to return to the Region of Circuit. He will meet them there." Just as suddenly as he had appeared, the messenger vanished. The women looked at each other in shock and then started laughing and crying. Miryam simply grinned from ear to ear. As they headed out of the vault, Magdala lingered. Taking out her phone, she took pictures of the wax and the lock. She wanted proof in case anything was tampered with later. She was afraid but also filled with joy. Without warning, Emmanuel stood before them.

"Hey, ladies." He smiled. Dropping to his feet, Magdala began kissing them and crying. Miryam went straight for his chest, and Sally stood with both hands covering her mouth. "I know, I know… but don't cling to me now; I can't stay with you yet. I still need to go up to Abba in the Higher Realm. You know– had to handle some business." He winked at them. "Now, go tell the guys that you've seen Me and to meet Me in Circuit." The women agreed.

"Yes, anything, Kyrios."

"I love you, Son."

"Love you, mama. See you soon. Now go!"

The women didn't want to draw too much attention, but they rushed as fast as possible to the car. Miryam didn't feel 49. She felt 16 again with news she couldn't contain. News that she knew would change the world! Pounding on the R.V. door, they blurted out to the guys that they had seen Emmanuel.

"What are you talking about?" Jack asked his mother.

"We saw Him!"

"How did you see him? Did you open the vault?"

"No, no, son!" Sally explained, "When we got there, it was open. We went in, but He wasn't there, so–"

"What do you mean He wasn't there? Had someone broken the lock? Oh, my– did they steal the body?" Dropping into a chair with his hand on his head, Jack was in shock.

"No," Miryam said calmly. "You are not hearing us. He is alive. His mission is complete. They may have killed Him, but they couldn't keep Him."

"Wait," Jack said, "You mean… what He said about, 'raising this frame in three days,' that was this? This is now? I mean– it? You're saying He–"

Simon was out the door. He was running as hard and as fast as he could toward Miryam's car. Jack raced out to join him.

"You're not going without me!"

"He won't be there!" Miryam called out to them. "You're supposed to meet Him in the Region of Circuit!"

Simon wasn't listening. He had to see for himself. Every red light felt like an eternity. As many times as Simon had driven in the city before, this time felt the slowest. It occurred to him as he sped past the landscape that he had seen this region in every season of his life. In the Fall, when things were drying up. In the Winter, when all was dead. In the Spring, when there was new hope. And in the Summer, when he was tested and tried. He had failed then, but he wouldn't fail again. Not for anything, anyone, or any amount of money. If he could just see Him himself. If he could just tell Him.

~~~

The two guards reported to Military Superintendent Pontius's office, who immediately sent them over to the only ones who cared: the Directors of the Church and the Educators of the Law. They tried to explain everything that happened but had a hard time; they passed out at the earthquake and vision of the Man in White. Sabeen was livid.

"Okay, here's what we're going to do. You are two fortunate men. Today you will become very wealthy. Why? Because when you're asked about this by the press, you will say that his followers came during the night and stole his body while you were sleeping. Do you hear me?"

"But if we were sleeping, how would we know it was His followers?"
~~~

"And, if we were sleeping, we would have to wake up at the sound of a lock like that being broken. Have you seen one of those locks? Besides, the lock isn't broken. It's perfectly intact! The door is open, but the wax and lock are unbroken!"

"Shut up!" Sabeen fumed. "We can break the lock. We can bust the wax."

"But the wax would have to be broken pulling outward, and we can only break it going inward." An elder offered.

"Are you really wanting to cover up the evidence of what has happened here, Sabeen?" Another questioned.

"Are you willing to lose everything we've spent our lifetimes' building?" she retorted, "For this, this–"

"Redeemer."

"Messiah."

"Savior," they all concluded.

"No. No, no, no. Now, stop it. Or you will all be off the payroll."

"Tell her," one of the guards said to the other.

"Tell me what?" Sabeen said with disgust. "There couldn't possibly be anything worse."

"Um– well. It's going to sound… crazy."

"All of this has been crazy. Spit it out." The guards exchanged weary glances. They took deep sighs.

"Just say it," one encouraged.

"There were others."

"Others? Other what's?"

"Bodies. People. Graves that opened and– people were coming out of them."

"Oh, my–" Sabeen flopped down. "You've got to be kidding. Zombies? You're adding zombies to your story?"

"No, not zombies… people. Like, some of the past religious leaders."

"You know what? This isn't a problem." The elders couldn't believe she was responding this way. "It's not a problem because no one is going to believe a word you say. You both sound crazy. Now, take the money and get out of my office."

The guards took their payoff and did as they were told.

"Others," she mumbled under her breath.

~~~

About seven miles out of town, an elderly man named Cleo was doing his usual laps around the Junior College track. He met up with his walking buddy Mac, and they began discussing everything that had been happening in town with the Festival, the brutal execution, and so on.

"Ugly times," Mac sighed.
~~~

As they talked, Emmanuel came and walked alongside them. They didn't recognize Him, so He asked them casually, "What are you guys talking about?" Their faces were downcast.

"Son, are you the only one in town who hasn't heard about what's been going on here the last few days?"

"I guess," He answered. "What things?"

The two men looked at each other like this kid must be living under a rock.

"About Emmanuel Paladin." Emmanuel shook his head no. Sighing, Cleo continued, "He was a true prophet."

"Do those still exist?" He teased.

"This one did. He was full of power in both His words and deeds before the Creator and the people. But those religious nuts handed Him over to be sentenced to death, and they executed Him. We had hoped that He would be the One who was going to redeem the world, but that was three days ago, so–"

"Wow. Is the news reporting anything?"

"Actually, yes. The mid-morning news said that some women went to where He was buried, but amazingly they didn't find His body."

"What… it was just… gone?"

"Well, yeah. They said there were some glowing messenger's from Theos there and said He was alive! Then some of those guys of His, well, they went too, but just like those women had said, they didn't see Him."

"One of them was his mom." Mac joined in.

"One of the men?"

"No! You nincompoop. One of the women."

"You guys seem pretty foolish to me. You claim to know things, but you believe the news? That's a world order for sure. Rather, you should believe everything the prophets before Him wrote. Didn't they say that the Redeemer would have to suffer such things before He entered into His glory?"

"Well, yeah. That doesn't sound unfamiliar." Cleo humphed.

Emmanuel started with the earliest authors of the Ancient Writings and explained all that had been written concerning Himself. By the 16th lap, the old men were done with their four miles.

"Hey, kid. You wanna get some coffee with us?"

"Sure, why not. Thanks."

As the men sat down at a table, Emmanuel took some crackers from the table's center and offered them to the men. As He did, their eyes were opened, and they recognized him as Emmanuel. Just then, He disappeared. The old men were astounded.

"What the…?!" Cleo flabbergasted.

"Cleo! Cleo!" Mac was slapping Cleo's arm.

"Dagnabbit, Mac! I'm sittin' right here! I saw it!"

"I knew my heart was just burning in my chest as He spoke! I thought, 'This kid knows an awful lot about the Prophets and the Ancient Writings not to be some sort of priest or something. By golly, it was Him! Right here with us the whole time! With *us!*'"

"You know I saw that execution on the news, man. He was deader'n a doornail. That kid was dead, Mac. D-E-A-D. Dead."

"Yeah, they did a number on Him."

"Oh, they slaughtered Him."

"But… He's back. He's alive."

"He's somethin' that's for sure. Appearing and disappearing. What do you call that?"

"Badass! That's what I call that!"

CHAPTER 37:

ABSOLUTE ASSURANCE

It had been a crazy morning. Miryam, Magdala, and Sally were adamant, and the midday news was already showing images of the opened vault. The guards were nowhere to be found, but reporters were seeking them out. The guys headed toward the Region of Circuit as the women instructed, then followed. There was a new caravan now, but with fewer cars. Just the guys in the R.V. followed by Miryam and Sibyl, then Sally and Magdala. As they drove, they speculated on what was happening and what was going to happen. They pulled into the Region of Circuit and decided to eat, but nowhere public. Better safe than sorry, they hit a drive-thru, parked somewhere shady, and kept the doors locked. They divvied out the orders and dug in. Some scarfed as though they hadn't eaten in days, some merely picked at their food from stress, and some sat quietly eating in anticipation. Suddenly, Emmanuel stood among them.

"Peace, brothers."

One would have thought a gunshot had gone off in their small quarters. Levi jumped a mile high and yelped. Jim yelled, and Simon froze. He couldn't remove his eyes and couldn't process his thoughts. None of them breathed. Jack screamed and rushed to tackle his cousin.

"I knew it! I *knew* it!" Emmanuel held fast for the monstrous hug.

"Whaaaat the– how did you–" Philip began.

"You might not want to start with *how* Philip." Emmanuel grinned. "Miss Me?"

"Kyrios," Simon whispered. Emmanuel smiled at him softly and blinked a slow blink. It was all Simon could do not to burst out in tears and throw himself at His feet.

Emmanuel was clean and looked refreshed. He seemed as though He had just showered and been to the barber. He looked good. He smelled good. He was good. Wearing a crisp, clean plain white t-shirt, spotless new blue jeans, and no shoes, He stood tall and organic. He raised His hand in a hello gesture and grinned. As He did, they saw the cleansed wound on His wrist where the spike had pierced Him. They inhaled. Was this happening? Jack pulled the other hand up and looked at the second wound. He gulped and met his cousin's eyes.

"This is… you're still my cousin, aren't you?" Jack wondered if being the Son of Theos and resurrected Redeemer of the World changed things on an earthly level.

"Sure," Emmanuel chuckled. "Look, I just stopped by to give you something." It seemed that every word surged from His mouth with love. How was He doing that? Radiating love?

"What? Seriously? You can't go now!" Jack argued.

"Jacky… guys, I've been given all authority in the Higher Realm, here and below. I've taken the keys of death, but the work on earth isn't entirely done. Just as I was sent, I'm now sending you. There is so, so much work to do, and you are my guys."

Again, Simon wanted to burst into tears. It was all so much to process. He had gone from being a gruff, no-bull businessman with no time to a completely sold-out, purpose-driven ball of mush. One of *His* guys. How did that happen?

"You're not a ball of mush, Rock," Emmanuel whispered. "Now, receive the Essence of the Creator."

With that, He breathed over them, and a translucent rainbow of waterless mist reached out to each of them. It looked like the Aurora Borealis and lit up the whole R.V. As they breathed it in, they became filled with the immaculate Presence of Theos Himself. It was almost like being drunk.

"Whoa–" Jim breathed.

"This is… heavy, man."

"Is this how you've felt?" Nathan questioned. "How did you walk straight?" The group chuckled and enjoyed the perfectly calm weight of the high.

"It doesn't always feel like that," Emmanuel said.

"I don't want it to end," Levi said. He'd never felt such perfect confidence and peace– no chatter in his brain and no fear.

"Well, that's the beauty. The Essence doesn't ever leave you. He will never forsake you or be absent. Not ever. Ask Him anything; for wisdom, for counsel, for direction, you name it."

"How will we know when He is answering?"

"Give it a shot," Emmanuel encouraged.

"Essence, er… Holy Presence–" The guys chuckled with Philip, who was most eager to learn. "How long will– whoa."

"What? What?!" the guys questioned. Emmanuel grinned.

"He spoke to me."

"What did He say?"

"What did you ask?"

"How do you know?"

"It's like… a perfectly clear, solid thought that comes quicker than I could have ever come up with. And an answer I would have never guessed. I didn't even finish the question!"

"It isn't always like that either," Emmanuel instructed, "But it can be. Ask Him to educate you on the difference between His voice, your voice, and the voice of the confuser– Teivel." The guys all began asking questions and awaiting their answers, both out loud and in their minds. "Look," Emmanuel continued, "This business carries a lot of power. I need each of you to go into every nation and tell them what you know. All that you have seen. Just like Johnny ceremonially immersed people in water, We want you to immerse those who believe– in The Presence, the Essence of the Creator.

"If you forgive anyone's transgression, they will be forgiven. But if you withhold forgiveness from anyone– it truly is withheld. So, act justly. Love Mercy. Walk humbly with your Creator."

They understood and were grateful to be trusted with such a commission and authority. It wasn't a gift just for themselves. When Emmanuel said He was sending them, He meant it. They were to distribute the gift of the Creator's Essence to any and all who would believe and receive it. Theos had officially opened the floodgates to Himself and wanted none to perish or remain powerless. Then, He opened their minds so they would understand the Ancient Writings. He told them all that was written about how the Redeemer would suffer and rise from the grave. How people would turn from wicked ways, and how forgiveness would come in His name to all nations– beginning with the City of Peace.

"You guys are the witnesses to all of these things. You've received His Essence; now I'm sending you out to accomplish all that Abba has promised, but stay in the city until you are covered with the dunamis power from the Higher Realm."

There were *more* gifts they would receive? It just got better and better. Simon understood in the peace of The Presence that all would be well, but he wanted to speak to Emmanuel privately and verbalize his remorse. He stood and was going to request a minute alone when just as suddenly as He had appeared, Emmanuel was gone. Simon breathed a sigh of disappointment. Drew knew his brother and felt his sadness, but he didn't realize the depth of why.

"Whoa–"

"That is crazy."

"Is He always going to do that now?"

"What are we supposed to do now? Where are we supposed to go?"

"Let's ask. Like He showed us." They all got silent and sought His Presence for an answer. In unison, they all grinned and said, "The City of Peace!"

"Of course!"

Thomas opened the R.V. door and stepped in. He had run an errand for the group when the excitement happened.

"Oooooh!" the guys let out.

"Dude, bummer! No way."

Thomas stood, looking at them with hesitation. He checked his shoes for dog poop. Cross talking over one another, they each started telling him about Emmanuel's visit.

"Right here! He was standing right here, not three minutes ago!" Thomas thought they were playing him with some less than funny initiation game.

"Yeah, yeah. Funny, guys."

"No, seriously, Thomas!"

"Dude, for real. Right there. There!"

"Okay. Aaalll right." He didn't believe them or know why they would keep it up. Did they really think he was that gullible? The guys insisted. "Look, unless I see with my own eyes the wounds I saw them strike into his wrists and ankles– I'm not going to believe it." The guys felt sorry he hadn't been there. "I hear you. But I was there. I saw him bleed buckets of blood. I heard him in pain. I saw them drive those spikes into him and stab him afterward just to make sure they'd done their job completely. I saw it– all right? Someone doesn't just come back from that."

It's true. Someone doesn't *just* come back from that.

~~~

As the guys headed to the City of Peace, they said their goodbyes to Miryam, Sally, Magdala, and Sibyl, who headed back to their homes. Magdala had begun a new life and would not be returning to the place she had called home. She wanted to stay with the guys but knew traveling with them in the R.V. would not be an option. They would soon split up as Emmanuel instructed them, and there wouldn't be a united road trip. So, she accepted Miryam's offer of returning home with her. There could be no greater honor than to learn life and service with the woman who had taught the Redeemer Himself.

Several days passed, and the guys were beginning to settle in on a ranch on the City of Peace's outskirts, owned by Levi's mother. They were each making plans of where they would go, how they would get there, where the funds would come from, and more. They would miss processing with each other and experiencing the thrill of people being healed together. They knew miracles would still happen. Emmanuel granted them the same power and authority that raised Him from the dead, and they had the Creator's Essence residing inside of them. How could they go wrong? It was just the
~~~

camaraderie that they would miss. Initially, they thought they would travel in twos. That way, no one would get off course, and they would each have accountability. None of them wanted to do anything that would put Kyrios in a bad light.

One evening, they met together for some barbeque and a campfire. Thomas sat gnawing on a rib bone when Emmanuel appeared seated beside him.

"Whoa!" Drew yelled. And they each turned to see Him. Thomas was the last to turn and almost choked on the rib. As he coughed, Emmanuel patted him on the back, then stood in front of him.

"Here, brother." He extended His wrists palm up. "Did you want to see for yourself?" Pulling up His shirt, He revealed the mark between His ribs that showed where He had been stabbed. "How about this?"

Thomas slid from his seat, dropping his plate on the ground. Falling with his face to Emmanuel's feet, he cried. "Oh, my Sovereign! Master…"

"Do you believe only when you can see Me? There is so much more reward for those who have not seen Me with their own eyes but can find it in their hearts to believe."

"I just– I saw what they did to You and I– I'm sorry. I'm sorry, Kyrios."

"No, no. Don't be sorry." Emmanuel knelt and helped Thomas stand. "Just understand. Faith is having confidence in what we hope for and being *certain* of what we do not see. Absolute assurance– even though we can't physically touch it."

"I understand."

And just like that, He was gone again. Simon had barely gotten to where He was before seeing Him disappear. That was twice; he had missed his chance.

~~~

Enough time passed that each of the duos had formulated a pretty solid starting plan. They were beginning to think they might not ever physically see Emmanuel again and didn't want to put off the assignment He had given them to tell the nations all they had seen and come to believe. They remembered the story He told them about the wicked servants not investing what they were given and didn't want to disappoint Him in this way. Jack's Redeemer Roadtrip channel was still racking up hits every day, and soon, they knew it would be up to them to add new footage.

Simon was starting to go stir-crazy. After three years on the road, he couldn't imagine going back to the life he once knew of locking himself in an office 'til all hours. 'I should have delegated all that years ago,' he thought. Only, he hadn't found any other cause worth living for until the road trip. He was grateful to be able to take his wife on this next leg of the journey. At least for the bits that she wanted to come. He considered buying a brand new R.V. and just selling everything else. Why not live on the road spreading
~~~

the news of the Redeemer forever. Nothing had ever brought him so much satisfaction, and he couldn't see himself as anything but the Rock anymore. He had no desire to be anything else.

"I'm going fishing," he announced to the guys. Simon knew where he could always go to clear his head.

"Wait!" Jack hindered, "I'll come with you!"

"Me, too!"

One by one, each of the guys agreed to come. Simon would have refused them, but he knew before long they wouldn't have days like these, so he didn't grumble too much. They loaded up and headed out to a nearby lake that Levi told them about and stopped just a couple miles shy of it to rent a boat. They were gone all evening and through the night. They laughed, remembering the last time they had all been on a boat together and how Emmanuel walked out on the water to be with them. How they wished He would do that now. Each of them kept an eye open for Him, even resisting the urge to sleep in hopes He would come. He did not.

Just as the day was breaking, they decided to head back to shore. When they were about a hundred yards out, a man called to them from the lakeside.

"Catch anything?"

"Nope."

"Nothing."

The man hollered back, "Try throwing a net out on the right side of the boat as you come in!"

Simon laughed to himself. If he hadn't caught anything after a whole night of trying, no stranger at the lakeside was going to have the secret recipe to catching anything, but before he knew it, Nathan and Thomas were throwing a good-sized net out. Simon sighed with slight irritation. The boat instantly started to drag. His first instinct was that something was wrong with the engine, but then he heard the guys whoop and holler. They weren't even able to pull the net in because of all of the fish that had swum into it. Jack froze and searched the lakeside for the man.

"It is Kyrios," he said. Simon looked at Jack and then for the man. Throwing the boat in neutral, he didn't wait to confirm it. He kicked his flip flops off and threw himself into the lake, heading for shore. By the time he reached land, the guys were pulling up in the boat.

"Bring some of those fish, and we'll have some breakfast," the man yelled. None of them asked. They knew it was Him. Simon, wanting to be obedient to the utmost, rushed to the boat and grabbed a bucket of fish to take to Him. As they approached, He had a charcoal fire going with perfect biscuits warming and all the fixings to the side. Simon was dripping.

"Looks like someone needs a towel," Emmanuel teased. "Did you bring one?" Simon shook his head no.

"I didn't think I would need one," he said seriously. The men all started laughing. They each hugged Him and dug into the biscuits. They were warm and fluffy. The butter melted on them quickly, and there was even jam. Anyone else and they would have wondered how they'd done it. This was the third time that Emmanuel appeared to them. They were so grateful to spend time with their friend and loved hearing His voice audibly. Each time it felt as if it had been years since they'd seen Him and didn't know how long it might last. When they finished eating, Simon was almost dry. He had been waiting for the right pause to ask to speak to Emmanuel alone. He didn't want to miss his opportunity a third time. Turning toward Simon, Emmanuel became serious.

"Simon, do you love me more than these other guys do?"

Simon froze with the weight of the question. "Yes, Kyrios; You know that I love You." Emmanuel did not actually want Simon to compare his love with that of the other guys. He wanted to invite Simon to love Him from a place of humility, not pride as he had done previously.

"It's important, then, that you are intentional in taking care of My people." Simon nodded. Nothing would keep him from it. He thought about telling Him about a new R.V. and his plan to tell anyone who would listen until the day he died. Emmanuel held up one finger and then lowered it.

"Simon, do you love me?"

Simon was slightly hurt that Kyrios would have to ask a second time but thought perhaps He was unsure after claiming three different times, not even to know him. Looking to the ground and shaking his head slightly, he returned his eyes to the Redeemer.

"Yes, Kyrios. You *know* that I love you."

"All right then. Make sure you take care of My precious ones." Emmanuel lifted two fingers and then lowered them.

Simon sat saying nothing more, although he had 202 things he wanted to say. After a long pause on everyone's part, Emmanuel asked Simon a third time.

"Simon," Simon sighed and didn't even want to look over. He didn't know if he could handle it if Kyrios had to ask him a third time. Didn't He believe him? Could He not trust him anymore because of the denials? "Do you love me?" He asked.

Simon was grieved. "Kyrios. You know *everything*. You know that I *love* You."

"Then do as I've asked you to." He knew Simon would. "I'm telling you now, you've always been strong and done anything you wanted whenever you wanted to. But when you're old, you'll be stretched and taken where you do not want to go." Emmanuel was cluing Simon into the way that he would serve and die on His behalf. Looking at him intensely, He said, "Always follow Me."

Emmanuel held up three fingers, then softened them into a loose fist and brought it to his chest.

Simon knew that never again would he betray this man who had changed not only his world but *the* world. Emmanuel did so many things that were not caught on video or written about in articles. If every one of them were written, the world itself could not hold all the books. For with every word written, not one could express the fullness of what He had done and accomplished so that everyone might know the Creator intimately. What words could explain the depth of love, devotion, and sacrifice He made?

CHAPTER 38:

CONFIRMATION

Rumors of Emmanuel's resurgence spread like wildfire. Jack did a vlog post confirming the rumors. The Tri-State Triton had Scout writing about it regularly in that he was the one who knew the most on the topic. Instead of followers dwindling after Emmanuel's execution, they were growing. Emmanuel appeared to a group of over 500 people at once to allow them to see for themselves that He was not a myth, a ghost, or just a made-up story by those who loved Him most. He was real and available to all. For 40 days, He revealed Himself to people. He also visited His family. His brothers and sisters, who hadn't always believed that He was the Redeemer, prophesied about for hundreds of years. He held his mother and strengthened them. They accepted Him as the Chosen One and received the Essence of the Creator so that they too could move forward, telling the world of The Way. The Way to the Creator. The Way to Redemption. The Way to Life.

The Beginning

From the Ancient Writings: The Prophet Isaiah, chapter 53.
New International Version.

The Prophecy regarding Emmanuel written 700 years before His birth:

Who has believed our message
and to whom has the arm of the Lord been revealed?
He grew up before him like a tender shoot,
and like a root out of dry ground.
He had no beauty or majesty to attract us to him,
nothing in his appearance that we should desire him.

He was despised and rejected by mankind,
a man of suffering, and familiar with pain.
Like one from whom people hide their faces
he was despised, and we held him in low esteem.
Surely he took up our pain
and bore our suffering,
yet we considered him punished by God,
stricken by him, and afflicted.
But he was pierced for our transgressions,
he was crushed for our iniquities;
the punishment that brought us peace was on him,
and by his wounds we are healed.
We all, like sheep, have gone astray,
each of us has turned to our own way;
and the Lord has laid on him
the iniquity of us all.
He was oppressed and afflicted,
yet he did not open his mouth;
he was led like a lamb to the slaughter,
and as a sheep before its shearers is silent,
so he did not open his mouth.
By oppression and judgment he was taken away.
Yet who of his generation protested?
For he was cut off from the land of the living;
for the transgression of my people he was punished.
He was assigned a grave with the wicked,
and with the rich in his death,
though he had done no violence,
nor was any deceit in his mouth.
Yet it was the Lord's will to crush him and cause him to suffer,
and though the Lord makes his life an offering for sin,
he will see his offspring and prolong his days,
and the will of the Lord will prosper in his hand.
After he has suffered,
he will see the light of life and be satisfied;
by his knowledge my righteous servant will justify many,
and he will bear their iniquities.
Therefore I will give him a portion among the great,
and he will divide the spoils with the strong,
because he poured out his life unto death,
and was numbered with the transgressors.
For he bore the sin of many,
and made intercession for the transgressors.

BIBLIOGRAPHY

1. Kyrios (kü'-rē-os) (Koor-ee-ahs) Strongs- G2962:
   koo'-ree-os; from κῦρος kŷros (supremacy); supreme in authority, ie (as noun) controller; by implication, Master (as a respectful title):—God, Lord, master, Sir
   https://wwwblueletterbibleorg/lang/lexicon/lexiconcfm?Strongs=G2962&t=KJV
2. Chapter 17- John Eldredge, Wild at Heart, Ransomed Heart Ministries. READ IT.
3. Chapter 32- Leif Enger, Peace Like a River, Barnes & Noble. John Eldredge, Waking the Dead
4. Katie Souza, Healing the Wounded Soul, Charisma House. www.katiesouza.com

SCRIPTURAL REFERENCES

1. Proverbs 23:31
   Alcohol. In the end, it bites like a snake and poisons like a viper
2. Luke 2:19
   Miryam pondered all of these things in her heart
3. Luke 1:46
   My spirit rejoices in the Creator who saves me
4. 2 Cor 10:5
   Whenever he came into her mind, she would take the thought captive
5. Matt 1:20-22
   Do not fear to take Mary as your wife… she will bear a son…
6. Luke 1:68-79
   Zachariah's prophesy regarding John the Baptist
7. Luke 1:80
   John grew and became strong in spirit
8. Luke 2:8
   Unto you is born this day… a Savior
9. Luke 2:19
   Mary pondered it all in her heart
10. Luke 2:
    Simeon's words in the temple

11. Matthew 2:13
    Herod seeks to destroy him
12. Luke 2:40
    The child grew, became strong; filled w/ wisdom, grace of God upon him
13. Song of Songs 4:11
    Your lips drip nectar, my bride. Honey and milk are under your tongue
14. Matt 2:20
    Return to Israel, for those who sought his life are dead
15. Psalm 27:15
    Quarrelsome wife is as annoying as a constant dripping
16. John 12:29
    …heard the voice, some thought it was thunder
17. Luke 2:46-51
    Missing, found him in his father's house
18. John 4:32
    I have food that you know not of
19. Hebrews 12:1
    Easily entangles
20. Matthew 14:1-12
    Herod married to Herodias (Gale married to Gailina)
21. Luke 3:3
    Voice of one crying out in the wilderness
22. Luke 3:8
    'bear fruit in keeping with repentance'
23. Luke 3:9
    Brood of vipers; cut down like a tree and thrown into the fire
24. Galatians 5:17
    Spirit vs Flesh
25. Multiple
    Right in their own eyes
26. James 1:15
    Desire leads to sin, sin when fully grown leads to death
27. Deuteronomy 8:3
    Man does not live by bread alone, but by every word…mouth of the Lord
28. Luke 4
    If you are the son of God…
29. John 2
    Do whatever he tells you. Water into wine

30. John 1
    In the beginning was the word…
31. Luke 4:18-21
    The Spirit of the Lord is on me… Today this is fulfilled
32. Romans 3:23
    All have sinned and fallen short
33. Romans 3, Psalm 14:1
    There is no one righteous, not even one…
34. Luke 4:36
    Words of authority and impure spirits obey…
35. Luke 5
    Bridegroom will be taken…then they will fast
36. Deuteronomy/Exodus Ten Commandments
    Honor thy father and mother
37. Psa 37:23
    Steps ordered by the Lord
38. James 1:22
    Don't just be hearers but doers of the word
39. Luke 6
    All the parables. Chapters 17 & 18
40. 1 John 1:9
    He is faithful and just to forgive us
41. 1 Cor 2:14-15
    Natural man doesn't understand, foolishness to him.
42. Eph 2:10
    Were dead in sin but alive in Christ
43. John 3:16
    God so loved the world that He gave His only son…
44. 2 Cor 10:5
    Taking thoughts captive
45. James 1:14-16
    Temptation lures and entices by desire. Desire births sin, sin to death
46. Gal 5:17
    Spirit wars with flesh
47. Gal 5:22
    Fruits of the Spirit
48. Rom 12:19
    Vengeance is mine
49. Jeremiah 3:8
    God sent Israel away w/ a decree of divorce for her unfaithfulness

50. Jeremiah 2:34
    On your skirts is found the lifeblood of the guiltless poor
    - (symbolized the way the strong trampled on the weak through oppression, financial enslavement, bribery, violence, and gross injustice
    - https://wwwchristianitytodaycom/ct/2018/may-web-only/patterson-sbc-divorce-god-hates-abusehtml

51. Mark 5
    Talaitha Koum
52. 1 Peter 5:8
    Be watchful; the devil prowls around like a lion waiting to devour
53. Mark 10:46-52
    Bartimaeus, the blind man, healed
54. Luke 8
    Speaking of John the Baptist (Causing them to stumble because of Him)
55. Isaiah 41:10
    Do not fear or be dismayed for I am with you…uphold you
56. Matthew 6:25-34
    Don't be anxious for anything
57. 1 Peter 3:15
    Always be prepared to give an answer for the hope you have
58. Matt 17:21
    Some only come out by fasting and prayer
59. Luke 10:17
    Even demons submit to us in Your name
60. Romans 10:09
    Believe in heart, confess with mouth…
61. Luke 9:50
    Is someone is not against you they are for you
62. 1 John 3:
    You will prosper and be in health even as your soul prospers
63. James 1:5
    Ask God for wisdom, He gives generously without reproach
64. Eph 2:8
    Freedom by grace through faith (saved)
65. 1 Peter 2:7-8
    They stumble because…disobey the message…were destined
66. Is 9:1-2
    The people walking in darkness have seen a great light
67. Isaiah 35:5–6

Eyes will be opened, and ears will hear

68. Isaiah 53:3
    He was despised, rejected by man, a man of suffering familiar with pain…
69. Psa 22:16
    Messiah delivered to the congregation of the wicked for judgment
70. Jer 31:3
    He loves you with an everlasting love
71. John 7:24
    Don't judge by appearances
72. Ephesians 4:15
    Judging must be done in love
73. Prov 6:10
    A little sleep, a little slumber and poverty will come upon you
74. James 4:17
    Anyone who knows what he ought to do and doesn't do it sins
75. Joshua 24:14-15
    Choose this day whom you will serve
76. Matt 12:30, Luke 11:23
    Whoever isn't for me is against me
77. Job 33:23-25
    I have found a ransom, a mediator…
78. 2 Cor 5:7
    Walk by faith not by sight
79. Romans 10:9
    Believe in heart, confess with mouth
80. Micah 6:8
    Do Justice, love mercy, walk humbly w/ your God
81. Hebrews 1:1
    Faith is being sure of what we hope for and certain of what we do not see

And more…

ABOUT THE AUTHOR

Leah Rodriquez DeSalles was raised in Modesto, California. In that we know endurance produces character, Leah's character far outweighs her stature. She is a short, fiercely loyal, relentlessly honest type of gal. Leah is happily married and lives in Phoenix, Arizona, with her husband, Rudy, and three dogs, Sumo, Dash, and Dot.

A note from the Author:

Thanks so much for reading this far, guys. I've got something to reveal to you– although this book is fiction, it is based on actual events. The good news is that Emmanuel is a real person! As a matter of fact, He is the only person to have ever lived that the world altered the timeline of existence for! Before Him was "B.C." After His birth is "A.D." That's pretty significant! He really was sent as a ransom for all of our missing the mark. If you have never known that redemption from all of the wounds in your soul was possible, know it now. Please know that with the acceptance of the reality that Emmanuel lived, traveled, healed people, brought deliverance, became a substitute for all of our missing the mark in life, and rose from the dead (Yes, there's proof. Check it out, dig deep!), we can– with absolute assurance– be made acceptable to live, breath and have our being in the perfect presence of Theos, Abba, the Creator– God.

If you'd like to accept His sacrifice, simply appeal to Abba now by saying:

Abba, I believe that You sent Emmanuel to be a ransom for all of my missing the mark. I long to know more about You, about Him, and enter into the immortal life that allows me to live with Your Essence and the Higher Realm. I receive You all. I thank You. Have Your way. Teach me. In the name of Emmanuel, Amen.

Awesome! Now be sure to check out the Ancient Writings! They are a trip!!! Some people call them the Bible.

www.ingramcontent.com/pod-product-compliance
Lightning Source LLC
LaVergne TN
LVHW010603100826
845148LV00014B/2820

* 9 7 8 0 5 7 8 8 5 4 3 5 9 *